GUARDIANS
OF THE GRYPHON'S CLAW

To Lilah:

Heed your call to Adventure!

FROM THE FILES OF THE DEPARTMENT OF MYTHICAL WILDLIFE

GUARDIANS OF THE GRYPHON'S CLAW

A SAM LONDON ADVENTURE

TODD CALGI GALLICANO

DELACORTE PRESS

Text copyright © 2017 by Todd Gallicano
Jacket art and interior illustrations copyright © 2017 by Kevin Keele

All rights reserved. Published in the United States by Delacorte Press, an imprint of Random House Children's Books, a division of Penguin Random House LLC, New York.

Delacorte Press is a registered trademark and the colophon is a trademark of Penguin Random House LLC.

randomhousekids.com

Educators and librarians, for a variety of teaching tools, visit us at RHTeachersLibrarians.com

Library of Congress Cataloging-in-Publication Data is available upon request.

ISBN 978-1-5247-1365-2 (hc) — ISBN 978-1-5247-1366-9 (lib. bdg.) — ISBN 978-1-5247-1367-6 (ebook)

The text of this book is set in 13-point Fournier MT.
Interior design by Ken Crossland

Printed in the United States of America
10 9 8 7 6 5 4 3 2
First Edition

For Squishy and the believers

AUTHOR'S NOTE

The following account is based on a case file that originated with the Department of Mythical Wildlife (DMW). In an effort to inform the public of this previously unknown government agency, my sources have provided me with copies of files from the DMW archives. As far as I can determine, "Guardians of the Gryphon's Claw" is the department's first case involving Sam London.

DMW case files consist of witness interviews, investigative notes, research materials, and reports offering comprehensive explanations of the events that transpired. Due to the often dry, fact-laden nature of this information, I have created a dramatic interpretation of the file's contents. All the details have been maintained, but the narrative has been enhanced for the reader's enjoyment. I have also included several references to the source material within the text and have appended a legend of abbreviations, codes, and terms to assist in decoding the DMW's distinct classification system.

Since these files are classified, dates have been omitted and some names have been altered to protect the identities of witnesses and individuals still in the department's employ.

—T.C.G.

PROLOGUE

It was the moment Penelope Naughton saw the troll at International House of Pancakes that changed everything. She had never actually laid eyes on a troll before—at least, not in real life. Depictions in Hollywood movies were the extent of her exposure to the mythical creatures. But this wasn't Tolkien's Mordor or Rowling's Hogwarts; it was Eureka, California. A town best known for its Victorian mansions, art festivals, and the state's oldest zoo.

That being said, Penelope couldn't help but notice how similar this troll appeared to the ones she had seen on the silver screen. The creature was large, with tan, leathery skin. His ears were enormous mounds of wrinkled flesh with pointed tops and lobes that drooped past his chin. The massive nose on the troll's face was crooked and upturned, exposing nostrils with copious amounts of dark, twisting hair.

His wide-set eyes featured two distant pitch-black pupils swimming in pools of yellow. He had long, hairy arms that reached down toward his knees and ended in rough-skinned hands with sharp fingernails. The smallest part of the troll was his head, which looked particularly diminutive given the size of his frame. Compared to a human, this creature was entirely disproportionate.

Upon seeing the troll, Penelope felt her rational mind check out and instinct kick in. She sprang to her feet, pointed, and screamed so loudly that a startled cook flipped a pancake with enough force that it stuck to the ceiling. While the patrons and staff were understandably rattled by Penelope's outburst, the troll seemed more panicked than surprised. His expression was that of a child caught with his hand in the cookie jar; of course, the troll's hands were the size of cookie jars. He appeared to purposely avoid eye contact with Penelope as he scurried from his booth and disappeared out the exit.

If this experience hadn't been strange enough, Penelope couldn't shake the feeling there was something familiar about the creature. It was as though she knew him. But how could she? It had to be her recent viewing of *Lord of the Rings* that had caused this momentary lapse of sanity. Yes, that was surely it. After all, no one else seemed bothered by his presence. He was just a big guy enjoying his breakfast. There was no such thing as trolls.

* * *

Forty-eight hours later, Penelope was on her way to Redwood National Park and she couldn't get there quickly enough. Her doctor had recommended she not return to work for at least six months. The thirty-three-year-old's condition, which was diagnosed as a rare type of sudden amnesia, didn't appear to be triggered by any physical trauma and only affected the last three years of her life. Penelope could easily recall her childhood—a simple one in the suburbs of Tallahassee, Florida. She remembered her schooling and the angry looks she received for wrecking the curve in science class. But most importantly, she retained her love of nature.

It had always been Penelope's dream to work in the outdoors, and her aspirations crystallized at age twelve during a visit to Everglades National Park. Ranger Woodruff Sprite was an eccentric sort who had encouraged and mentored Penelope along her path, which eventually led to Oregon State University. There she secured a bachelor's degree in zoology and animal biology, as well as a master's in forestry. The first part of her career was spent indoors in a lab, developing tools to aid the U.S. Fish and Wildlife Service, the U.S. Forest Service, and the National Park Service in protecting animals and conserving natural habitats. Six years later, Penelope's work culminated in her landing her dream job: park ranger at Redwood National Park. That was where her memory inexplicably stopped.

Penelope had been recuperating from her amnesia at a friend's house, but her real home was in the park. She couldn't even remember moving into the on-site housing the National

Park Service provided to all rangers, but she hoped her return might jog her jumbled memory. Unfortunately, when she arrived at her two-story cabin in the heart of the forest, it didn't look at all familiar. It was small, a touch shoddy, and surrounded on all sides by the beautiful redwood trees that made the park famous. They towered to awe-inspiring heights on trunks so thick you could carve a car tunnel through them.

Penelope ascended the creaky staircase to the front door of the cabin. As she wrestled with her keys, a noise from the forest froze her. She held her breath and listened intently, waiting for it to repeat. And it did. It was the whinny of a horse. The sound struck a chord with her. She knew that whinny—

"Gus?" she reflexively called out.

Penelope was down the steps and into the forest in an instant. The memory wasn't clear—it was more of a feeling or intuition. But the name she knew. Gus. He was a friend. And she couldn't wait to see him again. She followed the sound as it took her deeper into the woods and off the trail. She started to run, racing through the thicket as fast as her legs would allow. She plowed through a tightly packed group of trees and into a clearing, where she could finally see her Gus. But she couldn't quite believe what she was seeing.

Gus was a brilliant white horse with a coat that shimmered in the sunlight. The sparkle was almost enough to distract Penelope from an even more extraordinary realization: Gus had wings. Magnificent feathered wings that spanned at least ten feet and flapped slowly against the wind. As she tried to digest this impossibility, she immediately became aware of a man standing next to Gus, clutching his reins.

"Penelope?" the man asked, betraying a slight Southern drawl. "You're back early. I thought Dr.—"

"Who are you?" Penelope asked quickly.

"Ah. A little too early, it seems," said the man, adding with a smile, "I'm Vance. Vance Vantana, and this is—"

"Gus," Penelope interjected.

"Yeah. Gus," Vance replied. "You remember. Very good."

A moment of silence as Penelope took stock of her situation. The stranger was handsome, she thought. Tall, around thirty-five, with an athletic build and a rugged look more befitting a crime-fighting Texas Ranger than a park ranger. But there he was, dressed in the standard ranger uniform—the distinct green jacket and pants along with the signature beige campaign hat.

"It's good to see ya again," he said as he approached, his hand extended.

"Again?" she wondered. Had she met this man before? Now that she thought about it, his face did seem familiar, but she couldn't place him. And then Penelope's eye caught the sun's reflection off Vance's badge and she noticed something odd about it. Instead of the typically issued badge, bearing the image of a buffalo and the words "U.S. Department of the Interior," this one featured a picture of a beast that had the body of a lion and the head and wings of an eagle. She immediately recognized it as the magical creature known as a gryphon. The words surrounding the animal also gave her pause—"U.S. Department of Mythical Wildlife."

Preoccupied with the badge, Penelope didn't bother shaking Vance's hand. He withdrew it awkwardly.

"Trevor, Gus, and I were worried about you," he said.

"Trevor?" Penelope replied quizzically.

Vance motioned to the edge of the forest, where a hulking figure emerged. Penelope's eyes widened with surprise as she found herself staring at none other than the troll from IHOP. She suddenly felt the world go dark. Vance jumped to Penelope's side, catching her as she fainted.

"Great. You freaked her out again," Vance scolded the troll.

The troll shrugged innocently and responded in a high-pitched voice, "I didn't mean to, and she scared the heck out of me first, remember? I couldn't even finish my Rooty Tooty Fresh 'N Fruity."

"Tragic," chided Vance. "Well, pick her up and take her on home. Once she wakes, explain things. And bring Carl—he's always had a way of calmin' her down."

As Trevor turned and started for the cabin with an unconscious Penelope cradled in his arms, Vance placed a halting hand on the troll's shoulder.

"Find out anything you can about what happened, Trev," Vance whispered ominously. "Her amnesia was not natural."

Chapter 1

THE DREAM

Once again, Sam London found himself wandering in the desert.
After fourteen consecutive nights of the same dream, this
brown-haired, blue-eyed twelve-year-old had reached his
breaking point. As he looked out on the now all-too-familiar
landscape, an overwhelming sense of frustration billowed up
inside him. He wondered if tonight would prove as utterly
pointless as all the other nights spent in this place. Then again,
maybe this dream did have a point lurking about, but Sam was
simply missing it by waking up too soon. Whether it was the
alarm ringing him out of bed for school or his mother's op-
eratic singing in the shower—the only place she claimed had
Carnegie Hall–like acoustics—Sam was consistently roused
to reality before anything of significance occurred.

Adding to Sam's frustration was the fact this was a lucid dream, which meant he was fully aware he was dreaming.

Unfortunately, for some reason it wouldn't allow him to take advantage of this favorable circumstance. The only other time Sam had experienced lucid dreaming, he had bestowed superhuman powers upon himself and saved the world from an army of bloodthirsty werewolves. In contrast, on night three of Sam's desert odyssey, he attempted to defy gravity, only to learn that falling in a dream hurts about as much as it does in reality, at least until your eyes open. No matter what he tried, the Sam in this dreamworld was, as he considered it, as "un-special" as the Sam in the real world.

That word "un-special" was a wholly Sam creation. He used it to describe people who lacked a definitive skill or purpose. In Sam's eyes, some kids were born to play sports, some had a genetic predisposition to genius, and others were natural artists with boundless creativity. Sam London couldn't boast any of these qualities. He was just your average kid of average height with average looks and average grades. And except for its recurring nature and other peculiarities, his dream was like Sam—pretty average.

Each night for the last two weeks, Sam was transported to a desolate two-lane road surrounded by a seemingly endless desert. The only hint of civilization was a gas station that sat about a half mile up the highway. The night before last, Sam was able to reach the station and have a look around. Much to his dismay, the structure proved as stark as the landscape. The shelves in the mini-mart were bare, and worst of all, the ICEE machine refused to function. But Sam was not the type to give up easily. He held on to the hope that this dream would reveal a surprise or two. Though he did entertain the thought, if just for a moment, that this environment was on some level a metaphor for his life.

In addition to inspecting the gas station, Sam had used his time to explore several rocky outcroppings that peppered the terrain. Though he had yet to find anything of interest, there was one remaining possibility. The largest of the outcroppings was positioned about three hundred yards from the station. Sam had been avoiding this formation, as it was the tallest and consequently the most intimidating of the bunch. But tonight was the night to leave no stones unturned, no matter how high they were stacked.

Time was not on Sam's side. His alarm clock was ticking down to seven a.m. At any moment he could be yanked from his slumber—and his search. With that squarely in mind, Sam sprinted to his target—a mountain of granite boulders piled high atop granitic bedrock. The formation stood at least thirty feet and culminated in a plateau, which could very well be hiding the answers Sam so desperately sought. He picked his first "step," a large misshapen boulder that was easy to climb. His sneakers slid a bit against the gritty rock face—his hands could have used some of that chalk real climbers relied on. But soon enough he was within a few feet of his goal. Yet this part of the climb would prove especially difficult, as the rock had given way to loose bedrock and leverage was a precious commodity.

Sam reached out for a crook in the surface. Grabbing hold, he attempted to pull himself to victory, but the rock crumbled beneath his grip, and he suddenly found himself sliding back toward the ground. He scrambled, his arms moving like the tentacles of a panicked octopus, trying desperately to hold on to anything that would stop his rapid descent. He finally made contact with an area of the rock that jutted out a few inches. He clutched it and began the process of pulling himself back up the side of the formation.

By the time Sam hurled himself over the edge of the plateau, he was thoroughly exhausted and downright filthy. He stood up and surveyed the scene. Except for the spectacular view, this plateau was just as exciting as the ground below. He sighed—the frustration had officially transformed into resignation.

"Why?" Sam said aloud for the universe to hear. The universe didn't bother to answer. He decided he would no longer wait for his alarm or his mom to rouse him from his slumber. He was going to protest the dream by waking himself up. He quickly found it was easier said than done. Sam tried jumping up and down but remained in the desert. He shook his head briskly but only succeeded in making himself dizzy. He shut his eyes tightly, squeezing hard, then opened them again to see . . . he was still there. So Sam went for all three moves: he shook his head, clenched his eyelids, and stomped his feet hard on the rocky surface.

"Wake up! Wake up! Wake up!" Sam shouted.

He brought his foot down hard on the plateau and the earth shook beneath him, a quick and powerful tremor that drove him to his knees. A cloud of dirt plumed around him and he choked on the dusty air. Sam was blinded by a veil of grime, but as the murkiness melted away, he found he was no longer alone in this desert. When the dust settled, Sam's eyes narrowed and his lips parted in absolute bewilderment. The creature that stood before him was at least fifteen feet tall. It had the head of an eagle framed by a majestic crest of white feathers. Its beak was hooked downward to a sharp, lethal point. Emerald-green eyes glowed in the sunlight. Wings that were a mix of tan and pure white feathers extended several feet from its body. Although at first glance it appeared to be a bird, Sam's eyes were distracted by the beast's chest, which was covered not in feathers but in fur. A chestnut-colored coat spread across its body to its four powerful legs, massive paws, and a long, tufted tail. This eagle was also a lion.

Sam stood as still as a statue. The answers were before him, but he had forgotten the questions. He tried to form words as the creature stared down at him. He could feel its warm breath against his face.

And then he heard the faint sounds of an overcaffeinated radio deejay.

"Good morning, Benicia! Wakey, wakey! This is your wack-wack-wacky morning zoo with Bob and Bob!"

"Oh no. Not now . . . ," Sam groaned, realizing his alarm clock had gone off. It couldn't have come at a worse time. He fought to stay in the dreamworld, to ask the questions he had been saving up these past two weeks. Even the creature seemed disappointed as Sam drifted back to reality.

Sam awoke in his bed, alert and practically vibrating. He slammed his hand down on the alarm to silence it, then slipped out from under the covers and headed straight for his bookshelf.

Sam's room was a testament to all the efforts he had made to find his special gift that would enable him to stand out. A guitar and a drum set sat in one corner, the discarded remnants of his attempt to find his musical muse. A short distance from the instruments was a collection of sports paraphernalia: a hockey stick, a soccer ball, even a cricket bat. His most recent endeavor was positioned in front of the sports equipment—an easel holding a canvas. From the looks of it, Sam appeared to be documenting his lucid werewolf dream in acrylic. But even by subjective standards, the result was an unmitigated disaster.

The rest of Sam's room was devoted to animals both real and imaginary. Dragons and pandas, panthers and abominable snowmen, it was a hodgepodge of creatures represented through posters, figurines, and stuffed animals. For as long as Sam could remember, he'd always had an affinity for animals, especially the mythical variety. He thought they were cool, and he loved that each was special in its own unique way, a trait he no doubt envied. Some would later note that Sam's specialty lay all around him and he was simply oblivious.

Sam's bookshelf was chock-full of tales of fantastical creatures. Through picture books, encyclopedias, and graphic novels, Sam's obsession sprang to life. He ran his finger along the spines of his impressive collection until he reached his selection. He pulled it out and cracked it open. The book was titled *The Visual Guide to Extraordinary Animals* and provided an illustrative catalog of creatures most people considered make-believe. Sam shuffled to his destination, spread the pages wide, and gazed at the creature from his dream. The artistic rendering was so vivid it could have been a photograph.

"A gryphon," Sam said aloud as he read the page heading. His eyes shifted to the description:

One of the most ancient and powerful of all extraordinary animals. Highly intelligent and immeasurably strong, the gryphon is the guardian and protector of the world's magical creatures. Few men have laid eyes on a gryphon and lived to tell the tale. Those who have survived reported unusually good luck in the days that followed. Even those individuals who didn't actually see a gryphon but were merely in its presence experienced a surge of luck, often related to wealth.

Although they are not violent by nature, a gryphon will attack if provoked. Examples of provocation include endangering the creatures a gryphon is sworn to protect or threatening a gryphon's gold. Gold is considered a weakness of this extraordinary animal. It is highly attracted to the precious metal and is known to horde it in massive amounts. As such, most of the human deaths associated with these creatures are due to a victim's foolish attempts to steal the gryphon's gold.

It was always every man for himself at breakfast in the London household. Sam was usually the first one downstairs, and he'd snag himself a bowl of cereal or the occasional doughnut—if by some miracle they had made it into the grocery cart that week. This morning he sat at the tiny kitchen table and sipped a glass of orange juice as he thought back on his nightly adventure. He wondered if just dreaming of a gryphon would bring him good fortune. God knew he and his mom could use it. She had been working two jobs for as long as Sam could remember. During the day she was an art teacher at the local high school and at night she taught art history at a nearby community college. She happened to be an extraordinarily gifted artist, and Sam had always hoped her talent had been passed on to him. The werewolf painting had effectively dashed those hopes. As for working two jobs, his mom claimed it was necessary in order to save money for Sam's future. She constantly encouraged her son to dream big and dream often, and she wanted to make sure he never felt trapped in any way.

"Oh good, you're up," Sam's mom said with relief as she entered the kitchen.

Her full name was Odette Alexandra London, but everyone called her Ettie. She was thirty-five years old, with long auburn hair, crystal-blue eyes, and a slender, if lanky, build. Ettie was pretty, even prettier when she smiled, which she did often. Sam's mom was exceedingly upbeat. Though Sam couldn't help but believe there was something missing from her life. Like him, Ettie didn't have many friends. She also never dated, even though she had been single since Sam was a baby. She didn't talk much about Sam's father, Marshall London, and Sam had no memory of him. The only picture Sam had of his dad was taken before he was born. It was of Ettie and Marshall at Fontana Lake in North Carolina. The two of them were smiling happily as they stood beside each other on the shore with ducks, geese, and swans floating in the distance.

Sam wondered what happened to that seemingly happy couple. Although he was curious about what led his father to leave, he rarely discussed the topic with his mother. He didn't believe she had totally gotten over it—as evidenced by the fact that whenever he asked about his dad, Ettie would respond with "Let's not dwell on the past, Sam" and quickly change the subject.

"I was worried you hadn't showered yet," Ettie confessed, adding with a tinge of guilt, "I'm pretty sure I used all the hot water."

Sam wasn't surprised. She always used all the hot water. Her concerts often went long and apparently required a lot of steam. Ettie grabbed the carton of OJ from the fridge and poured herself a glass. She settled in across from Sam and exhaled. Sam remained quiet, his mind in overdrive.

"I picked up cookies yesterday," she offered. "The variety pack you like. They're in the cabinet. You want to take a package for lunch?" Sam nodded, still not entirely present.

"I just said the word 'cookies' and you didn't even blink. What's wrong? You're not sick or anything, are you?"

"No, I'm fine, Mom. I'm just thinking."

"Thinking? This early in the morning?" She considered him. "You had that dream again, didn't you?"

Sam nodded. "And this time it was different."

"It was?" Ettie said, intrigued. "Talk to me."

"You really want to know?" Sam asked.

"Are you kidding? Of course I want to know. I've had to hear about this dream every day for the last month—"

"Two weeks."

"Well, it's felt like a month. What was so different?"

"I saw something," Sam said in a cryptic manner.

"Okay. What?"

"It was a . . . gryphon," Sam responded tentatively.

Ettie smiled and nodded, as if she'd been expecting this. "Oh. A gryphon. One of those lion-bird things, right? That's cool." Sam spotted the underlying skepticism and quickly countered.

"It's not like that, Mom. I think it means something."

"And I think it means something too, sweetheart. I think it means you read a lot of those books. And have all those posters plastered on your walls."

Sam had known she was going to say something like that. And maybe she was right. But something inside him didn't think so. He thought it meant there was something special about this dream, and it was up to him to find out what.

SL001-180-20

Form FD-11

DATE: ███████

Ettie dropped Sam off at Benicia Middle School and headed the few short blocks away to Benicia High School. Sam's hometown of Benicia, California, was quaint and historic. It happened to be one of the very first capitals of California, serving in that capacity between 1853 and 1854. It sat on the north side of the Carquinez Strait, which was a narrow waterway that connected to the Suisun Bay. It was just enough to give the city a coastal feel.

Sam hadn't been asleep very long when his teacher, Miss Capiz, nudged him awake. If that wasn't bad enough, the unsightly pool of drool that had formed on his desk had now become evident to nearly everyone in the class. It sparked much laughter among his classmates, along with a few cries of "Eww!" from the female students. The whole episode was awfully embarrassing, and more than enough to get him held after class. Miss Capiz questioned Sam about his sleeping habits at home and he told her about the desert and the gryphon. Sam wouldn't normally divulge this sort of information to a relative stranger, but the Philippine-born teacher was supportive of his obsession, even letting him do a book report on *Secrets of the Loch Ness Monster*.

At the mention of the gryphon, Miss Capiz widened her dark oval eyes, which appeared even darker when framed by her pin-straight black hair. She relayed the tale of the sarimanok, a mythical bird creature from her home country that, like the gryphon, brought good luck. At least it was a happy story, Sam thought, unlike the time when Miss Capiz recited the frightening tale of the aswang, a mythical vampire-werewolf that craved human flesh, especially that of children. He had nightmares for a week. Miss Capiz seemed to enjoy telling these stories, so Sam always did his best to listen and nod appropriately. He liked to stay on her good side as much as possible. Sam knew a few students who had gotten on her bad side early in the school year. Ever since then, she reported every detail about their classroom behavior and performance to their parents. Miss Capiz asked Sam to keep her apprised of his research and sent him off with a warning—another class-time nap would trigger a call home. He was pleased to have avoided her wrath.

When the lunch period arrived, Sam chose to skip the afternoon meal in favor of a gryphon-centric fact-finding mission in the school library. He narrowed his search to a few books he found through the catalog system and took off through the maze of shelves. Sam's stomach grumbled angrily as he pulled *The Great and Powerful Gryphon* by Dr.

Henry Knox from the shelf. The author was familiar to Sam—and to anyone who fancied fantastical creatures. Knox was a well-known cryptozoologist and wildlife biologist who had written dozens of books on the subjects of both magical creatures and cryptids. Cryptids are animals or plants the scientific community doesn't recognize as actually existing. The study of cryptids is known as cryptozoology and is considered by some a pseudoscience. Knox's work in the discipline was unusual, given his position as a respected scientist. Sam remembered reading that he had attributed his interest to that of a hobbyist and nothing more. According to Knox, whether or not these creatures existed in our world, they lived in our imagination, and that was worth acknowledging and exploring.

Sam's interest was immediately piqued by the illustration on the book's cover. He gasped as he gazed upon an uncanny drawing of the gryphon from his dream. There was no mistaking it—this was the same gryphon he'd seen last night. A caption below the image read "Phylassos—the father of all gryphons, protector of magical creatures, and guardian of good." The emptiness in Sam's stomach made the pit that was forming even larger.

Sam wondered if perhaps he had seen the picture before in one of his many books by Knox and it had lodged itself in his subconscious, just waiting for the right moment to appear and have the most impact on his sanity. His rational side loved that explanation. The mind likes to play tricks, he thought. This had to be a trick. Of course, the other side of him was screaming the opposite. It was telling him he was right to believe this was more than just a trick. This inner debate raged until the bell rang him back to reality. Lunch was over, and his teacher would be expecting him in fifth period in six minutes. He borrowed the book on his way out, intent on learning everything he could about gryphons. His homework would have to wait.

*　*　*

Like every other weekday, Sam's mom dropped him off at home before heading off to the college to teach her night class. Sam was happy to have the alone time. He grabbed a cookie from the variety pack, switched on the television, and dropped onto the couch in their living room/home office/dining room. Space was tight in the two-bedroom condominium his mother rented, but it was cozy, clean, and most importantly, cheap. He retrieved the gryphon book from his backpack, eager to pick up where he'd left off.

Sam had just begun his quest for knowledge when the noise of the television distracted him. The voices on the TV were making it difficult to read. Music would be better, he concluded. Sam grabbed the remote to switch over to a music-only channel but hesitated when he noticed a story on the local news. A reporter was standing in front of a gas station where a winning lottery ticket had recently been sold. What made the story particularly newsworthy was that this station had already sold several winning lottery tickets in the last two weeks. As a result, a mass of people were now lined up outside, many having driven hundreds of miles to buy a ticket at the "lucky" gas station. Lottery officials had launched a formal investigation, since the chances of the same merchant selling multiple winning tickets were astronomically low. The reporter interviewed a few of the dedicated lottery players, who had made the trek all the way out to Death Valley, a remote area in Eastern California. The cameraman panned to show just how isolated the station was. And that was when Sam's life got exponentially more exciting. The "lucky" gas station was the gas station from his dream! Not only that, the pan revealed the rocky outcropping that was the very same pile of rocks where the gryphon had appeared.

It was real. The desert he had found himself in every night for the last two weeks was none other than Death Valley, California. Sam knew he had never been there before. He hadn't even seen it in photos. His rational mind waved a white flag. The fact was, his dream had come to life. But the question remained: to what extent? Sure, the gas station was there, and the rocky outcropping as well, but what about the gryphon? Was the legendary Phylassos standing atop those rocks, awaiting Sam London's arrival? There was only one way to find out.

Chapter 2
PHYLASSOS RETURNS

When you find yourself in a place with the word "death" in its name, it's hard to feel hopeful. Sam had arrived in Death Valley National Park, after an eight-hour bus ride from Benicia. The bus was one of two daily coaches that provided service between the Bay Area and Las Vegas, Nevada. As a result, it was mostly filled with retirees looking to gamble a portion of their fixed incomes and enjoy a ten-dollar surf and turf. Sam had purchased his ticket online using the prepaid credit card he'd earned for taking care of his neighbor's cats when she went on an around-the-world cruise. It was a job Ettie had initially wanted Sam to do for free for the retired economics professor who lived next door, but the neighbor insisted on paying Sam for his work while teaching him "a valuable lesson about managing money."

Even with the printed ticket in hand, Sam knew that his

age, and the fact he was riding alone, would raise a red flag with the driver. So he pretended he was traveling with the old woman who was boarding in front of him. He also made sure to sit next to her for the entire trip. The old woman, on the other hand, was under the impression Sam was nineteen years old and suffered from a rare condition that stunted his growth and caused him to appear very young. Sam relayed this tall tale as they waited to board, and only after the woman had expressed concern he was a runaway.

Lucky for Sam, this bus route to Sin City ran right through Death Valley on Highway 190. It also just happened to have a scheduled stop at the famous gas station—one of two breaks the bus took for snacks, bathrooms, and to "get in a stretch," as the driver put it. When the bus rumbled to a stop near the station, the first part of Sam's plan was complete, the second was just about to begin, and the third hadn't even been contemplated—namely, getting home and explaining himself to his soon-to-be nervous wreck of a mother.

Sam had hatched his plan the night before, soon after the television news report and accompanying revelation. He'd stayed up most of the night researching Death Valley, reading about gryphons, and determining how he was going to reach his destination. When he did eventually fall asleep, it was only for a spell, and he didn't dream, or at least, he didn't remember dreaming.

That morning had brought the first real test of whether Sam's scheme had any chance of working. He'd had to convince his mother he was too sick to go to school, but not sick enough to trigger a visit to the doctor; after all, his mother was a consummate overreactor. One false move and he'd spend the day languishing in a doctor's waiting room. As a teacher, Ettie was particularly sensitive about students claiming to be sick simply to miss class. That meant if Sam had any chance at all of persuading her, he would need to use a unique kind of deviousness, a kind Sam had little to no experience employing. After much deliberation and with some reluctance, he determined that success required—no, demanded—a painful sacrifice.

"I ate too many cookies and I don't feel very good," Sam said woefully as he stood in his mother's bedroom doorway. He clutched his stomach and displayed his best sick face, which consisted of a furrowed brow and pursed lips. He knew this unorthodox strategy would mean the end to the celebrated cookie variety pack, but a kid has to do what a kid has to do, especially if that kid has a date with a mythical creature in the middle of Death Valley. The occasional moaning and a few frantic runs to the bathroom were added to close the sale. It was touch and go as Ettie questioned him about his symptoms, but Sam took great care to avoid mentioning any that could indicate a more serious affliction. He even went the extra step of throwing out the pack of cookies in dramatic fashion and declaring unequivocally, "I don't want us to get these ever again!" Ettie finally bought it.

Teachers making cell phone calls in the middle of the school day didn't set a very good example, so it was unlikely Sam's mom would attempt to reach him. Just in case she tried,

Sam laid some groundwork by telling her he hadn't slept all night because of his stomach issues, so he'd be getting his rest during the day. Of course, if she really needed to get in touch, she could text him. There was still the chance Ettie would stop home between jobs and check on him. If that happened, the jig would be up several hours earlier than planned. Sam tried to keep a positive outlook.

According to an Internet encyclopedia Sam visited in his nightly research, Death Valley had earned its ominous moniker after a group of pioneers became stranded there during the winter of 1849 and were convinced they were going to die. The valley has the distinction of being the hottest, driest, and lowest spot in North America. It was named a National Monument in 1933 and officially became a National Park in 1994. Besides getting familiar with the area's history, Sam finished reading Knox's book on gryphons. So when the bus finally reached the gas station, he felt more than ready for whatever might lie ahead. He was well informed and well rested, having drifted off to sleep moments after departing. Yet nothing could prepare him for the surreal feeling of stepping into a real-life version of his own dreamscape. He had been there and yet he hadn't all at the same time.

The bus driver pulled to the side of the highway several yards before the station. Sam stepped off the bus, took a moment to get his bearings, and then surveyed the scene. Gas station: check. Rocky outcropping: check. This was definitely the place.

"The bathrooms are clean and the snacks aren't too

spendy," said the old woman. "If you play the lottery, it's the luckiest place to buy a ticket in the state."

"I try not to gamble," Sam replied. "It's hard, you know, with my condition and all. They always think I have a fake ID. It's not worth the trouble."

"You poor thing," she offered with the utmost empathy. Sam felt a little bad about lying to this complete stranger, as well as to his mother, but he saw these momentary ethical lapses as absolutely necessary to ensure the success of his mission.

The bus driver reminded the passengers to be back on the bus in thirty minutes, no exceptions. If you hadn't boarded after a half hour, you'd be unceremoniously left behind. Sam didn't pay him much mind, since he had no intention of completing the trip to Vegas. He headed inside the gas station to use the restroom and have a look around.

The owner had displayed photographs of himself with all the station's lottery winners. The winnings from tickets sold at this location totaled over $120 million, including the most recent Powerball jackpot of $97 million. Sam grabbed a package of cookies and ambled up to the counter. The clerk's name tag read "Milad." He appeared to be in his late teens and thoroughly unhappy with his choice of employment. As Milad rang up the sale on the register, Sam decided to engage in some subtle probing.

"Pretty lucky place," Sam said.

"I haven't won anything," Milad replied with more than a hint of bitterness.

"Sorry to hear that," Sam offered. Having established a line of communication, he got down to business. "Random question, but have you ever seen anything unusual around here? Like say out on those rocks?" He pointed to the outcropping.

"Unusual like what?" asked the clerk, his irritation growing.

"Like an animal. Sort of a strange animal," added Sam. The clerk stared back at him blankly. "Here." He retrieved the book from his backpack and showed Milad the image on the cover. "An animal like this."

"You're asking me if I've ever seen one of these . . ."

"Gryphons," Sam finished his sentence. "Yes. Have you?"

Milad widened his eyes. "Yeah. Tons of them. Out in those hills."

Sam's excitement could not be contained. "Really?"

"Of course not. Those aren't real. What do you think I am? Stupid? Get lost!"

Sam was suddenly being moved aside as another customer squeezed in front of Milad. The clerk's rebuke had rattled Sam. His rational side reawoke to rub his face in it. *See, I told you*, his inner voice taunted. *This is crazy.* But he was already here, already committed to the plan, and it was time to see it through. He stuffed the cookies into his backpack, exited the station, and started toward destiny.

Sam ran-walked most of the way and chalked up his surprising endurance to those loathsome squat thrusts in PE. He took just a brief moment to catch his breath at the base of the outcropping before he began his ascent. The rocks felt grittier, the air drier. There was clearly more at stake for Sam here than in his dreamworld. Most obvious was that falling could prove fatal. After all, this was not something he could wake up from. No alarm or shower aria would help him escape reality. And what of the gryphon? What if it appeared? What would Sam do then? It wasn't exactly a cuddly little kitten. If it existed, the accounts in the books were likely true, and that meant the creature was dangerous. Although Sam had made sure he wasn't wearing any gold that day, this simple precaution might not prevent the gryphon from seeing him as some kind of pint-sized plunderer. These thoughts weighed heavily on Sam, and his frayed nerves were a constant reminder that any outcome—good or bad—was possible.

Sam scaled the pile of rocks in the same manner as in his dream. He even avoided the loose rock he slipped on during his nocturnal climbs. He pulled himself onto the plateau and brushed himself off. It was as stark as he remembered it, but the wind blew with a slight whistle from this height. Sam could see a few cars speeding down Highway 190, trucks fueling up at the station, and the bus still pulled up alongside the roadway. He turned back toward the empty plateau and scanned the skies in the hopes of spotting something, anything, that might silence the skeptical voice in his head. He wondered if he needed to re-create the exact moment from his dream when the gryphon appeared. Perhaps there was a secret signal that coincidentally was the effort Sam undertook to wake himself up, a unique combination of actions that summoned gryphons.

As Sam prepared to follow through, his attention was caught by a glint on the horizon. He didn't know what it was, but it was headed right for him. It started as a speck against the expansive blue sky, approaching from the other side of the valley. It grew larger as it grew closer, and Sam stood transfixed. He squinted to try to enhance his vision. The speck was soon large enough to make out. It was a gryphon.

SL001-180-30
SUBJ: Hartwicke, Gladys
SOURCE: WS, BG
DATE: ████████

Gladys Hartwicke was nosy. She had always been nosy. Of course, she considered that an unflattering label for those who simply "cared much too much" about family, friends, and complete strangers. The Bay Area native came from a family of four sisters and two brothers, yet she never felt the desire to start a family of her own. As a result, she treated her many nieces and nephews as if they were hers. She lavished gifts upon them and was keenly interested in whatever they were up to in their lives. No detail was too minute, and she had a knack for questioning people until they were too exhausted to answer. But this was the price you paid to have Gladys in your life.

The roots of her penchant for making everyone else's business her own could be traced back to grade school. She was the student who made certain everyone was seated and quiet before class began. And heaven forbid there were students lingering outside the classroom. Gladys made it a point to inform them of the consequences for being tardy. Yet she was also the student who always offered others help when she knew they were struggling in a particular subject. In other words, she made it her responsibility to ensure everyone followed the same rules and were taken care of when needed. Buried beneath her well-intentioned, albeit meddlesome, nature was a generous heart. She really did care. So it was no surprise when Gladys Hartwicke alerted the bus driver that a certain diminutive passenger had gone missing.

"The young man who boarded behind me, he hasn't gotten back on yet," Gladys said to the driver when he finished reminding the other passengers of the bus's imminent departure. "I saw him walking into that desert," she added.

"Young man? You mean the boy you're traveling with?" asked the driver.

"He isn't traveling with me and he isn't a boy." She leaned in and whispered, "He has a condition. He's actually nineteen. Isn't that just awful?"

The driver shrugged. "The bus leaves in five minutes. He's either on it or he's not."

"Well, you can't just leave him here."

"Actually, I can. I got a schedule to keep. Or I get docked. There'll be another bus coming through here in a few hours."

"I'm sure he just lost track of time. These young people today, you know they don't wear watches anymore. They have those phones and gadgets, and out here they never work right," Gladys explained. "I can go and get him. I just need ten minutes."

"The bus leaves in five, ma'am," the driver reminded her.

"Please?" Gladys begged. Pleading with her eyes.

"I guess I can pad in another five," the driver offered reluctantly. "But not a second later—"

Gladys was already on her way. She borrowed a sightseeing couple's binoculars and spotted the "young man" heading toward a large pile of rocks in the distance. She returned the binoculars and headed after him.

Her seatmate had been asleep most of the trip, so she hadn't even been able to coax out a name. The best she could do was yell "Young man!" to try to grab his attention. Unfortunately, the hot, dry air coupled with her aged lungs made it difficult to get much volume. She was simply going to have to catch up with him. Gladys calculated she had at least fifteen minutes for the retrieval—she was counting on the driver not being so heartless as to leave once he spotted them making their way back. It was a gamble, but Gladys was a gambler.

By the time Gladys reached the rocks, the target of her pursuit had already climbed to the plateau above. Exhausted and out of breath, Gladys knew she was unable to follow him to the top, but if she only got high enough, he might hear her call out. Fueling her initiative was the frightening thought she'd had on the way to the outcropping: What if this mysterious passenger had been lying about his illness? What if he really was just a kid? The notion both terrified and motivated her. His safety suddenly became her responsibility, and that was a mission Gladys Hartwicke was born to accept.

The flapping of the creature's massive wings sent up a swirling column of dust that blanketed the plateau and rose hundreds of feet into the air. In Death Valley, these whirlwinds of dirt were often called sand augers—twisting, dust-filled tornados that fed off the desert floor as they moved across the landscape. Sam had forgotten about this part of the dream and closed his eyes and covered his mouth a moment too late. When he heard the wings slow and felt the haze begin to settle, he cautiously opened his eyes. They instantly stung from the dissipating cloud of dust, and he coughed as particles of desert sand forced their way into his throat. But it was all suddenly worth it—the stinging, the coughing, the lying, the possible grounding for eternity—for what he saw

34

standing before him was truly extraordinary. Phylassos had returned.

How do you break the ice with a centuries-old legendary creature? Sam had considered a few possibilities. First off, he could simply say something. The question was, what, exactly? "Fancy meeting you here." "I'm your biggest fan." "Please don't kill me." The options were endless. And even if he could narrow the list down to the perfect opening line, would the gryphon understand him? Did it speak English? Did it speak at all? Idea number two was to wait for the gryphon to make the first move. Sam crossed that one off the list pretty quickly, since that could involve making Sam its next meal. The most promising option was to give the gryphon a gift. An offering to build its trust and establish Sam's good intentions. Sam reached into his backpack and pulled out the only thing he had to offer: the package of cookies he had purchased from the gas station.

Sam extended his arm toward the gryphon, his sugary offering held loosely in the palm of his hand, as if he were feeding a small pet. The gryphon eyed Sam with a blend of curiosity, incredulity, and trepidation. That is to say, it looked confused. Sam couldn't help but notice the real-world gryphon was even more magnificent than its dreamworld counterpart. The dream, though realistic, still possessed an otherworldly feel. There was an oversaturation of color and light that didn't exist here in this desert. As Sam stared up at the creature now towering above him, he could truly appreciate how regal the gryphon was. It exuded an almost "angelic" presence and energy that was unlike anything Sam had felt before. Its piercing green eyes sparkled under true sunlight, and Sam could sense the powerful intelligence that lay behind them. He found it difficult to stay focused with his eyes so eager to wander. They darted from the gryphon's delicately feathered wings to its intimidating and fearsome-looking claws to the majestic crest that framed its head. Its pure white feathers bristled in a softly whistling desert breeze.

After a few anxious moments of the creature shifting its gaze from Sam to Sam's gift, Sam concluded that it was not going to take the bait. So he tossed the entire package toward the gryphon and stepped back. The creature leaned cautiously toward the gift without breaking its gaze. It sniffed at the package, then flipped it over with its formidable beak. It finally took its eyes off Sam for a moment, then suddenly turned back to him.

"Too many preservatives," growled the gryphon in a deep, almost whispery voice. The creature snatched up the package in its beak and hurled it back at Sam. "Not healthy for either of us."

It could speak! *Of course it could,* Sam thought. The book said gryphons were highly intelligent. Still, hearing the creature vocalize for the first time took Sam by surprise. He was speechless.

"But I thank you for the gesture. It was very thoughtful," added the gryphon.

"Are you Phylassos?" Sam blurted out practically all at once. The gryphon's eyes widened at the mention of this name. And Sam could have sworn he saw a smile creep across the creature's face.

"At my age, one would think I had seen all the tricks the universe had to play," the gryphon replied. "Yet here you are, standing on this rock in this desert at this very moment, knowing my name, and I do not know yours."

"I'm Sam London. You were in my dream."

"You were in my dream," said Phylassos with what Sam could officially declare to be a smile. "A dream so vivid I have journeyed to this place many times in the hopes it would hold the answers to my many questions."

"You mean, you don't know—"

"—why you and I have been brought together?" Phylassos interrupted. "I'm afraid I do not. But I trust a higher power is at work in these unusual events. There is a reason this meeting is occurring, Sam London, but knowing the universe as I do, I suspect that reason may not make itself known to us for some time."

Phylassos stepped toward Sam and leaned down so he was only a foot from his face. "But I must implore you not to speak of this to anyone. Do you understand?" Sam nodded. "No one is to be trusted, because not everyone is what they seem," the gryphon added in a measured and foreboding tone. "Tell me, Mr. London, what do you know of the gryphon's claw?"

The answer was easy: nothing. Sam had only seen gryphon claws in illustrations—except the four that were currently sitting in front of him, of course. Sam was just about to respond when his attention was caught by a distinct rustling noise that could only be generated by one thing: falling rocks. And it was coming from right below them. The gryphon had straightened instantly at the sound and moved silently to the edge of the plateau. Its mighty paws didn't touch the desert floor but floated a few inches above the surface—a feat accomplished with the gentle flapping of its wings. The beast peered over the edge to glimpse their unexpected guest.

It was Gladys Hartwicke.

Gladys didn't know what she was looking at. She had never seen anything like it. She was standing on a boulder several feet below the top of the outcropping, having slid a few feet after grabbing a loose rock. She had already ventured much farther than she expected to, but she could have sworn she heard voices—two voices, as a matter of fact—coming from the plateau, and she was determined to find out who the strange young man was talking to. The answer was looming over her, but she was too terrified to even contemplate it. As the creature's gaze narrowed, Gladys felt an overwhelming sense of dread. Her siblings always warned her that "caring too much" for people would one day get the better of her. Apparently, that day had come.

Sam's would-be rescuer did what anyone would likely do in the same situation: she screamed. If only she could have found that same magnitude of breath earlier as she was calling out for the "young man," Gladys might have avoided this moment. Her scream was surprisingly loud, and given the landscape and the stillness of the air, it had no trouble traveling across the desert floor and echoing throughout the valley. She continued her panicked cry even as she stumbled to the ground and quickly scrambled back up to race to the station. She would later claim it was pure adrenaline that propelled her across the valley and sustained her perpetual shriek. And as Gladys Hartwicke ran for her life she made this solemn pledge: if by some miracle she survived this day, she would from this time forward mind her own business.

Phylassos looked back at Sam. "You were followed," he said with unease. Upon seeing Gladys, Sam realized his plan had required a little more planning.

"She's harmless," Sam explained. "She's just a woman I was sitting next to on the bus. She must have gotten worried when I didn't come back. I'm sorry. It's my fault. I can fix this—"

Sam was already climbing back down the rocks. Phylassos peered over the edge. "Don't, Sam," he warned. "Let her go."

"No, I can make this right. Just stay here. I'll be right back," Sam responded. And he was instantly off and running.

Although Sam was gaining on his seatmate, it was becoming clear she would make it to the highway before he could reach her. He was already preparing himself to lie through his teeth and tell the woman—and anyone who heard her side of the story—that it was all just a hallucination. Her claim that a half lion, half eagle was on that rocky outcropping was simply a result of the harsh desert sun and the dust in her eyes. It was actually Sam, and only Sam, standing on that ledge. How could anyone believe otherwise?

Sam screamed after her, "Wait!" in the vain hope she would stop running and let him explain. But she was too terrified to even notice. He at least expected her to stop at the highway's edge; unfortunately, much to his shock and dismay, she never paused before crossing the busy roadway. Gladys barreled across the pavement as if completely oblivious to the cars speeding toward her. For Sam, what happened next felt like it was occurring in slow motion.

SL001-180-31
SUBJ: Larkin, Jane
SOURCE: WS
DATE: ████████

Twenty-one-year-old Jane Larkin of Bakersfield, California, was the first driver to veer off the road to miss Gladys. She was returning from Las Vegas with her boyfriend, Vincent, after celebrating her birthday. Jane spotted Gladys almost immediately, but her reaction was less than ideal. Instead of veering onto the shoulder, a frazzled Jane jerked the steering wheel to the left and careened into the eastbound lane. She hit the brakes as the car leapt across the yellow line and headed for the gas station. Unfortunately, the brakes on her late-model sports car hadn't been serviced in some time, and the car was still moving at quite a clip when it smashed into a vehicle that was being refueled.

SL001-180-32
SUBJ: Halsey, Reginald
SOURCE: WS
DATE: ▉▉▉▉▉▉

Monterey, California, residents Reginald Halsey and his wife, Claire, were gassing up on their way to Henderson, Nevada, to visit two of their six grandchildren. They had always wanted to see Death Valley, and this trip was the perfect opportunity. Claire was inside the store when Jane's car slammed into their luxury sedan. Reginald had seen it coming and dove out of the way. The impact sent the gas hose springing from the tank and spewing fuel onto the pavement. Reginald was about to grab for the hose and stop the release of gasoline, when he looked back toward the highway and realized it would be too late.

SL001-180-33
SUBJ: Caulfield, Frank
SOURCE: WS
DATE: ████████

Frank Caulfield's '79 pickup truck was a classic and looked that way. It was dented and rusty and sounded like six washing machines were working overtime under the hood. He had recently gotten a call from his brother-in-law in Las Vegas about some construction work at a new casino. Having been unemployed for a few months, Frank had little choice but to sell most of what he had, put the rest in a U-Haul trailer, and venture east for the much-needed paycheck. When Jane's car turned into his lane, Frank reflexively hit his brakes. But the speed at which he was moving made the truck unstable, and the vehicle turned slightly as it screeched to a halt. The turn was enough for the U-Haul trailer connected to the back of Frank's pickup to tear free from its hitch, tip over, and skid toward the station. Sparks sprayed from beneath the trailer as it hurtled across the pavement.

People had already sensed the impending disaster and were running frantically from the scene. Everyone—from Jane to Reginald to Milad to Frank to anyone else in the vicinity— was scrambling to get enough distance between themselves and the potential firebomb. Everyone except Gladys, that is. She had frozen like a deer in headlights at the sight of the first collision and remained that way even as the U-Haul skidded into the station. Sam gaped in horror as the sparks from the trailer ignited the puddle of gasoline. The ensuing flames followed the fuel source and raced toward the pump. Sam was the only one not running and still watching when Phylassos swooped down from the sky and snatched up Gladys in his claws. Sam was euphoric, but then the fire reached the pumps and the gas station erupted into a massive fireball. Sam lost sight of the gryphon and Gladys as a mushroom of flame went shooting skyward. Sam was thrown back from the tremendous force of the blast and everything went black.

Chapter 3
DR. VANTANA

SL001-180-34

SUBJ: Salazar, Cynthia

SOURCE: BG

DATE: ▉▉▉▉▉▉

There were a great many reasons why San Francisco
reporter Cynthia Salazar knew she had found her calling,
the most essential being the alliteration of her name,
which she loved reciting on television at the close of
her segments. She always delivered it with the same
inflection—an emphasis on the "Cyn" and a rolled "r"
to cap off Salazar. Besides her TV-friendly name,
Cynthia's predisposition to delivering news went back
to her childhood, when she was, without fail, the first
to tell you what happened, how it happened, and who it

happened to. Rest assured, if you lived in her hometown of Modesto, California, and there was a rumor spreading about you, Cynthia Salazar planted the seed and tended the crop. If there was a story you didn't want anyone to know, she would make sure everyone knew. She was a thrill seeker, but the thrill didn't come from bungee jumping or snowboarding or some death-defying stunt; it came from uncovering and sharing people's private information.

Although she would never admit it, the consummate gossip hound found that delivering bad news was somehow more exciting than delivering good news. Good or bad, she always added her own spin to a story, depending on how she felt about the people involved. That particular habit was one she had carried from childhood into her professional life.

Stuck in Bakersfield after the news van got a flat tire, Cynthia commiserated with her cameraman about how they never got the "big" stories. The day before, she'd been reporting live from a gas station in the middle of the desert. A gas station that just so happened to sell a few winning lottery tickets. *Big whoop*, she had thought. She hadn't wanted to come down to cover such a non-story in the first place, but the station producer had insisted, and she needed to stay on his good side. After all, he would be choosing the new evening-news anchor once veteran reporter Peggy Peggleman finally retired.

Cynthia couldn't stand Peggy, especially the way she over-emphasized the "p's" in her name.

Cynthia was sitting in the news van waiting for her cameraman to load the rest of the gear when she heard something interesting come over the police band radio. Apparently, there had been an explosion at the so-called lucky gas station.

"How big?" was the first question her producer asked when she called him with the news.

"From what I'm hearing, it was completely destroyed," Cynthia replied enthusiastically. "We're on our way there now. I think we should go live at five o'clock. It's an exclusive lead."

Cynthia's producer agreed. As they headed out to the station, Cynthia began writing out the story. She didn't have much to go on, but that wasn't important. What was important was having a great opening line. She settled on "It was a life-and-death struggle in Death Valley today." Much to her cameraman's chagrin, she spent the rest of the trip practicing the line with various intonations. He hadn't seen her this excited in quite some time. The truth was, Cynthia Salazar couldn't wait to deliver bad news.

The gas station Cynthia had reported from hours earlier was now just a smoldering mass of debris. The emergency vehicles were still arriving on the scene as Cynthia prepared for her live report. But the bad news proved to be not so bad after all. In fact, Cynthia's opening line would have been more accurate had it read "There was a miracle in Death Valley today." That was a change her cameraman suggested after learning that everyone involved had miraculously survived. No one surveying the damage would have believed such an outcome was remotely possible. Even a bus parked near the station and filled with elderly passengers managed to emerge unscathed. That was attributed to the quick reflexes of the driver, who threw the idling coach into reverse at the moment of the first collision and got enough distance between the bus and the station to avoid calamity. Cynthia knew that all the talk of miracles combined with the fact that the explosion wasn't intentional or suspicious meant her major news event had become a minor one. Unfortunately for her career aspirations, there was no chance this report would go national.

As the five o'clock news team prepared to lead off the newscast with Cynthia's coverage, the ambitious reporter saw one last chance to ratchet up the excitement level. She had gotten word that the woman who ran onto the highway and caused the chain reaction that led to the explosion was being transferred to an ambulance. When Peggy Peggleman handed off the newscast to Cynthia at the top of the hour, Cynthia delivered her opening line and the details of the accident before rushing to interview the woman at the center of it all.

"Why did you do it? Who were you running from? Was someone trying to harm you?" Cynthia yelled to the woman over the clamor of the emergency vehicles.

"It was a winged lion," responded a wide-eyed Gladys

47

Hartwicke. "It saved me. It swooped down and saved me. The boy. The boy knows everything. . . . He was speaking to it on that rock."

Cynthia pulled the microphone away, but it was already too late. Through her earpiece, she could hear the news team back in the studio laughing hysterically.

"Obviously, she is still in shock," Cynthia added in an attempt to hide her embarrassment.

"Maybe you should stick around down there a little longer, Cynthia," Peggy Peggleman suggested wryly. "There may also be a bigfoot sighting."

As the laughter continued, Cynthia Salazar delivered her closing line. "This is Cynthia Salazar reporting live from Death Valley. Back to you in the studio." She didn't even bother with her special pronunciation. It was the most deflated, uninspired way she had ever said her name.

Sam London awoke as he was being loaded into an ambulance. The sirens and the lights were disorienting, and it took Sam a moment to register what was happening. As soon as he did, he quickly felt his body to ensure that all his limbs remained intact. The nearby paramedic noticed and assured him he was still whole. Externally, Sam was fine, but internally, he was dealing with a nasty headache and an overwhelming sense of guilt. The obliterated gas station, the charred husks of cars, and all the people impacted by the accident: everything was ultimately the result of Sam's actions. He didn't want to be taken to the hospital; he just wanted to go home, crawl under his bedsheets, and hide from the world. But it was made clear by a California Highway Patrol officer that he didn't have a choice. He reluctantly told them who he was, and when asked why he had come to this place, he explained that he'd wanted to buy a lottery ticket for his mom from the "lucky" gas station. As for the reason behind wandering out into the desert—a fact relayed to officers by the bus driver—Sam said he was just trying to snap a great picture of the landscape and lost track of time. They didn't even bother asking him about Gladys and her "hallucination."

It was a little more than two hours later when Ettie arrived at the hospital. Sam had spent that time getting poked and prodded by doctors and searching his book for any mention of a gryphon's claw. He found nothing about the claw in Knox's book and wondered why it was important enough to cause the gryphon such concern. When his mother entered the room, Sam immediately began apologizing. But Ettie just raced to the bed and embraced her son, crying tears of relief. She held him for what seemed like an eternity but was probably just a solid minute or two. When she finally let Sam go, she looked into his eyes for an extended moment.

"You are in so much trouble," Ettie said with a mix of comfort and disappointment. "It was that dream, wasn't it?"

Sam nodded. Ettie shook her head, still digesting the day's events. For the next thirty minutes, she relayed the anguish she had endured after stopping home between jobs to look in on Sam and finding him missing. She checked with the neighbors, called the local hospitals, and eventually contacted the police. She wound up spending over an hour at the Benicia police station imagining all the possible outcomes, none of them positive, until a detective appeared with news about the accident and Sam's condition. Fortunately, the bus company had a plane ready to take relatives of riders to Bakersfield. They were especially concerned about Sam's situation and the potential legal ramifications that came with having allowed a minor to board without a parent or guardian.

When Ettie's nerves finally subsided, she began complaining about how hungry she was. The doctors planned to keep Sam a few more hours until his tests came back, and Sam had already been served his hospital dinner. With her stomach loudly rumbling, Sam suggested she slip down to the cafeteria to snag some sustenance. It was only a few minutes after Ettie left that a man in a white doctor's coat appeared in Sam's room. Sam was watching the news reports of the explosion and didn't even realize the man was there until he spoke.

"They're callin' it a miracle," said the doctor. Sam didn't recognize him as one of the physicians who had been treating him. "But I think it had more to do with luck, don't you?" He spoke with a slight Southern twang.

That word "luck" sent a shiver up Sam's spine. Sam knew, given his reading about gryphons, that people who encountered the creatures experienced good luck in the days that followed. But it wasn't until this man said it in relation to the accident that it dawned on him: it wasn't a miracle that had saved all those people; it was the luck of the gryphon. But how would this doctor know? Was it simply coincidence that he used the word? Maybe he just didn't believe in miracles.

"And that's not to say I don't believe in miracles," the man added, to Sam's surprise. "But miracles often leave far less devastation."

The man switched off the television and walked toward Sam. Sam guessed he was in his thirties, probably the same age as his mom. He was tall and good-looking and wasn't wearing a wedding ring. Handsomeness and marital status were two traits Sam automatically considered whenever he encountered men who could be possible suitors for his mother. He'd started doing that some years ago, when he noticed an underlying loneliness in Ettie. The man was carrying a large black duffel bag, which he carefully placed on the bedside chair.

"Who are you?" Sam asked.

"I'm Dr. Vance Vantana. I'm here to ask you some questions about what happened today and to run a few tests. Nothin' that involves needles," the man explained with a warm smile.

"Well, I already told the other doctors and the police everything," Sam responded, almost defensively.

"Not everything," Vantana suggested. With that, the doctor pulled a deck of cards from his pocket. "I'd like to try somethin', Sam. Is it all right if I call ya Sam?" Sam nodded.

Vantana pulled a card from the deck and turned it so Sam couldn't see its face. "Can you tell me what card I'm holding?"

"I'm not very good at these sorts of things," Sam said. "I tried the whole magician act a few years ago. I'm not coordinated enough."

"Then humor me. Take a wild guess," Vantana replied.

Sam concentrated on the card and then on Vantana, just to see if he was communicating anything through his stare. He wasn't. Sam took a shot in the dark. "Five of clubs." Vantana flipped the card, revealing a nine of diamonds. "I told you I wasn't good at this," Sam reminded him.

"Let's try again," said Vantana. "This time, we'll make it a lil' more interesting. Five dollars if you can guess the card." He pulled another card from the deck and held it up for Sam.

"That'll just make me feel worse about not getting it right," Sam quipped.

"Give it a go," requested the doctor.

Sam focused on the card, squinting, as if that might enable him to see through the rigid paper. He was about to guess four of hearts when something stopped him and he blurted out "Seven of spades."

Vantana turned the card to reveal a seven of spades. Sam gasped. "Looks like I owe ya five dollars. Tell me, Sam, what was different 'bout that one?" Vantana asked.

"I wasn't going to guess that card. I was going to say four of hearts, but right before I was about to speak that one jumped into my head and I just said it," Sam explained with bewilderment. Vantana had Sam do the card test a few more times, each time producing the same unusual result. It was only when the doctor offered money that Sam was able to guess correctly. He even tried a trick involving a ball and three cups. Sam could not for the life of him guess which cup contained the ball, until Vantana replaced the ball with a quarter. In all the excitement, Sam didn't have a moment to consider the implications of it. He was too thrilled to have found something he was good at. Especially something involving money. So Sam was hardly paying much attention when Vantana asked him a question as he was moving the cups.

"How did Phylassos look?"

Sam responded without thinking. "Amazing."

Vantana stopped the cups and Sam pointed to the middle one. "There. I . . ." Sam suddenly realized what he had said— and more importantly, what Vantana had asked. He looked up at the doctor and swallowed nervously. Vantana was smiling back at him. Sam thought quickly.

"I'm sorry, did you just ask me how Philadelphia was? It sounded like you said 'How did Philadelphia look?' And it looks amazing. In pictures I've seen. Liberty Bell, cheesesteaks . . ." Sam spoke rapidly, trying to cover his verbal tracks.

"Both you and Gladys Hartwicke show the distinct signs of havin' encountered a gryphon. Luck. Luck when somethin' is on the line. Be it life, death, or a few bucks," explained Vantana calmly. "And your signs, Sam, are incredibly strong. Of course, I've never tested anyone who's been in the company of a gryphon before. Phylassos has not appeared in quite some time."

Sam remained silent. He wasn't sure he could trust Vantana, so saying nothing seemed like the best strategy for the time being.

"Did he speak to you?" Vantana quietly asked. Sam stuck to his plan. "I know you don't trust me yet, Sam. That's a good instinct. But you're going to have to learn to trust me, and quickly."

"Quickly?" Sam said, puzzled.

"Yep," Vantana replied, his voice taking on a more serious tone. "Because you and I need to get as far away from here as possible."

"I'm not going anywhere with you," Sam declared. He instinctively moved his body back against the pillow. "Are you even a doctor?"

"I'm not a medical doctor. I have a PhD in zoology and mythological studies. I work for the government." Before Sam could follow up, Vance added, "And there'll be plenty of time to answer all your questions. But that time isn't now. I can assure you I wasn't the only one who saw Gladys on the news talking about a winged lion. The word has no doubt spread around the world. And that means there are forces out there who will be very interested in knowing why Phylassos chose to appear to you and you alone. Not to mention the fact that technically, you are the luckiest boy on the planet right now, a condition that could be exploited for less than noble reasons. In other words, you're in a great deal of danger, Sam

London. We need to find answers and we need to keep you safe. And I can't do either of those things here."

Vantana's attention was suddenly pulled away by a smell in the air. He lifted his nose and sniffed curiously toward the window. A moment later, he shook off his unease and turned back to Sam.

"Ready?" Vantana asked as he grabbed his duffel bag.

"Even if what you're saying is true, I can't go anywhere; my mom will freak out," Sam said.

"You're right. She will freak out," agreed Vantana. "That's why she can't know you're gone."

"How wouldn't she know? I'm either here or I'm not," Sam replied.

"Not exactly."

Vantana placed the black duffel on the bed, unbuckled it, and removed what looked to be a cross between a dog and a raccoon. It was covered in reddish-brown fur with stripes of black beneath its large auburn eyes. The raccoon-dog's ears were furry and perfectly rounded. It made a distinct purring sound that was higher-pitched than a cat's but just as soothing.

"His name is Nuks. He's an obake tanuki. I need you to hold your head directly over his. Can you do that for me?" Vantana asked.

Sam recognized the word "obake." He had read about these creatures in his books. They were animals from Japanese folklore that possessed magical abilities. Could this adorable creature sitting on top of him really be an obake?

Sam followed Vantana's odd instructions and leaned forward until his head was extended over the animal. Nuks took the signal and nestled his snout into Sam's neck and spread his paws on his chest. The purring sound Nuks had been making grew louder and faster and then abruptly stopped. Sam felt a shot of pain as Nuks dug his claws into Sam's skin. Sam was instantly paralyzed, frozen, as he watched something extraordinary happen.

Nuks's body began to grow, slowly and steadily stretching out until the creature was as large as Sam. He grew in proportion, with his back legs lengthening to match Sam's legs, his front legs expanding to the size of Sam's arms. Then the creature's hair began to disappear, as if it were being absorbed back into his skin. In just a few moments, this small, furry creature had managed to transform into a human. Sam regained control of his body, and he pulled back to find that the animal's face was still that of a raccoon-dog. But then Nuks met Sam's stare and its face started to change, shrinking and expanding, until Sam London was gazing upon . . . Sam London.

"You're a shape-shifter!" Sam exclaimed.

"You're a shape-shifter," Nuks responded in an animal-like growl.

"Good," said Vantana. "Keep talking so Nuks can match your vocal resonance."

"My vocal resonance?" Sam asked.

"My vocal resonance?" Nuks repeated. This time the voice was much closer to Sam's tone.

"That was better," Sam observed.

"That was better," Nuks replied, now perfectly matching Sam's "vocal resonance," as Vantana called it.

Vantana handed Nuks a hospital gown, which the creature put on. He also grabbed Sam's clothes from the closet and tossed them his way.

"Get dressed," Vantana said anxiously.

As Sam dressed, Vantana went to the window. It was a casement design, the kind that was horizontal and opened out from the bottom. He moved the lock lever and pushed, letting in a rush of cool night air. Vantana put his nose to the opening and took a long whiff. He then quickly shut it.

"Nuts," Vantana sighed.

"What?" Sam asked. "What is it?"

Vantana looked back at Sam and replied matter-of-factly, "Gargoyles."

Chapter 4
SEEING IS BELIEVING

After witnessing the shape-shifting raccoon-dog transform into his exact duplicate, Sam London was convinced that Dr. Vance Vantana was the real deal. Sam didn't consider himself vain, but he had never really seen himself like this—up close in three dimensions. He second-guessed his hairstyle and wondered if his ears stuck out a little too much. Then he speculated about the possibility of growing his hair out to disguise his ears. Two birds, he thought. Vance must have sensed his mind wandering.

"Hurry," Vantana said.

The mysterious doctor hadn't uttered much besides "Hurry" and "Let's go" since he'd made the ominous declaration that gargoyles were near. Under any other circumstances, that warning would have seemed positively loony, but considering the events of the last few hours, Sam didn't know what to believe. According to Vantana, someone was always within earshot in the hospital, and the utmost secrecy had to be maintained, hence his reason for remaining tight-lipped when it came to divulging any more information. He did, however, reveal one interesting fact when Sam was returning the gryphon book to his backpack—

"You've read Dr. Knox's book?" he asked, a touch of surprise in his voice.

"Yeah, he's the best. You know, when it comes to creatures like that." Sam pointed to the tanuki. "You read his books too?"

"You could say that. I helped write that book you're holdin'."

Sam was poised to follow up on this exciting revelation, but Vance was already at the door to the room, motioning for Sam to follow.

"No time, kid. We gotta move."

As they approached the elevator bank, Sam took up a position in front of the second of the two sets of doors. He was convinced this car would arrive first, and fortunately, he was wrong. The doors to the first elevator sprang open and Ettie emerged. Sam leapt behind Vantana to hide. The doctor quickly recognized the danger of the situation and casually shifted his body to conceal Sam. Ettie had paused after she left the car, appearing to get her bearings. But she didn't look Sam's way before figuring out the right direction. She continued down the hall as Sam slipped into the elevator. He thought back on what Vantana had said about the luck of the gryphon, namely that it kicked in when something was on the line. Maybe that meant more than just life, death, and a few bucks. Maybe it kicked in to protect Sam in ways he couldn't anticipate, as though it instinctively knew what was in Sam's best interests.

After the near disaster at the elevator, the two exited the hospital and ran-walked through the parking lot.

"How do you know Henry Knox?" Sam asked as he wound his way between the parked cars, following the doctor.

"He was my mentor," Vantana replied. He took a whiff of the night air and added, "We need to pick up the pace."

"What do you mean 'mentor'? Was he your teacher or something?"

"Yeah, in a way. But not like a schoolteacher, if that's what you're gettin' at. He was the one who hired me. The one who brought me into the department," explained Vance.

"Is that where you're taking me? To see Dr. Knox?" inquired Sam, hoping Vance would answer in the affirmative.

"I wish," Vantana said. He glanced at Sam solemnly. "Henry disappeared a few months ago."

"Disappeared?"

The doctor nodded. "But I'm hopin' you'll be the key to findin' him. If anyone'd know where he is—that is, if he's still alive—it'd be Phylassos."

"Alive? You mean, you think he could be—"

"I don't know, Sam," Vance answered with a certain resignation in his voice. The doctor stopped for a moment and hit a button on the small black remote attached to his key ring. A white SUV chirped back at him, as if to say "Here I am." Vance turned and headed its way.

"You said Dr. Knox recruited you into the department. And before, you said you worked for the government. What part of the government?"

They had reached the truck, a Chevy Tahoe, and Sam noticed a green stripe on its side, an insignia on the car doors, and a low-profile siren on its roof. The stripe led to the words "park ranger," and the insignia was an upside-down arrowhead bearing the words "national park service," along with images of a tree, a mountain, and a buffalo.

"You're with the National Park Service? You're a park ranger?" Sam asked, quizzically.

"Sort of. Get in." Vance opened the passenger-side door and waited for Sam to climb inside. Sam wasn't budging. "Trust me, kid, this is not where you want to be right now. I'll explain everything on the way."

"On the way where? I'm not getting in that car until you tell me who you really are—like who you work for and what this—" Sam was interrupted by a terrifying noise that reverberated across the starlit sky. It was the strangest sound he had ever had the displeasure of hearing. It was best described as a guttural squawk: a loud cry that was a mix of vulture and grizzly bear but with a speck of gargling. The gargle element reminded Sam of his mother gargling with mouthwash before bed; of course, this was much more frightening than anything in Ettie's presleep routine. Except for maybe those green facial masks she fancied—Sam had endured many a nightmare about those.

"Did you hear that?" Vance asked. Sam nodded slowly. "That'd be the distinct sound of a gargoyle—" Another cry joined the first one. "Correction. Two gargoyles . . . ," Vance added with concern. And then the night erupted in a chorus of the creatures. Vance swallowed. Sam's eyes widened.

"I'll get in."

"Good idea."

"Wait. What about Nuks? If those things are after me, then—"

"They'll know he doesn't smell like a human right quick. But it should buy us some time to get a bit of distance."

Sam climbed into the SUV without another word. Vance jumped into the driver's side, started the engine, and peeled out of the lot.

The noxious odor that assaulted Vance Vantana's olfactory senses in Sam London's hospital room was an unnatural blend of wet animal fur and quick-dry cement. The only other time he had encountered this unpleasant aroma was years earlier, when he was assigned to shadow a well-known real estate developer in New York City.

The developer had purchased a dilapidated nineteenth-century building on the Lower East Side of Manhattan, and instead of heeding calls to preserve it as a city landmark, he had ordered it torn down to make room for an extravagant new high-rise. Unfortunately, the building happened to be a gargoyle's nest. The bumptious developer was jogging in Central Park on a chilly January morning when the gargoyles attacked. Luckily, Vance was on the scene and managed to subdue the creatures by using an ingenious device invented by his colleague Penelope Naughton, a ranger at Redwood National Park. She had built the gargoyle equivalent of a dog whistle, and it worked like a charm. The creatures ceased their attack long enough for Vance to negotiate a truce.

It was his keen sense of smell that had led him to that moment, as well as to this unfolding situation—a sense his grandfather attributed to his unusual background. Vance Vantana was part Cherokee Indian, and the other part had roots that went all the way back to America's famous frontiersman Davy Crockett. Over the years, Vance had found ways to enhance his sense of smell with the help of Ranger Naughton and Dr. Knox. These enhancements were another unique aspect of his job with the DMW. But more about that later.

Vance hadn't counted on running into gargoyles tonight and wasn't prepared. He had the distinct feeling this impending encounter wasn't likely to prove as easily handled as that fateful morning in Central Park. "What were they after?" Vance wondered as he maneuvered the SUV northbound on Highway 99, a less-traveled state highway that ran parallel to Interstate 5. Considering the unpredictable nature of recent events, he felt it would be best to remain on roads with sparse traffic "just in case." Of course, he hadn't known gargoyles to be the type of creatures to attack without cause, only to answer a threat to their existence. But how was this boy a threat? It was still too early for Vance to answer that question. He simply didn't have enough information.

All the doctor knew was that a twelve-year-old boy had chatted with Phylassos—the greatest gryphon to ever live, and one that hadn't been seen in decades. For some unknown reason, the elusive creature had chosen to appear to a random child. Vance couldn't help but feel a twinge of jealousy. Maybe a little more than a twinge. Of all the humans in this world Phylassos could have spoken to, it should have been Vance Vantana.

He had so many questions for the gryphon, questions he had been saving since he was a boy in the backwoods of Tennessee. Now this boy—this Sam London—had his own questions. In some ways, Sam reminded Vance of himself as a child, and that made him feel familiar. It was this familiarity and the fact that the gryphon likely had some reason for choosing Sam that helped Vance overcome his initial envy.

Once they were safely in the car and cruising down the highway, Sam let it rip. "Are you going to tell me what's going on? Who do you work for? Why are we being chased by gargoyles? Where are we going?" Like a verbal machine gun, the twelve-year-old pelted Vance with a barrage of questions. Vance knew that each query would lead to another and another as down the proverbial rabbit hole they would head. Vance had to admit he enjoyed telling people the truth about the world they thought they knew. He had been on the other side of that conversation once before, on the day that changed his life forever. The opportunity to enlighten a fellow human didn't come often, but when it did, oh, how fun it was.

"Okay, okay. Slow down, partner," Vance said, looking over at Sam with a smirk. "You're probably not gonna believe what I'm about to tell you."

"I just saw a gryphon and had a dog transform into my twin, and I'm apparently being chased by gargoyles," Sam reminded the doctor.

Vance chuckled. "You're doin' pretty well with all this. Most folks would've probably freaked out by now. I know I did at first."

"You did?" Sam asked. Vance nodded reassuringly.

"Things have been movin' rather quick, Sam. But it's time to put all the cards on the table. There's somethin' you need to know about the world around you. Truth is, the whole of humanity—except for a select few"—Vance motioned subtly to himself—"don't see the world as it actually is. There are things out there that human eyes cannot perceive. They've been hidden from view."

"Why?" Sam asked.

"As a punishment . . ." Before Vance could explain all about the gryphon, humanity's curse, Alexander the Great, and the Department of Mythical Wildlife, his attention was caught by a blur in the side mirror. It was difficult to make out against the night sky, but it was big, and there was more than one. "Objects in mirror are closer than they appear" was about to take on a whole new meaning.

*   *   *

"Hang on!" Vance yelled. He dropped his arm across Sam's chest and swerved. But when Sam looked out at the road ahead of them, there was nothing to see. No other cars, no animals had wandered in front of them. What was Vance doing? The SUV sped up—Sam glanced over at the speedometer and saw the car was now going eighty, climbing steadily toward ninety. There was traffic up ahead, and Sam braced himself for what looked like an inevitable collision. Vance took his arm off Sam and grabbed the wheel with both hands. There were a car and a truck coming into view and effectively blocking the roadway from Vance's attempt to pass. The doctor steered left and crossed the divider. They were now headed toward oncoming traffic. The headlights of an approaching tractor trailer nearly blinded them as they hurtled toward it at breakneck speed. The truck's horn blared, but Vance was undeterred.

"What are you doing!" Sam exclaimed.

At the last possible second, Vance wrenched the SUV back into the northbound lanes, barely avoiding a nasty head-on crash.

"Grab the silver briefcase behind my seat," Vance ordered. Before Sam could say a word, "Now!" followed firmly.

Sam reached back and pulled a small, shiny briefcase out from behind the seat. Vance snatched it from Sam's hand and set it on his lap. He popped it open and Sam peered over to

66

get a look at what was inside, but it was too dark in the car to make it out.

"Well, I'll be, Sam—there's Phylassos!" Vance pointed out the window excitedly.

Sam spun his head around to look. "Where?" he asked as he scanned the darkness.

Sam felt a sudden shooting pain in his upper arm. He turned back just in time to see Vance injecting a dark red fluid into his body, right below his shoulder. Sam pulled away, but not fast enough. The injection was complete, and Vance yanked the hypodermic needle out of Sam's arm. Sam grabbed his shoulder, rubbing it in pain. It felt like a dozen bee stings all in the same spot. He stared daggers in Vance's direction.

"Ow! What did you do? What is that?" Sam cried.

"I'm sorry, kid. I had to. You need to see."

"See what? See that you're crazy? That you're some kind of sicko?"

Suddenly, the SUV was rocked by an unknown force, yet they were still moving. Vance pointed ominously to the hood of the car.

"To see that."

Sam turned toward the front of the SUV and his mouth fell open. There was a creature on the hood. A moving, breathing nightmare of a creature. The impact he'd felt was the beast landing on the car, its immense weight denting the hood. Its skin was smooth and hairless and was colored a dark sickly gray. Its head was that of a demon—horns protruded from its temples; it had a wide nose that snorted like an angry horse, black eyes without pupils, and a mouth with two long white fangs that curved over its bottom lip. It had two arms and legs, but each limb ended in a handlike appendage with five talons instead of fingers. And then there were its wings. They reminded Sam of the wings of a bat. They extended from its back, spanning at least seven feet, and were composed of the creature's gray skin, which was stretched to the point that it appeared almost translucent. It cried out with that same terrifying squawk they had heard back at the hospital.

Sam screamed in horror as Vantana swerved in and out of lanes in a vain attempt to shake the beast loose. The gargoyle didn't budge. It leaned forward and punched at the windshield with a clenched fist. The glass remained intact.

"Thank God for safety glass!" Vantana exclaimed with relief.

The creature reeled back for a moment and stared into the vehicle. Sam could see the gears spinning in its head. This monster was thinking, working things out. After a brief pause, it leaned forward once again. This time it pointed with one of its talons and with the tip traced a square in the glass. It struck the windshield in the middle of the tracing and the glass square popped in. Sam caught it in his hands.

"Uh . . . Vance?" Sam muttered, almost too paralyzed to speak. Vance was preoccupied with avoiding accidents with other cars and keeping an eye on the side mirror. God knew what else was coming. The gargoyle reached into the car and grabbed the edge of the now-open square. It tore the windshield from the SUV as if it were peeling an onion. That got Vance's attention. He looked at Sam, who looked back at him. The two screamed in unison.

"Hit the brakes!" Sam finally called out.

Vance slammed his foot down on the brake pedal and the SUV skidded along the road, kicking up dust and gravel in its wake. The momentum was too much for the gargoyle to handle. It careened off the hood, and Vance gunned the engine. But the gargoyle simply stretched out its wings and flapped them a few times, catching itself and remaining airborne. Vance zoomed ahead and passed the beast, which easily turned and kept pace with the SUV. It flew alongside them and stared menacingly into the car.

The SUV was rocked again, and the cries of more gargoyles could be heard over the noise of the punishing wind rushing through the open windshield. They were on the roof now. Another appeared, flying along the passenger side. One of the rooftop gargoyles reached down into the SUV, grabbing for Sam. Vance tried the brake trick again, but this time the gargoyles were anticipating it. They held on to the hood with their foot claws and one was able to pull Sam out from behind his seat belt. He tried to hold on, but the vinyl was too slippery in his perspiring hands. He quickly lost his grip.

"Sam!" Vance yelled, and reached for him, grabbing Sam's arm. The gargoyle was in the air now, flapping those massive wings. Vance and the gargoyle were having a tug-of-war with Sam's arm. It didn't last long. Sam wailed in pain and Vance's hand began to slip. The two of them locked eyes for an extended moment as they both realized what was about to happen. Sam could see the fear and desperation in Vance's expression. It was odd for him to see such sentiments in an adult. Whether it was his mother, a teacher, doctor, police officer, or even Vance—up until this moment, Sam had always found that adults projected confidence around children. The fact that Vance appeared to have lost control of the situation finally broke Sam's tough exterior.

"Vance!" Sam screamed in absolute terror. He could feel his eyes welling up with tears.

"No!" Vance yelled as Sam's hand finally slid from his grasp. As if in slow motion, the gargoyle lifted Sam from the SUV and took flight.

Chapter 5

CUT TO A CHASE

Classification 470 (Personnel Records)

Vantana, Vance

Activation Date: ███████████

By the time Vance Vantana was ten years old, he had
become one of the best trackers in Blount County,
Tennessee. His father had started schooling him early,
taking him into the Great Smoky Mountains when he
was just five. The two spent three weeks in the woods,
hunting and fishing and surviving in the wilderness. It
was on this trip, and the many others that followed,
that Vance's father taught his son not only how to live
in nature but how to understand it.

No doubt influenced by their Cherokee heritage, the
Vantana family were strong believers in the power of

animal omens—according to them, the animal world was constantly communicating with humans, but it was up to humanity to decipher their language. It was a language of symbol and totem. If you could read the signs, you just might avoid danger.

Vance hadn't been reading those signs that night in Bakersfield; he had been too caught up in the excitement. And now he was paying the price. He had just witnessed his charge, a boy named Sam London, getting plucked out of his car by a gargoyle. It wasn't long before Vance lost sight of Sam; luckily, he didn't lose the scent. The gargoyle's scent, that is, not Sam's. Upon meeting Sam for the first time, Vance noticed he wasn't able to pick up the boy's smell. This was a strange phenomenon that Vance had yet to encounter when dealing with an animal, human or otherwise. Every creature smelled a certain way, except this boy. But he would have to get to the bottom of this oddity later; Sam was in mortal danger, and Vance was his only hope. He threw the SUV into four-wheel drive and pulled the car off the highway and onto the desert floor. He could only pray he would find the boy in time.

Sam watched the SUV grow smaller as the gargoyle flew farther away. The rest of the "flock" was now following. The creatures remained low and soared silently over the desert landscape. As they continued on their path, Sam spotted a small town and scattered neighborhoods. He couldn't see Vance's SUV anymore, and he wondered if he would see anyone ever again. What did these creatures have in store for him? Sam's heart was racing, thumping so hard he could feel it in the tips of his fingers. His tears had dissipated, replaced with sheer terror. It was a fear of the unknown, a dread that he could be facing his end. He thought of his mother and what he had put her through these last twenty-four hours. If anything happened to him, would Nuks continue the ruse? He hoped for his mother's sake the creature would take his place, but that didn't seem very likely. At some point he would return to his normal form and Ettie would know the truth. Sam's seemingly innocuous dream had led him to a reality he would have never imagined possible. In that moment, he wished he had just left the gryphon well enough alone.

Angry with himself, Sam squirmed in the gargoyle's grip. The creature's claws were digging into his shoulders. He could feel the skin breaking, and knew he must be bleeding. He shifted again to help avoid the pain, but he must have shifted too much. The gargoyle lost its hold on Sam. He was now in a free fall—heading perilously toward the waiting earth.

Sam fell fast, but he didn't fall far. His death cry, which he let loose as soon as he realized he was no longer in the gargoyle's grip, was short-lived but impressive. When he hit the ground, he thought, *Wow, death isn't all that painful. It kinda feels like jumping into a pool.* He quickly concluded that he had fallen into a pool. He took in a mouthful of water, and the chlorine instantly stung his eyes. But he was alive. He pushed off the bottom and sprang to the surface, popping out like a piece of toast. He was immediately struck by the flash of lights and an abundance of noise. Talking. Conversations. He was disoriented and swam to the edge. A moment later he was being lifted out of the water by a man in a suit. But this was no ordinary man.

"Who are you?" the man asked with a menacing growl. Sam couldn't answer; he was too stunned by the man's appearance. He was about the same size, physically, as a man, even spoke like a man, but he had the head and body of a dog. His skin was covered in short, dark fur. His face was utterly canine—a long muzzle with a moist nose and pointed ears. He looked like an upright German shepherd. And he didn't seem particularly thrilled with his surprise guest. He snarled at Sam, as did the other dog-people gathered there. Sam could discern seven or eight of them in total—both males and females.

"Answer me, boy," the dog-man said more forcefully. The creature spoke with a British accent and had streaks of gray in his fur, leading Sam to conclude he must be older.

All Sam could muster was a very uncouth "You're a dog."

The growls and snarls suddenly stopped. The others gasped at the utterance and awaited their friend's response. The dog-man eyed Sam for what seemed like an eternity and breathed his warm, wet breath against Sam's face. And then the dog-man began to chuckle, softly at first, but it soon transformed into a laugh. A big laugh. As though Sam had told the funniest joke ever. The others took that as their cue and also began laughing. Amid the laughter—

"Very perceptive. You look worried. Are you a cat in disguise?" the dog-man asked. That spurred more laughs, and then one of the others spoke up.

"Maybe we should eat him and find out."

The dog-man responded, "Yes, Chad, I believe you're quite right. It has been a long time since we've feasted on cat. Though I remember it tasting like chicken . . ."

Sam panicked and screamed for help at the top of his lungs. "Somebody! Help! Please!"

"Shhhh," the dog-man silenced him. "This is a quiet neighborhood."

"Sam!" a male voice yelled from the night. The dog-people looked toward the sound's origin and found Vance Vantana hurriedly entering through a gate at the side of the pool's deck. He rushed toward Sam, but the dog-people growled and moved to intercept. The dog-man waved his hand and the others instantly stopped.

"Vance? Vance Vantana? Is that you, old friend?" the dog-man asked.

"Chase?" Vance replied, much to Sam's surprise. "What the heck are you doin' so far from ol' Blighty?"

"This is home now. Well, one of them, anyway. I thought you knew I had retired," the dog-man, apparently named Chase, answered.

"I heard about that. Just didn't expect you to retire here," said Vance. "In the middle of nowheresville."

"The dry air is good for my lungs, and you get a lot for your coin. I assume you're here for this tiny human?" Chase offered Sam, whom he still held suspended a few feet off the ground.

"Yep. Sorry 'bout that. I'll take him off your paws." Chase handed Sam to Vance like a rag doll and Vance quickly placed him back on solid ground. "Are you okay?" he asked Sam in a genuinely sympathetic tone. Sam nodded.

"Thank God I landed in that pool," he said.

"Would you care to tell me what in heavens is going on?" Chase inquired.

"Sam and I—we were being attacked by a pack of gargoyles, and one of the little monsters managed to get their claws on him."

"Gargoyles?"

"It's a long, long story," Vance said without going into detail.

"Well, I suppose it's just blind luck, then, that you landed in my pool," Chase said to Sam, who nodded in return. "Or was it the gryphon's luck?"

Sam's eyes immediately shifted to Vance, who simply grinned at the mention.

"Word travels faster than a Tennessee squirrel in a snake pit," Vance quipped.

"After all these years, when someone sees 'him,' it's awfully big news," Chase explained. "Does he"—he nodded at Sam—"have the sight or—"

Vance shook his head.

"What did you give him?" Chase asked curiously.

"Magnapedaxin thirteen."

"Let's hope it's more stable than twelve," Chase responded with a smirk. Sam looked at Vance, concerned.

"What's he talking about?"

"I'll explain later," Vance whispered. He shifted his attention back to Chase. "I reckon it is. It's runnin' through these veins as we speak."

"Always Penelope's guinea pig."

"She needs someone to test this stuff on. And I've got a heckuva good nose, but without that enhancement, I sure as God made little green apples wouldn't have picked up the scent of those gargoyles so far out. Bought us some time, for certain. I take it they didn't return?"

Chase shook his head. "I imagine they saw my guests and decided it wouldn't be wise to crash this party. Cynocephali and gargoyles—we were never very chummy. Though I'm a touch disappointed they didn't descend on us. I miss the action, Vance. There was never a dull moment," he said with a nostalgic smile. He looked directly at Sam. "I am, however, happy you dropped in, quite literally, on our little garden soiree. Perhaps you could help me quell a burning curiosity? I wonder, what did Phylassos say to you?"

"I already tried. This one is still a bit slow to trust," Vance said.

"Smart boy. Well, I am at your disposal, Dr. Vantana and Mr. Sam . . . ?"

"London," Sam offered.

"My favorite city," Chase remarked. "I am more than ready to come out of retirement, if required, particularly now. It sounds as though there are very exciting developments on the horizon for us all."

"I hope you're wrong about that," Vance said pensively. "Well, we best get to leaving and let you all enjoy your party. Apologies for the interruption."

"You're not going anywhere," said Chase.

"Excuse me?" Vance responded.

"It's much too late. Mr. London here is soaked to the bone and has been through quite a scare. You'll stay here tonight and enjoy my legendary hospitality. You can continue on your way in the morning."

Chase offered Sam his paw. "Let's see if we can't find you something dry to wear."

Sam looked to Vance for approval. The doctor considered for a long moment, then finally nodded. Sam smiled. He liked the sound of getting out of his wet clothes and getting some sleep.

The answers to all Sam's questions came later that evening as he sat at Chase's dining room table and nursed a hot chocolate. He had to admit, for a dog-man, Chase made a mean cup of cocoa. Sam reminded himself that he had to stop referring to Chase as a "dog-man." According to Vance, Chase was part of an ancient and proud race of mythical creatures known as the cynocephali. They were believed to have originated in Southern Asia before migrating to Greece sometime during the fifth century BC. Sam had come across the cynocephali in one of Knox's books. Given their canine appearance, they were initially considered savages by the humans who encountered them. Although their race had aggressive tendencies, there were those who aspired to be accepted into civil society. Sam wanted to learn more about Chase and his mysterious brethren, but that would have to wait. It was time to just get the basics squared away.

As the dryer spun the excess water from Sam's clothes, he settled into the dining room chair, snug in one of Chase's plush robes, and listened to Vantana and Chase describe a world he never knew or could ever have imagined existed.

"I work for the Department of Mythical Wildlife," Vantana explained. "We're sort of like the Department of the Interior's invisible cousin, the one who's in hidin' and no one ever talks about."

"And I work, or rather worked, for the Agency for the Welfare of Mythical Beasts," added Chase. "We're the British counterpart to the Americans."

"You said mythical, right?" Sam clarified.

"Yep. That's right. We manage the relationship between mythical creatures and humanity," revealed Vantana.

"But—"

"I assume you've always believed that such creatures do not exist," Chase concluded. "And yet here I am, right in front of you. And you've already seen a gryphon and a few gargoyles."

Sam nodded.

"They are all around us, Sam. They always have been," Vantana explained.

"But no one else can see them?" asked Sam.

"Humans can't see them," Chase replied. "At least, not all humans. You can now because Dr. Vantana gave you something."

"That injection. In the car," Sam responded. Vance nodded. "You called it mag . . ." Sam tried to remember the name he had heard earlier.

"Magnapedaxin thirteen," Vantana interjected. "It's a serum that was synthesized from the blood of—"

"Blood? From what?" Sam interrupted, completely unnerved at the thought that blood other than his own was now pulsing through his veins.

"I believe the animal is referred to as a Sasquatch," Chase answered matter-of-factly. "Isn't that right, Vance?"

"We call them bigfoot, or bigfoots, I suppose."

"Bigfoot? You shot me up with bigfoot blood?" Sam said, exasperated.

"Calm down, kid. It's not gonna kill ya. It's the only way humans can see these creatures."

"By injecting them with bigfoot blood?"

"By injecting them with a serum synthesized from the blood of mythical creatures," Vance corrected him. Sam was understandably overwhelmed, not only by recent events, but by the implications of what Vance and Chase were describing. And to top it all off, his heart was now pumping with the blood of a bigfoot, the legendary apelike creature of the American Northwest. It was named after the large footprints discovered by California road workers in 1958. Though mainstream science dismissed the idea that such a creature existed, Sam had been an ardent believer in bigfoot and currently had the proof right inside him. Of course, it wasn't likely anyone would believe him; he still wasn't sure he believed it himself. None of this made any sense. How could these creatures be living among humans and not be detected? Why did it require their blood to see them? Sam remembered something Vance mentioned in the car, before the gargoyles attacked.

"You said that humanity was being punished and that's why we can't see them."

"That's right."

"Punished for what?" Sam asked.

Chase and Vance exchanged a look. Chase smirked. "You want me to take this, old boy?"

"Be my guest," Vance said.

"Have you ever heard of Alexander the Great?" Chase asked.

"He was a general from a long time ago, right?"

"Something like that."

Sam sat quietly as Chase and Vantana took turns telling him a story that sounded like it belonged in the pages of a fantasy novel. They explained that in the third century BC, Alexander the Great became king of Macedon, a territory in northern Greece. A brilliant military commander, Alexander led his forces across Persia, conquering all in his wake. As his power grew, so did his arrogance. He became so imperious he thought himself a god. To prove he had no rival, Alexander ordered his men to catch two gryphons. He had the creatures tied to a chariot and forced them to fly him toward the sun. Alexander wished to stare into the face of God. But when he reached the very edge of the sky, he saw nothing. When he returned to earth on the backs of the crippled, dying gryphons, he was confronted by an old man who he believed to be his creator. Alexander offered him gifts and welcomed him into his kingdom. But the old man revealed himself to be Phylassos, the king of all gryphons and protector of magical creatures.

"He could change his shape?" inquired Sam at this point in the story, intrigued.

Vance nodded. "So the yarn has been spun."

Chase continued the tale. "Phylassos was furious with Alexander. For centuries, humanity and magical creatures had lived in peace. But this moment had illustrated the danger humans posed to creatures like these. Humanity's hubris would only grow more profound, and that meant animals like gryphons and the others would never be safe. Humans would find ways to exploit them and use them to serve their contemptible ways. And so Phylassos cursed humanity: from thence forward, humans would remain blind to the magical beasts surrounding them. Creatures of all shapes and sizes were given a choice: they could follow Phylassos's order or take on a more agreeable form."

" 'Agreeable'?"

"You now see me as my true self, Sam, but others see me as human," Chase explained with a modicum of disappointment. "It is our lot in life to never be seen as who we really are."

"That's a bummer," replied Sam.

"I appreciate the sentiment," Chase offered. "We are not the only species who must hide in this manner. Trolls and others appear as human to those without the sight."

"And so that's how it has been? Ever since Alexander the Great?" Sam asked.

The two men nodded.

Chase added, "Over time there has been a select group of individuals whom Phylassos has trusted to help ensure this wall of perception is never broken. Dr. Vantana and I are not the first in our positions."

"So just because humans can't see these creatures doesn't mean that the creatures can't—"

"See them. Or interfere with them." Vance completed Sam's thought. Sam nodded and yawned. "I think it's time you went to bed," Vantana concluded.

"He does appear tuckered out," Chase observed.

Sam had more questions, but Vance was right. He could feel his eyes growing heavier by the moment. After all, he had been awake for well over twenty-four hours, having foregone sleep the night before to plan his desert excursion. It was becoming increasingly difficult to stay attentive, and Sam didn't want to miss a thing.

Vance tucked him into the bed in Chase's guest room.

The doctor was very gentle when he wished to be, Sam noted. It was the first time he could remember ever being tucked in by someone other than his mother. Sam couldn't help but wonder if this was what it would feel like to have a father. Vance was strong and confident and caring. He'd be perfect for Ettie, Sam thought. But trying to make a love connection between those two would require an awful lot of explanation. It exhausted Sam just thinking about it. As Vance walked to the doorway and switched off the light, Sam managed one more question.

"Dr. Vantana—where are we going tomorrow?" he asked through the darkness.

"It's Vance, Sam. And I've got a lot of questions for you, about Phylassos," he replied as he stood silhouetted in the entry. "I need to find the answers. It'll be the best way to keep you safe. Get you back home with your mother."

"Who has the answers?" Sam asked.

"Carl," Vance said assuredly. "Carl can help."

Chapter 6
CARL CAN HELP

Penelope Naughton was still adjusting to a life she didn't remember. Each new day offered fresh revelations that were both mind-boggling and oddly familiar. It was a distinctly peculiar feeling. It was also one that had manifested itself just a few weeks prior at the International House of Pancakes in Eureka when she spotted a troll having breakfast and began questioning her sanity. Ironically, it was the troll, Trevor, who'd been by her side ever since, helping her fit together the jigsaw-like pieces of her past.

"Traybee steps," Trevor would often say when Penelope recalled aspects of her life. Traybee steps were the first steps baby trolls took when they were learning to walk. Of course, trolls were quite large as infants, so traybee steps didn't correspond perfectly to human baby steps. They were much, much bigger, and therefore, when Trevor said "traybee steps," it meant Penelope had made a giant leap in understanding. The last time she had taken a traybee step was the day she returned to the park. After passing out in the woods, she awoke in her cabin, where Trevor explained the existence of mythical creatures and her role in protecting them from humans, and vice versa.

Since then, Penelope had eased back into her role as park ranger at Redwood National Park. The most enjoyable part of her job was tending to the tourists and campers who passed through the legendary gates. She handed out maps, answered questions, and enforced the rules efficiently and affably. But there remained other aspects of her occupation that required further acclimation. Specifically, dealing with the mythical wildlife that roamed the forest. She had come to learn that, like her, many of the nation's park rangers had been briefed on the existence of mythical creatures and were responsible for their well-being. But Penelope's responsibilities to these animals went much further.

Science had always been Penelope's strong suit. Someone once told her the things you're very good at are often the things you are most humble about. When people paid Penelope compliments regarding her scientific prowess, she was always quick to point to some other scientist, past or present, who was—as she put it—so much smarter than she was. But the fact was, she was an exceptional scientist, and more importantly, she enjoyed her work. She recalled using her skills with the Department of the Interior, but it was this particular morning that she remembered using these same skills for the

Department of Mythical Wildlife. She was out making her rounds in a remote area of the park when more of the pieces of that puzzle began to come together.

"Are you going to follow me forever?" Penelope asked Trevor, who was less than a foot behind her.

"Dr. Vantana said I got to—I got to until you're not sick in the head anymore," the troll stammered.

"Sick in the head?" Penelope was annoyed by Trevor's indelicate choice of words. He looked down at her, unsure what to say or whether a reply was even necessary. Penelope noticed his confusion—a response Trevor seemed to display on many occasions. "Never mind," she added. "And what about him? Is he always going to follow me like a lost little puppy?" She motioned to the woods that surrounded the narrow hiking trail. Trevor followed her gesture and spotted the white winged horse named Gus slowly shadowing them.

"Gus? Well, yeah. He's kinda like your best friend," explained Trevor.

Great, Penelope thought. *My best friend is a horse. Well, at least he can fly.*

"Fly," Penelope heard a voice whisper. She stopped and Trevor nearly ran into her. She eyed the troll quizzically.

"What?" Penelope asked him.

"What?" Trevor replied with his requisite confused expression.

"Did you just say something?"

Trevor shook his trollish head. His appearance still took some getting used to for Penelope. He was hard on the eyes, but also sweet and surprisingly gentle. He grew less ugly with each passing day. Penelope considered his answer, peered around suspiciously, then continued on her way.

"Fly. Fly us?" the voice whispered again. Louder this time, and sounding like a question. Penelope froze, and this time Trevor couldn't slow his forward momentum. He slammed into the ranger and she tumbled to the ground. Trevor panicked.

"I'm sorry. I'm sorry, Ranger Naughton. I'm so sorry," Trevor pleaded. He pulled her to her feet with his long, hairy arm and went about brushing the dirt off her clothes. He was a little rougher than necessary, and Penelope backed away.

"What did you say?" she asked with authority.

"Sorry?" Trevor responded.

"No, before that. You said 'fly' or 'fly us' or something like that."

"No, I didn't."

"Fly us . . . ," the wispy voice called out once more.

"There!" Penelope exclaimed. "Did you hear that?"

"I didn't hear anything, Ranger Naughton," Trevor insisted.

"What are you implying? That I'm hearing things now?" Penelope asked, incredulous. "I suppose that's part of the job? Hearing voices in my head?"

"No, that's not—" And then Trevor's gaze moved from Penelope to Gus. His purple-red lips curled into a smile and he began to giggle. A low-toned growl of a giggle that exposed his large, discolored teeth, a few of which came to sharp points.

"I know, I know!" Trevor declared in his childlike voice. "You hear Gus. Gus is talking to you. I can't hear him, but you can."

"Gus? The horse?" Penelope replied. Trevor nodded happily. Penelope's eyes darted to the forest, where she spotted the winged creature. He was looking directly at her. When she met his gaze, a rush of memories flooded her mind. Memories of the two of them in the forest side by side, Penelope brushing his gleaming white coat, and of flying. Lots of flying. She could instantly recall riding on Gus's back as they soared high above the redwoods. But that wasn't all. There was one other memory that returned.

"My lab," she said wistfully. Trevor grinned.

"Dr. Vantana said you'd remember and that I couldn't tell you about it. You had to remember it for yourself. I don't know why. . . ."

As Trevor rambled on, Penelope closed her eyes and let the memories sweep over her. She could now picture her laboratory perfectly in her mind's eye. A silvery gray room with lab tables and computers and Erlenmeyer flasks—conical-shaped glass vessels holding liquids of various vibrant colors. She recalled working in the lab, mixing those concoctions, using the computers. The rush of recollections was overwhelming, like being a child on Christmas morning, racing down the stairs and seeing all the presents under the tree. Penelope discovered that she had been the lead scientist for the DMW and had perfected the ways humans were able to see mythical creatures. Her serums, developed from the red blood cells of these creatures, had minimized the amount of blood needed to provide the "sight" to humans. Her methods strengthened the potency of the injections and provided the department's officials a veritable menu of creatures to choose from. This was important since these injections didn't merely give humans the "sight"; they also bestowed upon them the magical abilities of the creatures whose blood was used. *Diminished* magical abilities, of course. Penelope had mastered the formula to ensure there wasn't too much power, which could prove fatal, and not too little, which would give humans the "sight" and nothing else. And then she remembered her own injection.

"I can hear Gus because he's inside me. His blood is . . ." Trevor nodded. "Equavolaxin," she recalled.

"Those horses there, they talk with their brains," Trevor added. "And you can also fly with them and go really high. I've seen you do it. You once went so high I couldn't see you anymore."

"Of course," Penelope said, realizing, "I can breathe up there because of the injection." She spun toward Trevor. "Where's my lab?"

"Where you left it?" he said, uncertain.

"Never mind. I think I remember," she declared as she stepped into the woods. She reached Gus, petted his silvery mane, and said, "Let's fly."

The horse whinnied in excitement and lowered his body to allow Penelope to climb on. She mounted the horse and Gus galloped forward, flapping his feathered wings. As Gus took flight, rising above the redwoods, Trevor heard Penelope joyfully cry out, "Traybee steps!"

The anticipation of what another day held was too great to keep Sam London in bed much after dawn. There was also something else propelling him from his slumber: the distinct smell of breakfast. His nose could discern several elements of the impending feast, including bacon, toast, and a dish with onion. The delectable combination of scents crept in under the door and rose a few feet to find Sam lying on the mattress. He slowly sat upright, as if the appetizing aroma had reached out with wispy fingers and pulled him to a seated position.

Judging by the quality of the hot cocoa Chase had prepared the night before, Sam assumed this morning's meal was likely to be as delicious as it smelled. As he climbed out of bed, he noticed that his clothes had been placed on a red velvet wingback chair in the corner of the room. They were dry and even appeared to have been pressed. The chair and the simple wood-framed bed were the only two pieces of furniture. Sam concluded that cynocephali were minimalists when it came to interior decorating. The entire home was mostly empty and didn't evoke any particular style. He had hoped to see a few pictures of Chase's family. He wanted to find out if there were different breeds of cynocephali. He was dying to lay eyes on a man-sized Chihuahua. Unfortunately, the house was devoid of personal effects. Sam considered this an interesting cultural observation. These dog-people must not be a nostalgic sort.

Sam got dressed and followed his nose to the dining room, where he found the large mahogany table set with polished silverware and a smorgasbord waiting to satiate his hunger. Among the spread were several identifiable items and a few that appeared alien.

"Good morning, Mr. London," said Chase as he entered with a plate overflowing with fried eggs. "Hungry?"

"Starved," Sam replied.

"Please." Chase gestured to a chair. As he did, Sam observed a small white patch on Chase's arm. A single colorless spot. Chase noticed. "Family birthmark. I guess I should be thankful they didn't name me Spot," he joked.

Sam peered around. "Where's Dr. Vantana?"

"He's having a new windshield put on the car. The hazards of playing with *les gargouilles.*"

Sam sat down, pulled his chair close to the table, and got right down to business. It was all as tasty as he'd predicted. Chase also indulged, but not nearly with the same abandon. He appeared amused by Sam's appetite. He explained that they were eating a "full English breakfast." There were fried eggs, fried tomatoes, bacon, sausage, toast, and a dish called bubble and squeak, which Sam initially believed was fancy dog food for cynocephali. It was actually a vegetable dish, but

Chase had quite a chuckle at Sam's original determination. Yet with all the delicacies to choose from, Sam enjoyed the cookies Chase had set out the most. They were small and rectangular in shape, with a slight coconut flavor and the word "NICE" etched on their face. Chase referred to them as biscuits and confessed that he'd had a weakness for the sugary treats since childhood. The conversation then turned to Sam.

"Why do you suppose Phylassos chose you?" Chase inquired. Sam shrugged as he took in a mouthful of eggs. Chase squinted at Sam and added, almost to himself, "What makes you special?"

Sam was quick to respond. "Nothing. Nothing makes me special. I promise." If only Chase could see his room, Sam thought. The cynocephalus would bear witness to all the failed attempts to find that one special skill. Chase considered Sam's answer but didn't seem to believe it. As Chase eyed him, Sam looked around the dining area. It was as sparsely decorated as the guest room.

"Why don't you have any pictures of your family?" Sam asked.

"Observant, I see," Chase replied. "Cynocephali do not prize familial relationships or any relationship based solely on genetic correlation. It can prove binding. As such, we have no need to make proud or opportunity to disappoint. We see relationships as purposeful, and purposes have beginnings and ends."

"Do you care about each other?" Sam wondered.

"We care very deeply, but not about any one individual. About all of us. About our collective future," Chase explained.

"Do you have a family?"

"I have offspring, but when cynocephali children are born, they are raised separately from their parents."

"So you don't know your own children?" Sam asked.

"I know of them. But we interact as fellow cynocephali. Nothing more. Enough about us. I have a great many questions about Phylassos. His appearance could mean many things to us as a species."

Sam kept stuffing his mouth to avoid answering Chase's increasingly pointed questions. He went through a whole package of biscuits and could tell the cynocephalus was growing frustrated. Fortunately, Sam was saved by the appearance of Dr. Vantana, who had returned from having the car fixed and was eager to leave. Sam thanked Chase profusely for his hospitality, which turned out to be as legendary as promised. Chase reiterated to Vance his willingness to lend a hand if needed, and Vance nodded and expressed hope it wouldn't come to that. Before they pulled away in the newly repaired SUV, Chase slipped a box of NICE biscuits to Sam for the ride to Redwood National Park.

"A gift for you, Sam London," Chase said as he handed them over. Sam smiled big.

"Thanks! I might eat them all before we reach the park," Sam proclaimed.

"They're hard to resist."

Sam waved to the cynocephalus as they drove off. He would miss his unusual new friend, especially his cooking.

Once they were on the road, Sam figured it was a good time to finish the conversation he and Vance had begun the previous evening.

"Before yesterday, when was the last time someone had seen Phylassos?" he inquired.

"Technically speakin', the last time he appeared to a human—or anyone, for that matter—was in 1945, shortly after the Potsdam Conference and the atomic bombing of Japan. It was a secret meetin' with the leaders of the world, informin' them that a balance needed to be kept. He wouldn't allow humanity to destroy the planet. After all, they weren't the only ones on it."

"So he revealed his existence and the existence of mythical creatures?" asked Sam.

"He had to. But they were all sworn to secrecy."

"But why would these leaders care about keeping it a secret?"

"Because if they didn't, Phylassos couldn't protect them," Vantana explained. He noticed Sam's confusion and continued, "You see, not all magical creatures agreed with Phylassos's curse on humanity. Many believed they should rid themselves of these humans. The use of nuclear weapons only added to that belief. Phylassos warned these leaders that in order to keep this balance, he would need help. Some way of protecting that secrecy and handling any incidents that might arise."

"The DMW," Sam concluded. Vance nodded.

"There were individuals like the cynocephali who had taken on that mantle in the years prior, but Phylassos felt it was time to bring humanity in on the cause. And there just so happened to be one of the world's foremost authorities on mythology in attendance. His name was Dr. Arrigo Busso. And he brought along his twelve-year-old protégé—Henry Knox."

"Dr. Knox was there?" Sam responded excitedly. Vance grinned.

"He was indeed. The two of them were charged with creating agencies like the DMW in every country. Since then, there have been rumors of Phylassos sightings and some supposed communication with the gryphon, but nothing like Potsdam or the other day with you. Now, are you going to tell me what Phylassos told you or what?"

"I have a few more questions," Sam replied.

"Shoot," said Vantana.

"Are you married?"

Vance eyed him. He wasn't expecting that query. "No."

"Girlfriend?" Sam followed.

"This is an odd line of questionin'," Vantana observed. Sam shrugged.

"Just trying to get to know you. See if we have anything in common. I'm also not married and I don't have a girlfriend," Sam responded.

"Really? I'm surprised. Just haven't met Miss Right yet, have ya?"

Sam shook his head. "Not yet. But I'm still young."

Vance smiled at that. He sniffed the air. "Why the heck do I smell coconut?"

"Oh. Those are the NICE biscuits Chase gave me for the road. They're really good."

"Well, I guess a dog would know his biscuits."

Sam chuckled. "You could smell the coconut?"

"I've always had a good sense of smell. Of course, the serum enhances it."

"How?"

"A serum can enable a human to manifest some of the abilities of the creature whose blood is used. Bigfoots have a killer nose."

Sam took a deep breath through his nostrils, but he couldn't smell the coconut from the cookies. He tried again. This time he took short sniffs like a bloodhound; however, he still couldn't detect the slightest scent from the cookies.

"What are you doin'?" Vance asked quizzically.

"I'm trying out my enhanced sense of smell," Sam explained.

"And?"

"Nothing. There's no difference. Does it work for everyone who takes it?" Sam asked.

"So far. Maybe it just takes time to develop," Vance suggested.

"Did it take time with you?"

Vance thought about that for a moment. "Well, maybe it's 'cause you're a kid."

"I doubt that would have an effect. If anything, it should be stronger in my case 'cause I'm smaller," Sam answered with certainty. Even after being injected with superpowered bigfoot blood, Sam was still just Sam.

The two of them finished out the trip in silence. Sam sulked over his lack of supersmell, while Vance sat frustrated with Sam's continued refusal to answer any of his Phylassos-related questions. Even so, they were both quite comfortable. They had serendipitously stumbled upon one of the many things they had in common.

Trevor the troll found himself sitting across from Sam London in Ranger Naughton's cabin. It was quite thrilling for him, since Sam had become a bit of a celebrity in the world of mythical creatures. Word had spread of the boy's encounter with the legendary gryphon, and the world was abuzz with rumors and conjecture around Phylassos's appearance. Trevor had heard of the incident from his second cousin Toby, who in turn heard it from his fourth cousin Tommy, who heard it from his half sister Tina. Troll families, though large, remained close-knit. They were creatures who valued family and friendships above all else and took great pride in the number of people they could call friends. In fact, trolls could quickly tell you the exact number of friends they had at any given moment. At this particular point in time, Trevor claimed eight hundred and two friends. He hoped to make it eight hundred and three. The addition of Sam London would be a triumph not only for Trevor but also for the entire troll race. Trevor could boast that his latest friend was one of the most famous humans in the mythical world. And any trolls related to Trevor would by simple fact of familial relation obtain bragging rights.

"So you're a troll?" asked Sam London with boyish wonder. Trevor nodded. "Are there many of your kind in the world?" Trevor nodded again.

"We're pretty much everywhere. Some creatures have ind-ind-ind—"

"Indigenous?" Sam offered.

"Yeah. In—" Trevor struggled. Sam assisted once again.

"—digenous."

"—places they live. But my kind, we can make ourselves comfortable anywhere. Except for like the ocean or inside a volcano."

Trolls weren't good swimmers, and as for volcanoes, trolls didn't get along well with the Cherufe, a volcano creature who refused to share. Sharing happened to be the cornerstone of the troll culture. No matter how small a morsel of food a troll possessed, he or she would always share it equally among friends and family. In fact, the act of sharing was so important, it was the method by which they established a new friendship. So when Sam offered Trevor one of his British "biscuits," the troll lit up and smiled so wide his ears crinkled. Eight hundred and three.

* * *

The broad grin on Trevor the troll's face proved more un-nerving than comforting for Sam London. Perhaps it was the color and sharpness of the teeth that caused the traditionally joyful expression to appear almost menacing. But Sam knew that the troll's grin, though a touch frightening, was well-intentioned. Vance had informed Sam about Trevor before they reached Penelope Naughton's cabin.

"He may not be pretty. Heck, he may even give ya night-mares. But just remember, he's a big ol' teddy bear," Vance explained with his signature smirk.

The doctor had also taken time before they arrived to ex-plain Penelope's role within the DMW and mention her re-cent bout of amnesia. Penelope's cabin sat off a small service road deep in the forest. It was surrounded on three sides by giant redwood trees and had a rustic wood facade and a stone chimney. Once inside the quaintly decorated home, Vance in-troduced Sam to the ranger and the troll, then disappeared with Penelope down a staircase that was hidden behind a painting. The painting was of a winged horse drinking from a pond. Sam noticed that the painting was signed simply *Trevor*. As Trevor munched on his cookie, Sam had to ask.

"Did you paint that?" He gestured toward the frame. Trevor nodded, crumbs falling off the small tuft of hair on his chin.

"It's good. My mom is an art teacher, so I'm a well-informed critic. It's very imaginative."

"Oh. I didn't imagine that," the Troll corrected Sam. "It's a portrait. You'll meet Gus later."

Sam let that sink in as he looked back at the painting. The frame suddenly swung back open and Vance and Penelope emerged.

"Come on, Sam. You've got an appointment," Vance said as he grabbed his jacket and hat. Sam climbed to his feet and reached out his hand for Trevor to shake.

"It was nice"—Trevor pulled Sam into a hug—"meeting you," Sam strained to say.

"Wow," Vance quipped. "You two are friends already? That was quick."

It was later on in their adventure that Dr. Vantana would reveal to Sam what sharing meant to trolls. The simple act of giving Trevor a cookie resulted in making a lifelong friend. Sam finally broke free from the troll hug, which felt like a bear hug, only sweatier. He said his goodbyes and followed Vantana to the door. Penelope pulled him aside before he exited.

"Dr. Vantana tells me you have not exhibited any enhancements following the injection of Magnapedaxin thirteen," the ranger whispered. "Is that still the case?" Sam sniffed the air and nodded. She pursed her lips to the side in a perplexed manner. "That's very unusual."

"I'm not surprised," said Sam. "It figures it wouldn't work on me."

"No, it doesn't. There's a reason, Sam. It's just a matter of scientific investigation. I'll get to the bottom of it. I promise." Penelope smiled and mussed Sam's hair.

*   *   *

The sun was just beginning to disappear past the horizon as Sam followed Vantana off a trail and farther into the woods. Sam had never visited Redwood National Park and was overwhelmed by the size of the trees. Dr. Vantana explained that the tallest of the trees was known as *Sequoia sempervirens* and the largest in diameter was *Sequoiadendron giganteum*. Sam was in awe of these massive spires of wood and leaves. They were nature's version of skyscrapers.

After forty-five minutes of hiking, they came upon a giant redwood trunk that was damaged during a lightning storm and had fallen to the ground. The slope of the terrain propped the trunk up several feet from the surface, enabling Vantana and Sam to walk beneath it.

"It's just through here," Vantana said as he stepped underneath the hollowed-out trunk.

Sam followed the doctor, and when he emerged on the other side, he suddenly noticed a change in the landscape. The trees now surrounding them were even larger than the ones they had passed along the way. Four times as big as the biggest redwood they had come upon just a quarter mile back.

"Are these still *Sequoiadendron giganteum?*" Sam asked.

"Nope. These are *Sequoiadendron collosaeus*. The true giants of the forest. Not many humans have laid eyes on them, Sam. This is a section of the park that is hidden from our kind for reasons you'll come to understand."

Sam could hardly fathom the magnitude of what he was seeing. He felt as if his eyes were betraying him. These trees were just too big to be real.

Dr. Vantana led them down a beaten path until they reached a pond surrounded by several *Sequoiadendron collosaeus*. Sam recognized the pond as the one in Trevor's painting, sans the winged horse. Exhausted, Sam plopped down on a rock to catch his breath. Vantana was busy scanning the terrain and muttering to himself.

"Are we there yet?" Sam asked, out of breath. "We're not going to camp the night, are we? I really don't like camping. I'm not very good at it. I didn't last very long in the Boy Scouts. They wanted me to learn all these knots. Do you know how long it took me just to learn how to tie my shoes?"

"Shhh," Vance silenced him. "I always get a little mixed up here. North is noon; we're looking for four o'clock." Vance pointed his left arm northward, then moved his right arm like the small hand of a clock until he reached four o'clock. His hand was now directed at one of the trees that lined the pond. It looked big enough to park two dozen cars around its base and soared into the sky so high Sam couldn't see the top. Dr. Vantana walked toward the tree, and Sam gathered himself and followed. Once they were at the base, Vantana put out his hand and began feeling the rough, creviced bark. This went on a full minute before Sam finally asked—

"Uh . . . what are you doing?"

"Lookin' for the button," Vance replied, frustrated.

"Button?" Sam asked. "Button for what?"

Vance abruptly stopped his hand and grinned. "The elevator." He pushed in on the tree bark and Sam could distinguish a button-shaped indentation. It lit up with an auburn glow and was followed by the distinct ding of an elevator arriving. Sam watched in amazement as the bark vibrated and wrinkled, then split and slid open. This tree apparently had an elevator. It looked like one you would find at an upscale apartment building, well lit, with sequoia-paneled walls. A familiar classical piece played over the elevator speakers; Sam remembered it from music class as a composition by Mozart. Vance stepped inside, but Sam hesitated.

"They carved an elevator into a tree?" Sam asked in disbelief.

"Not carved into the tree. It just appears that way. It's actually part of a structure that was built around the tree." The doors began to close and Vance stopped them with his arm. "I don't feel like climbin' today, Sam. You're gonna have to get in."

Sam entered the elevator and Vance let the doors close. The control panel had hundreds of buttons. Each was labeled with a floor number and a time. Vance's finger hovered above the panel and then settled on one of the buttons. The forty-seventh floor at eight-fifteen. Sam concluded that, like the arrangement of the trees around the pond, this was also configured in relation to a clock. Upon the push of the floor button, the elevator immediately shot upward. Sam grabbed the handrail to steady himself. The ascent was quick and not entirely straight up. Sam could feel the elevator shift sideways—and he realized it must be circling the tree. The sensation was akin to being shot up a spiral staircase at high speed. Sam's ears popped, and he began to feel light-headed. Vantana was watching.

"You get used to it," he offered.

Sam wasn't sure why he would ever need to. When else would he be traveling in an elevator that was part of a giant redwood tree? The elevator halted as suddenly as it had started. Sam had to grip the handrail to keep from falling over. The doors slid open and Sam's eyes went wide. He was staring out onto a massive tree branch that stretched outward into a sea of intermingled branches. There was nothing on either side of this branch except a steep drop to the ground. The branch itself was about as wide as a two-lane roadway. Vance motioned for Sam to get off.

"This is your stop."

"*My* stop? You're not coming with me?" Sam asked.

"I think it's best if you talk with him by yourself. Maybe you'll tell him all the stuff you won't tell me," Vance said with a snarky smile. Sam wouldn't admit it, but he had come to trust the doctor, even if he wouldn't share with him exactly what the gryphon had said. He'd been instructed to be careful with whom he spoke about their meeting, and he was taking that warning seriously. He also felt safe around Vance and didn't much like the thought of the ranger not being with him for his encounter with the mysterious "Carl." Rather than admit this feeling, Sam steeled himself and stepped out of the elevator and into the open.

"Well? Where is he?" Sam asked.

"In his house. Waitin' for you. You gotta go knock on his door, Sam."

"Knock on his door?" Sam repeated.

"Or ring the bell, whichever strikes ya."

"What door? What house?"

Vance pointed. "That one right there." Sam followed his finger and saw nothing. He peered back at Vance, his disbelief evident in his expression.

"Look harder," Vance suggested firmly.

Sam turned his eyes toward the branch once again. This time he focused and scanned the scene carefully. His gaze concentrated in one spot for a second or two; then he saw it. There was something on the branch just a few yards ahead. Sam squinted, thinking it might help him discern what he was looking at. It was a structure of some sort, but it was camouflaged so as to be almost completely invisible. It was as if Sam were seeing through the structure itself. As though it were entirely transparent. It was only visible because the edges of the structure didn't seamlessly transition into its environment. This visual wrinkle in the air betrayed the outline of the structure just enough for Sam to spot it. The more he stared, the clearer it became.

It was a house of simple architecture. One that reminded Sam of the colonial homes he had seen in history documentaries. It had four windows and a front door covered by an arched portico, held up by two pillars. The structure was exactly the width of the branch. It was a tree house unlike any Sam could have imagined. As he started toward it, he immediately noticed that this house was much larger than he'd thought. The front door was twice as tall as a normal front door. Carl must be big, Sam deduced. He glanced back at Vantana, his nerves dancing a jig in his stomach.

"Go on. He won't bite," Vance said reassuringly. "You're small enough that he could just swallow you whole." The doctor chuckled at his joke, but Sam wasn't amused. He got to the door and found that both the knocker and the button for the bell were too high for him to reach. He clenched his hand into a fist and banged against the wooden surface. Even at this proximity, the camouflage was impressive, making it appear as though Sam were knocking on air.

"Door's open. Come on in," a voice called from inside the house. It sounded mature in its tone—Carl must be old, or older than Vance, anyway. Sam leapt up and grabbed the knob, turning it in the process and pushing it open. He swung into the home, still clutching the giant doorknob. He let go and dropped to the ground. When he looked back toward the elevator, he saw that Dr. Vantana had already gone.

"You may wait in the study. I'll be in, in a moment," the voice added. Sam glanced around at his surroundings. It was a well-appointed home. The entryway led into a hallway with stairs leading to a second floor. The decor was antique in nature, bordering on ancient. There was a stone bench in the hall with etchings that appeared, to Sam's unarchaeologically trained eye, to be Egyptian. The walls were adorned with paintings from several eras, all sharing a common theme: nature. There were forests and mountains, hills and valleys, desert landscapes and coastal views. Carl had managed to bring a little of the outside inside.

Sam noticed an open set of double doors leading to a living room, and another door that led to what Sam concluded was the study. The living room had couches that were, like the front door, twice the normal size. There was a coffee table made from an old tree, which appeared to have been involved in a fire, since it was covered in scorch marks. The far wall had two windows that were separated by a massive fireplace and offered breathtaking views of the park. Atop the fireplace was a mantel with photographs, and above the mantel was a giant painting of Phylassos. Sam quickly determined that it was the same image of Phylassos from Dr. Knox's book. He strained to make out the photos on the mantel, but they were too small and far away. He was just about to step inside for a closer look when he heard a thump from a nearby room, followed by pounding footsteps. Sam quickly retreated to the study.

The study was more like a library with a desk and chairs. The room was lined with massive bookshelves that reached all the way to the top of the cathedral ceiling and were filled with tomes of varying sizes. The desk sat in front of a bay window that offered more extraordinary views. It was built from a dark mahogany wood and decorated with intricate carvings of mythological creatures. The backs of the two leather chairs in the room had similar carvings. Sam's eyes wandered and focused on a framed picture displayed on a credenza behind the desk. The photograph was of Dr. Knox standing next to a very large creature. Before Sam could comprehend what he was looking at, the voice returned, and this time it was in the room and standing directly behind him.

"Mr. London. It is an honor to meet you," the voice said humbly. Sam slowly turned to face his host. "If I'm not mistaken, your heart is pumping some of my blood around in that body."

Sam could barely manage a nod.

"Call me old-fashioned, but I believe that makes us family. And *mi casa es su casa*. Welcome home, Sam."

Carl was Sam London's newest family member, and he was also a bigfoot.

Chapter 7
A CLAW FULL

"My name is Vance Vantana, fresh from the backwoods, half horse, half alligator, a little touched with the snapping turtle; can wade the Mississippi, leap the Ohio, ride upon a streak of lightning, and slip without a scratch down a honey locust; I can whip my weight in wildcats—and if any gentleman pleases, for a ten-dollar bill, he may throw in a panther. So now that I've introduced myself, how about you return the favor? Come on. I can smell ya from here."

Thirteen-year-old Vance Vantana stood somewhere in the Great Smoky Mountains and called out to the seemingly empty forest that surrounded him. He clutched an aged hunting knife in his right hand. The blade was about ten inches long with a carved wood handle.

Vance had a habit of introducing himself using an old quote from Davy Crockett. He'd found the colorful description in a biography of Crockett borrowed from the school library. He enjoyed seeing a person's reaction to his unique introduction, but this time he didn't get the opportunity.

On Vance's thirteenth birthday, his father gave him the one present money couldn't buy: permission to hunt and camp by himself. Vance had been lobbying for approval since age seven, but his parents refused. When Vance read that Davy Crockett had gone out on his own at age thirteen, he immediately informed his father and the two made a deal: Vance would be allowed to explore the backwoods of Tennessee without a chaperone only when he turned thirteen and only if he stayed in school. Davy had dropped out of school at the same age to begin his adventures, and Vance's father didn't want his son to get any more ideas. On the day of his thirteenth birthday, Vance awoke just as the sun began to creep over the horizon and set out into the wilderness. What Vance didn't know was that this excursion would prove to be more than just a rite of passage.

For at least two years prior, Vance had been tracking a scent through the woods that was unlike any other he had encountered. Unfortunately, the trail often went cold or led to nothing, or he was called back to camp by his father. But on this day, Vance Vantana's birthday, the young tracker had managed to corner the smell and whatever was emitting it. So there he stood, waiting for it to reply to his introduction. The scent was at its strongest and was best described as musty and thick, like an old basement. But there was more to the odor than that. Vance could detect hints of lavender and chamomile. He wondered what kind of creature would attempt to mask its natural scent with flowers. The only animals Vance knew that tried to cover their smell in this manner were humans, yet there was no way this thing he had been tracking could be human. It moved too quickly. He couldn't even get eyes on it. It was a virtual phantom.

"You and I been doin' this dance since I was eleven. I think it's high time I met my partner, don't you?" Vance let that hang in the crisp mountain air for an extended moment. "I'm thirteen now. I'm an adult, and that means I can come into these woods whenever I like. I won't get tired of this, but I reckon you will." A brief pause, and then he added, "Don't be afraid; I ain't gonna hurt ya." He slowly slid the knife back into the sheath that was slipped under his belt.

Whatever it was didn't care for being considered "afraid" of anything. There was a sudden rush of air and a massive thump. Something was standing right in front of Vance, but he couldn't see it. He could sense it just a few feet away, but the space was empty. And then he heard it moving toward him. *Thump, thump, thump.* Until it was just inches away. Vance took a quick breath and held it. He could feel the creature's breath on his face and knew it was studying him. It exhaled and blew Vance's coonskin cap right off his head.

"I ain't scared of you," Vance said haltingly. He tried to look tough, but his quivering bottom lip betrayed his fear. A low, growling laugh followed, and then a second of silence. Vance swallowed, trying to nudge those butterflies in his throat back down to his stomach. But his attempts to hide his dread didn't matter. The "invisible" creature let loose with a roar so loud, it was as if the sound passed through Vance's entire body. He could feel his organs shake and his spine shudder from the force of it. It was an animal call that was entirely alien: part bear, part gorilla, and all terrifying.

Now, Vance was a brave boy, probably the bravest boy his age in the world at that time, but he was also smart. "Right smart in the head," his father used to say. Those smarts kicked in, and Vance did the only sensible thing: he turned and ran for his life, screaming the whole time. He didn't get far, though, since he slammed face-first into a hickory tree. He was out cold before he hit the ground. The roar suddenly ceased.

Vance awoke to the gurgling sound of a running stream and could tell simply by the way the water rushed over the rocks exactly which stream it was. It was an offshoot of Chilhowee Lake, which was part of the Little Tennessee River. He slowly opened his eyes to find he was propped up against a tree a few feet from the stream. He had an awful headache that pulsed with his heartbeat and a stinging pain in his left shoulder. He clutched it and tried to rub the pain out. Things were still a little fuzzy.

"Hello, Mr. Vantana. It is good to finally meet you in person," someone said in a plain and soft-spoken voice.

Vance looked to the source and his eyes slowly focused on an older man, perhaps in his late forties. He had a kind smile framed by a closely trimmed dark brown mustache and beard that sported streaks of gray. The hair on his head shared similar strands of gray and was hidden under a short-brimmed brown Stetson. His face, though youthful, was beginning to show the inevitable signs of age in the wrinkles on his forehead and around his green eyes.

Sitting to his right was the park ranger, a Norwegian fellow by the name of Orry Avskogen. Vance had encountered Orry several times during his trips into the Great Smoky Mountains National Park. Orry was a tall, burly man. He had a pitch-black beard and long hair, which he kept pulled back into a ponytail. He was an intimidating presence with eyes as black as coal.

"Who are you?" Vance asked the man next to Orry. Then Vance redirected his question to the park ranger as he gestured toward the mystery man. "Who is he, Ranger?"

"My name is Dr. Henry Knox. I have been following your exploits for some time, by way of Orry and Rupert, of course." Knox motioned to his right and left. Vance's eyes drifted over and he was suddenly staring at a massive human-like creature. He immediately knew this was what he had been chasing. It was at least eight feet tall and covered in brown hair that grew from every inch of its body except its face. It had large eyes shadowed by a pronounced brow. The nose reminded Vance of a gorilla's, only slightly narrower. Its head was oval in shape, and its facial hair was trimmed like muttonchops. The skin that was hairless was a light brown and faintly wrinkled. As for its mouth, it was wide and smiling to reveal perfectly white teeth.

Vance moved his body swiftly, leaping like a gazelle to

position himself behind a tree for protection. He peeked around the trunk to get another look at the beast. It continued to stand there with its big hairy arms folded, but now it was laughing. That irked Vance to no end.

"I don't believe you two have been formally introduced. Rupert was the object of your obsession," Knox said. But Vance wasn't listening; he was glaring at the creature.

"What's so funny you grinning like a mule eatin' saw briars? You laughing at me?" Vance stomped toward Rupert, growing angrier with each step. "I wasn't scared, ya know," he declared, which only caused Rupert to laugh more, and now Orry joined him. "I'll show ya who's scared." Vance put up his fists, ready to fight the creature, but Rupert unfolded his arms and offered his giant hand to the boy.

"My laughter is not meant as an insult, I assure you. My apologies if that is the way you interpreted it. I simply take great mirth in the utter absurdity of this situation. I stand here in front of a boy who has managed to succeed where so many of his elders have failed. The wisdom of age or experience mattered not. It was a thirteen-year-old boy who cornered the elusive, legendary bigfoot." Rupert spoke with a gentleness and elocution that hardly matched his exterior.

"A bigfoot?" Vance reacted to the mention of the name with disbelief. Rupert nodded.

"I am honored to make your acquaintance, and I hope to be your friend." Rupert's hand remained open, waiting for Vance to make his move. The boy eyed Rupert and then his hand. He glanced at Knox, who smiled and nodded ever so slightly. Orry just watched with a smirk and a twinkle in his black eyes.

Vance reached toward Rupert's hand, and the bigfoot took the boy's hand into his own. They shook, tentatively at first and then with strength.

"Now that you and me are pals, mind tellin' me why I couldn't see you before?" Vance asked. "You were invisible. Like some kind of ghost."

"Ah, yes. I can explain that, Vance. And once you understand, I will offer you a rather unique opportunity," Dr. Knox responded.

"Opportunity to what?"

"To help us," Knox answered. "But I must warn you, this information will change your life forever. Think you can handle that?"

"I think Mr. Vantana will be just fine," Rupert interjected. "Isn't that correct, Vance?"

"Bigfoot here is about as smart as he is hairy," Vance quipped. "C'mon, Doc, let's have it."

More than two decades later, Dr. Vance Vantana stood at the base of the *Sequoiadendron collasaeus* after just having left Sam London with Carl. He was the oldest and wisest of all bigfoots, and Vance hoped he would be able to wrest some information out of the kid. Once Sam went inside, Vance returned to ground level to wait for him. As he watched several bigfoot creatures return to their homes in the trees, he reminisced about his first encounter with Rupert, who was Carl's uncle. But with that memory came memories of Henry Knox, and those only made Vance frustrated. He was worried about his missing mentor, and he was more determined than ever to find him.

The trip down memory lane was cut short by the appearance of Penelope. Ranger Naughton flew in on Gus and landed a few feet from Vance. She leapt off the winged horse and hurried toward the doctor.

"I just got a disturbing call from the Agency for the Welfare of Mythical Beasts, a man by the name of Chriscanis," Penelope announced anxiously. "He didn't give me his last name."

"He's cynocephali. They don't have last names," Vantana replied. "What was so disturbing?"

"There was a break-in at the British Museum."

Vance reacted swiftly to the news, instantly alarmed. "What did they take?"

"He wouldn't say," Penelope replied. "He said he needed to speak with you directly. He sounded . . . concerned."

Vantana considered this, the stress becoming more and more noticeable on his face and in his body language.

"What's this about, Doctor?"

"It's about us all bein' in a heap of trouble."

* * *

Sam London clutched the picture that had been sitting behind Carl's desk. It was a photo of Dr. Henry Knox and a bigfoot creature. Knox was much younger than in the photo Sam had seen of him in one of his books. The creature looked similar to the one sitting across from Sam sipping tea. But the picture wasn't of Carl. Carl didn't have as much gray in his coat, his skin was a darker shade of brown, and his eyes were midnight blue. He also had a scar on his right cheek in the shape of a small semicircle.

"That's Uncle Rupert," Carl noted as he took another sip from his cup. The tea was naturally sweet and had an unusual reddish hue, which made it appear vaguely like blood. Sam found it to be a touch disconcerting at first. But it was a favorite of Carl's, a variety from Africa known as rooibos. The bigfoot took the photo from Sam's hand and placed it back on the table. He leaned forward.

"I was very pleased to hear that you had an encounter with Phylassos. As I'm sure Dr. Vantana has explained, this sighting is of great significance to our world," Carl continued. "I'm assuming he spoke to you. Have you told anyone what he said?" The refined nature of Carl's speaking voice was disarming and in contrast to his outward appearance. Sam shook his head in response to the bigfoot's question. "Good. You're being cautious, as well you should be. But at some point, Sam, you're going to have to learn to trust someone enough to share the gryphon's message."

"I know," Sam responded quietly. Carl smiled and set his

cup on the table. He eyed Sam for a moment, causing him to shift in his chair and take another gulp of the tea.

"Did Dr. Vantana tell you about the curse?" Carl asked. Sam nodded. "Did he explain how it came to be?"

"Yeah," Sam answered. "He and Chase told me about Alexander the Great. How Phylassos appeared to him as an old man. And then he cursed humans because of what they did to the gryphons."

"But did he describe how the magic works? How the curse has persisted for all these centuries?"

"No," Sam replied.

"Magic is a very particular thing, Sam. And magic that powerful is a tall order, even for a creature as extraordinary as Phylassos." Carl grew more animated as he continued. "You see, it's not as simple as casting a spell. Spells are not strong enough to curse an entire race, making them blind to a huge part of their world. No. It required something unique. It demanded that humanity be an unwitting participant in the curse."

"Unwitting? What do you mean?"

"There is an old saying: 'Never give a gift to your enemy, for it can be used to hold power over you.'"

"Alexander gave Phylassos a gift?" Sam asked. Carl nodded.

"On behalf of all humanity. It was a gift that further infuriated Phylassos, and convinced him that the punishment had to be severe." Carl leaned forward now, and softly said,

"Alexander had a claw ripped from the body of one of the dead gryphons." Sam's eyes widened at the mention of the claw. "He had it dipped in gold. And when he presented it to the person he believed was his god—"

"But was really Phylassos in disguise," Sam interjected.

"That's right. When Alexander gave it to him, he declared that it was a symbol of man's power on earth and his dominion over lesser creatures."

"I imagine Phylassos didn't like that very much," Sam said.

"No. He most certainly did not," replied Carl. "But he accepted this horrible gift so he could enchant it with a curse."

Sam bit his lip and looked down. Carl was right; he had to learn to trust someone with what he knew. He took a deep breath and said, "Phylassos asked me about the gryphon's claw."

"What did he say specifically?" Carl asked with urgency.

"He wanted to know what I knew about it. He seemed . . . concerned. But then we were interrupted. And he told me I shouldn't trust anyone because no one is what they seem," Sam confessed. Carl nodded. "Why would he be asking about it?"

"The gryphon's claw is what has kept this curse in place over all these years. If something were to happen to it—if it were, let's say, destroyed—the curse would be lifted. Humans would finally see the world as it really is." Carl let the implications sit with Sam for a moment. "I believe the claw is in danger. Something or someone is looking to destroy it.

And I also believe there is a reason Phylassos appeared to you, and you alone."

"Why? What possible reason could there be?" Sam wondered.

"You can help us, Sam. Help us protect the claw and our world."

"But how exactly would I do that? I mean, I'm just a kid, you know? I haven't even gotten some of the bigfoot smell powers like Vance has."

"It may not be apparent at the moment, but I trust it will become clear in time. Your meeting with Phylassos was no coincidence, I can assure you," Carl said with authority. "I am curious, though—what brought you out to the desert?"

"A dream," Sam replied.

"Was it a recurring dream?" asked the bigfoot with interest. Sam nodded. Carl's face broadened into a grin. "Certainly not coincidence."

There was a loud, hurried knock on the front door.

"Carl? Sam?" Vance's voice called out.

"We're in the study," Carl answered. A second later, Vance entered the room, a dire look in his eyes.

"We've got ourselves a situation," Vance said. "There was a break-in at the British Museum this morning."

"Let me guess—the gryphon's claw cup was stolen," Carl predicted with a half smile.

"Well, ain't you smarter than a tree full of owls. How'd you know so quick?" Vantana asked. Carl peered over at Sam and Vance followed his gaze. "Phylassos told you? And you couldn't trust me with that information? What is it? Am I not hairy enough?"

"He just asked if I knew about the claw," Sam responded defensively.

"If he brought it up, he must have known it was in danger," explained Vance. "You and I gotta get out there and have a look-see." He was eyeing Sam as he spoke.

"What do you mean, you and I?" Sam countered.

"I mean Sam London is going to London."

Chapter 8
LONDON'S CALLING

The photograph on the wall of US President Lyndon Baines Johnson led Sam to conclude that the vacant ranger cabin they were staying in hadn't been used in quite some time. The stale odor, dust, and cobwebs confirmed it. Sam struggled to get comfortable in the creaky wooden bed that hadn't been slept in since the 1960s. According to Dr. Vantana, he and Sam would be traveling to England the next morning and so they should, as Vance put it, "go to sleep with the chickens so we can wake up with the cows." Sam had never ventured out of the country and informed Vance that he didn't own a passport. Vance assured him he needn't worry. When Sam reminded him of the strict security measures at airports, Vance just chuckled and said, "Why ever would we go by plane? We need to get there quickly."

The cabin was in Shasta-Trinity National Forest, which

was a two-hour drive from Redwood National Park. Vance informed Sam they would have another two-hour drive in the morning and a short hike, then sent him to bed as soon as they arrived. But just because Sam was told to sleep didn't mean he was able to sleep. He wondered how his mom was faring and whether Nuks's ruse had proven successful. Was Nuks attending school in his place? Was he keeping up with Sam's schoolwork? Was the raccoon-dog smarter than Sam? But most importantly, would the magical creature stay on Miss Capiz's good side? He hoped for the best and finally caught a few hours of shut-eye.

The doctor woke Sam just before dawn and he stumbled out to the car, trying his best to remain half-asleep. He succeeded and zonked out for the entire trip to Castle Crags State Park on the eastern side of Shasta-Trinity National Forest. When Sam emerged from his slumber, he found Vance parking the SUV in a clearing covered with loose gravel.

"Rise and shine, kid. We gotta get a move on," the doctor said.

"A move on to England, right?" asked Sam. Vance nodded. "Unless there's an airport around here, I'm guessing you weren't kidding about not taking a plane."

"I wasn't," Vance replied matter-of-factly. "We have a bit of a hike ahead of us and you need to eat somethin'." The doctor offered granola, a bottle of orange juice, and some beef jerky. As Sam ate, he glanced out the windshield at the view before them. The area was covered in a thicket of Douglas fir trees, and rising out of the tree line was a massive rock face.

The granitic formation soared hundreds of feet into the air and resembled an ancient castle. The rocks that jutted out of the top looked like towering spires that had been carved by hand.

"What's that?" Sam asked.

"Castle Crags," Vance answered. "Looks like one of them British castles, doesn't it?" Sam nodded.

"Mother Nature can do some pretty cool things. I've never been to the Grand Canyon, but I've seen photos and . . ." Vance was smiling.

"What?" Sam asked.

"Scientists would have you believe erosion did all that." He gestured to the crags. Sam eyed him, waiting for the reveal. "It's a fortress. Carved out of that rock over two thousand years ago."

"Of course. By who? Bigfoots?" Sam asked sarcastically.

"By the dvergen, smart guy. For their king, a dwarf named Vestri."

"You're telling me dwarves carved all that? As in Snow White and the Seven . . ." Sam gestured to indicate someone small in stature.

"Actually, that's a misnomer. Dwarves are the same height as humans. They're tall and husky. Not like what you see in movies," Vantana explained. "Word to the wise: I'd avoid any mention of the whole shortness issue if and when you meet a real dwarf. It's a sore subject."

"Right," Sam replied. He was still having trouble believing all this, but given recent events, he realized he should start taking Vance more seriously, no matter how crazy his claims sounded. The doctor reached back and retrieved a worn leather sheath from behind the passenger seat. Inside was an old hunting knife. He slid the sheath into his belt.

"Why do you need that thing?" Sam asked nervously.

"We might get hungry. Need to slice up some fruit or vegetables." The doctor was a bad liar, Sam thought. "Let's go. I want to get in before dark."

Sam grabbed his backpack and followed Vance up a dirt trail on the west side of the parking area. The trail climbed steadily and joined with a narrow pathway, which continued for nearly a mile. This trail was lined with rocks on one side and a winding creek on the other. They reached a hundred-and-eighty-degree turn in the path where the creek and rocks parted ways.

"We hike off-trail the rest of the way," Vance announced as he stepped off the path and followed the creek. The thundering sound of rushing water grew louder by the moment, and as they hiked over a hill, Sam learned why. The creek originated from a waterfall—a spectacular sight of water cascading down a jagged rock face at the base of Castle Crags. It soared forty feet in height and poured over the uneven outcroppings.

"Burstarse Falls," Vantana said. "As the story goes, the name is a bit of a warnin'. Those rocks are mighty slippery. You gotta be extra careful when you're climbing them or you'll fall on your, uh . . . backside."

"And it'll burst?" Sam asked with a grin. Vance nodded with a smile.

"Something like that."

Sam suddenly realized what this meant. "Hold on a sec. Why would I be climbing those rocks?"

"'Cause you and I have to get behind the waterfall."

"Let me guess—there's some super-secret doorway to England behind it," remarked Sam mockingly.

"Not exactly. It's the entrance to the dvergen subway," Vance informed him.

"Dvergen. That means 'dwarf,' right?" Sam clarified.

"You're learning," Vantana said. "Now follow close."

Vance stepped carefully along the boulders that lined the creek and led to the waterfall. Sam was right behind him, taking it slow and steady. The doctor was correct about the rocks being slippery. The constant flow of water against the granite coupled with the moss that had grown onto the rocky surface rendered it especially slick. Sam nearly bit it while crossing to the final rock before the waterfall, but the doctor's quick reflexes kicked in. He grabbed Sam's wrist and held him up until he could regain his footing.

"Thanks," Sam said as he caught his breath.

"Well, I can't have you dyin' on me now. We're just gettin' started."

As Sam approached the waterfall, he noticed there were a few feet of space between the water and the rock face. Vantana was poised to head inside, but then sniffed the air and glanced back toward the forest.

"Looks like we got ourselves a going-away party." Vance gestured behind him and Sam turned. There were creatures emerging from the woods—creatures Sam had seen only in the pages of books. His eyes went to a group of several animals that were the size of deer but resembled rabbits. Their heads were adorned with long beige antlers. Jackalopes, Sam concluded. Near the jackalopes were small humanoids floating a few inches off the ground. They were pale-skinned with wispy white hair and light blue eyes—so light they appeared translucent. Their clothing was made of foliage and their backs sported white gossamer wings that flapped so quickly Sam could barely tell they were moving. The creatures reminded him of hummingbirds. Fairies, he deduced. There were also creatures he didn't recognize, including a fish with vaguely human features that stood at the edge of the creek, and a horse-sized animal with the head of a boar and a large horn that sprang from the front and back of its head.

"What are they all doing here?" Sam wondered.

"They came to see the boy who saw Phylassos," replied the doctor as he continued toward the waterfall. Sam gave the "going-away party" a small wave, then caught up with Vance. The doctor put his hands on the slick rock face and muttered several words in a language Sam didn't recognize but Vance said was Ancient Nordic. The moment Vantana finished the phrase, the rock shifted. A door-shaped cutout opened, swinging a few feet inside. Vantana entered and Sam followed. The rock door came to a creaky, lumbering close behind them, plunging them into darkness. Vance pulled out a small flashlight, which gave off more light than its size would suggest. Sam could see that they were in a tunnel carved out of the stone. It was smooth and rounded and led to a steep stone staircase, which they descended.

When they finally reached the bottom, they stepped onto a platform that sat within a larger tunnel, like a big-city subway station. The walls displayed colorful carvings of ancient battles between warriors dressed in red and black armor. Instead of a subway train to the side of the platform, there was a massive black metal contraption in the shape of a bullet. It was open on both sides with several rows of tall metal grates, but no seats. The front of the "bullet" was covered with a thin transparent material that resembled crystal, and the rear sported rocketlike tubes that extended a few feet.

"Climb on in," Vance said with a flourish of his hand.

Sam eyed Vance worriedly. "Is it safe?"

"Safe enough."

Sam stepped inside the machine and began walking toward the other side.

"Right there is good," Vance remarked. "Press your back against that metal grate."

Sam followed Vance's instructions while Vantana climbed in and positioned himself behind the control panel at the front of the machine. The controls consisted of dials and levers that appeared ancient in design and were covered in cobwebs and dust. Vance brushed them aside with his hand.

"How old is this thing?" Sam asked with trepidation.

"Pretty old. But dwarves are excellent builders."

The doctor pulled a metal lever attached to the floor. The entire contraption suddenly dropped several feet, slamming to the cave bottom. It also began to hum, as if power was instantly coursing through its metal skeleton. Thin metal wires snaked out from behind Sam and Vance. They wrapped themselves around the two passengers, securing them to the machine. The dwarf version of seat belts, Sam determined. Sam's arms were at his side when the wires settled in, and as a result were now stuck in place.

"My apologies, Sam. I should have told you to raise your arms," the doctor said guiltily. "Then again, it's probably better this way." Vantana's hands returned to the control board, where he adjusted a few dials. He then pulled back on a sliding panel, revealing a rudimentary map of the world etched onto a silver surface. Sam could see the familiar continents represented, but there were other landmasses as well, one of which was clearly marked "Atlantis."

Vance touched an area of California and the silver bubbled beneath his fingertips. A metallic black thread sprouted from the surface, and Vance took hold. He pulled the thread across the United States and over the Atlantic Ocean and hovered above England. As he lowered the end of the thread to the map, the silver bubbled up to grab the end and sucked it down, pulling it taut. Vance peered over at Sam, who squirmed in his bindings.

"Ready?"

"I don't know," Sam responded.

"Just breathe like normal. And when you feel like you're going to throw up, don't pay it any mind. Your body will be traveling way too fast to regurgitate."

Sam was still considering these words when the doctor reached out and pulled a lever on the control board. The hum of the machine turned into a rumble, and the entire contraption began to vibrate furiously. It caused Sam's teeth to chatter, so he clenched them together and felt the vibrations through his body.

"Hang on!" Vance exclaimed as he yanked another lever on the panel. The rockets on the back of the machine exploded to life, and the machine shot forward like a bullet leaving a gun barrel. This was no roller coaster—it was pure terror. Sam had never felt anything like it. The skin on his face was being stretched by the force of the acceleration as the machine hurtled through the tunnel with a massive roar. It twisted and turned and twisted again. They spun upside down, then sideways, then dropped deeper into the earth, only to shoot back up a moment later.

Sam squinted as he looked at the map on the control board. He could see that the thread was shortening. The end that had sprouted from California was being pulled across the continent. From the looks of it, Sam and Vance were moving through entire states in mere seconds and rapidly approaching the East Coast. Vance had his flashlight aimed ahead of them, but all Sam could see was the darkness just ahead of the light and the smooth tunnel walls. Then the machine took a sharp turn straight down, careening toward the center of the earth.

"We have to get below the continental shelf," Vance yelled over the earsplitting sound of the rockets. The machine was in a momentary free fall, until the tunnel shifted and they were suddenly level once again. The wire on the map showed them moving across the Atlantic Ocean and closing in on the United Kingdom. It was at this point that Sam's breakfast attempted to make a second appearance. He swallowed, but the sensation persisted. It was climbing up his esophagus and into his throat, where it decided to linger. He wanted to throw up, needed to, but he couldn't. Vance was right. The tremendous velocity at which they were traveling was too much for his body to counteract. Of course, he wasn't looking forward to the machine stopping. He didn't even want to entertain the thought of what would happen then.

As they approached the coast of England, the machine began its ascent and was soon shooting straight up. To Sam's amazement, the pressure on his body was pushing his breakfast back down where it belonged. When the machine finally leveled out, Sam felt perfectly fine. The nausea was gone. The machine continued on its path, and as they crossed beneath the English Channel, it passed through a strange shimmering cloud, like a glowing silver fog. It tingled against Sam's skin, but it wasn't wet.

"What in the name of John Henry?" Vance muttered. The machine emerged from the haze and kept moving toward London.

"What was that?" Sam asked.

"Haven't the slightest. But we're almost there." Vantana gestured toward the map, where the metal thread was almost gone. Only an inch left, and then it disappeared. Sucked back into the map.

But the machine didn't stop. Vantana reached out and pulled on a lever. No effect; they just kept moving. He frantically turned dials and pulled switches. Still nothing, and now they seemed to be picking up speed.

"What's happening?" Sam yelled as the contraption barreled through a winding set of tunnels, turning them upside down, then right-side up again. Finally the rockets sputtered and stopped firing. The machine slowed and came to an abrupt halt near a platform that appeared identical to the one at Castle Crags. The metal wires binding Sam and Vance retracted.

"That cloud we passed through—it did something to this thing," Sam concluded.

Vance nodded. "Yeah, I suppose it did. Question is why."

"Where are we?"

"From the looks of this tunnel, I'm guessin' Smoo Cave in Durness, Scotland." Vance helped Sam onto the platform. "We'll have to figure out another way to get where we're going."

The two started up a steep staircase until they reached a stone door. Vantana spoke a few more of those Ancient Nordic words and the door opened. They walked onto a ledge behind another waterfall. This waterfall was deep inside a grand limestone sea cave, with the water flowing through a large skylight-like opening in the ceiling to form a small lake. Vance and Sam stepped along the ledge until they could climb down to a wooden viewing bridge. They followed the bridge to the main cavern and headed toward the opening of the cave.

Daylight was dwindling as they approached the exit. Sam peered out to find they were at the end of a long sea inlet, surrounded on both sides by limestone cliffs that rose a hundred feet into the air. Two wooden stairways on either side led up an emerald-green hill to the tops of the cliffs. The falling water was punishingly loud and nearly obscured another sound, which had subtly joined the cacophony. It was an intermittent clanging of metal against metal that followed the sounds of Sam's and Vance's footsteps. When Vantana reached the cave's entrance, he paused and turned his head slightly to sniff the air. Sam sidled up to him.

"Don't move," Vance whispered. The sounds Sam heard suddenly stopped. "We're not alone," Vance added. Just as the doctor turned them back toward the waterfall, some kind of creature crashed down on top of Sam.

Sam struggled against the mysterious assailant. "Vance! Help!" he screamed as he wrestled his attacker. Sam squirmed underneath and finally got a good look at what he was fighting. It was small, around his size, with a red cap on its head, a long nose, teeth that were sharpened into points, blood-red eyes, and long, talonlike fingers. It wore iron boots and wielded a spear-shaped weapon with an iron ax blade at its tip. The creature slashed at Sam, who deftly swung his backpack to protect his chest. The creature reared back and moved to take another swing, but its arm froze in midmotion. It peered up to find Dr. Vantana staring it down. Vance lifted the creature off the ground and tossed it across the cavern floor, where it landed in a heap with its partner. Vantana pulled Sam to his feet.

"Thank you," Sam said anxiously.

"No time for thank you; we have to get out of here." Vance pointed to an adjacent cave. "They have friends." Sam turned to see dozens of the creatures charging toward them. Like a mass of fire ants, they were crawling along the ceiling, the walls, and the cavern floor. "Run!" Vance ordered.

The two raced out of the cave and up one of the staircases. It was a steep climb, and Sam struggled to maintain speed as they ascended the cliff. The stairway rounded back toward the cave, and Sam could see the creatures following in a swarm. The stairs ended near a roadway with rolling hills on one side and a small town in the distance. Vance took off across the road and into a meadow, making a beeline for town. Sam glanced back and could see the goblinlike creatures still pursuing them, their axes at the ready.

"What are those things?" Sam yelled to Vance as they sprinted toward the woods.

"They're called redcaps. Don't ask why their caps are stained red."

"Those are stains?" Sam's realization sent a chill down his spine. "Bloodstains?" he asked. Vance didn't answer, confirming Sam's deduction. "But they're slow, we can outrun them, right?" Sam asked. Vance shook his head.

"Redcaps don't tire. They may be slow, but they're steady. When we start to falter, they'll be ready to pounce."

"What are we going to do?" Sam hollered, his breathing growing more labored. He could feel his body slowing down, and the implications terrified him.

"Our best bet is to try to lose them in the hills, look for a forest, maybe hide. They can't smell worth a darn, and they ain't the smartest ducks in the pond." Darkness was falling fast, and Sam stayed close to the doctor as he led him across a sheep pasture. They climbed hill after hill until Sam could hardly catch his breath. He was losing ground and slowing them down. As they came storming down a steep hillside, Sam slipped on the wet grass and tumbled to the base. Vance tried to pull him back to his feet to continue, but as he did, Sam could see that it was already too late. The redcaps were marching down the hillside, dragging their axes behind them, devilish smiles on their twisted faces. Dr. Vantana grabbed Sam's hand and held it tightly.

"We're gonna be all right," Vance told Sam reassuringly.

"No, we're not," Sam replied, resigned. Vance grabbed him.

"Yes, we are, Sam London. I'm Vance Vantana, fresh from the backwoods. Half horse, half alligator. And I'm here to protect you!" Vance unsheathed his knife and took up a fighting stance as the redcaps pulled their axes to the ready. "All right, you vile little monsters. Let's see what you're made of."

Chapter 9
THE LORD OF THE HUNT

Vance Vantana never got a chance to protect Sam London from the bloodthirsty redcaps, but it wasn't because he wasn't tough enough. The monstrous creatures inexplicably halted their forward march. An eerie hush fell upon the Highlands as the redcaps stood stoically, glaring at Sam and Vance with crimson eyes. The doctor wasn't sure what to make of their unusual behavior. They had the duo right where they wanted them and were not known to be a merciful race. In fact, given the slim odds of survival and the redcaps' reputation, Vance had already devised a last-ditch plan that would involve him taking out a dozen or so redcaps, clearing a path for Sam to escape, and then hanging back to fight the horde until he could fight no longer. It would provide just enough time for the boy who'd seen the gryphon to get to safety, but it would surely cost Vance his life. Luckily, this new development put the grim scenario on a temporary hold.

"I guess you must have scared them," the boy speculated.

"I always did have a—" Vance's self-flattery was interrupted by a low rumbling noise and a vibration in the ground beneath their feet. Their teeth chattered as the sound quickly turned thunderous and the shaking grew violent. It felt like an earthquake, but one localized to where they stood.

"Look!" Sam exclaimed as he pointed to a crack forming in the ground. The tear in the earth was widening and spreading toward them. With no place to run, Vance knew they couldn't avoid the inevitable. He grabbed Sam.

"Whatever happens, don't let go!" Vance instructed. The rupture finally arrived at their feet and the earth promptly swallowed them whole. They were instantly free-falling into a black abyss. Neither of them could even catch their breath enough to scream. Like a cat, Vance twisted his body midair to ensure that when they landed, he would break Sam's fall. They finally hit the bottom with a pronounced thud.

"You okay?" Vance whispered to Sam, who was crumpled on top of him.

"Yeah. I think so," Sam responded. "How are you?"

"I feel kinda like the name of that waterfall," Vance quipped.

"Burstarse?" Sam chuckled. The chuckle turned into laughter. It was just the release they needed from the anxiety and fear that had overwhelmed them just moments earlier.

Sam found the ground and rolled off Vance. As he did, Vance spotted a light approaching in the distance.

"Someone's comin'. Get behind me," he ordered. Sam quickly did as he was told. The light grew closer, enabling Vance to determine that they had landed in a large tunnel. The illumination ahead emanated from a lantern carried by a woman in a flowing green dress. She had long red hair and almond-shaped green eyes. Vance could immediately tell she was a sidhe, a type of fairy from the Celtic lands who was considered an omen of death. The doctor sighed—things were not looking up.

"Who is she?" Sam asked.

"A sidhe," Vance replied. The woman reached out her hand and beckoned them to follow.

"A sidhe?" Sam repeated.

"Also known as a banshee. Come on." Vance stood and moved to follow the woman. Sam grabbed the doctor's arm.

"We're going with her?"

"The fact that she hasn't killed us yet is a good sign. I wanna avoid giving her a reason to," Vance responded. "Let's see what she wants." Sam nodded reluctantly and climbed to his feet. The sidhe turned and started back down the tunnel.

"Pssst!" Sam whispered as the two cautiously followed. Vance stopped and turned back.

"What?"

"I think you dropped this." Sam handed Vance his knife. In all the commotion, Vance hadn't realized he'd lost it.

"Thanks, kid. This blade has got a lot of history." Vance was about to slide it back into its sheath when the beautiful sidhe suddenly spun around. She opened her mouth and let loose with a high-pitched scream, transforming into a monstrous creature: an old hag with leathery skin, rotted teeth, and mangy white hair. Her scream paralyzed Vance and Sam. The doctor had never encountered a sidhe before but had heard stories of their keening, a kind of death cry that would instantly immobilize the strongest of men. It felt as if all his nerves were firing at once, leaving him completely frozen. The knife fell from his rigid hand and the sidhe bent down to retrieve it. Once she had it in her grasp, the scream stopped and her appearance returned to her previous, more pleasing state. Vance could move again. He looked to his side and found that Sam could move as well, though the boy appeared terrified.

"We still ain't dead," Vance remarked, trying his best to put a positive spin on the situation. They continued through a winding tunnel that led deeper into the earth. They heard drums in the distance, and the sound grew louder as they proceeded. The passageway finally ended in a massive cavern.

"Whoa," Sam said as he sized up the place. Vance was equally impressed. It was easily the largest cave he had ever seen. But it was more than just a cave. It resembled the interior of a Gothic cathedral. The underground marvel consisted of a long hall with a vaulted ceiling more than a hundred feet tall. The walls of the cave were decorated with intricately carved scenes of natural landscapes and mythical beasts, and the hall was lined with enormous stone sculptures of more magical creatures. At the end of the cavern was an altar that rose a few feet from the ground and featured a large stone throne covered in vines and decorated with brightly colored gems. Almost as impressive as the size of the cavern was the fact that it was filled to capacity.

An army of redcaps lined the walls, slamming their ax handles on the ground in unison to create a constant, almost hypnotic beat. They parted to form a narrow aisle, and the sidhe led Sam and Vance toward the altar. As they got closer to the front of the cathedral, Vance spotted several other creatures in attendance. There were a dozen or so sidhes; a few fomorians, mythical giants with the heads of goats; and several woodwoses, wild forest men covered in hair. The wild men grasped the reins of four barghests, huge, ferocious creatures that were part wolf and part bear with sharklike jaws.

When they reached the altar, they were greeted by a striking woman with jet-black hair and dressed in a long white robe. It was Marzanna, a powerful Eastern European sorceress associated with death, nightmares, and winter. Not exactly Glinda the Good Witch. It was times like these Vance wished Knox were still by his side.

"Silence!" Marzanna demanded. The audience quickly grew quiet and she eyed her prisoners. "Welcome," she said tauntingly.

"I am Dr. Vance Vantana with the Department of Mythical Wildlife. And I order you to release us immediately," Vance declared with authority. Judging from the laughter that spread through the room, the crowd must have thought he'd told a joke. The redcaps resumed slamming their ax handles on the ground. Marzanna smirked.

"Perhaps you don't quite understand the situation." Vance spoke slowly, as if to schoolchildren. "You all are in violation of the law. There will be consequences." The audience wasn't impressed, as the sneering continued.

"And whose law have we broken, Doctor?" a booming voice bellowed through the great hall. The creatures in the room instantly turned silent and dropped to their knees in reverence.

"Your grace," Marzanna announced as she curtsied toward the hulking figure that stepped onto the altar.

"Phylassos's law? The mighty king of mythical beasts?" the creature asked sarcastically. "Is he *your* king?" he asked the audience.

They responded with an angry "No!"

"I'm their king," the creature sneered. He was humanoid in appearance, nearly the size of a bigfoot, with forest-green skin, golden hair, and giant antlers that protruded from the top of his head. There was a reddish-yellow snake wrapped around his neck that sported curled ram horns.

Sam nudged Vance. "Who's that?"

"Cernunnos. Otherwise known as the not-so-jolly green giant," Vance replied. The doctor had dealt with this forest-dwelling beast before, and each experience had proven exceedingly unpleasant. Cernunnos fancied himself the Lord of the Hunt and the real protector of magical creatures; as such, his ego stretched far beyond the tips of the antlers on his big green head. He made it his mission to come to the aid of those accused of violating the laws of noninterference, and to help the guilty go into hiding.

"On your knees, humans. You are in the presence of Lord Cernunnos," Marzanna announced. Sam looked to Vance for direction.

The doctor shook his head slightly. "I'll handle this."

The doctor walked toward the altar steps. "You and I got a serious problem, Cernunnos." Suddenly, vines sprouted from the ground beneath Vance's feet. They twisted and wound themselves around his legs and arms, rendering him totally immobile. Another vine crawled up his back, wrapping around his neck and covering his mouth, gagging him. He struggled against the restraints, but they proved too strong. And then he was lifted into the air by the vines and carried until he was dangling above the wolf-beasts. They snapped at him, just inches out of reach.

"Looks like you have the problem, Doctor," Cernunnos said icily. The audience roared its approval.

The experience of the last hour had made Sam once again question the decision to seek out the gryphon. In the time since their meeting in Death Valley, Sam had been carried off by gargoyles, chased by ugly midgets with axes, and paralyzed by a banshee, and he was now about to watch Dr. Vantana be served as dinner to a bunch of hungry wolf-beasts.

"Let him go!" Sam pleaded. Cernunnos focused on him and smiled broadly.

"My friends," Cernunnos said as he gazed out on his audience. "We welcome a very special guest into our midst. Samuel London, the human who saw the gryphon!" As Cernunnos gestured to Sam, the audience erupted. He silenced them with a simple wave of his hand and walked toward the boy.

"You're merely a child," Cernunnos observed. He looked back to the crowd. "He's a child!" he announced mockingly. The crowd jeered loudly. Cernunnos walked back onto the altar, dropped into his throne, and leaned back. Sam's attention was still on Vance, who remained barely out of the reach of the creatures. Sam took stock of the situation and concluded that a new strategy was in order.

He had encountered people like Cernunnos before. Individuals whose power—or rather, perceived power—made them arrogant. He recalled his encounters with the overzealous student safety patrol officers who monitored the halls at Benicia Middle School with an iron fist. Like them, Cernunnos appeared to think he should command more authority, and he seemed particularly sensitive to being disrespected. With that in mind, Sam decided it was time to treat the green guy like a self-important eighth-grade safety patroller and feed his ego.

Sam kneeled down on the cave floor in front of the altar and lowered his head. "You are correct, Lord Cernunnos. I am but a child. And so it is an honor for someone as young and powerless as me to make your great acquaintance." That got Cernunnos's attention. He leaned forward, his lips curling into a smile that bared pointed white teeth.

"I would humbly ask that you please release my friend from harm, my lord. I know you don't have to. But I beg you to show him mercy."

"And you can assure me he will offer the same respect to my throne as you, boy?" Cernunnos asked.

"I can, your grace."

The vines returned Vance to his position next to Sam and retracted.

"Thanks, kid," Vance said.

"Just play along," Sam replied. Vance rolled his eyes.

"Fine," he whispered reluctantly. He peered up at Cernunnos. "I wish to know what you . . . ," Vance started, but Sam quickly silenced him with a glance. The doctor tried again. ". . . what your lordness wants from us that he risks reprisal for holding us against our will and endangering our lives."

"Come now, Dr. Vantana, you're being dramatic. I have no intention of harming you or the child," Cernunnos responded.

"It didn't appear that way a moment ago," Vance followed.

"Looks can be deceiving. You should know that by now. And I have found fear to be an excellent motivator. Wouldn't you agree?"

Vance squinted at the creature. "I wouldn't know."

"Is that not how your gryphon operates?" Cernunnos responded with a wry grin. "It is the curse that keeps your race blind, but it is fear that keeps our kind from disrupting your so-called balance. Fear that one misstep could result in being stripped of our magic, or worse, being condemned to be absorbed by Gaia herself."

"I didn't make the rules," Vance countered.

"Lucky for us we've been so well-behaved." Cernunnos called out to the crowd, "Haven't we, my brethren?" The audience whooped and hollered. "I cannot promise that will always be the case."

"Is that a threat, Your Majestic Graciousness?" Vance replied with a hefty amount of sarcasm. Sam eyed the doctor with concern. He didn't want him being fed to the wolves again.

"I am not the threat, Doctor. Though someone shares my sentiments, I do not condone their actions," Cernunnos explained. "I was not the one who sent the gargoyles."

"What gargoyles?" Vance responded. Cernunnos narrowed his eyes at the doctor.

"How's the esteemed Dr. Knox? Still missing?" Cernunnos smirked. "A pity, no? I'm sure Phylassos would have preferred appearing to him rather than to the child."

"Is there a point to this?"

"Tell me, has the Maiden Council been informed of "— Cernunnos gestured toward Sam—"this?"

"I don't see why that would be necessary," Vance replied.

"Of course you don't," Cernunnos said. He eyed Vance, then Sam, with a curious intensity before his gaze settled back on Vance. "You asked earlier what I wanted, but I've brought you here because of what *you* want."

Cernunnos signaled Marzanna, who turned away from the crowd for a brief moment, and when she spun back around she was holding an object. She walked it over to Cernunnos, who snatched it from her hand and held it aloft to the crowd.

"The gryphon's claw!" he declared. In his hand was a golden chalice in the shape of a curved claw. The stem of the cup was golden, while the claw itself was dark in color. The thin end of the claw sported a small golden statue of a gryphon. The wide end was topped with a lid encrusted with emeralds. The crowd roared at the sight of the object.

Sam immediately looked at Vance for his reaction. The doctor's eyes were locked on Cernunnos, who met his stare. "Now, now, everyone. Before you grow too excited, I must reveal an awful secret. You see, my loyal subjects, this is not the claw you believe it to be. If I were to crush it to dust in my hand, Phylassos's unjust curse would not be lifted. For it is a fake. Another one of the gryphon's many tricks."

"I wonder then, Lord Cernunnos, why would you steal it?" Vance asked.

"Borrowed. And I needed some way to summon you here," Cernunnos explained. "The gryphon is concerned about the claw, is he not?"

Vance said nothing.

"I will tell you this: whoever is conspiring against your king would not be fooled by this trinket or the others. They would know that the real claw is—"

Cernunnos was interrupted by a growing disturbance near the rear of the cavern. Heads turned toward the commotion as the redcaps drew their axes to the ready. Sam maneuvered his line of sight to see what the fuss was all about and spotted a cynocephalus striding down the middle of the aisle toward the altar. He was young, the same breed as Chase, and wore a long-sleeved gray polo shirt, charcoal-colored cargo pants, and a matching beret. The logo on the left side of his shirt had the image of a gryphon with the words "Ranger Service" beneath it. He caught Vance's eye and winked.

"'Ello, mate. You should have called, told me you were planning a detour," the dog-man said with a British accent.

"It wasn't planned. And word to the wise, Chriscanis, old Green Bean is extra touchy today," Vance remarked.

"Of course," Chriscanis said. He turned his attention to Marzanna and bowed his head. "I request an audience with Lord Cernunnos." She eyed him suspiciously.

"What do you want, traitorous dog?" Cernunnos asked.

"I formally ask that you release the humans known as Vance Vantana and Sam London into my custody. Immediately." There was a spate of laughter in the room.

"No," Cernunnos responded matter-of-factly.

"I ask that you reconsider," Chriscanis added.

Vance whispered, "You're going to get us all killed." Chriscanis waved him off.

Cernunnos paused, as if actually contemplating the request.

"No, again," the creature replied to even more laughter. "Anything else? Do you want a bone?"

"Not right now. Thanks. Though I must inform you that by refusing this act of good faith, I am bound by my oath to the Agency for the Welfare of Mythical Beasts to place you, Lord Cernunnos, under arrest for violations of the laws of human interference and theft of a historical artifact—" Before Chriscanis could finish, the room exploded in protest. Vance shook his head in disbelief while Cernunnos snarled through his teeth. He silenced the crowd, then glared at the ranger.

"You, arrest me?" Cernunnos asked as he walked toward Chriscanis. The room became deathly quiet. Cernunnos leaned down toward the cynocephalus, getting inches from his face. He whispered loudly, "You're going to need an army."

"I thought I might," Chriscanis answered. He grinned, then let out a howling whistle that reverberated through the cavern. It caught Cernunnos by surprise, as did the chaos that followed.

The cavern was suddenly invaded by dozens of creatures. There were small humans with scrunched-up faces who were descending from tunnels they had dug out of the cave walls. Their heads emitted a bluish flame as they held swords that crackled with fire. They charged at the redcaps with abandon, calling out with terrifying war cries. Near the back of the hall, more creatures were pouring into the cave. They were cynocephali, but these dog-people weren't like Chase or Chriscanis. They were Chihuahuas. Man-sized Chihuahuas! If the situation weren't so dire, Sam would have jumped up and shouted a celebratory "Woo-hoo!"

Sam could immediately recognize that it wasn't just the difference in their breeds that set them apart from the two cynocephali he had already met. These dog-people were fierce. They carried themselves like true warriors—they were strong, intimidating, and completely fearless. They marched into the cavern gripping chains attached to nightmarish beasts with the upper bodies of monkeys and the lower bodies of wolves.

As Cernunnos attempted to digest the sudden turn of events, Vance grabbed Sam's hand.

"Follow me!" he ordered. The doctor weaved through the fray and the two took cover behind a large boulder. They both peeked over the top of the rock to get a glimpse of the battle.

"Who are those little guys on fire?" Sam asked.

"Bluecaps. Nasty little miners. That's miners with an 'e.' Lucky for us, they absolutely despise redcaps," Vance replied. "And those monkey-wolf-things over there are the shug monkeys. Very loyal, surprisingly trainable, and totally lethal."

"Those are Chihuahua cynocephali," Sam said as he pointed excitedly to a cluster of the dog-people who were fighting off a horde of the horse-headed giants.

"They're considered the warrior class of cynocephali.

Real tough hombres," Vance revealed. "It's not safe for us here. We need to find a way back to the surface."

At that very moment, a body soared over their heads, slammed into the cave wall, and crumpled to the ground. It was Chriscanis. He shook off his dazed expression. "This is your idea of a rescue mission?" Vance asked the ranger.

As Chriscanis got to his feet, he smiled and replied, "This is my idea of a *fun* rescue mission." He booted back a charging redcap, then spun to face a sidhe. The creature screamed her awful scream, but Chriscanis was unaffected. When the sidhe realized its scream wasn't working, it quickly retreated. Chriscanis tossed something to Vance: earplugs.

"We call them banshee busters. Never travel to the Celtic lands without them," Chriscanis said. "I'll have some of my mates clear a path for you. Just get yourselves up top and wait for me there. It's a bit of a dog's dinner down here, and I should probably clean it up."

"How ironic," Vance quipped. Chriscanis barked at the Chihuahua cynocephali, who shifted their attack and began clearing a path to the exit.

"Let's go," Vance ordered, and the two made a beeline for the opening.

* * *

Sam London and Dr. Vantana awaited the arrival of Chriscanis and his ragtag army near a series of government-issued jeeps parked along the roadside.

151

"You all in one piece?" Vantana asked Sam.

"I think so," Sam replied. "Who was that guy?"

Vance told Sam about Lord Cernunnos and the creature's belief that he was the real protector of magical creatures.

"But I thought Phylassos was the protector," Sam remarked.

"There are some who believe the gryphon isn't up to the task," Vance responded. He took a moment to peer around, then continued, "Sam, the balance that was struck is tenuous at best. Cernunnos was right when he said that fear is what has, in a sense, kept the peace."

"What about the curse?" Sam wondered.

"The curse keeps them hidden, but there have been a growing number of incidents between humans and mythical creatures. Now, it had always been the fear of reprisals from Phylassos that helped curb these incidents, but as the years passed with no sign of the gryphon, many creatures that abhorred the arrangement grew more brazen. Of course, there was still Dr. Knox," Vance explained.

"What do you mean?"

"It was widely believed that Dr. Knox was in communication with Phylassos. He wouldn't talk about it, but there were instances when a lawbreaking creature would be captured or cornered and suddenly just disappear. Mind you, Phylassos never made an appearance. Knox would somehow get the gryphon a message and he would handle the situation."

"And now that Dr. Knox is gone?" Sam inquired.

"Since he went missing, things have gotten increasingly more complicated. That is, until you came along," Vance said, his smirk returning. "See, kid, you represent that connection to these creatures. The fear and the hope. It's why you'd be so important to someone like Cernunnos."

Their conversation was interrupted by the return of Chriscanis and his Chihuahua warriors. They looked the worse for wear.

"How'd it go?" Vantana asked as the cynocephalus grabbed a canteen of water out of his jeep and rehydrated.

"He called back his minions and we agreed to a truce," Chriscanis revealed. "In exchange, we forget the whole thing." The dog-man eyed Sam. "You must be Sam. I don't believe we've formally met. The name's Chriscanis."

"Good to meet you," Sam replied. Chriscanis moved to shake Sam's hand and realized he was still holding the claw cup.

"Oh . . . right, we reclaimed this. As well as this." Chriscanis pulled Vance's knife out of his back pocket and handed it over. "I'll make sure the cup gets back to where it belongs, and with better security."

"Thanks. And thanks for showing up. Impeccable timing," Vance said. "How'd you know?"

"My investigation into the museum theft uncovered evidence that it was the work of a banshee. There's only one egomaniacal forest creature who surrounds himself with the sidhe," Chriscanis explained. "When you failed to show at the dvergen subway station at the scheduled time, I suspected something might be amiss. I have to confess, I'm a little thunderstruck by his recklessness. Cernunnos has always proven to be a bit of a, well, pain in the proverbial backside, but this is troubling."

"I agree," said Vance.

"Is the cup really a fake?" Sam interjected.

"It is," Vance confirmed. "One of the many claw relics spread around the world to keep creatures like Cernunnos guessin', and to give us a heads-up when someone or something started getting unhealthy ideas about ending the curse themselves."

"So now we know it was Cernunnos who was behind it. That's good, right?" Sam suggested.

"Not entirely, I'm afraid," Chriscanis answered. "This wasn't the first relic stolen."

"What are you talking about?" Vance inquired.

"After the claw cup was taken, I reached out to other rangers around the world to warn them the relics in their regions may be in danger. I learned that nearly all of them had already been stolen."

"What?!" Vantana exclaimed. "Why wasn't the department notified of this?"

"It was. Apparently, they spoke directly with Dr. Knox and he told them to keep it a secret. But with Knox gone and the gryphon returning, they felt it was time they said something. I believe we may be dealing with a growing insurrection." Dr. Vantana sighed deeply.

"Sam, would you do me a favor and wait in the jeep?" Vance asked. "I just need a moment with Chriscanis."

"Well, why can't—"

Vance interrupted Sam's protest. "I'll explain later."

Sam wasn't happy about being sent to the jeep. *This is what adults do,* he thought. *Send you out of the room when they have "grown-up" things to talk about.* Sam believed "grown-up" things were code for "more interesting."

"Fine, I'll go. But first tell me: if that cup was a fake, then where's the real claw?" Vance and Chriscanis exchanged discomforting looks. "You don't know. . . ."

"It's complicated, Sam," Vance replied. "Please?" He gestured to the jeep.

Sam rolled his eyes and trudged to the vehicle. "Whatever!" he said with as much of a whine as he could muster. He climbed into the jeep and watched as Vance and Chriscanis walked a few yards down the road.

Moments later, he spotted one of the Chihuahua cynocephali passing by. "Excuse me?" Sam called to the creature. The cynocephalus turned toward him. "I'm Sam. Sam London," he said, trying to establish a line of communication. "The boy who saw the gryphon?" The human-sized Chihuahua appeared unimpressed. "In the cave back there, we found out the claw cup wasn't the real gryphon's claw. You know, the one that was cursed. I was wondering if you could tell me where the real one is."

The dog-man eyed Sam for a moment, then turned and started to walk away. Sam wasn't about to give up. "Gosh, I don't know why everyone is so scared to talk about it." The cynocephalus stopped and spun back around.

"I am not scared," the creature said in a deep, coarse voice with an irritated, insulted tone.

"Well, you certainly act like it," Sam countered. The cynocephalus snarled at him, and for a moment Sam thought he might have gone too far.

He backed off. "Hey, I'm just sayin'. I asked a simple question and no one wants to answer me. So they either don't know or they're too freaked out to tell me."

The Chihuahua stared at Sam for a few moments. "There are many claws. And many stories."

"Which story do you believe?"

"According to the oldest of legends, the gryphon's claw rests in the possession of the Guardians."

"The who?" Sam asked.

"An honored group of magical warriors who are sworn to protect the claw with their lives. If the tales are true, they are the most formidable force on earth."

"Where are they? Where can we find them?"

"You don't find them. Those who have sought out the Guardians have never returned," the cynocephalus said. "We do not speak of such things. Phylassos would not approve."

Sam attempted to follow up, but the Chihuahua walked off. A moment later, Chriscanis climbed into the driver's seat of the jeep and Vance approached the passenger side.

"Listen, Sam. Chriscanis is going to take you to another dvergen subway and then escort you home."

Sam was surprised to hear that word. "Home?" he asked with a mix of shock and dismay.

"I am glad to have met you, Sam London. Perhaps we'll cross paths again." Vance continued, "You can let Nuks know he's free to go."

"Wait. I'm going with you," Sam replied adamantly.

"No, you're not. It's too dangerous. I've already put you in harm's way enough."

"But I have to go. I'm the one who saw the gryphon, remember?" Sam protested. "He picked me for a reason. Carl said so."

"I'm sure he did. But where I'm going, you can't follow. It's that simple."

Sam met Vance's gaze. "You don't understand, Dr. Vantana. I have to go. I have to see this through," Sam pleaded, his voice cracking with emotion. "This . . . this might be my one thing. The thing that makes me special. I can't give up. I have to know for sure." Sam could feel the tears welling up in his eyes. It was as if his entire life had come down to this moment. Vance looked away.

"I'm sorry, kid," the doctor said guiltily. He turned to walk away, escaping Sam's disappointment. Sam bit his lip and thought hard. This couldn't be the end of the adventure. He had to know what was so unique about him that he was the one chosen by the gryphon.

An idea began to form in his head. He was tapping into the same deviousness that had gotten him on that bus to Death Valley a few days earlier. He knew very well that what he was about to do wasn't entirely ethical. But his desire to determine his one special trait was just too strong to ignore. He owed it to himself. He owed it to the gryphon.

"Ready for another ride in the dwarven death trap?" Chriscanis asked with a smile. Sam jumped out of the car. "Guess not," he heard the dog-man quip.

"You're going to seek out the Guardians," Sam called out to Vance. The doctor froze but didn't turn to face him.

"Who told you about them?" Vance asked.

Sam swallowed. The point of no return, he thought.

"Phylassos," Sam replied.

Vance spun around. "You're lyin'."

Sam shook his head. "He told me there existed an honored group of magical warriors who protect the claw and that I needed to seek them out. He gave me a message for them. I didn't tell Carl because I wasn't supposed to talk about it."

Vance marched toward Sam. "What was the message?"

"I have to deliver it. In person. I promised."

"This isn't a game, Sam. Where I'm headed, people don't come back. You could die. Do you understand that?" Vance asked sternly.

"I understand," Sam responded. Vance didn't like this one bit. Sam could tell by the way he grimaced and loudly sighed every few seconds. The doctor seemed to be having quite the vigorous internal debate.

"If you're lyin' to me . . . ," Vance started. At that point, Sam knew he had him.

"I have to go," Sam asserted. "You know I do."

Vance paused for a moment and then muttered something that sounded like "Come on," in a defeated tone.

As they walked back toward Smoo Cave, they heard a voice call out, "Wait up!" Chriscanis ran to join them.

"Oh no. Heck no. Not you too," Vance declared.

"If the human child gets to go, I get to go," Chriscanis replied defiantly.

Vance was exasperated. "I am not responsible when we all die, are we clear?" he said bluntly.

"No worries, mate. If we're dead, we won't be able to blame you," Chriscanis remarked with a grin. He nudged Sam. "I love a good field trip. Especially ones that'll likely prove fatal."

Chapter 10
THE GUARDIANS

SL001-180-60

FD-11

DATE: ▮▮▮▮▮▮▮

Art teacher and single mom Odette London wasn't sure who the boy was who had returned from the hospital in Bakersfield, California, but she was certain he was not her son. He was her new and dramatically improved son. Ever since the fiasco in Death Valley that had left several cars totaled and a "lucky" gas station in charred ruins, Ettie had noticed a distinct change in Sam's behavior—a change for the better. The first and most welcome example of Sam's transformation was his exceedingly affectionate nature. When Ettie dropped Sam off at school before the accident, a simple hug or—God forbid—kiss on the cheek would be met with impassioned protests and embarrassed whines of "Mom!" But since their return from Bakersfield, Sam refused to get out of the car or even open the door without a proper kiss and hug. She could even spot him in the rearview mirror standing on the curb and waving as she drove away.

It was also difficult to believe Ettie had once criticized Sam for watching too much television and playing too many video games. Nowadays, Sam had boundless energy, and she would often find him running in circles in the backyard. In addition, New Sam, as she liked to call him, didn't complain about her cooking. In fact, she even caught him foraging in the trash for leftovers one night. He explained he was quite hungry and, after seeing a commercial about starving children overseas, felt guilty about throwing away perfectly good food. Other peculiarities that sprang up with regard to food included New Sam's sudden penchant for nuts and berries. Cookies were replaced with fruit, and potato chips were swapped for pumpkin seeds.

The only distinctly bad behavior Sam now exhibited was an odd way of dealing with bullies at school. Sam had had run-ins with bullies in the past, but he always managed to brush off their comments and avoid messy physical confrontations. But his most recent encounter with trouble went much differently. Ettie was called to the school after an incident involving Sam and a few boys who had been teasing him about being a "mama's boy." Apparently, Sam had ignored these verbal taunts but reacted when one of the bullies pushed him. His response was a growl. At first blush, this would seem silly, and likely ineffective at dissuading his tormentors. However, the bullies swore that when Sam growled he revealed a row of sharp teeth and fangs. It was enough to send the boys running to the teacher, to whom they confessed their story.

Although the school principal acknowledged the sheer absurdity of the situation, he suggested to Ettie she have a talk with Sam about this bizarre behavior. "Boys shouldn't growl like wild animals," the principal advised. "It's uncivilized." Ettie nodded and assured him she would put a stop to it.

Sam was tremendously distraught after the meeting with the principal. He apologized profusely to Ettie on the car ride home and for the next several days. He even did extra chores around the house without being asked. Ettie found the story of growling amusing, if strange. Stranger still was Sam's belief that he would have to sleep outside that night as punishment for his behavior. When she informed him, rather incredulously, that he wouldn't, her son became overjoyed. He kissed her goodnight, gave her an extra-firm hug, and retreated happily to his bedroom. It was that night Ettie decided to make an appointment for Sam with a psychologist.

The real Sam London was having second thoughts. Actually, he was having second, third, fourth, fifth, and sixth thoughts. And they were all the same: he shouldn't have accompanied Vance to find the mysterious Guardians. Lying about having a secret message for them and going along on this dangerous journey had turned out to be his worst idea ever. In fact, it was looking like it would be his last.

It had been three days since Vance, Chriscanis, and Sam hopped a dvergen subway to the Phoksundo waterfall in Nepal's Shey Phoksundo National Park. They were met at the station by a Nepalese park ranger by the name of Raju. He was a stern-looking fellow with a long black handlebar mustache. Sam could tell the ranger was disturbed by the presence of a child on this journey. Raju stared intently at him as he explained all the arrangements he had made and all the dangers they would face, the most treacherous of which was the extreme, unforgiving cold. Normally, an expedition of this type would require several Sherpas, a mountain people known for their Himalayan navigation skills, but the secrecy and perilous nature of the mission meant they could only take one Sherpa guide. Sam was sure Vance was pleased he wouldn't have to be responsible for more lives if things went south.

As Raju warned, the weather was not kind. Sam never imagined he would find an opportunity to wear seven pairs of socks at once; yet even that was not enough to keep out the bone-chilling cold. Besides the cold, there were the effects of the high altitude. The Sherpa guide, Chriscanis, and Vance all seemed perfectly fine in this air. Sam, on the other hand, felt nauseous, dizzy, and tired. Although the yaks provided to them were supposed to be used to carry their supplies, once it became evident Sam was not conditioned for this kind of trek, he was allowed to use one of the creatures for transportation. It was a shaggy, heavy beast, with long, coarse hair, handlebar-shaped horns, and an unremarkable disposition.

As for food, the group was subsisting on the Sherpa version of a potato pancake, which Sam concluded shouldn't have been considered a pancake at all. Pancakes invoked images of syrup and butter. Just the thought brought Sam back to Chase's house. He could imagine himself eating the proper English breakfast. Heck, after being subjected to these flat potatoes, Sam would have given anything for some of Chase's bubble and squeak or even one of his mom's dinners, the latter being the clearest indication of his desperation. Besides the potato pancakes, there were lots of vegetables, and lentils. Sam had never tried lentils before and quickly concluded he would never try them again. The only bread to be had was immeasurably dense.

"As dense as a collapsed star," Chriscanis joked. Sam slathered the weighty chunks with butter until he learned it was yak butter. Then he got sick to his stomach. Chriscanis noticed Sam's disgusted expression and quipped, "You look like you might *yak*." He laughed heartily at his joke.

Tenzing, the Sherpa guide who was accompanying them, turned back on the third day of the journey. He announced that he'd had a change of heart. He had a family he could not abandon and, despite pleas from Vance, headed home. All the yaks, except the one Sam was riding on, followed the Sherpa. According to Chriscanis, Tenzing's departure was an ominous development, since he was the most capable guide among several Sherpa villages. Apparently, where they were headed was more intimidating than Mount Everest.

The terrain had changed from green and lush to white and stark. It was also becoming more treacherous. Hills turned into rocky hills, which changed into steep rocky hills and finally transformed into snowy, rocky, steep mountain passages. The trio and the yak hugged the icy ridges of a small mountain range and moved farther into the Himalayan valley. The trail was not easily identified, but Vance seemed to always know the right direction. Sam chalked it up to those legendary tracking skills he'd heard so much about. But on the fourth day, Vance's confidence began to waver, along with everyone's energy. He was starting to second-guess himself and appeared increasingly frustrated. The punishing blend of snow and wind caused frequent whiteout conditions that made navigation nearly impossible.

By the end of the fourth day, they reached a vista that was located a thousand or so feet above the valley floor. As the sun began to set and Sam winced at the prospect of another night spent in the icy cold, Vance stopped and pointed firmly to the horizon. The snowfall relented just enough to see what had captured Vance's attention. It was a mountain. A massive mound of snow and ice that lay in the shadow of Everest.

"There it is!" Vance announced over the howling wind.

"Phylassos's mountain? Are you certain?" Chriscanis asked as he eyed the impressive sight with a pair of binoculars.

"If the legends are true," Vance replied.

"So that would mean the Guardians are just—"

"At its base," Vance noted. "In the village of Kustos."

"Phylassos has his own mountain?" Sam asked. He hadn't heard this part of the legend before. Vance nodded.

"It's his home. And it's where some believe the real claw is kept."

Chriscanis gave Vance a congratulatory slap on the back. "I was moments away from losing faith in you, old chum."

"That'll teach you," Vance said with a smile. He led the trio down a steep path toward the valley floor. "We'll find better shelter from the cold and wind down there," he explained.

Sam gazed up at the mountain. Before now, his stare had always been drawn to Everest. Earth's highest mountain rose a staggering twenty-nine thousand feet above sea level. It was a breathtaking sight—so breathtaking it was difficult to notice anything around it. Perhaps that was the point, Sam thought. With everyone so distracted by the world's tallest peak, they never paid much attention to what might lie in its shadow. Sam hoped Phylassos was home. It would be nice to see him again and to apologize for the events in Death Valley. Sam was contemplating what he'd say to the gryphon when he heard a strange swishing sound.

His eyes immediately darted to the source of the noise. The ridge was collapsing. Snow was breaking off the path's edge and sliding down to the valley below. Sam looked up at Chriscanis and Vance, his eyes wide with terror. The ground beneath Sam's yak gave way. Instantly, Sam and the beast were sliding down the side of the ridge. He gripped the yak with all his strength and was immersed in a massive cloud of ice and snow.

As they hurtled toward the valley floor, Sam could feel his leg scrape against the jagged rocks. When the two finally came to an abrupt halt, their stop was punctuated with a loud, disturbing crack. And then Sam's world went dark.

It had been nearly an hour since Dr. Vance Vantana had watched Sam London and his yak slip off the mountain's edge. This was exactly what the doctor had feared. He hadn't wanted to take the boy on such a dangerous journey to begin with, but Sam claimed he had a special message from Phylassos intended for the Guardians. Although Vance suspected this was a ruse devised solely to obtain approval to come along, he didn't want to entertain that thought. It would only make him feel worse about what had happened. Fact was, he enjoyed having Sam around; it was a pleasant change from the usual day-to-day for a ranger with the DMW, and it played a major role in his agreeing to Sam's request. However, it also meant that Vance now held himself personally responsible for the boy's safety.

The darkness of night was creeping steadily across the valley floor, making it increasingly difficult to locate the boy.

They were running out of time to tend to any injuries he might have sustained if he had miraculously survived the fall. The doctor breathed a giant sigh of relief when he heard the distinct howl of Chriscanis, followed by—

"Over here! I found him!"

Vance rushed toward the cynocephalus's voice to find him standing over Sam and the yak. Sam was still unconscious, and the yak was disoriented from the fall. Vance quickly sprang into action and with Chriscanis's help eased the bewildered yak back on its feet. Once it was out of the way, Vance could see the injuries to Sam from the fall. The look on his face must have been grim, because a very groggy Sam noticed.

"What?" Sam cried softly, as if in pain. "What is it?" Vance saw the tears forming in the boy's eyes. A second later they started to tumble down his cheeks. "I can't feel my leg," he said, distressed.

Chriscanis gestured for Vance to stay quiet. "Let me handle this," the cynocephalus whispered. He leaned down to Sam. "It is because your leg is cold," he answered calmly. "But it is also cut and most likely broken."

"It doesn't hurt," Sam responded anxiously. "Shouldn't it hurt?"

"It's too cold out here, buddy," Vance said, trying to sound as calm as Chriscanis. He wasn't used to this feeling. This sense that he lacked control of the situation. He was someone who always remained calm under fire. But there was something about this boy that seemed to negate all that. With Sam, Vance felt like a worried parent.

"So I'm okay?" Sam asked with a glint of hope.

"I'm gonna make sure of it." Vance tried to sound confident. He couldn't help but feel the cynocephalus's judging eyes on him. "You rest now, Sam," he added, avoiding Chriscanis's look. "We're going to find a splint for your leg and get settled for the night."

When Sam's leg was splinted and he had nodded off for a nap, Chriscanis confronted Dr. Vantana. "We won't make it, Vance," he said matter-of-factly. "He's burning up. Maybe if we turned back now, we could save his leg."

"It's too late," Vance replied solemnly. "He wouldn't survive."

"Then what do you propose we do?" a frustrated Chriscanis asked.

"We charge ahead to Kustos. If the legends are true, the Guardians can help him."

"So we are relying on legends and conjecture?" Chriscanis countered, exasperation in his voice. "We're talking about the boy's life. . . ."

"Don't you think I know that? But it's our only play. We gotta get there before he gets worse. There are limits to their magic."

"And you think we'll make it across that valley in time?" Chriscanis asked. "It could very well be the same distance to the nearest Sherpa village."

"We have no other options," Vance responded with

resignation. "I'll do whatever I can to make sure we don't lose him."

Sam awoke a half hour later, hungry and restless. Chriscanis did his best to distract him with stories of his adventures as a ranger with the Agency for the Welfare of Mythical Beasts. Meanwhile, Vance was determining the best route to the base of Phylassos's mountain. He knew Chriscanis was right—getting to the village before Sam was too far gone was a long shot, but he had to believe there was a chance.

Midway through one of Chriscanis's stories about the real Loch Ness monster, Sam blurted out, "I lied." Those two simple words grabbed the attention of both adults. Sam added, "I don't have a message for the Guardians from Phylassos. I just said that—"

"So I would let you come along," Vance finished his sentence.

Sam nodded. "I'm sorry," he said with a genuineness that seemed to capture the weight of his dire situation.

"Well, I figured you were lying like a no-legged"—Vance caught Chriscanis's curious eye and adjusted—"cat."

Sam was surprised by the subdued response. "You mean, you're not mad?"

"I'm mad at myself for buyin' that bill of goods. I should have known better. But you gotta let sleeping"—at another glance from Chriscanis, Vance corrected himself—"cats lie.

Heck, when I was your age, if I was in the same situation, I probably would've done the same thing."

As the night wore on and the three huddled inside their tent, Sam made another confession.

"I miss my mom."

"I do too," Chriscanis added. Sam perked up at this.

"You know her?" Sam asked, surprised.

"Of course," Chriscanis replied. Then he realized. "Oh, I see. You have heard about the cynocephali way of dealing with family." Sam nodded. "Yes, it is true. But some of us, myself included, have rejected those archaic traditions."

"What about your father?" Vance piped up.

"I don't know him. For the males of our kind, old habits die hard." Chriscanis sighed. "I envy humans. You cherish family. Celebrate it. You even have reunions. It's quite charming."

"Not all of us are like that," Sam offered. "It's just my mom and me. I've never met my dad."

"Maybe you have and just don't know," Chriscanis suggested. "I often tell myself that. Perhaps I have already encountered him along my many travels."

"I've seen a photo," Sam added. "I've never met him, even by accident."

The trio soon drifted off to sleep for the night. But before Vance fell into his slumber, he thought about what Sam and Chriscanis had discussed. He could not imagine not knowing his father. By Sam's age, Vance and his dad had survived countless brushes with death in the wilderness. They had spent more time together before he was ten than some kids spend with their parents in an entire lifetime. It strengthened their relationship and gave Vance the opportunity to absorb much of his dad's knowledge. Knowledge that had already saved his hide a number of times. Vance reminisced about those near-fatal moments until he finally succumbed to his tired eyes and fell asleep.

The doctor's slumber was cut short by the sound of the wind howling. He awoke with a start and looked over to see Sam sound asleep and Chriscanis missing. Vance bundled up and stepped outside to find their companion. When he emerged from the tent, he noticed something unusual—the wind wasn't blowing. The night was still. His eyes turned toward the sound he'd thought was the wind and spotted his friend, howling at the moon. Vance quickly headed over, but when he reached the cynocephalus, Chriscanis didn't acknowledge him. He simply continued howling.

"What in blazes are you doing?" Vance exclaimed.

"Sam needs to meet his father," Chriscanis answered, before proceeding with his howl.

"What are you trying to do? Howl him here?" Vance asked incredulously.

"The boy cannot meet his father if he dies. Our only hope is to get him to Kustos," Chriscanis explained. "But you and I both know he will not make it."

Vance couldn't argue with him. Fact was, even with all the navigational planning Vance had done to ensure the shortest route to Kustos, there was a very good chance that what the cynocephalus said would turn out to be true. The frostbite on Sam's wound had deepened and caused an infection. They were prepared to deal with a possible injury, but not on this scale. The medications they had didn't appear to be helping, except to make the boy sleepy. If only they had found Sam a little earlier, they could have done more.

"I am howling to ensure we get him to Kustos on time," Chriscanis clarified.

"Not sure I follow."

"You are relying on the legend that the Guardians are healers, correct?" the cynocephalus asked.

Vance nodded. "I've found that in this line of work, legends are one of the only things we can count on."

"I agree. And so I assume that adage also includes the legend of the roc?"

"As in the giant bird Marco Polo spotted in the thirteenth century? The one that supposedly lives somewhere over the South China Sea?" the doctor answered. Chriscanis nodded. "Well, I've never actually seen one."

"Very few have. And almost all of them were cynocephali," Chriscanis revealed. "You see, our kind have the unique ability to summon the beast. When I was very young, I saw it done with a distinct howl."

"And then what? We ask it for a ride?" Vance wondered.

"Something like that. But first we have to bait it."

The cynocephalus gestured toward the yak, which was tied to a post that had been driven into the ground. "Given the steep slope of the valley, the wind currents, and the size of the roc, once it snatches the yak in its talons, it will have to fly across the valley to gain sufficient speed to clear the mountains."

Vance grinned. "Oh, I get it. We're gonna bide our time, wait for it to grab the yak, then take hold of the rope tied to the yak and hitch a ride across the valley, dropping right at the Guardians' doorstep."

"Exactly. And we can strap Sam to my back," the cynocephalus suggested.

"Complicated and risky—I like it. Of course, it's all gonna depend on whether Big Bird makes an appearance," Vance reminded him.

"Yes, well, that—" The two were suddenly plunged into darkness. They had been speaking under the intense moonlight, which was bright enough to negate the need for flashlights. Vance looked up to where the moon had been a moment ago only to see a black spot. Then the spot moved. A huge shadow passed over the full moon and a loud whooshing sound accompanied it, followed by an even louder screech. The whooshing grew in volume; Vance quickly identified it as the sound of wings flapping. Massive wings.

"I'll retrieve Sam. With all that medication, he'll probably sleep through the whole thing," Chriscanis said with a smirk.

"I'll ready the ropes on the—" Vance froze. "Where's the yak?" The yak and the post had vanished.

"Great Scottish Terrier!" Chriscanis exclaimed. He pointed to the tent. The yak was retreating inside.

"That yak ain't as stupid as it looks. He must have sensed he was about to become supper," Vance hollered as he ran toward the tent. Chriscanis followed close behind. And then the roc swooped down. The bird was tremendous, easily the size of a jumbo jet and just as loud. It stretched out its giant talons to grab the yak, but the creature was already too deep into the tent. So the roc snatched up the entire tent. It flapped its giant wings with increasing force, pulling the tent stakes from the ground and yanking the entire structure skyward. Vance and Chriscanis exchanged a panicked look. They sprinted forward and leapt for the dangling tent ropes. Vance missed.

Luckily, Chriscanis grabbed the rope he had reached for and, quickly realizing Vance was going to miss it, reached with his other hand to grab hold of the doctor.

"Thanks!" Vance exclaimed.

"My quick doglike reflexes," he replied with a smile.

"Look out!" Vance yelled. The yak had lost its footing in the tent and slid out of the entrance. Chriscanis barely avoided being sliced by the yak's horn as it fell several feet to the snow-covered ground. The roc was flying the exact route Chriscanis had predicted. Things appeared to be going well until the tent began to collapse on itself.

As the tent broke apart under the strain of the roc's grip and the weight of the supplies, Sam's sleeping bag—with Sam still inside—began to slide toward the entrance. Vance quickly noticed the boy was seconds away from following the yak.

"Sam!" Vance called to Chriscanis, who spotted the impending catastrophe. Unfortunately, both of the dog-man's arms were in use at the moment.

"I can't reach him in my current predicament," the cynocephalus yelled down to the doctor. "I will swing you over to the other talon. You grab hold of it and I'll grab Sam."

"Better make it snappy," Vance replied, his eye on Sam, who was now barely inside the tent. With each flap of the roc's winds, Sam's sleeping bag was jarred and sliding farther. Chriscanis began swinging Vance toward the roc's talon as they soared across the valley floor. Vance lifted his legs to avoid passing trees. Swinging like a pendulum, Vance got closer. He stretched out his arm, but it was still inches away.

"Let go," Vance ordered Chriscanis. "Let me go and save Sam!"

"No," the cynocephalus called back. "We can do this."

At that moment, Sam's sleeping bag shifted and started its final slide out of the tent.

"Let go!" Vance pleaded.

Chriscanis swung Vance one final time and released his grip on the doctor as Sam's sleeping bag fell from the tent. The cynocephalus grabbed hold of the corner of the bag, but the material was too slick and his paw began to slip. And then another hand grabbed the other corner. It was Vance! The doctor had used the momentum of that last swing to grab the roc's talon. The two rangers held on to the sleeping bag as tightly as they could.

"How much of that medicine did you give him?" Vance asked, eyeing the dozing Sam.

"Looks like just enough," Chriscanis replied, satisfied. "The bird will reach its lowest altitude as it begins its ascent on the western slope." He nudged his head forward. Vance looked ahead and saw that they were rapidly approaching the mountain.

"I take it we'll be closest to the ground just as it goes vertical?" Vance surmised.

Chriscanis nodded. "I propose we drop Sam first to avoid falling on him when we hit."

"Agreed," Vance responded. "On your word." The roc was barreling toward the slope. Sam had slipped entirely into his sleeping bag. Chriscanis watched their progress intently. As the bird turned vertical, they were just a few feet from the ground.

"Now!" the cynocephalus yelled. The two let go of the bag and watched as Sam fell to the ground, disappearing into a snowbank. Vance and Chriscanis followed right behind, letting go of the roc's talon and sailing to the waiting earth.

Once on the ground, the duo quickly found each other and then stumbled down the slope to where they had dropped Sam. As they pulled his sleeping bag out of the snow, the boy slowly started to regain consciousness.

"What happened? Where am I?" Sam asked groggily.

"Save your strength," Vance advised.

"Climb on," Chriscanis ordered Sam, motioning to his back. A still-half-asleep Sam climbed onto the cynocephalus's back and the trio hiked down the slope. Chriscanis pointed out several darkened structures jutting out of the snow. They headed toward them and found what looked to be the ruins of a village. As they passed under a worn wooden arch, they noticed streetlamps that lined the main path, but the place appeared deserted. It was a Himalayan version of the American ghost town.

"Looks like we got here a thousand years too late," Chriscanis suggested.

And then the streetlamps suddenly began to glow a fiery shade of orange. One by one, the lamps radiated a warm hue, as if the lights were following the group as they ventured deeper into the village.

Vance was walking a few feet ahead of Chriscanis and Sam when he came to a sudden halt. The flight in the extreme cold had impacted Vance's supersensitive nose, drying it out and rendering it almost useless.

The streetlamps were heating up the pathway, in addition to lighting it, and had now turned red-hot. The extreme warmth moistened Vance's nasal passages, and he inhaled deeply through his nostrils. Instantly, he could tell they were surrounded.

Chapter 11

TASHI

Sam London knew his prognosis was grim. Despite assurances from Dr. Vantana, he had come to terms with the dire state of his leg and now his life. The numbness had already traveled to his other leg and was slowly inching up his back. Sam wondered if this was the feeling of life leaving his body. He was terrified by the thought. Apparently, the village of Kustos was his only hope. He had overheard the doctor and Chriscanis talking when they thought he was asleep. He didn't hear everything, but he did glean the critical nature of his injury and that the legendary Guardians might be able to help. Unfortunately, there was a massive frozen expanse sitting between him and his possible survival. He was skeptical that they would make it across the valley in time, and from his eavesdropping he learned that Chriscanis didn't think they'd make it either. It was for this reason their current situation was so puzzling.

"How did we get across the valley so quickly?" Sam asked the cynocephalus, who was carrying him piggyback. The two had entered the village following Vance, who had taken point.

"We flew," Chriscanis answered matter-of-factly.

"Seriously," Sam said, believing he was being teased. But before Chriscanis could answer, he was silenced by the doctor's hand, which popped up like a stop sign. As Vantana peered around anxiously, Chriscanis sniffed the air, growled, and instantly crouched in a defensive posture.

"What? What is it?" Sam whispered. Chriscanis didn't respond. Sam scanned the village. As far as he could tell, it was just a collection of abandoned wood structures. They had doors and windows, but no lights. The only illumination was the strange glowing streetlamps above them. Sam was quickly feeling suffocated by his numerous layers as the warm lights melted the snow beneath their feet. "This place is a ghost town," he said.

"And the ghosts have us surrounded," Chriscanis replied, his eyes sweeping their perimeter. The doctor had retreated to Chriscanis's position, and the two stood back-to-back.

"There," the doctor said to Chriscanis in a hushed voice. He was pointing toward the entrance of the village. A figure was walking toward them.

"And there." Chriscanis gestured the opposite way, where another figure had appeared. More of them began to materialize out of the shadows, advancing from all directions.

"Looks like everywhere," Sam added. The figures were

taking their time in their approach, remaining stone silent as they lumbered slowly and methodically toward the group. It was all quite unnerving.

Chriscanis set Sam on the ground. "Stay between us," he directed.

"I'll do the talkin'," Vantana said. "Don't make any sudden moves."

They were soon encircled by a few dozen figures. Sam could now see they varied in size but were all dressed in thick yak hides. Each wore the same large cylindrical fur hat on their heads and carried a gray walking staff. Their faces were masked by bushy fur collars, except for their eyes, which peeked out from the narrow opening beneath their hats.

"My name is Dr. Vance Vantana. I am with the Department of Mythical Wildlife," the doctor explained slowly. "We mean you no harm. We are here for—"

"The claw," a calm voice spoke out from the crowd. "You seek the gryphon's claw." The male voice belonged to one of the taller figures in the group. He sounded older, and as he emerged from the crowd, Sam could see he was leaning heavily on his staff for support. But as he came closer, the man slowly began to stand up straighter and taller. A ruse? Sam wondered.

When the man spoke again, he did so with an authoritative and serious tone. "Those who seek the claw must die."

"Next time, I'll do the talking," Chriscanis whispered to the doctor as the figures began closing in, their staffs now at their sides, wielded like weapons.

"Wait," Vantana pleaded. "We don't want the claw. We've come with a warning—"

"We do not require warnings," the man interjected, sounding insulted. "We have protected the gryphon's claw for over two thousand years. Guarded it with our lives."

"And we are honored to be in the presence of the legendary Guardians," Vantana said. He bowed his head in reverence. Sam couldn't help but think he had taught the doctor something back in Cernunnos's lair. Vantana continued, "We are here because we believe the claw is in danger."

"The claw is always in danger," the man replied. "Let me guess: you wish to have a look at it? To ensure its safety?"

"Well, actually—" Vance started, feeling optimistic.

"A most pathetic attempt at trickery," the man concluded. "Kill them."

"It's pathetic because we're not trying to trick you," Sam declared as the figures descended on the trio. Vantana pulled out his knife, ready to fight. Chriscanis growled and got set for battle.

"Please!" Sam cried. "I have seen the gryphon!"

The Guardian gestured for the others to stop. He moved closer to Sam, staring at him with almond-shaped eyes, but the doctor and Chriscanis blocked his path.

"That's far enough. If you've got a beef, you've got it with me," Vantana said firmly.

"And me," Chriscanis added. "Spare the child."

"The child," the man repeated those words, as if fascinated. There were murmurs among the crowd as they began to finally notice Sam. The Guardian spoke again. "You . . . you are the boy from our dreams."

"Me?" Sam asked. The Guardian nodded. The doctor and Chriscanis exchanged a surprised glance.

"We saw you standing on a towering rock in a vast desert. You and the mighty Phylassos." The Guardian gave Sam a sideways look. "You gave him cookies?"

Dr. Vantana looked back at Sam, dumbfounded. "You did what?"

"It was all I had," Sam explained, thoroughly embarrassed. "I meant it as an offering. So he wouldn't try to eat me."

"We know who you are, Sam London. I am called Yeshe. I am the village elder and leader," the Guardian said, before adding, "You may travel to Phylassos's cave, and there you will find that the claw is safe."

"So you've seen it, then?" Vantana asked. The Guardian eyed him for a moment, as if trying to read his intentions.

"No one has. Not for two thousand years."

"Then how do you know it's safe?" Sam responded. His voice was strained by the pain from his wound.

The Guardian moved toward Sam to get a better look at the boy. He suddenly squinted, as if feeling Sam's suffering. "You are gravely injured," he said with surprise.

"That's right," the doctor confirmed.

"His wound is growing worse. He will not survive the night, and the trip to the cave takes two days," Yeshe explained to Vantana matter-of-factly. Sam's eyes darted to the doctor in panic.

"Calm down, kid. It'll be fine," the doctor assured him. He looked back to Yeshe. "There are legends about your people. Legends that say the Guardians of the gryphon's claw are great healers. We're hoping these stories are true."

Yeshe nodded. "They are indeed, Dr. Vantana." Sam lightened a bit at this revelation. Things were looking up. "But our healing comes at a price. . . ."

Sam felt a surge of pain through his body, causing him to shriek. Vantana felt Sam's head. His expression was dire.

"Will this price make him any worse?" the doctor inquired. The Guardian eyed Sam, concerned.

"Tashi," Yeshe called. A Guardian appeared out of the group. This one was not much taller than Sam. The Guardian walked up to him and gestured for Chriscanis and Vantana to move aside. The two parted hesitantly. Tashi kneeled down next to Sam and placed a hand on his head. Sam caught the Guardian's emerald-green eyes. They reminded him of Phylassos's, with one exception: Tashi's eyes emitted a soft glow.

"Give your pain over, Sam," Yeshe instructed. Sam glanced at the Guardian leader, confused. "Don't look at me. Look at Tashi. Visualize your injury and then give it over. Use your eyes."

Sam had no clue what Yeshe was talking about. *Give my pain over? Use my eyes?* It didn't make any sense, but he thought he'd best give it a try. He met Tashi's gaze, and once he was locked in on the warrior's glowing eyes, he could feel a change. The world slowed to a crawl. The sounds that had enveloped him seconds earlier faded into the distance. He suddenly felt completely alone with Tashi. As if they were the only two beings on the entire planet.

As Yeshe had instructed, Sam started visualizing his injury. He pretended he was telepathically communicating with Tashi, like a mutant in one of the comic books he enjoyed. He relived the injury in his mind's eye and could have sworn he heard Tashi whisper inside his head. *Good*, the voice said.

It was a moment later that Sam heard Tashi's leg snap, just like the sound he'd heard when the yak fell on top of him. With a hand still on Sam's head, Tashi met the boy's gaze with brilliant green eyes. The Guardian's brow furrowed in pain, and Sam stopped visualizing his injury. Tashi grabbed his arm and squeezed, mentally whispering, *Don't*. So Sam continued imagining the injury, and as he did, he began to feel pins and needles in his feet.

"My feet!" Sam exclaimed. "I can feel them!"

"Do not stop," Yeshe advised.

Sam did as he was told. It was an odd, disconcerting feeling. Not only could he now feel his feet, but he could feel the bone in his leg move. It was shifting under his skin, becoming whole once again. Soon the pain had subsided and the numbness disappeared entirely. He gazed down at the bandage on his leg and pulled it back: the wound was gone. He looked at Tashi, whose eyes were now tightly shut. The Guardian crumpled to the ground next to him. Sam quickly moved to his healer's side. Tashi was trembling, and then the trembling turned to an increasingly violent shaking.

"Help!" Sam called to the other Guardians gathered. "Do something!"

"Once a Guardian absorbs the pain of another, they must find the strength to heal themselves," Yeshe explained.

"Will Tashi be okay?" Sam asked with tears in his eyes.

"That is up to Tashi." Yeshe nodded to two Guardians, who scooped up their fellow warrior and disappeared into the crowd.

Sam was overwhelmed by the possibility that he might have injured his healer. Perhaps even fatally. He wanted to turn back the clock and refuse the healing in the first place. But that was impossible. He was overcome with exhaustion. His head felt like it weighed a thousand pounds, and his eyes refused to stay open a moment longer.

"Sam? You okay, buddy?" the doctor asked, his words fading as Sam fell into a deep, rejuvenating sleep.

Sam London awoke several hours later to a headache and the clamor of medieval combat—which consisted of the clanking of swords and the thump of weapons hitting wooden shields. He found himself in a large room with a dozen beds—a barracks, he concluded. Sam noticed that Vance and Chriscanis were not with him, so he climbed out of the bed and headed for the door. As he opened it, he was hit with a bone-chilling gust of wind that sailed through the main thoroughfare of the village. He was now very awake. The Guardians were going about their business—some moving through the town with food and other supplies, while others were training at the base of the mountain. In the midst of this snowy expanse, these legendary warriors trained with swords, wooden staffs, and their bare hands. He moved toward them to get a closer look.

"What do you think, Sam?" asked Vantana, who sidled up to him, along with Chriscanis. "Think you could take one of them on?"

Sam shook his head. "I don't think anyone could take any of them on." He watched two Guardians cross swords with such force, a volcano of sparks erupted into the air. They appeared to be experts in just about every method of self-defense Sam knew existed. And they were faster and jumped higher than humanly possible. Sam had seen his share of action movies, and nothing could compare to the fierceness he was witnessing firsthand.

"Tough as nails, these Guardians," Vantana observed. Sam nodded in disbelief.

He watched as one of the Guardians lost his staff in a particularly thrilling fight. It flew through the air and landed at Chriscanis's feet. The cynocephalus leaned over to pick up the seemingly innocuous weapon and quickly learned it was anything but. A flash of blue light shot up from the ground and out of the staff. The problem was that it used Chriscanis's body as a conduit. The surge pulsed through his muscles, causing them to instantly contract. Sam watched bolts of electricity move through Chriscanis's body as it sought the staff in his hand. A Guardian appeared and wrested the staff from the cynocephalus, whose muscles finally relaxed. His short fur was standing on end.

"That is a shekchen. It is a Guardian weapon, and as such can be wielded only by a Guardian," Yeshe said as he joined them.

"Good. To. Know," Chriscanis said haltingly.

"How does it work?" the doctor asked.

"It's like a lens that draws out the energy inside Gaia and focuses it," Yeshe answered.

"Gaia?" Sam inquired.

"Earth," Vantana replied.

"You see, Sam, the earth has an innate energy," Yeshe explained. "Think of it as an electrical current that runs through the entire planet. To us, it is the living, breathing energy of Gaia herself. Guardians can channel that energy and use it when necessary. Our bodies are not like yours. That is why we alone are able to harness this power."

When Yeshe was finished explaining the shekchen, he led the trio into a mess hall. Though the food looked much more appetizing than what they had been surviving on for the journey, it still left Sam longing for his usual fare. He asked about Tashi and was told the Guardian's condition was still unknown.

Over breakfast, the Guardian leader revealed more about his people. The origins of the Guardians dated all the way back to the initial meeting between Alexander the Great and Phylassos.

"You mean when humanity was cursed?" Sam asked.

Yeshe nodded. "There were about a dozen humans who witnessed the exchange and sought forgiveness from Phylassos. There were slaves, warriors, even doctors in Alexander's army who recognized the evil that had been done."

"I remember this part of the tale," Dr. Vantana interjected. "The first Guardians pledged to protect the gryphon and the curse for eternity."

"In many ways, we are part of Phylassos," Yeshe revealed. "Our blood is not completely human. The gryphon endowed us with special abilities to help us in our mission."

"What kinds of abilities?" Sam inquired, leaning in.

"According to Knox, not only do the Guardians possess certain powers, they are invincible." Vantana turned his attention to Yeshe. "Is that right?"

"As long as the claw is under our guard, we are protected from mortal injury or disease."

"So that means Tashi is going to be okay?" Sam asked with a new sense of optimism.

"Like everything in this world, Sam London, it is not always that simple. Our human minds are still quite strong. As such, they hold great power over our physical bodies. It is faith, and faith alone, that can recognize and embrace the gryphon's power within us."

"You mean, you must believe in this power for it to be real? To work?" Chriscanis inquired.

Yeshe nodded. "It is a rite of passage for all Guardians, when we face our own mortality and must find the strength to overcome our own thoughts. That is what Tashi is confronting as we speak. If Guardians emerge from this trial, they are stronger and have proven they can be true protectors of the claw."

"And once you do get through this . . . you become immortal?" Dr. Vantana asked.

"Oh no. The gryphon would never have cursed us with such a thing," Yeshe replied, smiling. "There is a time we spend here and a time beyond. We age just as you do, and when the moment comes for us to leave this plane for another, we are ready and excited to step into the next stage of existence."

Chriscanis followed. "But if the claw was destroyed or—"

"Or simply taken from our guard, the legends say we would become vulnerable. No longer protected by the gryphon's magic."

When they finished eating, Sam helped Vantana and Chriscanis gather their belongings and prepare for the journey to Phylasso's cave. The Guardians provided additional supplies and even gathered to see them off.

"The cave of Phylasso is heavily protected and cannot be entered without a Guardian," Yeshe revealed. "So I have decided to send you with one of our most courageous and capable warriors." At that moment, the crowd parted and Tashi stepped forward.

"Tashi!" Sam exclaimed. "You're okay!"

Yeshe grinned. "All healed in time to escort you. We wish you good fortune. Farewell." Yeshe bowed to his visitors, as did the crowd. Sam, Chriscanis, and Vance bowed back.

Tashi ventured ahead of the trio and started up the slope of the mountain. As they began their ascent, Sam kept glancing back toward the village. The Guardians were still gathered and watching. But as the wind sent the snow swirling into the air, visibility diminished, and soon Sam could no longer see them.

The first few hours of the journey were uneventful, just a lot of walking up a steep, narrow, winding path. Dr. Vantana insisted on walking between Sam and the edge of the trail. Even if they were traveling with a healer, the good doctor wasn't taking any chances. Tashi walked a few feet ahead of them, shekchen in hand.

"I just don't get it," the doctor said to Chriscanis in a hushed tone. Sam listened intently. "The Guardians think the claw is just fine, evidenced, I'm sure, by the fact that Tashi up there survived healing Sam."

"Yet Phylassos was concerned enough about the claw to mention it to a complete stranger," Chriscanis added.

"It's got me wonderin' if old greenie was being honest about not sending those gargoyles," the doctor posited.

"But if Cernunnos didn't, who did?" the cynocephalus asked.

"That's what I can't make heads or tails outta," Vantana replied. "But I am awfully curious to get to this cave. Maybe the claw is in danger in some way we don't yet understand."

When night fell, the group set up camp, and Chriscanis and Vantana tried to start a fire. The temperature, which was already below freezing, fell a few more degrees. Sam had prepared for the weather by piling on the layers once again, but he was still thrilled by the prospect of a fire for warmth. Unfortunately, the relentless wind was making it impossible to ignite the kindling. The doctor and Chriscanis were huddled over the pile of wood, feverishly trying to achieve combustion. They didn't even generate a spark. Sam noticed Tashi quietly observing from a few feet away. After a few moments, the Guardian pulled a spherical object out of a bag, walked over, and placed it atop Chriscanis's woodpile.

"Pardon me, but we're trying to start a fire here," the cynocephalus said. "Perhaps you could move that—"

"Hang on," the doctor said to his companion. He turned his attention to the Guardian. "Tashi . . . is that a warming bell?" Tashi nodded. Sam craned his neck to get a better look at the object. It was white, almost translucent, with a rounded top that flared out at the bottom like a bell. But it didn't stay white for long. The object began to glow a light orange, which deepened to a fiery red within seconds.

"What exactly is a warming bell?" Chriscanis inquired.

"It's what was linin' the main street of Kustos. Didn't dawn on me till now. They're like lights that only glow hot when they sense a creature who seeks the claw," the doctor explained. "They work as a warning for the Guardians."

"Ah. So that's why those streetlamps only lit up when we entered the village," Chriscanis recalled. He placed his hands near the bell. "It is quite hot."

"So we're the ones triggering it?" Sam wondered.

"That's right," the doctor confirmed. "Now come over and get yourself warm." Sam gladly followed the doctor's orders and basked in the heat. The bell warmed the camp for the rest of the night.

*   *   *

The next morning, the group awoke early and continued their journey. The ascent grew steeper with each passing hour, but the clouds had finally receded and the sun made a welcome appearance.

As they moved ahead, Sam noticed the mountainside was intermittently blanketed in shadow. When Sam looked upward for an explanation, he was baffled by what he saw: the sky was clear. If the clouds weren't creating the brief moments of shade, what was?

A second later he spotted the culprit, although he couldn't quite believe what he was seeing. It was the largest bird he had ever laid eyes on. He nudged Dr. Vantana in disbelief and pointed. The doctor looked, then turned to Chriscanis.

"You didn't do any howlin' in your sleep, did ya?" Vantana asked while gesturing to the circling creature. Chriscanis peered skyward and his face went grim.

"Holy Himalayan Mastiff! It's the roc!" the cynocephalus exclaimed.

"The roc?" Sam asked. He had heard that name before. If memory served, it was a giant mythological bird mentioned in Henry Knox's book.

"I suggest we pick up the pace," Chriscanis advised anxiously as the roc began to descend.

The doctor grabbed Sam's hand and hurried up the slope. The trio sped past Tashi, who seemed confused by their sudden burst of speed.

"It's a long story," Vantana said to Tashi. "But we have company." Tashi spotted the roc but didn't appear fazed by the creature or the impending doom Vantana and Chriscanis believed it would bring.

When the doctor noticed that the Guardian wasn't keeping up, he turned back and shouted, "Keep moving! It's lookin' for food!" That last declaration sent a chill up Sam's spine, which he could somehow feel despite the frigid temperatures. But Tashi didn't budge. The Guardian turned to face the creature as it swooped down. Vantana pulled Sam to the side of the mountain, protecting him with his body. Chriscanis joined him, also positioning himself to shield Sam.

The monstrous bird screeched a cry so piercing, the doctor, Chriscanis, and Sam reflexively covered their ears. Tashi stood firm. The roc landed on the edge of the slope and flapped its massive wings, sending up a tornado of ice and snow. The gust was powerful enough to blow the hat right off Tashi's head. A mane of long black hair tumbled out and billowed in the rushing wind.

"Well, I'll be a Shetland sheepdog!" Chriscanis declared.

"Ain't that somethin' . . . ," Dr. Vantana followed.

"Tashi's a girl!" Sam declared. Not only was Tashi female, she also appeared to be around Sam's age.

They all watched with surprise as Tashi slammed her shekchen to the ground. A torrent of blue bolts shot up from the earth and through the staff, erupting into a brilliant burst. It reminded Sam of the plasma lamp in his science teacher's classroom. The clear glass sphere housed an electrical discharge that when touched would make your hair stand on end. The Guardian then let out a screech with the same resonance as the roc's call, though not as loud. The creature instantly responded to her, slowing its flapping wings.

"What in Dalmatian?" Chriscanis uttered in disbelief.

"Is she—" Sam started to ask.

"She sure is," Vance answered. Not only was Tashi a healer and a warrior, she could also talk to giant birds. That was three special skills to Sam's none. He was in awe.

As Tashi walked toward the roc, Sam heard her make several cawing sounds in a soft voice. She reached her hand out and the bird leaned forward, allowing the Guardian to gently rub its beak. The roc closed its eyes, like a puppy having its belly rubbed. She whispered to the creature and it responded with gentle squawks and a low-pitched staccato screech. Tashi stepped back and bowed her head to the bird. The roc bowed its head in return and flapped its giant wings once more as it lifted off the mountain slope and took to the air.

As the roc flew away, Tashi headed back toward Sam, Vantana, and Chriscanis. She eyed Vantana and Chriscanis with irritation.

"It doesn't like you two very much," Tashi said.

"Us?" Vance responded. "What did we do?"

"If you wanted a ride for the boy who saw the gryphon, all you had to do was ask," Tashi scolded them. "You didn't have to bait him. It is demeaning." She retrieved her hat and ventured forward.

"How was I supposed to know?" Chriscanis said guiltily to Vantana.

"Ya learn something new every day," the doctor quipped.

"Hold on," Sam shouted to his companions. "We rode *that* across the valley?"

Chriscanis smirked. "We didn't ride so much as hang on for dear life."

"That's the last time I fall asleep before you two," Sam concluded. "That is way worse than any slumber party prank." Vance and Chriscanis shared a laugh at Sam's assessment.

By the time they reached the top of the mountain, the sun had just begun to set. The journey had grown easier in the last few hours, though Tashi spent most of that time shooting disapproving looks at Chriscanis and Vantana. Sam had tried to make conversation with her, but she reminded him to save his energy and his oxygen.

"I didn't know about the roc," Sam told Tashi. "I just want you to know that." Tashi peered over at the boy, her eyes emitting that faint emerald-green glow.

"He told me," the Guardian responded with a slight reassuring smile.

"Can you talk to all animals?" Sam asked.

"Those who wish to listen. Now we must be quiet, or the snow lions will hear us."

Sam wondered what that meant. The foursome reached a clearing at the mountain's peak. It was only a few yards wide, but that was enough for them to pause and take a short respite from the wind. Sam spotted a large opening in the face of the mountain. The cave was pitch-black inside, but as they approached the entrance it began to glow.

"Warming bells?" Sam asked Tashi, who nodded.

The cave was only about twenty feet deep. At the back of this outer cavern were massive doors carved into the rock. The carvings depicted two gryphons from the side, standing on their hind legs, ready to attack.

"Is that—" Sam started, but was silenced with a stern glance from Tashi. He looked back to the cave and noticed two statues sitting on either side of the doors. They resembled the decorative lions Sam had seen all over San Francisco's Chinatown. The statues sported flowing manes of curly hair carved into the marble, as well as wide-open mouths that made them appear almost cheery. These must be the snow lions Tashi had spoken of, Sam concluded. But how could they hear anything? They were only statues.

Tashi thrust the end of the shekchen to the ground. "Don't advance any farther," she said in a loud whisper to the group. But the doctor was already a half step beyond the staff. "Freeze," she said firmly. Vantana immediately did as he was told. Sam looked to Tashi, who for the first time since he'd met her appeared nervous. Everyone stood stone still for a few moments, eyeing Tashi with concern. When she finally relaxed, Sam and the others let out anxious breaths. Sam concluded they had all just dodged some invisible danger that only Tashi was aware of. But their silent celebration was short-lived.

The marble snow lion statues began to crack and split open with a ground-rattling rumble. Sam watched slack-jawed as two creatures emerged from the broken chunks of marble. They were part giant Lhasa apso and part African lion. They sported turquoise manes and gleaming white coats.

"Those are the guards?" Chriscanis asked, amused. At that very instant the snow lions spotted their guests and opened those big, cheery mouths.

"Get down!" Tashi commanded. She dropped to the ground, along with Sam and Dr. Vantana. But Chriscanis was still standing. Tashi yanked him down just as the snow lions released terrifying roars. It was the single most fearsome thing Sam had ever heard. It made the gargoyles' squawks sound almost delightful.

The sound shook the mountain like an earthquake and sent a powerful blast of wind barreling toward the group. Sam could feel his body begin to move, pushed by the force of the gust. And as the blast strengthened, his body moved faster, sliding straight toward the edge of the mountain. Sam scrambled to grab something that could stabilize him, but his hands kept slipping. Tashi spotted Sam's struggle. She slammed her shekchen to the ground and reached for Sam's hand just as it slipped again. The shekchen was acting as an anchor against the gust of wind, and Tashi was now fully extended, with Sam desperately holding on to her.

Dr. Vantana and Chriscanis were losing their own battles with the punishing rush of air and were both sliding quickly toward the edge. The doctor reached out and clamped onto Sam's foot, while Chriscanis grabbed hold of Vantana's leg. All four were stretched out to the maximum their bodies would allow, and clutching each other for dear life. But the wind blast grew stronger, and Tashi's shekchen slipped. The entire group slid farther toward the edge, with Chriscanis tumbling over the side.

Tashi let out a cry and slammed the shekchen back to the ground, halting their movement once more. Chriscanis dangled over the edge of the mountain, still latched on to Vantana's leg, the thousand-plus-foot drop looming beneath him.

And though it seemed things couldn't get any worse, the foursome was then lifted off the ground by the force of the wind and hovered a few feet in the air. Tashi strained to touch her fingers to the earth. Sam's leg began to hurt from the weight of Vantana and Chriscanis, and he couldn't stop himself from wailing in pain.

"Sorry, buddy!" the doctor screamed over the deafening roar.

Tashi finally made contact with the ground. It was just the tip of her finger, but it was enough. A surge of electricity shot through her body and into the staff, sending a shower of sparks soaring upward and arcing across the sky. The snow lions' roars abruptly stopped. Everyone slammed back to the ground and Chriscanis climbed over the edge to safety. Tashi quickly got to her feet and faced the snow lions.

She growled as she pointed to herself. The snow lions bowed their heads and scurried backward, clearing a path to the doors. Tashi turned to the group.

"Stay close to me and do not look the snow lions in the eye, do you understand?"

"Sure," Sam responded confidently.

"Not you," Tashi replied. She pointed to Dr. Vantana and Chriscanis, who didn't care for being scolded by a child yet again.

"Of course," Chriscanis responded, annoyed.

Tashi continued forward and the others followed closely. When she reached the door, she twirled her shekchen and touched the tip to the stone surface. The doors rumbled and slowly creaked open. She fired her shekchen as she stepped inside, and the discharge split in several directions. The bolts of energy ignited torches that lined the cavern's walls and illuminated the space. The cave was massive, a voluminous hall carved out of shimmering rose quartz and packed with gold. Gold cups, gold coins, gold everything. Sam had never seen so much gold, and yet with all the treasure surrounding him, his eyes were immediately drawn to the center of the room. There was a pedestal of rose quartz rising from the gold-covered floor. Atop the pedestal rested a golden object.

"Is that . . ." Sam stepped closer to get a better look, and glanced at Tashi, who nodded. The golden object was the gryphon's claw. The magical claw that had cursed humanity for over two thousand years. Sam considered the immense power that sat just a few feet from him. If the claw was some-how destroyed, then mythical creatures who had been hidden from human view would suddenly be visible.

"Well, I'll be," Dr. Vantana muttered as he stepped closer. "Take a look at this, Chris." But Chriscanis was more inter-ested in the copious amounts of gold scattered about.

"I'm assuming that stealing the gryphon's gold would

spell certain doom?" the cynocephalus asked wryly as he examined a golden goblet.

"No," Tashi replied nonchalantly. She picked up a gold coin and hurled it out of the cave. The instant the coin passed the stone doors, it exploded into dust and vanished. "Only a gryphon can remove the gold from its lair."

"Hey, the warming bells are off," Sam observed when he saw the coins pass the entry.

"We're not seeking the claw anymore," the doctor reminded him.

"Oh yeah, I guess that's right," Sam said.

The doctor moved in closer and studied the relic. "Looks perfectly fine to me," he concluded.

"As Yeshe foresaw," Tashi said. She pulled down her jacket collar, revealing her entire face and reminding Sam how young she was.

"Now what?" Chriscanis asked.

The doctor stepped away from the claw and back toward the entrance. He paced on the only ground not carpeted in treasure.

"So why would the gryphon be worried about it if it was sittin' pretty in his cave?" Vantana asked, puzzled.

Sam's eyes were on the doctor, but he suddenly spotted something odd behind Vantana. He tried to alert the others but only managed a faint "Um . . ."

"I don't know, mate. Doesn't make a lot of sense to me," Chriscanis piped up. Sam's eyes had now grown into saucers. Tashi noticed.

"Um . . . guys?" Sam tried again to get their attention.

"False alarm, perhaps?" Vantana suggested.

"Dr. Vantana?" Sam said loudly, finally getting the doctor's attention.

"Yeah, Sam?"

"The warming bells . . . they're lighting up," Sam said as he pointed behind Vantana to the entryway, where the orange glow had returned.

"Not now, Sam," Vantana replied. "I'm more interested in why—"

"We're no longer seeking the claw," Tashi stated, before dropping into an attack stance, her shekchen at the ready.

Dr. Vantana froze and sniffed the air, immediately looking grim. "Oh gre—" He didn't get a chance to finish. A monstrous white creature leapt through the entryway, smashing into the doctor and sending him careening across the cavern. He slammed into Chriscanis and the two landed in a heap. The creature roared as he stood up. It was about eight feet tall and covered in silver fur, like a bleached version of Carl, but angry. Really angry. It had steel-blue eyes, three-inch claws, and a mouth filled with razor-sharp teeth, which it was currently baring.

"Yeti!" Tashi cried as she wielded her shekchen and prepared for battle. The yeti spotted the pedestal and headed directly for it. Only Sam London stood between the magical gryphon's claw and one of the fiercest creatures ever to walk the earth.

Chapter 12

THE SNOWMEN ARE FROSTY

SL001-180-70

SUBJ: Tashi of Kustos (SA)

SOURCE: BG

DATE: ████████

It was time for Tashi to die. The Guardians called it the
Age of Mortality, when young warriors faced their greatest
fear—death. The ritual, if it could even be called that,
was different for every individual. In fact, no Guardian,
not even the elders, knew exactly when a warrior would
be tested or what form the test would take. But it was a
critical rite of passage for any Guardian seeking to take
his or her place among the protectors of the gryphon's
claw. Tashi was still a few years behind the average
age when most would face the test, but her skills were

By the time the three strangers entered Kustos, Tashi was
deeply frustrated. She had become one of the most skilled
fighters in the village, yet everyone still treated her like
a child. So it was quite the surprise when the village elder,
Yeshe, called on her to step forward. The youngest stranger
of the trio had been injured, apparently gravely, and Tashi
was to heal him. Tashi immediately recognized that healing
the boy would be her test. There was no mistaking it. The Age
of Mortality had been reached, and Sam London was Tashi's
ticket to fulfilling her life's ambition. She would rescue him
from the brink of death and risk her own in the process. She
was reminded of an old saying Yeshe often repeated: "Be
careful what you wish for."

Fear was an alien concept to the Guardians. Tashi had
never been scared, so it was difficult for her to recognize the
feeling when it appeared. The sensation was one of overwhelming dread, as though something could—or rather
would—go terribly wrong. The boy's life and Tashi's future
were hanging in the balance, not to mention the fact that the
gryphon was depending on her. After all, he had chosen to
appear to Sam London above so many others. This had to

mean the boy was important to the protection of the claw. And protecting the claw was a Guardian's sworn duty.

Tashi was also keenly aware that once she undertook this healing, her life and Sam London's life would never be the same. There was a reason Guardians who reached the Age of Mortality were not tested through healings: they created an unbreakable bond between the healer and the healed, a connection so powerful it became part of the Guardian's existence from that day forward. When Guardians faced death and beat it protecting the gryphon's claw, their bond with the creature was complete. Their instincts were instantly altered, and their lives would be forever dedicated to the claw's protection.

But this was different. Saving Sam would create an enduring connection with him, as well as with the gryphon. It would mean that in addition to Tashi's mission to protect the claw, Sam's life from this point on would fall under her guard. Once the healing had occurred and the link had been established, protecting Sam would become instinct. It would be a part of her life and a part of his, for as long as they lived. Considering he was not a Guardian and did not live in Kustos, she wondered how this would be achieved. But that was a consideration for another time; she first had to save him.

Tashi had never known pain like the kind she experienced when she healed Sam's injuries. Of course, like many young Guardians, Tashi had been hurt in trainings, but she had never been gravely injured. This feeling was understandably unique. When she absorbed Sam's wounds, she could feel her life energy being drained from her body. One moment she was staring into his eyes and completing the transfer, and the next her world turned pitch-black.

At its heart, the test the Guardians faced was a mental battle, a war between their perceived reality and their beliefs. It was no secret that the gryphon's blood pulsed through Guardian veins, and that as long as the claw was under their guard, they were protected from death and disease. That was part of the gryphon's magic. Unfortunately, the only thing standing in the way of that magic was the Guardians' all-too-human mind. If they didn't fully believe or accept the power the gryphon had bestowed upon them centuries earlier, their sense of mortality grew stronger, clouded their thoughts, and put their lives in danger.

Tashi struggled to trust in the gryphon's power when bleeding from a fatal wound. A voice in the back of her head whispered, *What if?* Those two simple words were worse than any injury because they meant her faith was fading. At that moment, Tashi's body was rocked with a wave of excruciating pain. She was instantly overcome by a sense of despair and hopelessness. Her body went numb and her vision clouded like steam on a windowpane. Her ears were bombarded by a piercing ring, which spiraled upward in volume until it abruptly cut out and she was left listening to the loud, steady thump of her heartbeat. But the beat began to weaken. Tashi's pulse turned softer and slower. The once-powerful drumbeat that marked her life was fading as though the drummer were marching farther and farther away. And then it was heard no more. Tashi of Kustos had succumbed to her injuries.

The darkness that followed was terrifying but brief. In a brilliant flash, the black void turned a gleaming white. As the brightness subsided, Tashi could see she was now standing on a rocky cliff in the middle of a vast desert. She recognized her surroundings as those from a dream she had—the dream of Sam London meeting Phylassos. What surprised her even more than finding herself in this place was the fact the gryphon was standing just a few feet away. Tashi dropped to her knees in reverence to the king of magical creatures.

"Rise, young warrior," the gryphon said in a low growl. Tashi climbed slowly to her feet, her head still bowed. "Look upon me, Tashi of Kustos." The warrior finally lifted her head and met Phylassos's gaze. "Are you fearful?" he asked. Tashi shook her head adamantly. "Yet here you are. Do you not believe in me? In my power?" She shook her head again. "Yet here you are," the gryphon wryly repeated. Tashi's face registered a realization.

"Wait . . . ," she responded, confused. "Am I . . . ?" The gryphon nodded. Tashi became instantly agitated. Her brow furrowed and her body tensed. "No!" she exclaimed. "No, that is not possible!" She pounded a fist against her chest in defiance. "This heart shall beat again," she declared. "It must."

"Why must it?" the gryphon inquired.

"Because Guardians cannot die. You have deemed this so."

"Have I?" the gryphon said coyly. Tashi nodded. "But death is powerful, is it not?"

"Not as powerful as you," she replied.

"Are you certain? Mustn't each of us face the King of Terrors? The final enemy of all flesh?" the gryphon posited, a twinkle in his big green eyes.

Tashi stood taller and spoke the words she had grown up reciting every day of her young life: "I am a Guardian of the gryphon's claw. Since the day of Alexander's folly, we have sworn to serve the mighty Phylassos, father of all gryphons and protector of magical creatures. The gryphon's blood flows through our bodies. Pumps our warrior hearts. It grants us power over death. The strength to choose when we fight our last battle. *And today is not my day.*" Tashi stressed those last six words with a steadfast and steely determination. The gryphon smiled when she was finished, and it was at that instant the young warrior felt a thump in her chest. It was a pounding beat that shook the ground beneath her feet. It was followed by another and another, until her heart was pumping once again.

"I shall live to protect the gryphon's claw," Tashi vowed with fearless resolve.

The gryphon leaned in and whispered loudly, "But that, Tashi of Kustos, is not your life's only purpose."

Tashi considered Phylassos's words. "Sam," she said. "Sam London."

The gryphon nodded. "There will come a time when you must choose between the safety of the boy and my own." Tashi's eyes widened with concern. "When that moment comes, you will know who to choose," Phylassos added.

"But . . ." Tashi needed more than that. She was sworn to protect both; how could she ever choose between them? She woke with a start to find herself in the barracks, her anxious parents sitting vigil nearby. They leapt to their feet, overjoyed that their daughter had succeeded. The test was complete. Tashi had overcome death and could take her rightful place as a Guardian of the gryphon's claw. They brought her her favorite food and drink to celebrate, but Tashi was too distracted by thoughts of her vision and the prophetic words of the gryphon. She wondered about this future choice she would be forced to make and prayed for the wisdom to make it. One thing was certain: she and Sam London were now bound for all eternity—a truth with implications she didn't yet fully understand.

Sam had heard the expression "deer caught in headlights" before. In fact, he had witnessed its inspiration one night when he and his mom were returning from a movie. The road was shrouded in a thick, soupy fog, and they pulled around a corner to find a deer standing in the middle of the street. Ettie slammed on the brakes and brought the car to an abrupt halt just a few feet from the terrified creature. It stared into the light, frozen like a statue. Finally, Ettie honked the horn and the animal scurried off into the woods.

Sam London currently found himself playing the part of the deer in that scenario; the car was a yeti, also known as an abominable snowman. Sam's muscles clenched and his heart raced. He had slipped into fight-or-flight mode, and it was time to choose. Fortunately, the decision was made for him. A streak of lightning flashed across the cave ceiling. In an instant, Tashi was standing in front of Sam, crouched in a defensive posture. She spun her shekchen and met the yeti's chest with the weapon's tip. A charge shot through the staff and into the creature. The yeti vibrated off the ground and was then propelled backward twenty feet. Tashi spun around to face Sam, whose jaw was still in a fully dropped position.

"That was awesome!" Sam exclaimed. He was growing more impressed with Tashi with each passing hour. But she wasn't fishing for a compliment; she was all business.

"Run!" she commanded.

Sam wasn't about to argue. He turned to make a getaway, but as he did, he had a sudden realization. Everyone else was doing their part to protect the claw—Dr. Vantana and Chriscanis were in a heated battle with two other yetis near the cave entrance, while Tashi had just rescued him from certain death. But what was Sam contributing to this struggle? The answer was nothing. Whether it was the gargoyles, the redcaps, or the recent yak debacle, Sam London seemed to always need rescuing. It was high time he did something heroic, he thought. Without a moment to lose, Sam reached up and snatched the gryphon's claw off the crystal podium, then ran for the innermost part of the cave.

Sam glanced back toward the others as he leapt over the treasures scattered on the cave floor. He had noticed that things had gotten eerily quiet all of a sudden and was curious to see whether they had won the battle. That wasn't the case.

The yetis had simply ceased fighting, and just stood there, motionless. Tashi, Vantana, and Chriscanis were puzzled.

"Looks like they may have had enough," the cynocephalus suggested.

The three yetis pivoted toward Sam. Sam peered down at the golden claw in his clutches and had a frightful realization.

"Uh-oh," he muttered.

The creatures charged him. There was no escape; he had gotten himself cornered, and the yetis were closing quickly with long, leaping strides. Sam spotted the doctor running behind the monsters.

"Throw it, Sam!" the doctor ordered. "Throw it!"

Sam cocked his arm back and launched the claw toward the doctor. It didn't come close. The claw spun through the air and nailed one of the yetis in the head. Luckily, the blow dazed the beast long enough for Vantana to scoop up the precious relic and toss it to Chriscanis.

"Sorry!" Sam yelled.

"If we live, remind me to teach you how to throw," the doctor offered as he scrambled away from the yetis.

The creatures spun around and headed for the claw's new possessor. Chriscanis waited until they were right on him, then threw it to Tashi. She made a leaping catch worthy of the major leagues and dropped back down into her combat stance.

"I'm open!" the doctor announced, waving his hands.

Just as the yetis were about to pounce on the Guardian, she shot the claw to the doctor, then used her shekchen to sweep the legs of the creatures as they headed toward Vantana.

They got back to their feet and continued their pursuit. The battle quickly devolved into a high-stakes game of Monkey in the Middle in which the monkey was a bloodthirsty yeti. But it didn't take long for them to wise up.

The yeti in the center—who sported a black streak of hair on his otherwise pale head—called to the others with a gravelly roar. The two yetis stomped over to their counterpart, and the trio leaned in and barked at each other.

"Are they . . . huddling?" the doctor asked.

"They are a communal species," Tashi explained. "Everything they do is by committee." Tashi cleared her throat and made several sounds similar to those emitted by the yetis. The striped creature turned to her and responded with the same noises.

"Are you talking to them?" a stunned Chriscanis asked the young warrior. Tashi nodded and continued her dialogue with the yetis.

"Why didn't you talk to them before?" the doctor inquired, a touch exasperated.

"They do not listen when they are in a rage," Tashi replied matter-of-factly. "They say they are tired of playing games. They want the claw."

"What a surprise. Tell them they can't have it," the doctor advised.

Tashi made a few more of the sounds, but the striped yeti appeared to lose interest. He turned back to his counterparts, and they continued their huddle. A moment later, the three yetis turned and started toward Sam.

"Why are they heading for me?" Sam said in a panic. "I don't have the claw!"

"They will use you as leverage," Tashi answered, as if the answer were obvious.

"Run, Sam! Before they can corner you," Dr. Vantana ordered.

Sam eyed the converging yetis and saw an opportunity. He ran toward the creatures at full speed.

"Good gracious! You're supposed to run *away* from the monsters!" Chriscanis exclaimed.

But Sam kept moving. Even the yetis appeared confused by his behavior. He sucked in a breath, then slid right between the legs of the striped yeti. The creatures were not prepared for the surprise move and took a moment to react. It was all the time Sam needed. He shot across the cave, leaping over jeweled cups and treasure chests filled with golden baubles as he made a bee-line for Tashi, Vantana, and Chriscanis. The trio were cheering by that point, amazed and elated by his daring move.

"Now what?" Sam asked Tashi, when he finally reached the cave entrance.

"The gryphon's claw is no longer safe here. We will bring it back with us to Kustos. Yeshe will know what to do."

The yetis had redirected and were now lumbering back toward the entrance. Sam and the others spun around and sprinted through the stone doors. As they rushed outside, Tashi hung back and hit the door with the tip of her shekchen. A pulse of electricity spread across the stone surface, and the doors began to close. The yetis were too slow to reach the entrance in time. The massive stone doors shut, trapping the creatures inside.

Exhausted by the encounter, the group took a moment to catch their breath.

"Oh, for a pug's sake," Chriscanis said.

They turned to see what he had suddenly become aware of: the cave was behind them, but there were now two dozen abominable snowmen in front of them. The yetis had friends, and they were lined up side by side, their teeth bared, ready to fight.

Dr. Vance Vantana knew the score. The quartet was grossly outnumbered and outmatched. It was time to surrender. He could immediately tell his decision was not well received by Tashi. The warrior had never backed down from a fight; it was an entirely foreign concept to her people. But Vance reminded her she wasn't the only one in this battle.

"We've got a responsibility to look out for the kid," Vance whispered to her as she gripped her shekchen, preparing to take on the beasts solo if necessary. "And we'll be useless to protect the gryphon's claw if we're all dead." Tashi eyed him, then finally nodded in grudging agreement. Vance winked. "Don't you worry. I still got a few tricks up my sleeve. Let's see where this goes."

*   *   *

The march to the yeti village was a bone-chilling struggle through ice and snow along a narrow, winding path that skirted the edge of the mountain. It was also downhill, which made slipping and falling to one's death an ever-present possibility. Vance hoped someone would come searching for the quartet and find their tracks until he saw the snowmen covering their trail. It was fascinating. Two yetis at the rear of the pack blew the footprints away, expelling a large gust of air from their lungs. The force of the wind returned the landscape to its pristine state.

"What are they going to do with us?" Sam asked, unnerved.

"I haven't a clue," Vance told him. "But we're still alive, and I always count that as a positive sign."

"Until we're not, that is," Chriscanis quipped. "I'm hoping they're vegans. But with fangs and an anger-management problem like that—"

Vance caught Sam's terrified expression and shot the cynocephalus a warning glare. Chriscanis instantly quieted. "Sorry, mate," he whispered to the doctor.

There was a part of Vance that was excited about the journey they were on, despite the circumstances. After all, he was a scientist at heart, and no human had ever laid eyes on a yeti village. Some believed they lived inside a cloud; others theorized that their village was invisible. Vance soon learned that there was truth to both of these notions.

When the yetis led the group through a slender passage between two mountains, they were engulfed in a fog so thick Vance couldn't see two inches in front of his face.

"It's like walking through cream of mushroom soup," Chriscanis observed.

"Dr. Vantana?" Sam said nervously.

"Take my hand, Sam," the doctor replied. "We'll be fine."

The doctor quickly felt Sam's hand clutch his own. The group finally emerged from the haze to find themselves looking down on a hidden valley. The yeti village wasn't invisible or in a cloud; it was concealed beneath a canopy of clouds and surrounded on all sides by mountains. From this height, Vance could determine that the village was structured in concentric circles. It reminded him of the bigfoot habitat in Redwood National Park. The two creatures were distant cousins, so the similarities weren't surprising. In the center of the village was an enormous dome of ice like a massive igloo.

When they reached the valley floor and Vance could get a closer look, he deduced that the circles represented different social levels of the yeti culture. Those on the lower end of the hierarchy occupied the outer rings. These yetis were workers who lived in single-room igloos built closely together. They growled and snarled at the group as they were ushered by. The yetis occupying the inner circles appeared more sophisticated and lived in elaborate ice dwellings with multiple rooms. They stood straighter and didn't bare their teeth in an aggressive way. On the contrary, they studied their guests in a pensive, inquisitive manner.

The group was led past the center of the camp and beyond the dome. Vance stole a glimpse inside the structure and saw dozens of yetis trading goods and holding meetings, while yeti youth were attending what looked like school classes. Outside that lay a sloping embankment. They were marched to the bottom, where they found a darkened cavern cut off by a large frozen door and vertical bars made of thick stalagmites and stalactites. The doors were opened and the foursome was pushed inside. The doors then shut, and two yetis remained to guard their new prisoners.

"We've been arrested by abominable snowmen," Chriscanis said, incredulously. "If we ever get out of this, it'll make one heck of a pub story."

"Despite the look of it, this is not a terrible development. We can rest up and consider our options. Form an escape plan," Vance explained. He glanced at Sam, who had dropped to the cavern floor, exhausted. "We'll find a way out of here," he assured the boy.

At that instant a voice called out from the darkness of the inner cave. It had an older sound to it with a tone that was familiar to Vance. "I was hoping the cavalry was coming to rescue me, not keep me company." Vance immediately looked toward the origin of the voice.

"Who's there? Come into the light, where we can see you," he demanded. A second passed and a figure emerged from the shadows. He was an older man, past seventy, with a gray beard and mustache, kind eyes, and a warm smile. Vance's eyes widened in disbelief. "Henry?" he said in amazement.

Dr. Henry Knox, the head of the Department of Mythical Wildlife, the author of countless books on mythical beasts, and the man who had disappeared three months ago, nodded.

"Miss me?"

Chapter 13

KNOX KNOCKS

It had been nearly three months since Dr. Vance Vantana had seen his mentor, Dr. Henry Knox. In that time, Vance had come to realize just how much he relied on the legendary scientist professionally and how much he missed him personally. They had met when Vance was just a boy. Knox had taken him under his wing and shown him a world he never knew existed or thought possible. He was part teacher and part family member—the latter became more pronounced over the years, as Vance devoted himself to his work and had little time to develop outside relationships. It was a major reason why Knox's disappearance was so devastating. It had helped Vance to believe that Knox was out there somewhere, alive, and that he would eventually return or be found. Of course, he hadn't expected to find him in a yeti prison. But there the old man was, tired and scruffy but in good health. Vance couldn't help himself—the rush of emotions was too great. He bounded over and embraced his mentor.

"Based on this welcome, I'm supposing you thought me dead," Knox posited. Vance broke the hug, looking sheepish. He tried to hide his embarrassment with irritation.

"Where the heck have you been?!" Vance questioned Knox like a mom whose kid had stayed out past curfew. "One day you were there and the next"—he snapped his fingers—"Poof! Gone."

"I'll explain it all to you later, if we get out of here alive. Perhaps you could introduce me to your friends?" Knox suggested.

"Right, right. Of course," Vance said. "I think you already know Chriscanis, Chase's successor."

Knox approached the cynocephalus. "Yes, I believe we've met, if briefly. Congratulations on your new position."

"Thank you, Doctor. Hopefully, I'll survive my first year," Chriscanis added wryly.

Knox set his sights on Tashi next. "The perfect posture, fierceness in the eyes, and an extraordinary strength of presence. You must be a Guardian." Tashi nodded.

Sam London was just too excited to wait for his introduction. He stepped forward and shot his hand out. "I'm Sam. Sam London. I'm a really big fan of yours, Dr. Knox. It's an honor."

Knox shook Sam's hand and studied him. Then he looked

at Vance. "You brought a boy on the most dangerous journey on earth?"

"He's very persistent," Vance explained with a guilty shrug.

"I am," Sam added.

Knox smiled. "You must be."

"He saw Phylassos," Vance revealed. Knox looked to Sam with surprise and the boy nodded his head affirmatively.

"Well then, I look forward to hearing more about you, Sam London," Knox said, impressed. "Now, what are you all doing here?"

Vance explained the events of the last few days and the recent battle in Phylassos's cave. Knox was displeased to hear that the yetis had secured the gryphon's claw. He called the entire affair confounding.

"The yetis have never been known as an ambitious species. Territorial, yes. Obsessively territorial. But certainly not power hungry," Knox mused.

"I reckon they're being manipulated. Like the gargoyles that attacked us outside Bakersfield," Vance surmised.

"It would seem so. But by whom?" Knox asked.

"Whoever it was, they knew to use us to gain entry into the cave. We were pawns," Chriscanis said.

"Indeed you were," Dr. Knox replied. He then turned his attention to Tashi. "Do you still have a charge left in your shekchen?" Tashi nodded. "Good. We will need it. And we must hope that your brethren have been alerted."

"You mean the other Guardians?" Vance asked. "How would they know?"

"The claw has been taken. They will sense it," Tashi explained. She shifted her attention to Knox. "But they still may not find us."

"They will. We just have to—" Before Knox could finish his sentence, there were two yetis opening the prison door. One of them pointed at Sam, then gestured for him to step forward. Sam immediately looked to Vance for help. Tashi, Vance, and Chriscanis took a position in front of Sam as Knox stood by, watching.

"Tashi," Knox said, "ask them what they want with him."

Tashi made several guttural noises and motioned to Sam. One yeti replied with a string of staccato barks. Tashi responded and the yeti followed. She turned to Sam. "They wish to ask the boy who saw the gryphon some questions."

"They can't be serious. I'm not lettin' him go off alone with them snowballs," Vance asserted. "I'm responsible for him." The yeti growled at Vance.

"You're not invited," the young warrior replied, in what was likely a refined translation of the yeti's utterance.

"Vance, it is our best opportunity. We cannot take on an entire village of yetis single-handedly," Knox explained. He faced Sam. "Sam, can you do this?"

Sam nodded. "I think so. What do you want me to do?"

"I want you to stall them for as long as you can. And when you see the signal—"

"How will I—" Sam started.

"You'll know. When you see it, you're going to take this . . ." Knox slipped Sam a small metallic device. It was capsule-shaped, with a button on the end. Vance's brow rose.

"Is that . . . ," Vance began to say, but was silenced by a nod from Knox.

"You push this button and then you run, boy. You run like the dickens. You find a place to hide and you stay put until you hear us call for you. Do you understand?"

"I think so." Before Sam could get a grasp on his orders, the yetis entered the cave and grabbed him. Tashi pulled Vance back to avoid an altercation.

"You will do us no good dead," Tashi reminded him.

"I agree, old boy," Chriscanis added. "Best if we stand down. Let this play out."

Vance attempted to relax, but seeing Sam dragged away by the yetis was tough. He had to keep reminding himself that Henry Knox had never failed him before. Time and again, Knox had saved Vance from dangerous situations. Vance wondered why he found it so hard to trust his mentor now. Perhaps it was because he had already been through so much with Sam. It took all his strength to call out and reassure the boy as he was led away. "You're going to be okay, Sam," he said. But he couldn't hide the uncertainty in his voice.

Not surprisingly, being dragged up an icy embankment by two abominable snowmen was an unpleasant experience. They weren't exactly gentle creatures. But Sam London couldn't help thinking the worst was yet to come. If they could somehow get over the language barrier without Tashi's help, the yetis would likely have questions to which Sam didn't have any answers. And then what? What would they do to him? It had already been a tumultuous day, punctuated by imprisonment in a yeti cave-jail and meeting Dr. Henry Knox. If the yetis hadn't taken his book bag, Sam would have loved to have Knox sign his book on gryphons. Yet instead of enjoying this encounter with the famous author, Sam was being sent by him to distract the yetis and give them all a chance to escape. Sam wondered what the device was that now sat snugly in his pocket, what it could possibly do to save them, and what the signal would be to use it.

The creatures marched Sam toward the center structure. What had been teeming with yetis just moments earlier was now completely deserted. The village was eerily silent, except for the haunting whistle of the wind as it wound through the icy buildings. When they rounded the massive dome, Sam finally got a look at his destination—or, more importantly, the creature that was waiting for him. It was six feet tall with sickly dark blue skin. It sported mangy black hair that fell just below its shoulders, and bloodshot eyes. The creature was dressed in a dirty black cloak that fell loosely around its body but was open in the back to allow for its wings. They were inky black, shorter than a gargoyle's, and flapped softly, constantly, and almost hypnotically, without ever pulling the creature off the ground. When it spoke, it did so in a breathy, rough voice that was high in pitch. This living nightmare was apparently female.

"Bring the boy closer," the creature said, gesturing to him with talonlike fingers. Sam could see razor-sharp fangs in its mouth and a long nose that hooked slightly toward its chin when it talked. One of the yetis pushed Sam closer as the hideous being leaned in for a better look. It ran a talon down Sam's cheek, then smiled a terrifying smile.

"Do you know who I am?" the creature asked in a vile whisper. Sam eyed her, studying her features. They were familiar to him. He searched his memory and then realized—

"You're the creature my teacher told me about. The aswang," Sam said.

"And you are the boy who saw the gryphon. Tell me, was Phylassos worried about his precious claw?" the aswang asked with an air of superiority.

"Claw?" Sam replied, feigning ignorance. The aswang pulled the golden gryphon's claw from within her cloak.

"This claw. The one that has sustained the unjust curse for all these centuries," the aswang said with a simmering anger. "The one that has forced our kind to live in the shadows, when it is we who should rule over simple creatures, like you."

Sam looked back to the prison: still no signal.

"They cannot help you now, boy," the aswang snarled.

She was right, Sam thought. He was on his own. He swallowed his nerves and relied on the one skill that had gotten him this far.

"You're talking about that claw as if it's the real one. You can't trick me," he said confidently.

The aswang eyed him. "I can smell the magic on it from miles away. Enough with your feeble attempts to—"

"I fell for it too," Sam bluffed. "Until I found out where the real one was. But don't feel too bad. Everyone knows how sneaky the gryphon is. To be honest, I'm a little upset at myself for not realizing it sooner. It's so obvious. I mean, why would he hide it here, of all places? Especially if he thought it was in danger. It totally makes sense that he would have hidden it—" Sam stopped and quickly cupped his hand over his mouth. When he pulled his hand away, he began again. "I can't believe I almost said it out loud. Man, would I be in trouble."

The aswang was listening to Sam with increasing interest and growing frustration. She eyed him, then the claw she held in her talons. "You lie, boy. This is the genuine claw." The doubt in her declaration was clear, and Sam hid his glee. It was time to ride this bluff as far as it would take him.

"Nope. It's not. The Guardian showed me the proof that it's a fake. But don't listen to me," Sam suggested. "Go ahead and break it. You'll see. It won't end any curse."

The aswang snarled, "Where is this proof?"

Sam stretched out his hand. "Here, I'll show you."

The aswang hesitated. "If this is a trick, I shall eat you whole."

"It's not. Just give it to me, already. I'm surrounded by abominable snowmen. What am I going to do?" The aswang eyed him, then slowly handed over the claw. Sam pretended to study it closely, and cast an eye toward the prison. *C'mon, guys,* he thought.

"Well?" the aswang said. "Show me, boy! Or I shall—"

"Eat me whole, I got it," Sam responded. "Just give me a second. It's not that easy to see. That's why it's a really good fake." He was running out of time. Still no signal, and the aswang was getting wise to his ruse.

"Enough of this. Give me the claw. If it is a fake, we will find out soon enough."

"We?" Sam inquired. "As in the yetis, or is there someone else? Like someone above you? I kind of thought there might be. No offense. But you don't seem like the top-banana type."

"Give it to me," the aswang said, irritated.

The moment of truth. Sam had played his hand and lost. He was about to return the claw when it finally happened. An electrical charge shot into the sky and illuminated the valley. Sam's eyes went to the origin—the prison! That was the signal. It was enough to briefly distract the aswang and the yetis so Sam could do as Knox had instructed him: run like the dickens. The aswang quickly realized Sam was making off with the claw. She yelled to the yetis, and the creatures were instantly in pursuit, the aswang leading the charge.

Sam clutched the claw tightly to his chest as he ran at a full sprint through the village and toward the narrow mountain passage they had taken to enter the valley. He pulled the cylindrical device that Knox had given him from his pocket, pressed the button on the tip with his thumb, and dropped it to the ground. He spotted a collection of wooden carts the yetis used for food and quickly dove for the closest one, sliding beneath it and hiding between the cart and a short ice wall. He peered back to where he had dropped the device and could see that it was now spinning. In fact, it was spinning so fast it began to lift off the ground like a miniature helicopter. He could also see that it was flickering with light. And that was when something extraordinary happened: the yeti village was suddenly overrun by Guardians in full warrior dress! The yetis reared back and total chaos ensued.

While the yetis scrambled to face their new opponents, Sam began to notice that something didn't seem altogether right about these Guardians. Sam focused on the one closest to him and could see that it shimmered. These weren't Guardians, Sam concluded. His suspicions were immediately proven correct when the aswang ran right through the one Sam had his eye on. These Guardians were holograms. The aswang grabbed the device that was projecting the images and crushed it in its talons. All the Guardians instantly disappeared. Sam's eyes darted over to the scores of yetis who had been preparing to face off with their imagined enemies. They froze, confused.

Suddenly, Sam was being dragged out from under the cart by his feet. His body slid across the ragged ice and into the open. He spun himself right-side up and saw the aswang pulling him toward her with her talons.

"I will have the claw, boy!" the aswang squealed. "And then I shall have you for dinner!"

Sam kicked at the creature and managed to connect with

her chin, stunning the aswang. He broke free from her grip, climbed to his feet, and took off running. The aswang regained her bearings and pursued, but now she used her wings to fly a few feet above the ground, swiftly closing the gap between them. She barked orders to the yetis, who joined the chase.

Sam glanced back to see that he was now being chased not only by the aswang, but also by an entire village of abominable snowmen. There was no way he was going to make it to the narrow mountain passage in time. Track was another one of those sports he wasn't very good at.

The aswang reached Sam and swooped down, slashing at him. The creature's talons tore the back of his jacket and caused him to lose his footing on the icy terrain. He tried to keep himself upright, but the momentum was too great. He tumbled to the ground and slid several feet. He could hear the aswang land behind him, stalking him like prey.

"No escape now," the aswang jeered.

Sam was tired, his breathing rapid and heavy. He began to feel a sense of resignation—it was similar to the feeling he had experienced with his near-fatal injury in the Himalayas. The difference was that the pain was replaced with paralyzing fear. And there was a sound filling his ears that seemed to make the situation all the more frightening. A dull roar that grew louder by the second. The ground was vibrating beneath him. At first he thought it was the yetis vocalizing before pouncing on him. But when he saw the aswang stop and peer around curiously, he knew it wasn't coming from the yetis. The aswang's focus had turned to the mountain passage, which was obscured by the low cloud cover. Sam followed the creature's gaze. And then, out of the dense white mass, the source of the roar made itself known.

Hundreds of Guardians emerged from the clouds and stampeded toward the village. They let loose a terrifying war cry and wielded their shekchens, ready for battle. It was an astonishing sight. The hapless yetis believed them to be holograms, which gave the warriors time to get closer.

"They're real!" the aswang tried to warn them, but her voice couldn't be heard over the noise of their boots on the ice.

The yetis' slight hesitation was all the Guardians needed to overcome their enemies and overwhelm the village. The aswang ignored the army and charged after Sam. She lifted him by his jacket and flapped her wings. The two were several feet from the ground when the aswang was struck by an electrical charge. She fell back to the ground, losing her hold on Sam and allowing him to roll away.

"Are you okay?" Tashi asked him as she rushed over with Dr. Vantana and Chriscanis. Sam nodded and Vance helped him to his feet.

"I think so," Sam said as he got his bearings. "What took you guys so long?"

"You'd be surprised just how difficult it is to break out of a yeti ice prison," Vantana replied. "You did good, kid. Real good."

"That you did," Chriscanis added. "You saved the whole lot of us."

"I thought I was toast when the aswang—" Sam turned to gesture toward the creature, but she was already gone.

"There she goes," Vance said, pointing to the sky. The aswang had taken flight and was disappearing into the cloud cover.

"And with her, the answers we need," Chriscanis concluded. Tashi let off a few bolts from her shekchen, but it was too late. The aswang had escaped.

"Did you get any good intel out of her?" the doctor asked Sam. "Anything that could help us figure out who might be behind this mess?"

"Not much, but she's definitely not working alone. She kept using the word 'we,' and she knew who I was," Sam revealed. "I think there's someone above her. Someone calling the shots."

"The aswang have always been trouble," Chriscanis said. "But I've never known them to be the type that enjoyed being bossed around."

"Nor the yetis," Tashi chimed in.

"Right, right," Vance added, pursing his lips as if trying to make sense of it all. Sam caught his eye and shrugged. The doctor smiled. "I think this belongs to you." He handed Sam his book bag. "I'm pretty certain this book bag has been places no other book bag has been."

"That's for sure," Sam replied.

Dr. Knox and Yeshe approached. Behind them Sam could

see that the yetis had ceased fighting and stood stoically, surrounded by Guardians.

"The yetis have surrendered," Dr. Knox announced. "They offered little information on the aswang. It contacted them a few months ago and preyed on their jealousy of the Guardians to persuade them to help retrieve the claw."

Sam looked at Tashi, curious. "Why are the yetis jealous of you?"

"They were the gryphon's sworn protectors before Phylassos cursed humanity. Once the curse was in place, the gryphon believed the claw would be best protected by those who weren't a part of it. That is why we were created. Our loyalty would never be questioned," Tashi explained.

Yeshe continued, "But the yetis rebelled and Phylassos punished them, prohibiting them from ever leaving these mountains."

"Apparently, one of the aswang's promises to them was their freedom," Knox added. The old man stepped closer to Sam and put his hand on his shoulder. He smiled kindly. "We owe you a great debt, Sam London. You are the hero of this day, if not the century. It is an honor to have met you, and I thank you for saving us and the claw."

Sam's grin would have made the Cheshire cat envious. "You're welcome. . . . Oh, and here." He handed the claw to Knox, who handed it to Yeshe. "Dr. Knox?" Sam asked sheepishly.

"Yes, Sam?"

"Could I ask you a favor?"

"Now is a good time. I would be hard-pressed to refuse a request from my liberator."

Sam pulled the gryphon book out of his book bag. "Would you sign this for me?"

"I think I could manage that," Knox answered with a wink.

The journey back to Kustos was Dr. Vantana's chance to question his mentor and fill him in on recent events. Knox was particularly intrigued by the gargoyle attack and the encounter with Cernunnos, who had always had a particular dislike for Henry. It appeared his grudge went back quite a few years. Knox didn't seem as disturbed by Penelope's sudden amnesia as Vance thought he would. Vance questioned him about the last time he'd seen Penelope, and Knox explained that he'd met with her right before he decided to go "silent," as he called it. Vance remembered Penelope talking about the hologram device when he'd been in her lab just days earlier. She had found the specs for the device, and evidence that she had completed it, but couldn't locate the actual unit. Now Vance knew that Knox had taken it. The doctor continued to wonder why there was no record of Knox's having removed it and why his leaving coincided so perfectly with Penelope's amnesia. Knox discounted it as merely chance.

According to Knox, he had been receiving messages from Phylassos regarding a threat to the curse and attempts to steal the claw. He learned through his sources that claw relics around the world had been stolen. However, because of the delicate and secretive nature of this investigation, Henry decided it would be best if he unraveled the mystery himself and didn't mistakenly tip off whoever was behind it. His search led him to Tibet, where he got caught by a group of yetis on his way to Kustos. Now that he knew about the aswang's involvement, the case would take him and Vance to the Philippines. Time was of the essence, since the creatures behind this conspiracy might already be adjusting their plan in response to the DMW's investigation.

With Vance and Henry heading to Southeast Asia, Sam would have to return home, although Henry couldn't be certain Sam's purpose had been fulfilled, either in connection with Phylassos or the investigation. It appeared he had done his part, and they were putting him in too much danger by including him any further.

Dr. Knox decided it would be best if they waited until their return to Kustos to break the news to the boy. As expected, Sam was quite upset, which in turn made Vance upset. To make matters worse, Henry directed Vance to counter the injection he had given Sam days earlier. It would dilute the bigfoot blood in Sam's body and return him to normal. Having the sight taken away was a devastating blow to Sam. Vance felt terrible, but Henry was right. Until Sam was of age, he would need to return to his life outside this strange new world. Constantly seeing magical creatures flitting about would make that impossible.

Fortunately, Yeshe compensated for the bad news by

arranging for Sam to receive a medal for his heroism and to be named an honorary Guardian of the gryphon's claw. Yeshe noted that the medal was forged with the same gold Alexander the Great had used to plate the claw. Chriscanis volunteered to escort Sam home, while Vance and Henry prepared to leave for the next stage of their investigation. As Vance said goodbye to Sam, he found that the connection he had made with this boy was stronger than he realized. He had always been a loner, but Sam London had him reconsidering his life and his solitude. Vance was most certainly going to miss him. Of course, he wasn't sure Sam's part in this mystery was over. He took solace in a sneaking suspicion that this would not be the last time they saw each other.

So many questions lingered in Vance's head about Sam and his meeting with Phylassos, and now the doctor had even more questions surrounding his mentor, Henry Knox, and his unusual disappearance. But the question that weighed on Vance's mind the most was simply: Where was the gryphon in all this? After everything that happened, why had he not chosen to appear again?

Vance couldn't help but feel that Henry wasn't being entirely forthcoming. What did his friend and mentor know about Phylassos? And when would he decide to tell him?

Chapter 14

NO PLACE LIKE HOME

*To Sam London, the boy who saw the gryphon and saved us
all. Your friend and biggest fan, Dr. Henry Knox.* This inscrip-
tion by Dr. Knox in *The Great and Powerful Gryphon* was one
of the few reminders Sam had of his extraordinary adventure.
He had already read and gazed lovingly at it several times
since returning home. It made him understandably nostalgic.
There was a world he never knew existed, a world in which
he felt like he finally belonged. In that world there was something special about Sam London. Everyone had heard of him,
everyone wanted to know him—for better or for worse. That
certainly couldn't be said for his life in Benicia, California.
Here he instantly went back to average.

It was two nights earlier that Sam had returned to Benicia.
He hadn't been pleased when Dr. Vantana had informed him
that he would have to leave Kustos and return home. And

while he appreciated and adored the medal awarded him when he'd been named an honorary Guardian, it felt like a deliberate attempt to soften the decision to send him back. However, the worst part was having the sight taken away. He had protested this decision passionately, but Dr. Knox had insisted. Knox believed having the sight put Sam and his mother in too much danger. If the DMW ever required his services in the future, they would reinstate it. But for the time being, it was important that Sam return to his mother the same way he had left. According to Vance, the loss of the sight wouldn't be immediate; it would take several hours to kick in. By then he would be home and wouldn't even know the difference. Sam found that hard to believe.

Sam said goodbye to Tashi, thanking her again for saving his life on more than one occasion. She just bowed her head, saying, "It was my honor and my duty, Sam London."

Sam wasn't sure what Tashi meant when she said it was her duty to save him. But he did notice one detail regarding the young Guardian that he hadn't had time to notice until now: she was cute.

Saying goodbye to Dr. Vantana proved much more difficult. They had been together since the night in Bakersfield. The doctor was the person who had revealed this incredible world to him. Sam had experienced so much these past several days, and the doctor had been by his side through it all. Vantana had saved him, taken care of him, and worried about him. Sam didn't know if he'd ever meet his real father, but if he did, he hoped he would be a lot like Vance Vantana.

Chriscanis, the cynocephalus, escorted Sam home before returning to England. Fortunately, the Guardians knew of a dvergen subway station that was less than a day's hike from the village of Kustos. Sam was starting to enjoy his rides on the dvergen subway, though the ancient nature of the contraption was at times unnerving. Chriscanis reminded him how ingenious dwarves were with these types of mechanisms, and that he didn't have a thing to worry about. They rode the subway back to the waterfall near Castle Crags, where Penelope had arranged for a car to be waiting. Chriscanis drove Sam back to Benicia, and the two spent the last few hours in the car talking about what it was like to be a cynocephalus.

"Too many of our species believe that our culture somehow makes us stronger," Chriscanis explained. "But I know the truth. I've seen it with my own eyes. Family makes you stronger." He then shared his secret desire to be human, to see what everyone else saw when they looked in the mirror.

"Don't you like being a cynocephalus?" Sam asked.

"When you work and live among humans, when you come to appreciate their . . . humanity, it is hard to feel like you belong."

Sam could relate to this sentiment. He confessed his own feeling of not belonging and how he thought of himself as "unspecial." Chriscanis grinned as Sam recounted all the activities he'd attempted in his search for that one unique skill.

They arrived at Sam's house in the late evening. As he walked Sam to the door, Chriscanis admired the quiet neighborhood. Realizing they would need to get Nuks's attention without waking Ettie, Chriscanis barked toward Sam's second-floor window.

Nuks peeked out, spotted the two, and was at the front door in seconds. He cracked it open, still appearing and sounding like Sam. He was excited to see his twin.

"Sam!" Nuks exclaimed in a loud whisper. "You're home!"

"Good to see you too, Nuks," Sam said with a smile.

"And that is my cue. Farewell, Sam London," Chriscanis said with a flourish and a bow. "We had a whale of a time."

Sam shook the cynocephalus's hand. "Yeah, we sure did. And just so you know, I consider you family now. You don't need to be related to qualify."

"Thank you, Sam. Thank you very much." Sam could tell Chriscanis was touched by his words. Sam waved to him one last time as he drove away.

When Sam entered the house with Nuks and closed the door, he inadvertently woke his mother, who had fallen asleep on the couch. She roused and slowly sat up. When she glanced toward the front door she saw two Sams. She snapped her head back in shock. As she rubbed her eyes in disbelief, Sam gestured for Nuks to hide. When Ettie looked again, she was met with just one Sam.

"That was freaky," Ettie said. "I saw two of you."

"Wishful thinking," Sam said, grinning. He walked to the couch and sat on the edge of the cushion. As much as he would miss being on an adventure, he sure was glad to see his mom again. She must have noticed the elation in his face.

"Are you okay, kiddo?" she asked, concerned.

Sam nodded and gave his mom a long, tight hug. "I'm just happy to see you," he replied.

"You're a strange boy, Sam London. But I'm not complaining. Not in the least."

Back in Sam's room, Nuks returned to his tanuki form and asked if he could stay. He promised to be the best companion Sam could ever hope for. He would be loyal and obedient and wouldn't make a mess. In fact, he even offered to help Sam clean his room. Sam wasn't opposed to Nuks's sticking around, but he was certain his mother would be. Nuks begged Sam to at least ask his mom and Sam obliged.

After explaining to Ettie that there was a very sweet rescue dog who needed a home, Sam braced himself for the inevitable and was surprised by Ettie's response.

"A month ago this would have been a big fat no way," she confessed. "But you've been so incredibly well-behaved lately—always helping out, doing your schoolwork—how can I say no? You deserve a reward, and if this is what you want, so be it." She then proceeded to give Sam a lengthy list of rules regarding the new pet, including the stipulation that this was a trial period. Sam happily agreed, but Ettie's reply had him wondering what Nuks had been up to since he'd been gone. It sounded as though the tanuki had set a dangerous precedent. A precedent that became clearer in the days that followed.

* * *

Sam's first day back at school was another reminder that he missed being on his adventure. Nuks had tried to get him up to speed on what he learned in the time he had been away, but Sam had trouble focusing. He woke up early and took his shower before his mom—a trick Nuks hadn't mastered, but the tanuki didn't seem to mind cold water. It was the most well-rested and cleanest Sam had felt since before he left for Death Valley. He headed to the kitchen for breakfast, thrilled to have normal food again. Unfortunately, he found that Nuks had heavily influenced the grocery shopping. Sam's favorite cereals had been replaced with granola, and his snacks consisted of dried fruits and nuts. Luckily, Sam had two more of Chase's British cookies. He ate one and saved the last for a special occasion.

Sam experienced more of Nuks's handiwork when Ettie dropped him at school and pulled him in for a huge hug and kiss. Sam reacted the only way he knew how.

"Mom!" Sam whined. "I thought we talked about this!"

Ettie eyed her son, confused. "What?" Then she seemed to remember—"Oh, that's right, we're cranking it up to two kisses and an extra-long hug. Okay, I'm in." Ettie kissed a horrified Sam twice on the cheek, then gripped him in a hug that seemed to last for hours. When Sam finally extricated himself from her embrace and the car, he was expecting to be instantly teased by a group of boys standing nearby. Instead, the boys spotted Sam and ran off as if they were scared of him. Nuks had informed Sam that he had an altercation with some bullies at school, and word must have spread not to mess with him. But things got even stranger when he entered

240

the school. He was being greeted warmly by fellow students he had never even spoken to before. "Hey, Sam!" and "How's it going Sam?" echoed through the hallway as he made his way to his locker. He waved and nodded in acknowledgment to these new acquaintances.

"Good morning, Sam," a female voice called out. Sam peered over his locker door to find the very blond and blue-eyed Nerida Nyx. Sam and Nerida had known each other for as long as Sam could remember. In fact, the two had had many a playdate when they were toddlers, a result of their mothers' close friendship. Although they had grown apart in recent years, they remained friendly, often waving to each other in the hall or discussing what their moms were up to. Nerida's mom, Tianna, and Ettie took the same yoga class and would hang out from time to time. Sam rarely talked about Nerida with his mom, as it usually spurred a great deal of teasing. Ettie was convinced Sam had a crush on Nerida and would often start sentences with phrases like "Well, when you and Nerida get married" or "When you and Nerida have kids . . ." The latter came when Sam was critical of his mother's parenting skills. But Sam would be lying to himself if he didn't admit to having a crush on his childhood friend. She was easygoing, smart, pretty, and enjoyed talking about mythical creatures.

"Good morning, Nerida," Sam replied with his warmest smile.

"Nice to see you," she added. Sam almost read into that a little too much, but Nerida was already talking again. "Are we still on for after school?"

Sam was stumped. What had Nuks arranged with her? And how could he have forgotten to tell him? Sam tried to figure out a way to respond without sounding like he didn't know. "Oh, right . . . after school. Was that today?" he replied, hoping to subtly procure more information.

"You definitely said today," Nerida clarified. "'Cause you said it's always better to forage for berries early in the week before the other animals get to them. Which, now that I think of it, sounds like you were referring to us as animals. But I guess that's technically true. . . ."

"Of course, foraging for berries . . . because you wanted to . . ." Sam was trying to find out how the heck this had happened.

"I wanted to learn how you did it. I mean, after you brought all those amazing berries the other day, how could I not?" Nerida answered with enthusiasm.

It pained Sam to say the following, but he had no choice: "I'm sorry, Nerida, but something's come up. Can we do it another day?"

"Oh, sure." Nerida was clearly attempting to hide her disappointment. "We'll do it *tomorrow*," she added emphatically. Before Sam had a chance to protest, the athletics coach walked by.

"Sam, buddy, don't forget tryouts are today at lunch. I'm counting on you!" he announced as he passed, a big, toothy smile plastered on his face. Sam stared back.

"Tryouts?" he repeated quizzically.

"Yeah," Nerida explained. "For track and field."

"M-me?" Sam stuttered in disbelief. He was certainly no runner.

"Yes, silly," Nerida replied. "The coach saw you at lunch. Running the track, jumping the hurdles. He said you were, like, the fastest kid he's ever seen. I mean, I didn't see it myself, but everyone has been talking about it." Sam nodded in a stunned daze. He closed his locker door and proceeded to his class.

"See you tomorrow, then," Nerida called out.

Sam nodded again, defeated by this turn of events. The raccoon-dog masquerading as Sam London had proven to be more popular than the real thing. It was a humbling revelation.

When Sam headed to Miss Capiz's class, he learned that she was out sick and a substitute teacher had taken her place. Although Nuks had turned much of his school life upside down, he had at least done a good job learning. The creature had been maintaining good grades while Sam was gone—in some classes, even better than Sam's. As the teacher droned on about a topic Sam wasn't interested in, he gazed out the window and let his mind wander. He wondered how many mythical creatures were roaming around Benicia . . . creatures he could no longer see. For all he knew, this substitute teacher could be a cynocephalus, or maybe even a dwarf. He couldn't tell. There was no more bigfoot blood running through his veins, and that left him glum. He knew something almost everyone didn't, a secret he could never divulge—and even if he did, no one would ever believe him.

Sam scanned the landscape until something caught his eye. For the briefest of moments, he could have sworn he saw

Tashi. She was standing on the lawn in front of the school, dressed in her Guardian clothing and clutching her shekchen. He did a lightning-fast double take, but she was no longer there. Was his mind playing tricks on him?

He quickly stood and asked to be excused to use the bathroom. Of course, he had no intention of going to the bathroom—he was heading outside to confirm he was merely seeing things.

He didn't have much time, so he raced to the spot where he'd seen Tashi, but there was no sign of her. Sam trudged back to the school and scolded himself for imagining such things. It had given him a surge of hope. For a few seconds, he'd believed Tashi had come to get him—to inform Sam he was needed once more. But as he settled back into his class, he told himself it was time to stop thinking about the past and start facing his reality in Benicia. He already had enough to deal with from the aftermath of Nuks's ruse. Daydreaming about Tashi wasn't going to help.

Sam faked an injury to get out of the track and field try-outs, then headed to the library to spend the rest of the lunch hour getting caught up on his classwork. After school, Ettie picked him up and dropped him off at home, per their usual routine. Once home, Sam hopped on his bike and took off to the grocery store to stock up on normal food. Nuks tagged along, apologizing on the way for not informing Sam about all the changes at school. The raccoon-dog stayed outside by the bike as Sam ventured into the market. Sam had just shut the door to the ice cream section of the frozen food aisle when it happened again. The reflection of the door revealed Tashi standing outside, peering through a window and into the store. Sam spun around, but sure enough, she was gone. When he got outside, he asked Nuks if he'd seen a Guardian, but the raccoon-dog shook his head, then whispered, "What does a Guardian look like?"

Sam didn't bother going into detail. Back at home, Sam relaxed on the couch with a package of cookies and switched on the television. He soon nodded off but was awakened by a knock on the front door. It was dark out by now, and Sam had strict rules to never open the door to anyone while Ettie was at work. He wondered who could be knocking at this hour. He climbed off the couch and headed over for a look. He noticed Nuks was missing and remembered him saying something about going outside to get some exercise. Maybe he'd locked himself out, Sam thought.

Sam pulled back the curtains on the living room window and was surprised to see Miss Capiz standing on his doorstep. She appeared anxious, her eyes darting around as if she was worried about being seen. Sam walked to the door and reached for the knob, then hesitated. Miss Capiz knocked again.

"Sam?" she asked in a hushed voice. "Sam, if you're home it is very important that we speak. Very important."

Sam wasn't sure what to do. The rules were clear—it didn't matter how well he knew someone; Sam was not to let anyone in the house when he was home alone. But Miss Capiz was his teacher, and she sounded distressed.

"I know about the gryphon, Sam," he heard her whisper

through the door. Sam froze at the mention of the creature. Miss Capiz knew? But how? "We must talk," she added quickly. "You're in grave danger."

"What do you know about the gryphon?" Sam asked.

"I know everything. You must trust me. Please, Sam, let me in; it's not safe out here."

Sam was at a loss. This was the last thing he was expecting. He called back to Miss Capiz, "How do I know you really are who you say you are? You could be some sort of shapeshifter trying to trick me."

"That is true, Sam, and wise. I appreciate your caution. You must continue that. As for whether I truly am Ina Capiz, your teacher, I can tell you the day before you saw the gryphon in real life you fell asleep in my class. Drooled on the desk, if I remember correctly." Miss Capiz gave a nervous laugh. Sam considered her words, took in a breath, then unlocked and opened the front door. "May I?" She gestured inside. Sam nodded and moved out of the way. Miss Capiz stepped into the living room while Sam shut and locked the front door. She sat down on the couch and Sam settled into the large recliner across from her.

"You said I was in danger?" Sam asked. "What do you mean?"

"There are forces who are seeking you. But I can keep you safe," Miss Capiz assured him.

"How?"

"We have to get you out of here, but first we need to find out how they're tracking you," she said.

"They're tracking me? Who? How do you know?" Sam replied, unnerved at the thought that there were creatures following him.

"I'll explain later. We must move quickly. Did you bring anything home with you from your journey?" she inquired.

"Just my book bag, my gryphon book, and a medal from the Guardians," Sam responded.

"I'll need to see this book bag. It may be the source," Miss Capiz said with concern.

"Okay . . . I'll go get it." Sam hurried up the stairs, grabbed his pack from his room, and headed back down. He had left the book bag at home that day for fear someone might abscond with it—it held too many memories to risk losing. Sam set the bag down on the coffee table and unzipped it. "This is the book." He pulled it from the bag and set it down. "The medal," he continued. "Snacks," he added, pulling out the last biscuit. But after he emptied it, he noticed something peculiar. "Why is it still so heavy? Everything is out." Miss Capiz rose to her feet and reached for the bag.

"Let me have a look," she said, and grabbed it. She guided her hand into the largest zippered compartment and felt around. Sam could hear a slight ripping sound—fabric being torn from its stitching. When Miss Capiz's hand emerged, it was clutching the golden gryphon's claw. Sam was too stunned to speak. How did that get in there? He had given the claw to Dr. Knox in the yeti village. Who had put it in his book bag? And why?

Nuks bounded through the patio doggy door but stopped

dead between the kitchen and the living room when he spotted the claw and Miss Capiz. The fur on his back stood on end, and he began to growl viciously at Sam's guest.

"Chill out, Nuks," Sam called to the tanuki. "This is my teacher, Miss Capiz. She's helping us."

"No, Sam," Nuks warned in a trebly growl. "Get away from her!"

"Don't be ridiculous. . . . She's my teacher," Sam reiterated. He looked to Miss Capiz, who eyed Nuks nervously. "Tell him, Miss Capiz."

Nuks moved in closer, growling louder now. He spoke slowly as he approached. "She is not human." With those words still echoing in his head, Sam faced his teacher and quickly realized he had made a terrible mistake.

Miss Capiz let out a terrifying shriek as she reared back and transformed. Her fingers lengthened and sprang into sharpened talons. Pitch-black wings burst through the back of her sweater. Her skin grew pale as her teeth narrowed into pointed fangs, and her eyes turned blood-red. Sam tripped as he flinched backward and fell to the ground.

Nuks lunged, but Miss Capiz swatted him away. The raccoon-dog flew back and hit the wall, taking a few framed photos with him as he slid to the floor, unconscious. Sam was still trying to process this terrifying information. His teacher was an aswang . . . and not just any aswang, but the one Sam had met at the yeti village. The one that had nearly killed him.

Chapter 15

UNGUARDED

As she watched Sam say his goodbyes, Tashi of Kustos was torn.
She and Sam had a connection. Tashi had healed him, which
had caused her to face a Guardian's greatest fear and emerge
triumphant. This miracle healing, followed by the Guardian
rite of passage, had formed an unbreakable bond between the
two. But now that bond was being tested by circumstance. As
a Guardian, Tashi's first duty was to protect the gryphon's
claw; however, her link to Sam meant she would be required
to protect him as well. How could she do both, especially
when Sam lived thousands of miles away? No Guardian had
ever faced this kind of quandary. After all, the village of Kustos rarely had visitors, and even when it did, the Guardians
didn't heal them. This case was unique, and Tashi hoped for
some wise counsel and clarification from Yeshe.

Fortunately, Yeshe had requested a meeting with Tashi

to discuss recent events. But when Tashi arrived at Yeshe's quarters, she was surprised to find that he was not alone. Dr. Henry Knox was also present. She bowed to both men, and Yeshe gestured for her to sit.

"Please, Tashi. We have much to discuss," Yeshe said with a smile.

Tashi sat down, then looked at her leader, but it was Dr. Knox who spoke next.

"Yeshe and I have decided you should travel to Benicia, California. To be close to Sam London."

Tashi was not expecting that, and it showed in her puzzled expression.

"I know you must be confused by this order. But I also know that like any Guardian put in an unusual position, you are struggling with your purpose," Yeshe concluded. "You are a Guardian of the gryphon's claw, of that there is no doubt. But you are also the boy's protector."

"But I cannot be separated from this place," Tashi noted.

"Of course you can. Your fellow warriors will continue their mission without you. And you will take your mission beyond these mountains, protecting the claw in a new way."

Dr. Knox spoke again. "You see, Tashi, Sam London will be left unguarded if you do not go. The universe brought the gryphon and Sam together for a reason. A reason we don't yet fully understand."

"Perhaps it was to save us in the yeti village or to expose the plan to steal the claw," Tashi offered.

"Perhaps. But what if there is more for him to do?" Knox asked. "We believe Phylassos would want this."

"Can we not ask him?" Tashi inquired. "The gryphon, I mean?"

"Tashi!" Yeshe scolded her.

"I simply meant if there was a way to contact him. To find out. To make certain," Tashi explained in her defense, as respectfully as possible.

"There is much about Phylassos that you do not know," the doctor responded. "But you will, in time. Right now, you must trust us."

Tashi nodded. "Then I will go. I will protect Sam London's life with my own, if I must. Please forgive my brief impertinence. You were correct, Yeshe. I was at odds with my purpose, but now I see how I can be both a Guardian of the gryphon's claw and a guardian to Sam London."

"Good, Tashi," Yeshe said. "Very good. You will leave at once."

Tashi rose and walked toward the door. She paused, then turned back. "Am I leaving forever?" she asked. The crack in her voice betrayed her feelings in the matter.

"Certainly not," Yeshe replied warmly. "Just as long as is necessary."

"And, Tashi . . . don't let Sam know of your presence. Unless, of course, it becomes unavoidable," Dr. Knox added.

Tashi nodded and exited.

Word of Tashi's new assignment spread quickly through

Kustos and was met with surprise. The implications of Yeshe's orders were entirely alien to the Guardian culture. Guardians did not leave their posts, yet here was one of their most gifted warriors being sent away by their leader. Many didn't know how to process it. Guardians were born in Kustos and died in Kustos. They said goodbye to another Guardian only at the time of their death, which came at the hour of their choosing. Tashi's parents were especially affected by this turn of events. They were saying farewell to their only daughter, but at least it was not forever. She had become the youngest Guardian of the gryphon's claw, and now she would be heading thousands of miles from the one thing she had worked so hard to achieve. It helped her parents to see that she was at peace with this decision, and that she promised to visit them in their dreams—a trick Guardians had inherited from the gryphon.

Before she left, Dr. Vance Vantana took her aside to thank her for protecting Sam and gave her Ranger Penelope Naughton's contact information.

"If you run into any trouble or you need anything, you contact Ranger Naughton. She'll know what to do."

As Tashi made her way to the entrance of the village, she found that all her fellow Guardians had gathered to see her off. Hundreds of villagers held their shekchens to the ground and sent a massive arc of electricity into the sky. It illuminated the entire valley in a swath of silvery blue light. It was an extraordinary gesture reserved for honoring those Guardians who had chosen to move on to the next plane of existence. But it was the only way Guardians knew to express the feeling of loss in any form. Tashi had never been an overly emotional individual—strong emotion was not the trademark of a warrior, and certainly not of a Guardian—yet, given this display by her peers and family, she couldn't help feeling touched. She quickly looked back as she headed toward the dvergen subway, and admired the village of Kustos, her home since birth, from afar, wondering if she would see it again.

* * *

When you're trained to be a Guardian, you are trained to survive in the harshest of climates. For Tashi, surviving in Benicia was a walk in the park, quite literally. She found a quiet park near the water, where she took up residency. She slept in a tree and foraged for food. Some of the local animals even gathered food for her, leaving it piled up at the base of her tree. She watched Sam's house at night and often slept during the day near his school. She was impressed with the massive building dedicated to educating human youth, especially when compared with the small wooden structures that passed for schools in Kustos. Tashi began to get the sense there were other magical creatures near Sam, both at school and at home. But that sense also told her they were harmless.

That is, until a more malevolent force overtook her senses. Tashi didn't know what it was, simply that it was close and evil in nature. Believing Sam might be in danger, she stepped up her surveillance.

The problem with shortening her proximity to Sam was the risk of being seen—a risk that turned into reality when

Sam caught sight of her at school. Fortunately, she hid when he emerged from the building to investigate. Later, when Sam visited a local market, Tashi became concerned for his safety among so many strangers—especially with the sense of dread still hanging over her. As she approached the window to keep a closer eye on Sam, she felt like she too was being watched. She peered over to see a tanuki staring at her from a few yards away. Tashi recalled that Sam had been replaced with a tanuki . . . this was the raccoon-dog she had seen with him earlier. She concluded that he was one of the harmless magical creatures she could sense around Sam.

"You are the tanuki who took Sam London's place?" Tashi asked in the creature's native tongue, which sounded like a series of squeaks, barks, and growls. The tanuki nodded.

"I am Nuks, and you . . . you're a Guardian," Nuks responded in awe. "You're Tashi. Sam told me about you."

"Yes," Tashi confirmed. She looked back to the window and realized Sam had spotted her. Tashi ducked and spoke to Nuks. "He must not know I am here." Nuks nodded in agreement.

"I think we should talk," Nuks whispered. "I am worried and I don't know why."

"As am I. I will meet you behind Sam's house at nightfall."

* * *

At sunset, Tashi made her way to Sam's backyard to meet with the tanuki. In general, magical creatures possessed an acute awareness or intuition that was highly sensitive to potential dangers. If Nuks was anxious, Tashi's instincts were correct, and it was just a matter of time before the evil that was lurking would make its presence known.

Nuks exited through the back door and spotted Tashi standing toward the rear of the yard.

"Hello again," the tanuki said as he approached. Tashi bowed her head slightly.

"Where is Sam?" she asked.

"He's asleep on the couch," Nuks replied, then added, "He's safe." Tashi nodded. "You're very far from home, Guardian."

"I am," Tashi said. "I was sent to look after Sam. Tell me, tanuki, what has you so concerned?"

Nuks shivered. "I really don't know, exactly. Just this feeling. If I weren't a magical creature, I would say it was the sense that a predator was near. Yes, that's it. As if there is something in the shadows waiting to strike. Do you feel it too?"

"I believe I do," Tashi answered. "We must remain vigilant, tanuki—"

"Nuks," he corrected her.

"I will be watching, but if you sense anything more, inform me at once." Nuks bobbed his head in affirmation. But it was at that very moment that Tashi herself sensed something more. The feeling was stronger than it had ever been, as if the evil was right next to them. Nuks also appeared to feel it. The tanuki looked around, as if trying to find the source. Tashi did the same. They scanned their surroundings, but there was nothing to see. "You check on Sam," Tashi ordered. "I will have a look around."

The night turned deathly still as Nuks went in to find

Sam. No wind rustling through the trees or crickets chirping. Tashi knew this was another bad omen. The evil hiding in the shadows was preparing to step into the light. Tashi readied herself for its arrival.

Back in the house, Sam London was defenseless. He didn't have Dr. Vantana, Knox, Chriscanis, or Tashi by his side. He didn't possess the hologram device or a weapon of any kind. And Nuks was lying on the floor, having been knocked unconscious. The aswang that was masquerading as his school teacher had the upper hand. And she also had the claw.

"It is time we finish what we started in the yeti village," the aswang snarled. "There is no one to protect you now, Sam London. And I am quite hungry."

Sam spun around and tried to run but didn't get far. The aswang grabbed his ankle and pulled him close, causing him to flip onto his back. She clutched his neck with her long, bony fingers and lifted him off the ground. Sam flailed about, trying to strike the creature with an arm or leg, but she kept him at just enough of a distance that he was unable to make contact. She apparently found his struggle amusing, and cackled evilly. Sam caught a glimpse of Nuks from the corner of his eye. The tanuki was slowly coming back to consciousness.

"Sam," Nuks muttered.

The aswang glared at Nuks, then back at Sam. She squinted her bloodshot eyes. "Don't worry, Sam. I'll eat him for dessert."

Nuks began to whimper, softly at first, but then the whimpers grew louder and stronger.

"He sounds scared. Are you scared?" the aswang asked. Sam couldn't answer—the grip of the creature's talons around his neck made it impossible for him to speak. He was terrified and completely helpless. "I can see it in your eyes." The aswang grinned menacingly.

"What do you see in mine?" a voice called out. The aswang spun to see who had joined them but was met by a blast of crystalline white powder. The creature screeched as the particles landed on her exposed arms and neck. They appeared to burn her skin on contact. Her hands sizzled and she recoiled in pain, causing her to release Sam and the claw. Sam dropped to the ground, snatched the claw, and scurried away.

"This way, Sam!" the voice cried, and that was when Sam finally recognized it. He looked up to see Tashi standing in the foyer wielding her shekchen. There was a Guardian in his house! Sam couldn't have been more ecstatic. She had arrived in the nick of time. Sam rushed to her side. "Get behind me!" she ordered. "You too, tanuki." Nuks scampered over, still feeling the effects of his fall.

"What is that stuff? Some kind of acid?" Sam asked, referring to the white powder Tashi had thrown at the aswang.

Tashi shook her head. "Salt. It is a weakness of the aswang."

As she flapped her wings, rising off the floor, the aswang shivered the salt off her body and hissed at Tashi. Tashi threw another handful of salt, but this time the aswang was ready. She dodged it, flying toward the entryway.

"Hand over the claw and we might let your friends live," she announced.

"You pose no threat to us anymore, creature," Tashi replied confidently as she charged her shekchen and aimed.

"I am not talking about you three. I speak of the pathetic ranger and the old man, who had the misfortune of meeting a few of my relatives in the Philippines."

Sam's heart dropped. Dr. Vantana and Knox were in danger? Tashi must have seen the concern in Sam's face.

"She's a liar, Sam," Tashi assured him. "She is baiting us."

"Yes. I am. And the bait is in Hérault. There, your friends will face their crimes."

"I don't believe you," Sam said defiantly.

"Then go and see for yourself. But remember to bring the claw. It is the only thing we will trade for their lives. If you can keep hold of it, that is. We won't stop coming," the creature warned. She flapped her wings and disappeared out the front door and into the night.

*   *   *

A few hours later, Sam and Tashi were on a bus bound for Redwood National Park. Tashi had shared Ranger Naughton's contact information, and Sam used his phone to alert her to their impending arrival. Sam didn't go into detail, just told her it was urgent that they meet. Ranger Naughton arranged to pick them up at the bus station and bring them to the cabin. After the attack by the aswang, the revelation that he now possessed the claw, and the information she had divulged regarding the fate of Dr. Vantana and Knox, Sam had one thought and one thought only: *Carl can help.* But to contact Carl, they would have to see Ranger Naughton and brief her on the situation.

Nuks agreed to return to Sam's form and continue the ruse while Sam and Tashi searched for answers. Sam felt bad about recruiting Nuks to take his place again, especially considering the state of the house after the aswang's attack. Nuks assured Sam everything would be fine. He would clean up as best he could before Ettie returned home and if necessary come up with a good excuse for the mess.

Once on board the bus, Tashi and Sam discussed the day's events and what they might mean. The Guardian was still struggling with the revelation that the claw had been hidden in Sam's backpack.

"It must have been Dr. Knox, working with Yeshe, who put the claw in your bag," Tashi concluded. "When they told me I was to travel here to guard you, they said I would also be guarding the claw in a new way. They must have known."

"But why hide it in my backpack?" Sam asked. "Wouldn't it have been safer in Phylasso's cave?"

"It would seem so," Tashi replied. "But the cave had been compromised by the yetis once before . . . and the gryphon has yet to be heard from. It is all quite puzzling. Perhaps there is information we are not aware of."

Sam considered what information could justify giving a twelve-year-old kid a relic that could change the world. He bristled at the thought that the key to the greatest secret ever kept from mankind was sitting in his twenty-dollar backpack. It was like holding a winning lottery ticket and waiting to cash it in. The entire wait was an anxiety-ridden affair made worse by a sudden hyperawareness of one's surroundings. Sam scanned the other faces on the bus, paranoid that someone knew what he had and was simply waiting for the right time to strike. Adding to his nerves was the thought that Dr. Vantana and Dr. Knox were in danger. He was more than ready to exchange the claw for their lives, if it came to that.

"Where is Hérault?" Sam asked the Guardian.

"I do not know," she answered.

"I still can't believe my teacher was an aswang," Sam confessed, embarrassed. "I almost ruined everything."

"She was in violation of Phylassos's law," Tashi noted. "The aswang have evil intentions in their hearts, and because of this, they were forbidden to leave their homeland."

"She's been my teacher this whole year," Sam said. "Do you think it could just be coincidence that I was in her class?"

"It seems unlikely," Tashi replied.

"So you're saying she was my teacher for a reason?"

"Perhaps."

"But why? How could she have known I'd be the one to see the gryphon?" Sam asked. "It doesn't make any sense."

Tashi simply shrugged. "No, it doesn't."

* * *

The bus would take several hours to reach the Arcata Transit Center in Arcata, California. From there, Ranger Naughton would be waiting to drive them the rest of the way to the park. They would arrive by morning. Three hours into the trip, the bus stopped in a town called Willets for a half-hour layover. Tashi and Sam got out to use the bathroom and pick up some food at a local fast food restaurant.

As they made their way back to the idling bus, Tashi walked a few feet ahead of Sam. It was exceptionally dark. Overcast skies had diffused the moonlight, and half the lights in the restaurant's parking lot were out. The lack of illumination left a large portion of the lot covered in darkness. Unfortunately, the two had to pass through this unlit area to reach the bus. Sam didn't think anything of it and entered the shadows behind Tashi. Suddenly, his body was yanked deeper into the darkness. Whatever it was, it pulled Sam by his backpack with such force it took his breath away and managed to wrench the bag off one of his shoulders. Sam was instantly on his back, his bag was now at his side—only one arm through a strap—and he could feel the cold, moist asphalt on the nape of his neck. He sensed the presence of several creatures, one of which was on his chest, grabbing for his backpack. Sam pulled it close and held on tight. He could hear the creatures screeching and could smell their rancid breath, but he couldn't see them. The stench of sulfur invaded his nose, burning his nostrils and causing his eyes to tear up. The bloodcurdling screams sent shivers down his spine.

"Sam!" Tashi called out. Before he could respond, a leathery claw clamped down over his mouth.

A pair of headlights from a passing car bathed the area in

a pool of bright white light, but Sam could still see nothing. His heart raced, and he was growing nauseous from the encounter. And then a strange sensation came over him. A wave of warm energy rippled through his body, crawling across his skin, all the way to his head. His eyes immediately began to sting, but when the pain subsided, the creatures attacking him were suddenly visible. And they were hideous. About three feet tall, with reptilian bodies. Their legs were long, like a kangaroo's, and their backs sported a row of sharp spines. They had red glowing eyes, protruding jaws, long fangs, and forked tongues. The little monsters were hopping on their hind legs and screeching, as if goading the one sitting on Sam's chest. That creature bared its fangs and moved in close.

Things looked grim until one of the surrounding creatures was lit up by a flash of shimmering blue light. The monster shook and convulsed, then dropped to the pavement with a pronounced thud. The other creatures took notice, including the one on Sam. It was the next to get hit. A bolt of electrical energy found the creature's back, sending a charge through its body and causing it to freeze. Sam threw the monster off his chest and climbed to his feet. Tashi was at his side in an instant, helping him get away from the remaining beasts. She sent a few bolts from her shekchen behind them as they rushed to the bus.

"Are you okay?" Tashi asked, her attention focused on the remaining monsters.

"I think so. What were those things?"

"They are called chupacabras. The word is Spanish for 'goatsucker,'" Tashi answered. "Did it bite you?"

"No. It tried, but you saved me just in time." *Of course,* Sam thought. *Chupacabras.* He had read several stories about these creatures, which came from Latin America. They looked exactly like their description in the stories, just a lot more terrifying. Sam and Tashi quickly reboarded the bus and headed for the back.

"The aswang warned us. . . . She said they wouldn't stop coming," Sam said.

"They are nasty beasts, the chupacabras. We are lucky you are alive."

"Tashi," Sam said softly. The Guardian turned to face him. "I could see them. At first I couldn't, but then something happened. I felt something strange and then I could see them."

Tashi raised a single brow, intrigued. "The chupacabras are among the cursed. They are not shape-shifters; therefore, humans cannot see them."

"But I did," Sam proclaimed. "I totally did."

"And you had the sight taken from you, did you not?"

Sam nodded. "Before I left Kustos. Dr. Knox insisted. He gave me an injection that took it away," he explained. "And it must have worked, because I didn't see them at first."

"Events grow stranger by the moment," Tashi concluded.

The bus left Willet and resumed its course for Arcata. Sam's unanswered questions kept piling up. Redwood National Park couldn't come quickly enough.

Chapter 16
TAKING FLIGHT

Penelope knew that her amnesia hadn't been caused by an accident. She hadn't fallen and hit her head or walked into a tree and knocked herself out. Her doctor found no evidence of cranial trauma. When she pressed for answers, he simply told her that dysfunctions of the mind can prove quite mysterious. One never knows what spurs changes in brain chemistry. But his assessment wasn't good enough for Penelope. This mystery was too personal and too important. In the absence of a clear-cut scientific explanation, the ranger began to conclude that her memory loss was not a matter of brain chemistry; rather, it was a matter of magic.

She was still learning every day about the world around her and the mythical creatures that populated it. She was aware of the presence of magic and the ability some creatures had to manipulate it, but because her analytical mind could not accept the word "magic," she referred to it as "strange science." She was determined to find out who had had the means and the motive to erase her memory. It was easier said than done. Even if she had been aware of such a plot and left clues to the answer, she couldn't remember where she had hidden the evidence. Fortunately, she stumbled upon it while cleaning. She was moving a refrigerator in the lab, when she heard an object fall and hit the floor. She peeked behind the fridge and spotted a notebook. It looked like the kind she kept for recording her experiments—black with a white, numbered label—but where the number usually was, this one was blank. It also had a large elastic band wrapped around it. It reminded Penelope of the diary she used to keep as a child. She had wrapped it with a large rubber band, as though that provided some protection for her private thoughts. She pulled the rubber band from the notebook and noticed creases on the cover and binding—telltale signs it had been well used. When she opened it, she learned why: it was a personal journal.

The journal started three years ago, when Penelope had begun her job at Redwood National Park. It didn't include entries every day, only when she had something important to express. She pulled up one of the lab stools and sat down, then flipped through the pages until she reached the last few entries, leading up to her amnesia. The first one she read, which was dated two weeks before her episode, seemed relatively benign. She discussed her latest experiments with

Gus's blood and the impact they had on their friendship. She also talked about a problem with a colony of jackalopes stealing food from human campsites. Toward the end of this entry, she came upon an interesting statement. While on a hike to confront the offending jackalopes about their illegal activity, Penelope had spotted massive footprints leading to a more remote area of the park. In the entry, she theorized that they were bigfoot prints and said she would follow up with Carl. The next entry didn't mention anything about the prints or the follow-up with Carl. Instead, it was dedicated to the surprise visit by Dr. Henry Knox, Penelope's superior. It read as follows:

> *Today was an unusual day. Upon returning*
> *from my morning rounds, I discovered Dr.*
> *Henry Knox waiting for me at the cabin. I think*
> *this is the first time I've ever seen Dr. Knox*
> *without Dr. Vantana by his side. I love sharing*
> *my work whenever I have the opportunity, and*
> *can always count on Dr. Knox to express much*
> *enthusiasm. He was particularly interested in*
> *the new holographic projector I built, which is*
> *intended to aid rangers in situations when they*
> *are outnumbered and need to appear to have a*
> *larger presence. The doctor had many questions*
> *about how the device works and how to create*
> *the illusion it projects. He also asked if he could*
> *borrow it, but I explained it is still a prototype*

and requires a further round of tinkering before
being allowed out of the lab.

The following I make note of here because
it was so odd. Dr. Knox inquired about any
"strange happenings" at the park. He asked
about the goats in the northern sector and
whether I had checked on them recently. When
I asked if that meant I should be keeping an
eye out for chupacabras, he suggested I keep an
eye out for anything unusual. The doctor left
before sundown, saying he was going to take a
look around. I have never seen him so pensive. It
makes me nervous.

Penelope's curiosity had been more than piqued, so she continued reading. The next entry relayed her follow-up with Carl, which had an intriguing outcome. Apparently, when she went to speak with Carl, she spied him heading into the woods alone. Penelope followed and found he was walking toward the area where she had seen the bigfoot prints. Unfortunately, Carl's sense of smell was much too keen for her to follow undetected for long. He became aware of her presence and turned back. She played dumb and asked if he had spotted any jackalopes in the area. He claimed he hadn't, so she went on her way but returned later that afternoon to track Carl's prints. As she did, she noticed that his prints were joined by additional footprints. The first set appeared to be human, but those disappeared after a few yards and were replaced with other animal-like prints that Penelope could not identify. She took some casts and returned to her lab to determine who or what Carl had been meeting.

The final entry before the diary went blank—and Penelope suffered her bout of amnesia—proved especially revealing. She wrote:

> *I have discovered a great secret. The kind I cannot disclose in this book. I intend to prove my theory today when I track Carl the bigfoot through the northern section of the park. I will be using a spray I synthesized from samples of Carl's fur that will duplicate his scent. If my scent matches his, he will not be able to distinguish it and I should be able to follow undetected. If my theory is correct and these meetings with Carl are taking place, I wonder what it might mean for the department and the curse. I can't help but conclude that we all must be in some kind of danger.*

Penelope closed the diary and returned it to its hiding place, wedged between the wall and the refrigerator. She dropped back down onto her stool, the revelations weighing heavily. She contemplated what she had read and what it all meant. What was Carl up to? And why did she sound so concerned in the entry regarding the curse? But most importantly, what was the great secret she couldn't reveal on paper? It was all quite confounding, made more so when taken together with the previous entries, especially the entry on Dr. Knox. Was Knox aware of this impending danger? Perhaps that was why he disappeared around the same time Penelope lost her memory. This was no coincidence, she surmised. With Dr. Knox still missing, there was only one other person she could talk to about the events surrounding her amnesia: Carl the bigfoot. He obviously knew something; after all, according to the diary, she'd been following him the day she lost her memory.

Penelope had been trying to meet with Carl ever since she'd returned, but he never made time to see her. Trevor the troll claimed it was simply because he was busy; however, in light of the information in the diary, Penelope started to believe he'd been avoiding her on purpose. She felt a knot in her stomach at the thought of meeting with Carl—how could she be certain he wasn't a threat? Given his commitment to the cause for so many years, a development like this would be devastating.

As Penelope prepared to leave to visit the bigfoot, she received a phone call from an unnerved Sam London. He spoke quickly, informing her that he had been attacked by an aswang and that he was headed to see her, along with a Guardian. She wondered if she had misheard that last part. Surely Sam wasn't referring to an actual Guardian from the village of Kustos. He must be confused. The last she had heard about Sam London was when Vance called, requesting to have a car ready for Chriscanis so he could bring the boy home. Vance hadn't said much else on the call, which Penelope had noted was cryptic. All the recent events, together with the journal entries, led Penelope to believe that Knox was aware of the coming danger and that danger was now at their doorstep.

Penelope left her lab and found Trevor sleeping on the couch in her living room. She closed the painting that doubled as the lab's secret door extra hard. Trevor roused at the noise and noticed he wasn't alone. He sat up, eyes wide.

"Did you hear about Sam London?" Trevor asked anxiously.

"How did you—" Penelope started, then realized. "Let me guess—a friend of a friend of a friend."

"Of a friend of a tanuki who went foraging with Nuks. He's the tanuki that took Sam's place," Trevor explained. "He didn't say much, just that Sam was attacked by an aswang."

"Yes," Penelope replied. "He called me. He's on a bus headed this way. What are you doing here?"

"I came to tell you the news, but when I saw you were in your lab, I figured I'd wait until you came out. I know you don't like to be bothered when you're in the lab," Trevor noted. "Aswangs are nasty creatures, Ranger Naughton. Why would they attack Sam?"

"I don't know, Trevor. I'm sure we'll find out soon enough."

Trevor rose from the couch and walked over to Penelope. He got in close, glanced around as if to make sure no one was within earshot, then whispered, "I did hear one other thing, but I'm not sure I should believe it."

"Sam is traveling with a Guardian?" Penelope guessed. Trevor gasped.

"So it *is* true!" the troll exclaimed. "Wow! I wonder if they have friends. I'm a good friend. I bet I'd be their first troll friend."

"Let's not get ahead of ourselves," Penelope cautioned. "I'm sure the Guardian isn't here to make friends."

"Of course," Trevor replied. "I'll do whatever I can to help. You can become very good friends with someone if you go through ad-ad-adversity with them." Penelope rolled her eyes. Trolls were way too obsessed with collecting friends—it was irritating.

"Do you mind if I stay here tonight?" Trevor asked. "It's awful late, and I'd like to be here when Sam arrives. Just in case he needs me. He's my—"

"Friend. Yes, I know," Penelope said, exasperated. She usually wasn't this cranky, but her mind was still swirling with thoughts of her journal. She refocused and tried to smile. "Sure, you can stay here."

"Thanks!" Trevor plopped back down onto the couch, which was clearly not made for a creature his size.

"I have to go out," Penelope announced.

"Now? But it's pitch-black out there. Where do you have to go that's so important?"

"I have to talk to Carl."

"I think you should wait till morning," Trevor advised. "He likes his sleep."

"Unfortunately, I can't wait. He's been avoiding me for too long. Haven't you noticed?"

"It was strange that he had time to meet with Sam but he

still hasn't checked up on you," Trevor admitted. "Especially since you two are friends."

"Well, it's time to find out why. Make yourself comfortable; I'll be back later," Penelope said, before heading to the front door. She opened the door to leave and came face to face with a dog-man.

"Ranger Penelope Naughton, I presume?" the dog-man said in a British accent.

"You're a cynocephalus," Penelope responded, shocked to finally see one in person.

"Indeed I am." The cynocephalus thrust out a paw. "The name's Chase. Agency for the Welfare of Mythical Beasts, retired."

Penelope took Chase's paw and shook. "Pleased to meet you."

Trevor was up and heading toward the door. "I know exactly who you are, Mr. Chase," the troll said. "I've always wanted to be friendly with—"

"Trevor," Penelope interrupted firmly. "This is likely not a social call."

Chase nodded. "You are correct. I have received some rather disturbing news regarding Vance Vantana and Henry Knox. I am hoping it is merely rumor."

Penelope realized that meeting Carl was not in the cards for her tonight. She gestured to Chase. "Come on in and tell me what you've heard."

* * *

The sun was just inching up over the horizon when the bus pulled in to the Arcata Transit Center. Sam and Tashi had taken shifts sleeping, though Sam was pretty certain Tashi never actually fell asleep. The slightest bump or mechanical noise would wake the vigilant Guardian. Sam did manage to get some much-needed rest despite his anxiety regarding Vantana and Knox, combined with the fact that he had the claw in his possession. As the day's first light hit his tired face, his body was brimming with the excitement of seeing Carl and getting some answers. It wouldn't be long now.

After the chupacabra attack in Willet, Tashi insisted on walking behind Sam as they headed to the parking lot to meet Penelope. But when Sam spotted the ranger waiting near her department-issued SUV, he took off running toward her. This sent Tashi into a tailspin. The Guardian sprinted after her charge but couldn't prevent him from reaching Penelope and delivering a welcoming embrace. When Tashi arrived at the car a second later, she yanked Sam backward by his shoulder and scolded him.

"Sam London!" Tashi exclaimed with fury. "I am bound to protect you. I cannot have you acting the fool, putting yourself in danger."

"Danger? This is Ranger Naughton," Sam replied. "We can trust her."

"I am sure that is what you believed about Miss Capiz," Tashi countered.

"My teacher turned out to be an aswang," Sam explained to the ranger. He shrugged. "How was I supposed to know?"

"Your friend is right," Penelope said. "You must be more careful now, Sam." The ranger turned to Tashi. "I'm Ranger Penelope Naughton. I'm human." Tashi eyed her for an extended moment, then nodded.

"I am Tashi of Kustos."

"An honor to meet you, Tashi," Penelope said. "Now, what is all this about an attack by an aswang? What would a creature like that want with you?"

Sam gestured for Penelope to lean in close. She obliged, intrigued.

"I have the gryphon's claw," Sam whispered. He noticed her skeptical expression and pulled his backpack around to his chest. He unzipped it and revealed just the tip of the shiny gold claw. It glinted in the light—the reflection was so blindingly bright, Penelope shielded her eyes. She cupped her hand to her mouth in disbelief.

Tashi peered around nervously. "I think it would be best if we go," she suggested. "We do not need to attract more attention to ourselves."

"Oh, yes. Right," Penelope replied. "Hop in."

The trio settled into the SUV and Penelope pulled out of the transit station and headed onto the highway.

"I can't believe you have the claw right there," the ranger said, still trying to process what she had just seen.

"Neither can I," Sam confessed. "It's why I need to talk to Carl right away."

Penelope pursed her lips. "I'm not sure that's a good idea." Sam eyed her, curiously. "It's a long story," she added.

"But he may be the only one who can help us. The aswang said they have Dr. Knox and Dr. Vantana."

"I've been made aware of that," Penelope replied. Sam looked at the ranger, surprised she knew. "I got an unexpected visit last night from Chase," she explained.

"The cynocephalus?" Sam interjected. Penelope nodded.

"He also heard the doctors were in danger. He's concerned and wants to lend a hand . . . or paw, I guess."

"Does he know anything else?" Sam asked.

"Just where they're being held. A region in Southern France. I believe it's called Hérault." Sam sat up straighter.

"Hérault?" he exclaimed. "That's what the aswang said. She also said I would have to trade the claw for their lives. I'm hoping Carl will know what to do."

"Carl can't be trusted," Penelope said with reluctance.

"Why not?" Sam asked.

The park ranger relayed the story of her private journal, the great secret, and how Carl was somehow involved. She suggested they discuss it with Chase and maybe contact Chriscanis to determine the best course of action. Carl was off-limits until she could ascertain which side he was on.

The remainder of the car ride to the park was spent with Sam updating Penelope on the events of the last few days. When Sam got to the part of the story with the holographic device, Penelope's expression turned to one of unsettling shock.

"What?" the ranger interjected, as if she had heard incorrectly.

"I don't know what it was called, but it was just this really cool device that projected holograms," Sam explained.

"Oh, I *know* what it does . . . it's my device. I built it," Penelope replied, the irritation evident in her tone. "Knox had it? And gave it to you?"

Sam nodded. "Did I do something wrong?"

She shook her head. "No, you're fine," she responded warmly this time. "Tell me more."

"Not much more to say," Sam said. "Dr. Knox told me to hit the button and run. It was awesome!"

"Really?" The remaining hints of Penelope's annoyance were instantly replaced with giddy excitement.

"It created hundreds of projections of Guardians," Sam revealed. "The yetis completely freaked out."

"So it worked?" she asked excitedly.

"Big-time," Sam said. "If it didn't, we would all be yeti leftovers now."

"Then what happened?"

"Then the aswang realized what was going on and destroyed the device," Sam answered.

"Destroyed?" Penelope responded, crestfallen. "As in . . ."

Sam nodded. "Yeah. Sorry," he said, noticing Penelope's solemn expression.

"It was my only prototype and I don't remember how I built it." She sighed.

"Oh, I didn't—" Sam started, but Penelope waved him off.

"Don't worry. It wasn't your fault. I'm just glad it helped

when you needed it to," she said. "I'll take it up with Dr. Knox when I see him again."

"*If* you see him again," Sam reminded her.

"We will," Penelope assured him.

When Sam told her about the chupacabra attack and the sudden sight, Penelope was insistent that she get a sample of his blood at the lab. The ranger postulated that whatever was giving him the sight now might have been preventing the Magnapedaxin 13 from working properly.

All caught up on the adventure, Penelope looked into the rearview mirror at Tashi, who was sitting silently in the backseat.

"How are you doing back there?" she asked the Guardian. Tashi didn't respond. "Is she always this quiet?" Penelope asked Sam.

"Depends," Sam replied. "She yells at me a lot."

"I do not yell at you," Tashi interjected. "If I raise my voice, it is out of concern for your safety."

Sam whispered to Penelope, "Her concern sounds a lot like yelling."

They arrived at the cabin to find Trevor waiting outside to greet them. He pulled Sam into a big troll hug.

"Sam!" he exclaimed. "I want to hear all about your adventures!" Then the troll noticed Tashi and couldn't contain his excitement. "You must be a Guardian," he said with boyish wonder. Tashi nodded and Trevor bowed his head.

"You do not need to bow to me, troll," Tashi informed him. "I am not the gryphon."

"Oh, right," Trevor replied, now slightly embarrassed. He offered his hand. "My name is Trevor. Pleased to meet you." Tashi shook the troll's hand. "I make a very good friend," he added.

"He does," Sam confirmed with a smile.

"Okay, enough," Penelope announced. "Everyone inside." The group entered the cabin and Sam spotted Chase standing in the kitchen.

"Chase!" he said excitedly.

"Sam London, I presume much has happened since last we met?" Chase inquired with a knowing smirk.

"That's an understatement," Sam replied. He slipped off his backpack and unzipped it. He was just about to open the bag when Tashi intervened.

"Sam!" she said with a scowl.

"What?" Sam responded, as if surprised by Tashi's reaction. "It's just Chase, for goodness' sake." He pulled back the fabric at the top of the bag and exposed the claw. Trevor immediately gasped at the sight and leapt back several feet. He hit the wall behind him and caused the painting that doubled as the lab door to spring open.

"You've got the claw!" Trevor exclaimed in disbelief. "The gryphon's claw!"

Chase's ears pricked up. "May I?" the cynocephalus asked as he reached for the relic. Tashi interceded and placed her hand on the bag in a protective manner. Chase got the message and backed off. "I'll just observe from a distance."

"That would be best," Tashi said.

Sam informed Chase and Trevor about the aswang's proposal—the gryphon's claw in exchange for the lives of Dr. Knox and Dr. Vantana.

"Then you must give it to them," Trevor insisted. "You've got to!"

"Let's be cautious, now," Chase interjected. "We can't be certain they would even hold up their end of the bargain. Perhaps there is another way?"

"What other way?" Sam inquired.

"We could travel to Hérault, find where they are being held, and see if we can stage a rescue," Chase suggested. "If not, we can consider trading the claw, but only if it is dire. Of course, I believe Dr. Knox would not want us to surrender the claw under any circumstance."

"But they could be—" Sam started.

Chase nodded solemnly. "It is part of our commitment to the cause," he said. "We must be willing to give our lives for the protection of all magical creatures. Unfortunately for us, we can be harmed, unlike Guardians."

"This is true," Tashi affirmed. "And it is the reason why I must go and rescue them. I will call upon my fellow Guardians if necessary. It is our life's purpose." She looked at Penelope, Trevor, and Chase. "Can I trust the three of you to protect Sam while I am gone?"

Trevor nodded. "Sure thing."

"Wait a minute," Sam interjected. "If you're going, I'm going."

"It is much too dangerous," Tashi protested.

"So was finding Kustos," Sam reminded her. "Plus, the claw was given to me. I'm not letting it out of my sight."

"I will go as well," Chase offered. "You will need help. And I am familiar with that area."

"I'm cool with that," Sam said.

"I am not 'cool' with any of this," Tashi maintained.

"We should take a closer look at this place," Penelope suggested. "See if we can determine where they're being held." She gestured for everyone to head through the secret door to the lab. The group moved down the narrow metal steps to a large, sterile room—an entirely different motif than the homey wood cabin upstairs. Sam took a long look around, excited to see the hidden space where Penelope performed her experiments. He saw refrigerators with glass doors filled with different-colored liquids in test tubes, and lab tables with intricate beaker setups and centrifuges. In a far corner there were scientific and metalworking tools, along with a collection of strange-looking weapons and devices that reminded Sam of the holograph projector. Near the front of the room sat a sophisticated computer system hooked up to two large monitors, and the wall closest to the stairs sported a giant flat screen.

Penelope stepped over to the computer and punched a few keys. The screen on the wall instantly displayed an image of France, then zoomed in on the southern part of the country. An outline wrapped around a large area.

"That's Hérault," Penelope said. "Sam." She pointed to him. "Let's get that blood sample, shall we?" Sam nodded apprehensively. Penelope grabbed a syringe from a nearby table as Chase, Tashi, and Trevor studied the image on the screen. Penelope took a vial of blood from a vein in Sam's arm. He grimaced, but stopped when he noticed Tashi looking his way. He didn't want to look like a wimp in front of a Guardian.

When she was done, Penelope grinned. "I'm excited to get you answers."

"And I'm excited to hear them," Sam said.

Chase pointed at the screen. "Well, if the doctors are indeed in this region, they are more than likely hidden within this wooded mountainous area."

"Agreed," said Penelope. "It actually makes quite a bit of sense now. Those gargoyles that attacked you and Vance, they're from the Hérault region."

"So is the Beast of Gevaudan!" Trevor added anxiously. "It's a terrible creature. A terribly terrible creature. One scratch of its claws is fatal!"

"We shall strive to avoid it, then," Chase said matter-of-factly.

"I have a weapon I can send you with to help against the gargoyles, and I can put something together for the aswang," Penelope offered. "But without knowing what else will be waiting, it's going to be tough to prepare."

"Then we must simply prepare for anything and everything," Chase countered with confidence.

Sam glanced over at Tashi for her thoughts on the situation, but the Guardian appeared preoccupied. Normally, Sam would conclude she was in one of her meditative states, but in this instance, she wasn't staring straight ahead; rather, she was gazing at the top of the stairs with a seriousness that concerned him.

"Tashi? What's wrong?" Sam asked quietly. The Guardian took a few seconds to answer. By then, Chase, Penelope, and Trevor had shifted their attention to her. She spoke but continued staring toward the lab door.

"I hear something," she said in a hushed tone.

The others exchanged nervous glances as Tashi started back up the stairs. Everyone followed. When Sam emerged from the lab, he found the Guardian standing with her back against the cabin's front door.

"Ranger Naughton, do you have a tunnel or passageway for escaping this cabin?" Tashi asked as the ranger entered behind Sam.

Penelope wasn't expecting the question. "Uh . . . no. I've never needed one. Why?"

Chase was at the window. "You need one now," he said, gesturing outside. "Chupacabras."

Penelope's eyes went to Sam. "They must have followed you." Sam rushed to the window to get a peek. Sure enough, the cabin was surrounded by hundreds of the little monsters. They snarled and stared hungrily at the cabin.

"They are waiting to gather an overwhelming force, and then they will attack," Tashi explained. She remained surprisingly calm, considering the circumstances. Trevor, on the other hand, was in a total panic.

"Attack? Attack *us*? Here? In here?" the troll stammered. "What are we going to do?"

"We cannot win this fight," Tashi stated plainly. "We are outnumbered and"—she eyed Trevor and Penelope—"outmatched."

"I can take care of myself, thank you very much," Penelope retorted, annoyed by Tashi's implication.

"Perhaps," Tashi replied, oblivious to having offended the ranger. "And though I would prefer to do battle, I cannot put Sam into danger that is avoidable. We must leave."

"How are we going to do that?" Trevor asked, practically hyperventilating. "They're all around us!"

"I could call on Gus," Penelope suggested. "He could fly us out two at a time. Maybe he can bring some friends."

"I do not recommend that course of action," Tashi said. "The horses would not survive."

"The Guardian is correct in that assessment," Chase confirmed. "Those creatures out there can jump quite high. As soon as one of your horses came down to pick us up, the chupacabras would attack . . . without mercy."

"I have a better idea," Sam blurted out. "Chase, Tashi— I'm going to need both of you to pull this off." Sam's idea was risky, borderline crazy. But if it worked, he'd be hailed a genius. Of course, at the moment, everyone was just staring at him with a heaping tablespoon of skepticism.

*   *   *

It was about an hour later when the group was ready to execute Sam's master plan. The chupacabras had taken the time to continue amassing their army. Meanwhile, inside the cabin, Penelope and Trevor were stationed downstairs, preparing to operate as the first line of defense should the creatures gain entry. Getting into the cabin would prove much more difficult for the chupacabras now that the windows were boarded up and furniture was blocking both the front and rear doors. Sam, Chase, and Tashi were upstairs in Penelope's bedroom, which occupied the entire second floor. It had a front-facing dormer window that they hadn't boarded up. The rest of the room's ceiling was in the shape of the roof, with its two-sided walls slanted to a peak in the center.

Sam looked at Chase. "Ready?" he asked with hope in his voice.

"I must confess, I'm feeling a tad silly. All my years with the agency and I never did this."

"First time for everything," Sam suggested.

"And you're certain it will work?"

"I've seen it work. . . . Well, I didn't actually see it," Sam corrected himself. Chase's eyes widened at his admission.

"Wait a minute—we are hinging our lives on a trick you never actually saw succeed?" he asked, incredulous.

"I know it did!" Sam exclaimed. "Tell him, Tashi." Tashi nodded once. Chase softened. With that, Sam opened the window and gave the cynocephalus the cue.

"Here goes," Chase said. He cleared his throat and started

to howl. Softly at first, but soon increasing in volume. The chupacabras gathered around the cabin all stopped snarling for a moment, confused by this strange sound. Unfortunately, the distraction was short-lived—the army of little monsters began advancing toward the cabin en masse.

"They're coming!" a terrified Trevor screamed from downstairs.

"Just make sure they don't get in!" Sam yelled back. "We only need a few minutes."

Chase continued to howl as the chupacabras descended. They were banging and hurtling their bodies against the doors and windows, desperate to get inside. Then they began to climb up the side of the cabin, hooking their claws into the wood siding and hoisting their bodies upward. One of the creatures reached the bedroom window and grabbed for Sam. Chase stumbled back and stopped howling as the creature continued to move into the house. Tashi poked it with the tip of her shekchen. The beast flew fifty feet backward, soaring above its compatriots before dropping to the earth with a resounding thud.

"Thank you," Chase said. He returned to the window and resumed his howling.

Sam gazed anxiously up at the sky. Tashi put her hand on his shoulder.

"It is a long way to fly," the Guardian noted. "We cannot expect—"

"He has to!" Sam declared. He hoped that stating it so

emphatically would somehow will the universe to comply. Then he heard the sounds of shattering glass and smashing wood.

"They're coming through!" Trevor shrieked.

"Howl louder!" Sam demanded. The cynocephalus eyed him, then turned up the volume.

Trevor and Penelope retreated to the second floor, slamming the door behind them. "There's too many," the ranger said. "I put out a distress call to the closest ranger station, but it'll take them a few hours to get here."

"We don't have a few hours!" Trevor said, on the verge of big troll tears. "They're going to eat us!"

Sam looked back up to the sky. "Please!" he whispered to himself. "Please!"

Sam's plea was finally heard. A massive shadow passed over the landscape, blocking the sun and enveloping the forest in shadow. The chupacabras froze and gazed up at the sunless sky. Even the creatures that had gotten into the house were scurrying out to get a look. What they saw was everything Sam had hoped for. . . . The roc had arrived.

"Yes!" Sam exclaimed, pumping his fist in celebration. Trevor, Penelope, and Chase all cheered. Even Tashi smiled . . . for a second. Sam caught the Guardian's eye and she quickly switched to her stoic expression. "I'll go first," she announced, and climbed out the window. Once Tashi pulled herself onto the roof of the cabin, she offered her hand to Sam. He took it, and she helped him up onto the slope. The two of them pulled Chase out next, followed by Penelope.

Then all four joined forces to get Trevor onto the roof. The troll was deathly afraid of heights and tensed up at the sight below.

Tashi stood at the edge of the roof, straddling the dormer and wielding her shekchen. She let out a high-pitched screech and the giant bird swooped down. It flapped its enormous wings as it hovered several feet from the house, its head near Tashi. She reached out and communicated with the creature the same way she had on Phylassos's mountain. After a few seconds, the Guardian turned to the others.

"He will fly us to Hérault. He says he would be honored to carry Sam London and the great gryphon's claw."

"Awesome!" Sam shouted. He was thrilled that his idea was working; unfortunately, the chupacabras had their own plans.

The creatures did something no one was expecting: they began to climb on top of one another, forming a pyramid of bodies that rose higher and higher until it finally reached the roc. Three of the beasts leapt onto the giant bird's back. The roc reared and took to the sky, trying to shake the chupacabras off. Sam was in shock and Trevor had turned to jelly.

"They . . . they attacked that bird," the troll stammered in horror.

"And now they're going to attack us," Penelope added ominously. "Everyone get ready!" She brandished an odd-shaped gun with a disk at its end. During their preparations, Sam had learned this was called a banshee gun—it re-created a banshee scream in a directed manner. Penelope used it to freeze several chupacabras as they climbed up the side of the cabin, while Tashi delivered electrical charges to the attacking horde with her shekchen. Sam hung back with Trevor and Chase, who appeared surprisingly unfazed by the situation.

"Perhaps we should just see what they want," Chase suggested. "Does that Guardian speak chupacabra?"

"They want the claw, and I'm not giving it to them!" Sam asserted.

The chupacabras were relentless. Soon the group was forced back and surrounded on all sides. There was no escape. As they braced for their last stand, a loud roar echoed through the park. But this wasn't one single roar; it was dozens of voices roaring in unison. The chupacabras halted their advance and turned toward the sound, but they couldn't get a fix on the source. It was everywhere at once. Sam's eyes darted to the perimeter of the chupacabra mass to see what had suddenly terrified them: it was an army of bigfoots!

The bigfoots emerged from the forest and stomped toward the chupacabras with Carl leading the pack.

"Woo-hoo!" Sam exclaimed. "The cavalry!" He watched the bigfoots make quick work of the chupacabras as they cleared a path to the cabin. Penelope wasn't pleased.

"Question is, are they rescuing us or simply coming for the claw themselves?" she wondered.

Meanwhile, the roc had managed to toss the creatures from its back, and returned to pick up its passengers.

"Sam! We must go!" Tashi ordered as the roc appeared above them. Sam looked at Penelope with concern.

"We'll be fine," she assured him. "Go!"

"But Carl . . ."

"I'll figure it out. Go get Henry and Vance." Sam nodded. "And take this—" She handed him the banshee gun. "It might come in handy."

The roc opened its talons just enough for Tashi, Sam, and Chase to climb inside. Once settled, Tashi put her hand on the inside the roc's talon and closed her eyes. In an instant, they were in the air and headed for Hérault, unsure who or what would be awaiting them.

Chapter 17

A RETURN TO GAIA

For the second time in his young life, Sam London wished he were unconscious. The first had been during a particularly brutal dental appointment. In this instance, it was thirty minutes into his flight with the roc. The last time Sam had flown with the creature, he'd been fortunate enough to be asleep and totally unaware. He concluded that was definitely the best way to travel when flying in the precarious grip of a massive mythical bird. His stomach had become a bundle of extremely nervous butterflies desperately trying to escape. Through the spaces between the roc's talons, he could see the earth thousands of feet below. If the creature desired, it could easily drop the trio and let them plummet to their deaths. As for his traveling companions, Tashi was perfectly at ease and Chase was actually resting his eyes. Sam couldn't understand that at all. He could feel the warmth of the roc's skin and the steady pulse of the creature's heartbeat. It reminded him that he was at the mercy of this bird, and he hoped it didn't have any uncontrolled muscle spasms that would cause it to relax its grip.

Thankfully, the flight was much shorter than Sam had anticipated. Though speedy, it was not as quick as the dvergen subway. Somehow Sam felt safer in that metal contraption, hurtling at inhuman speeds through tunnels carved thousands of years before he was born. The sentiment perfectly encapsulated Sam's true feelings about traveling with the roc. Approximately two hours into the flight, Tashi sprang from her meditative state.

"We are getting close," the Guardian announced. "I will let the roc know he may land."

"Wait a moment," Chase interrupted, his eyes now open. "I don't imagine this bird knows the area where we're headed. He could wind up dropping us a hundred miles from our destination. Let me take a look." He peered between the roc's talons to the ground below and studied it a few seconds. "We appear to be approaching Haut-Languedoc; it's a natural park in the northern part of Hérault. Looks like he does know where we're headed. Smart bird. Tell him he can land us at the opening to the gorges, where the river forks. Right outside town."

Tashi nodded, placed her hand on the roc's talon, and closed her eyes. Several seconds later, the bird began its descent. Sam's stomach took a short trip to his throat, but he resisted the urge to throw up. Puking on the roc might spur it to drop them.

"You look a touch green, my friend," Chase said with a smirk. "Close your eyes and take a few deep breaths. You'll be fine."

Sam followed Chase's suggestion and the nausea subsided. Twice on this adventure he had almost lost his lunch. The first time was on the dvergen subway, and now this. He was starting to miss good old-fashioned airplane travel.

The roc flapped its mighty wings and hovered a few feet from the ground. He then opened his talons just enough for the three to climb out. Sam felt relieved to be standing on solid ground again. The feeling was akin to stepping onto a dock after a rough boat ride. Sam's body could still feel the movement of the flight. It was several moments before things were back to normal. When they did stabilize, Sam took in his new surroundings. They were spectacular.

The roc had released them at the edge of a forest that led into a vast canyon. But this wasn't the kind of barren desert canyon found in the American Southwest. These massive rocks formed elaborate, breathtaking gorges that carved their way into the landscape, as if sculpted by hand. In the distance, Sam could see that the gorges led to a mountain range. The most stunning characteristic of these formations was how vividly green they were. The valley was carpeted with chestnut and oak trees and winding streams that fanned out in every direction like thin blue fingers reaching out to grab hold of the earth.

Sam spotted a small village on a hillside at the fork of a river. The houses were constructed of colored stone, and at the crest of the hill sat an ancient church. The outer part of the town featured remnants of fortifications from what appeared to have been a castle. Sam was absorbing the extraordinary sights when Chase sidled up.

"Mons la Trivalle. 'Mountain of the Three Valleys.'" As he spoke, the cynocephalus pointed to the three valleys that branched out from the town. Sam suddenly noticed the unique geography that marked the town's location. "And you see the mountain range in the distance?" Chase asked. Sam nodded, eyeing the sharp, jagged summits. "That is Caroux-Espinouse, the central massif—where the earth's tectonic plates push together. The canyons it formed are the Gorges d'Héric."

"It's incredible," Sam said, scanning the terrain. His attention was pulled away when he spotted Tashi walking toward them, the roc taking flight behind her. "Did you thank him for the ride and for not dropping us?"

"I expressed our gratitude," Tashi replied. She looked at Chase. "He told me he spotted something unusual as he made his descent."

"Oh?" Chase responded, curious. "What does a giant mythical bird categorize as 'unusual'?"

"A gathering of some kind. There were magical creatures there, but he couldn't get a good look."

"How far?" Sam asked.

"About a kilometer north, deep into the gorge," Tashi answered.

"Great," Sam replied. "We'll start there." And with that,

Sam tightened the straps of his backpack and charged into the woods.

"Oh no, Sam London. I will be leading the way," Tashi announced as she hurried to get in front of Sam. He grinned—having Tashi around made him feel like he had his own personal secret service.

The trio followed a stream that wound northward into the gorge. They hiked steep rocky terrain, pushed through thickly wooded forest, and traversed sandy mud with a viscous quality that sucked their shoes into the earth. It was thoroughly exhausting. Tashi took point, with Sam in the middle and Chase covering their tails. The Guardian showed no sign of fatigue and pressed on with an almost superhuman tenacity. Sam did his best to keep up and managed to persuade Tashi to allow a few breaks for water and rest.

"I do not want to be in this canyon when the sun sets," Tashi would remind Sam with every stop. Sam didn't want to either, and it was always enough to motivate him to continue moving, although he would still freeze at every sound that emanated from the surrounding forest.

"Did you hear that?" Sam would whisper whenever he heard the slightest noise. Tashi would pause, listen, and say, "It is nothing to be concerned about." And she would continue.

Sam's paranoia led him to recall what Trevor mentioned about this area. After hearing a rustling that Tashi dismissed, Sam looked at Chase. "Was it true what Trevor said?" he asked with trepidation.

"About the Beast of Gevaudan?" Chase replied. Sam nodded. "I have heard its wound is fatal," the cynocephalus confessed. "Though the stories of its rampage were revised by history and those who wish to keep it secret. The tales you've likely heard bear little resemblance to the truth."

"Why would the gryphon want to keep the real story a secret?" Sam wondered.

"Because it was a beast that defied the gryphon," Chase answered.

Defied the gryphon? Sam thought. This was sounding more interesting by the moment.

"How?"

"It attacked humans without remorse. It was a hybrid of two beasts—one magical, one not. These are the most dangerous."

"What kind of hybrid was it?" Sam asked.

"A lion and the mythical black dog," Chase replied. "Some believe it was an experiment gone horribly wrong—or right, depending on who you ask."

Sam had heard of black dogs before; he read about them in one of his many books on mythical creatures. They were phantom canines that roamed Europe. Legend claimed the creatures were the result of evil spirits; they would haunt areas where terrible things had occurred. They were known to stalk and slay lone travelers. As such, a sighting of such a creature was considered an omen of death.

"You said these types of hybrids are the most dangerous . . . why?" Sam inquired.

"Because the gryphon's curse is theirs to toy with as they please," Chase revealed. "They can choose to be seen . . . or not."

"And that's how it was able to do such harm," Sam concluded. Chase nodded.

"Those poor humans never saw the beast coming. The descriptions of it were given by those with the sight. Some hid its real appearance out of fear or simply out of disbelief that such a creature could exist. They claimed it was a wolf. But those who had seen it described it very differently, insisting quite correctly that it was no wolf."

"If I remember the story right, the Beast of Gevaudan was finally killed by a hunter," Sam said.

"No human could ever have hurt that creature," Chase corrected him. "Phylassos was enraged by the Beast's behavior and punished it by returning it to Gaia. But some believe that because it was a hybrid, it could not suffer a magical fate and roams the forests to this very day."

That thought sent a shiver up Sam's spine. "Returned to Gaia . . . Cernunnos mentioned that when he had us in his cave," he recalled. "What does it mean exactly?"

"It is when a magical creature moves on to the next plane of existence," Tashi answered, her interjection taking both Chase and Sam by surprise—she had been listening this entire time. "They become one with Gaia. They return to the earth."

"They die?" Sam asked.

"Not quite," Chase replied. "At least, not the way humans conceive of death. It is not a permanent separation from this world. Our energies are absorbed and live again in other ways, other forms."

"Did Phylassos try to do that with the Beast?" Sam inquired.

Chase nodded. "He did, but the creature was not entirely magical, so it proved useless."

"Why didn't the gryphon just kill it? Like, permanently?" Sam asked.

"Because the gryphon cannot kill a magical creature. It is the 'protector' of such creatures. To kill is not in its—" Tashi abruptly stopped talking. She put her finger to her lips, silencing her companions, then pointed upward. Sam looked to the sky and spotted what Tashi had heard. A dozen gargoyles flew overhead, followed by a few aswangs and several other creatures Sam didn't recognize. They looked like birds, but Sam could have sworn they had hideous human faces.

"Harpies," Tashi whispered. When the creatures passed, the Guardian turned to Chase and Sam. "We must be close. I recommend that we tread extra carefully from this point forward." Tashi started moving again, then halted at a loud rustling in the trees ahead, along with the distinct snapping of branches. Whatever made that noise had to be quite large, Sam concluded.

"You stay with Sam; I'll scout ahead," Chase whispered to Tashi.

"No," Sam said. "We should stick together."

"That is not a wise strategy in this circumstance," Tashi asserted. "One should scout and one should stay with you."

"I know you will not leave his side," Chase added. "So I will go." Chase started toward the noise.

"Wait. Take this—" Sam handed Chase the banshee weapon. "I have Tashi," Sam explained. Chase nodded and took the gun. He ventured forward and disappeared into the woods.

"Come," Tashi said to Sam, gesturing for him to follow.

"But we should stay here," Sam replied. "So Chase can find us."

"We require cover. We will be able to see when Chase returns," Tashi explained as she led him to the edge of a stream, which widened close to where they stood. A large cluster of rocks sat on the bank of the waterway. The center boulder was large and sloped inward on its southern face—an ideal spot for concealing themselves. Tashi crouched behind the rock and Sam followed suit.

"What are we going to do when we find them?" Sam asked the Guardian.

"We will come up with a plan and execute it," she replied matter-of-factly.

Sam eyed his bodyguard. "How old are you?" he asked. He had been wondering but never had a moment to inquire. He continued, "I mean, I'm twelve. And you look like you could be twelve too. You're a little taller than me, but I'm short for my age. The thing is, I don't know any kid who talks like you or can do what you do. It's like you're some kind of an adult trapped in a kid's body."

Tashi faced Sam, surprised by his question and ensuing explanation. "We start our training before human children even begin to form memories."

"You didn't answer my question," Sam noted, at which Tashi simply turned away. "And I guess you won't." The two sat for a few more minutes, and Sam had another thought: "What if we're outnumbered? It seems like we're always outnumbered. And you saw those things that flew over us. That's probably just a small sample of what's waiting."

"That is why we will make certain we are unseen," Tashi responded.

"Oh, yeah. We go stealth for sure. But I still—" Tashi pressed her hand over Sam's mouth, silencing him. She gestured to the woods behind them; Sam nodded, and she released her makeshift muzzle. Sam gulped down a dozen of those nervous butterflies that had taken up permanent residency in his stomach—it felt like they were multiplying by the second.

Tashi leveled her shekchen at the thicket of trees and let loose a small electric charge. The burst of blue energy shot out from the weapon and went careening into the woods, where it quickly dissipated amid the vegetation. At that moment, Sam heard something rustle in the bushes.

"For the love of Labradors!" a voice called out.

Tashi let loose another charge before Sam could stop her. This burst of energy had a wider spread. A millisecond later, a body sprang from the forest in a somersault and leapt to its feet.

"Chriscanis!" Sam exclaimed. The cynocephalus appeared shocked to see them.

"What in the bichon frise are you doing in France, Sam? And you"—he pointed to Tashi—"you nearly killed me."

"I was being cautious," the Guardian explained.

"Cautious is good," Chriscanis replied. "But being cautious should have kept you far away from this place."

"We're here to rescue Dr. Knox and Dr. Vantana," Sam revealed. The cynocephalus eyed him.

"And that, my friend, is precisely why *I'm* here. But this is not a place for you, Sam. These woods are too dangerous." Chriscanis turned to Tashi. "You must take him far away, immediately."

"I'm not going anywhere," Sam protested. "I have the claw. I'm the only one who can do this."

"You have . . ." Sam nodded, and Chriscanis's face went grim. "Good greyhound, Sam. Now you must go. Before it is too late."

"We can't. Chase is scouting ahead."

"Who?" Chriscanis asked.

"Chase. The man you replaced," Sam replied.

"He's here? With you?" Chriscanis asked anxiously.

"I am indeed," Chase answered as he emerged from the forest and approached. "My successor . . . good to see you."

Sam and Tashi stood up and walked out from behind the rock formation to join the two cynocephali. Sam noticed that

Chriscanis was unnerved by the sudden appearance of Chase and even shifted into a defensive posture.

"It took me some time to piece it all together, but it was always so clear," Chriscanis began.

"Whatever are you talking about?" Chase remarked with the slightest of smirks.

"The gargoyles. I kept returning to the gargoyles. That's what did it in the end, to have fallen into your pool in that random little town. The chances were . . . astronomical."

Sam was instantly interested in their conversation. His ears pricked up at the mention of the gargoyles and Chase's pool. He remembered that night vividly, and now he was trying to process what Chriscanis seemed to be implying.

"What do you mean?" Sam interjected. "What about the gargoyles? It was my fault. . . . I caused them to drop me." Sam recalled squirming in the grip of the creatures, which he assumed had triggered his fall.

"No, you didn't," Chriscanis revealed. "They let you go. On purpose."

"But that would mean . . . ," Sam started.

"Well done, young pup," Chase said as he fired the banshee weapon with three rapid shots. Sam felt the screeching wave of sound slam into his body and ripple across his skin. His muscles seized up and he was instantly a statue. It might not have been as painful as a real banshee scream, but it was just as effective. Sam could see Tashi struggling out of the corner of his eye. Try as she might, she could not move an inch. Chriscanis was on the other side of Sam, stiff as a board.

"It doesn't freeze the eyes, now, does it?" Chase mused aloud. He held the gun up, admiring it. "But Penelope has built a most delightful weapon. I hear it keeps its victims like this for several minutes. More than enough time, I would think."

"Tashi!" Sam exclaimed in muted fashion through stiffened lips.

"Sam . . . ," the Guardian muttered in response, battling the effect of the weapon.

"Now, now, don't fight it, children. It's more painful that way," Chase advised. Sam had to agree. Whenever he tried to move or speak the pain would intensify. It also seemed to linger longer the more you fought it. "I'll be taking that claw now, Sam."

Sam was still coming to terms with the shocking revelation that Chase was the mastermind behind everything. Sam was furious with himself. How could he not have seen this? Never mind the pain, he had to speak. "You . . . ," Sam started, fighting the discomfort.

"Me," Chase replied as he approached him. He unzipped Sam's backpack and reached in to retrieve the claw. Sam gathered all the strength he could to move, but only managed to flinch. "I can tell you're upset," Chase chided him. "Wondering why you didn't realize it sooner?" Chase pulled the claw from the pack. "Don't be too hard on yourself. You couldn't have known the gargoyles were working on my orders. But I simply had to meet the boy who saw the gryphon. The plan was already in motion, and you, my young friend, were a curious wrinkle. Fortunately, you aided this cause more than you know. And will help it a great deal more before this historic day ends."

Chase walked back around to face his prisoners. He held the gryphon's claw in his hand and studied it. "A bit smaller than I imagined. Especially for something so powerful it can render an entire species blind to the world around them. No matter, it appears easy to destroy. Your species is in for a big surprise," Chase sneered.

Sam thought about all the things he was going to do when the effects of the banshee weapon wore off. He envisioned himself defeating Chase, rescuing Dr. Knox and Dr. Vantana, and fighting off the horde of magical creatures gathered up ahead. It made him feel better to plan his revenge than to simply stand there, helplessly listening to Chase take his victory lap. Tashi looked Sam's way and he rolled his eyes. It was one of the few times he had seen the Guardian smile. Or at least, try to smile.

"But there are always surprises in life," Chase added. "You were one for me, your Guardian was another, and Chriscanis—I wasn't expecting you to make an appearance."

"I always expect the unexpected," Chriscanis said. "It's why I wore banshee blockers."

It took a second for Chase to not only register what Chriscanis had just said but also process the fact that he could say it. The young cynocephalus seized the moment and attacked with abandon. He launched at Chase, taking him to the ground. The two became a rolling mass of kicks and punches.

As they exchanged blows, the claw and the banshee weapon went flying. Sam wanted to shout "Get him!" with all his might, but what came out of his lips was hardly audible. The two cynocephali actually fought like dogs, nipping and growling at each other as they wrestled over the dirt, then went tumbling into the stream. Chriscanis was getting the better of the older and slower Chase. The young cynocephalus hurled his adversary backward, and Chase landed in a heap a few feet from Sam and Tashi.

"Hang in there, mates," Chriscanis said as he walked toward Chase. "We're almost done here." He grabbed the back of Chase's collar and pulled him up to his knees. Chase was clearly beaten—his hair matted, panting heavily, his eyes glassy. He muttered something with the little breath he could catch. "What did you say, old dog?" Chriscanis asked. "Was that a plea for mercy?"

Chase shook his head and exclaimed *"Bête!"* with his last ounce of energy. An instant later there was a blur of black fur and Chriscanis was gone. Sam's eyes scanned the area until he found his friend once more. But he wasn't alone—he was struggling with a massive beast. It had a thick black coat and glowing red eyes. Its mouth was enormous for its body size, sporting large white fangs the size of Sam's legs. It roared like a lion, but with a shriek that sounded like it belonged to a T. rex. As the beast tossed Chriscanis around like a rag doll, Chase rose to his feet and collected the claw and the banshee weapon.

"Ça suffit!" Chase called out, and the beast retreated from Chriscanis, who was now lying motionless on the ground.

Sam took one look at the creature and knew it was the Beast of Gevaudan. Just as Chase had described, the beast appeared to be part lion, part giant black wolf, and weighed several hundred pounds. Sam also knew that if this was the Beast and the stories were true, Chriscanis was badly wounded. He wanted to race to his side to help him. He struggled against the effect of the weapon . . . and felt his pinky move. The stiffness was dissipating. Seconds later Sam sprang forward and rushed to Chriscanis. The Beast moved to pounce, but Chase kept the creature still with a wave of his hand.

Tashi gripped her shekchen and crouched into her defensive posture. Chase noticed, but didn't seem at all intimidated.

"Stand down, Guardian, or I shall have my pet introduce himself to the boy," Chase warned.

"You will kill us anyway," Tashi replied. The Beast growled at her, but Tashi stood firm.

"If that is what I wished, I could have had the chupacabras handle it, or even seen to it myself, personally. No . . . this tale has unfolded much better than I expected. Now I have collected all the pieces I need for the final reveal. And you, Guardian, are a delightful bonus."

Sam found Chriscanis barely conscious. He checked the cynocephalus's body for a wound, and when he found it his heart sank. Chriscanis had been clawed by the Beast. Five bloody cuts from the creature's sharp claws stretched across the cynocephalus's torso. Sam knew what this meant, but he wasn't about to give up hope. He looked at Tashi. "Quick!" he exclaimed. "You have to heal him."

Tashi stood stoically and cast her eyes downward. Chase looked toward Sam.

"If she healed him, it would kill her and not help him much, if at all," Chase explained. He waved the claw in his hand and Sam realized: Guardians were susceptible to mortal injury when they did not have control of the gryphon's claw. He looked back at Chriscanis, who was fading in and out of consciousness.

"Sam . . . ," Chriscanis murmured. "You have to get away. . . . I can buy you some time. . . ." Sam tried to smile at the cynocephalus's bravery in the face of such overwhelming odds, but he was too devastated by the circumstances.

"I'm not leaving your side," he promised. Chase's shadow suddenly loomed over the two.

"Come along, boy," Chase ordered. "We have much to do."

Sam clutched Chriscanis's paw and looked up at Chase. "Help him! Please," he pleaded. "I'll do whatever you ask."

"That is beyond my power. He made his choice."

When Sam looked back down at his friend, something on Chriscanis's wrist caught his eye. There was a small, colorless spot in his fur . . . a spot Sam had seen before—on another cynocephalus.

"Your arm . . . your wrist," Sam said to Chase. "Show it to me." Chase eyed the boy for a moment, then pulled his sleeve up to expose his wrist. Sure enough, there was the same colorless spot in Chase's fur.

"I never thought my family birthmark was that interesting," Chase said, before pulling his sleeve back down. He noticed

Sam eyeing Chriscanis's birthmark and the realization washed over Chase's face. Chriscanis was not entirely aware of what was going on, but he could tell that something was amiss.

"What is it, Sam?" he asked in a whispery voice. "What's wrong?"

"Nothing," Sam answered. Then he turned his eyes to Chase. "I was just thinking how proud your father and mother would be of your bravery, your courage."

"My mother would be upset at me for this, I imagine . . . but my father . . . you think . . . ?" Chriscanis's voice trailed off, his eyes closing. Sam shook him and the cynocephalus managed to open his eyes again, if just barely.

"I know," Sam said in a comforting tone, meeting his gaze. "I'm proud of you. And we're family too, remember? We always will be." Chriscanis nodded, then coughed, a loud, agonizing hack that caused Sam to cringe and start to cry.

"I'm sorry . . . ," Sam said, holding on to his friend with all his strength.

"Just promise me . . . ," Chriscanis began. "Promise me you'll never forget that it is not who you are that makes you special, Sam, it's what you do. It's what you do." Sam saw one final, peaceful smile before Chriscanis of the Agency for the Welfare of Mythical Beasts succumbed to his wounds.

"No!" Sam exclaimed. All the anger and sadness and helplessness was too much. He just wanted to break down, but before he knew it, he was being yanked to his feet. It was Tashi. As soon as he saw her, he pulled her into an embrace and sobbed.

"He will be okay, Sam. He will return to Gaia," the Guardian said, trying to console him.

"I don't want him to. I want him to be here with us."

Chase grabbed Sam's wrist and dragged him forward. "Enough of this."

"He was your son!" Sam declared with equal parts shock and disgust. "How could you do that to him?"

"We do not fret about familial relations," Chase explained. "I am saddened by this loss because he was a fellow cynocephalus. A comrade. But he chose the wrong side. He stood in the way of our progress as a species destined for greater things."

"He was greater than you'll ever be," Sam said.

"We'll see about that in a few hours."

Sam watched through his tears as Tashi said a blessing over their fallen friend. The Beast growled at her and she turned to follow Chase. Sam's eyes didn't leave Chriscanis's body. He watched as the cynocephalus slowly disappeared. But it wasn't that he vanished; rather, he transformed. The spot where his body was lying became a grassy mound covered in sunflowers. One moment, Chriscanis was there, and the next, there was a beautiful new addition to the pristine landscape. It stood out amid its surroundings. There was something in particular about this spot that made it more colorful, more tranquil, more beautiful than everything around it. Sam's friend had returned to Gaia.

Chapter 18
PHYLASSOS REVEALED

Classification 470 (Personnel Records)

Vantana, Vance

Activation Date: █████████

"It's comin' up a cloud," Virginia Vantana would often say. The grandmother to Dr. Vance Vantana lived until her ninety-seventh year. And she lived all of those ninety-seven years in the same small town and the same quaint farmhouse. Virginia got to know her home so well she could always tell when something wasn't quite right. She would step outside on her porch, feel the breeze or glance at the horizon, and instinctively know if trouble was on its way. It didn't matter if it was weather-related or family-related, old Virginia had a sixth sense when it came to all sorts of unpleasantness. Whenever she did feel that trouble was just around the corner, she'd pull her grandson in close and whisper, "It's comin' up a cloud."

For Dr. Vance Vantana, Virginia's old saying couldn't have been more perfect for describing the events of late. Like his grandmother, Vance could feel it in his bones that something was not quite right. He'd had this nagging sense since Henry Knox disappeared, and it had only grown in intensity in the months that followed. It was as if there were a storm cloud looming on the horizon that was becoming darker and more ominous by the moment. It hadn't reached him yet, but Vance knew it eventually would. He just didn't know how devastating a storm it might be.

Dr. Knox and Vantana had left the Guardian village of Kustos and hitched a ride on a dvergen subway to the Philippines, an island nation in Southeast Asia that was situated to the east of Vietnam in the western Pacific Ocean. The subway left them off at the Aliwagwag Falls in the southern part of the country. They were a series of eighty-four cascading waterfalls that many dubbed the "stairway to heaven." Vance couldn't have imagined a more magnificent way to begin such a dangerous journey.

From the Aliwagwag Falls, the two headed for the Visayan Islands, a mountainous island group that was the purported home of the aswang. Vance had studied the creatures during his schooling, though he never expected to meet one.

They had been a main feature of Filipino folklore for ages, the country's version of a werewolf and vampire melded together. It always surprised Vance that Phylassos had allowed the creatures to coexist with humans, but the gryphon was the protector of all magical creatures. He couldn't choose favorites. Of course, Phylassos wasn't going to allow the aswangs to perpetrate their evil on unsuspecting victims, so he placed several restrictions on their behavior. Much like the yetis, the aswang were prohibited from traveling beyond their home. Phylassos also believed he could curb their horrific dietary habits with a little magic. After a spate of aswang attacks in the sixteenth century, Phylassos enchanted the creatures to reject their unusual hunger. But there were recent rumors the attacks had started up again, and that could mean one of two things: the creatures no longer feared the gryphon and his punishment, or the gryphon's magic was waning, which was a sign that would encourage other creatures to challenge the curse. If there was truth in either of those possibilities, Vance knew this trip would prove especially perilous.

The weather in the Philippines was a wet, searing heat that made Vance feel like he was trapped in a steam bath with a space heater on full blast. Vance couldn't help but chuckle at the irony that he had practically been fighting off frostbite just hours earlier, wishing for this kind of warmth. And now that he was deep within this hot tropical bisque, he yearned for the chilly temperatures.

As the two doctors made their way to the aswang home, they passed through Kuapnit Balinsasayao National Park and checked in with Ranger Torotao, a sarangay who ran a tight ship. These creatures were well-known in Filipino mythology and reminded Vance of the cynocephali, although instead of being a race of dog-men, sarangays were half bull. They were an exceedingly disciplined species who prized precision and hard work. Like the cynocephali, sarangays were seen as humans to those without the sight, but for those who could see their true form, they were a very intimidating lot.

Ranger Torotao was particularly excited to see Dr. Knox. He had heard about the doctor's disappearance and had been concerned for his safety. He was also enthusiastic for the chance to show off the work he had done in the park. Unfortunately for Torotao, Knox was not interested in a tour. He and Vance questioned the ranger about the aswangs and revealed the creatures' recent attempts to steal the claw. Torotao was shocked to hear of such brazen disobedience of the gryphon's law but could offer little insight into what might have triggered their seditious behavior.

"Once an aswang, always an aswang," Torotao said in his thick Filipino accent.

The ranger volunteered to accompany the duo, but Knox declined the offer. Vance was disappointed in his mentor's decision, as sarangay were fierce fighters. He would likely have been of great assistance if they encountered trouble. Later, Knox explained that he was still not entirely sure which creatures could be trusted, so he didn't want to take the risk. His explanation was followed by a series of questions regarding the gargoyles and the meeting with Chase. He would often bring the topic up, then drop it, then bring it up again. On the final ferry ride to the Visayan Islands, Knox took up his questioning once more.

"And the gargoyles just dropped Sam?" Knox asked.

"Yes," Vance answered. "He told me he squirmed a bit and the creatures lost their grip."

"Lost their grip . . . right above a pool?"

Vance confirmed the details repeatedly until he began to question his own understanding of the incident. He told Knox that at the time he chalked it up to the luck of the gryphon, which Sam certainly showed signs of exhibiting at the hospital in Bakersfield.

"Yes, I could see how that might have been a natural conclusion," the doctor replied. "And maybe you're right. Maybe it was simply luck."

Vance didn't think Knox believed that, but he also wasn't sure what it meant if it wasn't chance. Could Chase have had a hand in these recent events?

When they finally reached their destination, Vance took the lead, but Dr. Knox kept close behind. Vance was continuously surprised by the man's spryness. Even at eighty-something—he never divulged his age—the doctor always kept pace with a man several decades his junior. Though Penelope denied it, Vance wondered if she had fashioned Knox a secret concoction that enhanced his vitality. Maybe he could coax her into giving him some when he reached Knox's age.

As soon as they set foot in the thick, humid jungle, Vance could smell trouble . . . literally. It was a musky, rotting scent that filled his nostrils and made it impossible to discern the presence of any creatures. Of course, if this was what aswangs smelled like, the two doctors were surrounded. Vance hoped it was simply the stench of this jungle and not aswangs. He had armed himself with two items he knew would prove invaluable in a fight with aswangs, should their conversation with the creatures suddenly go south. The first was the simpler: a canister of salt. Unfortunately, Vance hadn't had time for Penelope to build one of her famous weapons, which would have likely shot sodium chloride–filled projectiles at the creatures. Instead, Vance would be relying on an old-fashioned saltshaker he'd "borrowed" from a restaurant they'd stopped at along the way. He left an extra-large tip to pay for the rental.

The second weapon he brought along was the most peculiar he had ever employed in his duties as a ranger for the Department of Mythical Wildlife. It was a picture of Virginia Vantana, his sweet late grandmother. The folklore behind the aswang mentioned photos of grandmothers as being effective in warding them off. If Virginia had been there with him, she likely could have warded them off by hand—she was a feisty one. He had slipped the photo of Virginia into his back pocket, prepared to use it when the time was right.

That time came quicker than Vance had expected. The odor he hoped might just be the jungle turned out to indeed be the stench of the aswangs. He and Dr. Knox were surrounded. They were lightning-fast and well organized, and they descended in droves. He didn't have much time to strategize a defense, so he went for the only weapon he could wield quickly: Virginia Vantana. He unleashed the photograph and held it aloft. He could almost hear his grandmother say, "Oh, Vancey, it is most definitely comin' up a cloud."

Sam London had never known sadness like the kind he knew that day. Until this moment, he had not experienced the loss of a friend or relative and had no understanding of what grief truly felt like. There was a hole in his chest, as if it had caved in on itself and created an emptiness that all the happy thoughts in the world could not fill. In the shadow of Chriscanis's death, Sam wondered how much time he had left and what would become of Tashi, Vance, and Dr. Knox. Would they all share the young cynocephalus's fate?

Chase led Sam and Tashi through the thicket of forest, the monstrous Beast of Gevaudan following on their heels— ready to pounce at the slightest misstep. They wove their way through the rocky terrain until descending into a steep embankment. The path narrowed and darted through a heavy curtain of foliage, which had formed from the closely packed tree line. Chase guided them through the vegetation, and they emerged on the edge of an expanse that lay deep inside the gorge, surrounded by cliffs. As soon as they reached the other side, Sam could hear a chorus of bellowing jeers that reminded him of his time in Cernunnos's lair. But this wasn't an ornately carved cave; rather, they were now standing amid the ruins of an ancient stone amphitheater.

Hundreds of mythical creatures covered the moss-coated seating area. Some of the creatures Sam recognized immediately. There were gargoyles, yetis, aswangs, cynocephali, harpies, and chupacabras. Others in the audience were a mystery to Sam. Tashi pointed as they walked.

"That is a kapre," she said, gesturing to a tall, dark-skinned man with a long beard. He was squatting and smoking a long pipe that emitted a thick black smoke. "They are from the same area as the aswang. Not usually aggressive, but then, perhaps it is just some of their kind."

"Like the cynocephali?" Sam suggested.

Tashi nodded. "Yes, there appear to be factions within various species that are seeking to end the curse."

Sam spotted other bizarre creatures, including one that was part snake and part human, as well as a translucent figure with fangs and wings.

"The yetals," Tashi noted. "From India. They are ghastly creatures, forbidden by the gryphon to leave their dwellings."

As Sam scanned the crowd of fantastic beasts, his eyes stopped on one particular creature. "Vance!" Sam exclaimed. Dr. Vantana was being held toward the front of the ruins, near the stage. He was guarded by two large, angry-looking gargoyles. Sam could immediately discern that the doctor was in a weakened state. He could barely look up at them as they approached.

"Sam . . . ," the doctor said in a strained, whispery voice. "I'm sorry. . . ."

Sam raced to Vantana and embraced him. The gargoyles growled, but Chase waved them off.

"A family reunion of sorts," Chase quipped. "Just like the kind you humans love, no?" he asked mockingly. "Though I am certain this reunion will end quite differently than what is customary."

Sam released the doctor from the hug and looked him over. "Are you okay?" he asked. "Are you hurt?"

"Mostly my pride, kid," Vance replied with his best attempt at a smile. "You?"

"I'm fine. But Chriscanis . . . he . . ."

"Returned to Gaia," Tashi interjected as she joined them. The doctor could see that Sam's eyes showed the signs of recent tears.

"I'm sorry to hear that. He was a good friend."

Sam looked at the ground and nodded softly.

"Where is Dr. Knox?" Tashi inquired. "Did he escape?"

"No . . . no, he didn't," the doctor replied solemnly. He then gestured to the stage. Sam and Tashi followed his pointed finger and froze at its target. Dr. Knox was imprisoned in an iron cage, the bars bent in as if fashioned by hand—likely the work of magic. He appeared to be unconscious and was chained by his ankle to the stone floor. Sam was horrified by the scene. He charged the stage, but was pulled back by Chase.

"Calm yourself, child," the cynocephalus warned.

Sam glared at Chase with fury in his eyes. "Let him go!" he demanded.

"I will do no such thing," Chase responded firmly. "Miss Capiz, can you control your student, please?"

"With pleasure," the aswang hissed from the shadows. She emerged from the crowd and moved up behind Sam. She clutched his neck with her long, bony fingers and dragged him back to where they were holding Dr. Vantana.

"Sam London, we meet again. And under more agreeable circumstances," the aswang said slowly in her menacing tone. Sam shook her off and gave her a scowl, then turned to Vance.

"What are they doing to him?" he asked.

"You'll find out soon enough," the aswang snarled. Sam looked at the creature with contempt.

Dr. Vantana shrugged. "I really don't know. They've had him like that since we got here."

"When did you arrive?" Tashi asked.

"Two days, three, maybe more? Last I remember we were ambushed by a horde of aswang. They made a beeline right for me and only me," the doctor revealed. "Now I reckon they wanted to use me as leverage to get Henry to surrender. I recall them threatenin' my life and then things went a little—well, a *lot* black. I woke up here and saw Henry up in that cage. I don't think he gave them what they wanted. Might be why you're here," the doctor said, looking at Sam.

"Do you have any idea why Dr. Knox gave me the gryphon's claw?" Sam inquired.

Vance looked sideways at Sam. "Come again?"

"The claw was in my bag when I returned home. Now Chase has it," he explained.

Vantana sighed. "Then it's over. He'll destroy the claw and end the curse once and for all. You can't put that genie back in the bottle."

"But . . . why not just destroy it, then? Why do that to Dr. Knox?" Sam wondered. Dr. Vantana shrugged.

"You can never explain crazy, kid." Sam couldn't argue with that. But he still believed there had to be a reason. Chase wouldn't just imprison an old man in an iron cage for fun—he was evil, but he was also purposeful. If he already possessed the claw, what else would he be seeking, and how could Dr. Knox help?

"Didn't you say Dr. Knox could communicate with Phylassos?" Sam asked Vance, an idea forming in his head.

The doctor nodded. "I'm pretty certain he can."

"Well, maybe Chase wants to summon the gryphon. Bring him here to witness the claw's destruction," Sam theorized. "And he thinks Dr. Knox can make that happen."

"Perhaps," Tashi said. "But that would be very unwise. The gryphon is a powerful creature."

"And it's not like Henry has Phylassos's phone number," Vantana added.

Sam shrugged. "It's the best theory I've got."

"Looks like we might be able to prove that theory right quick," Vantana said, nodding toward the stage.

The creatures in the audience were growing louder, the

various vocal outbursts creating a cacophony of strange roars and animalistic calls. Chase climbed onto the stage, and with a wave of his hand silenced the gathered horde.

"I wish to bid you all welcome," the cynocephalus announced to another round of roars. "We have gathered in this place to witness a momentous occasion. What you and I do here and now will be remembered for the ages, for it will right an ancient wrong—a blight that has persisted through fear and trickery. I tell you this day that we have nothing more to be afraid of. From this time forward, our kind will no longer be relegated to the shadows, forced to hide our true selves. Now is when we step into the light. Are you ready, my brethren? To end the curse and kill the gryphon, once and for all?" The audience responded with their resounding cheers of approval.

Sam looked at Dr. Vantana and Tashi, who appeared just as shocked as he was by Chase's declaration. "Kill the gryphon?" Sam asked the two. "Is he serious?"

Tashi calmly replied, "Even if he is, he is not capable." Sam tried to take solace in her confident tone, but the possibility made him queasy.

"Well, then," Chase continued with enthusiasm, "on with the show!"

The cynocephalus walked toward the cage that imprisoned Dr. Knox. He was lying on the floor, barely conscious.

"It is time to expose the lie, old man," Chase proclaimed. "Tashi, Guardian of the gryphon's claw, step forward. Your services are required." Tashi remained still. "Come now, Guardian. Let's not make this difficult for you." The two gargoyles guarding Dr. Vantana gave Tashi a shove forward. She stumbled but quickly spun around, ready for a fight. "That would be suicide."

"I do not fear death," the Guardian reminded him defiantly.

"Oh yes, I know. But you need not die now. There is no honor in that. Just hear me out," Chase offered. Tashi eyed the cynocephalus, then stepped toward the stage. Chase gestured for her to join him. She did, cautiously. When she reached the stage, Chase smiled. "Thank you. Now I want you to use your weapon—your shekchen—on Henry Knox." She stared at Chase, outraged by the notion.

"I shall do no such thing. And you may do what you wish to me; I don't—"

"Fear death, yes. We are well aware. Oh, my dear girl, your warrior prowess cannot hide your naïveté. You don't see the whole picture, now, do you? Your death is meaningless to me," Chase explained. "I have no intention of harming you. After all, you are committed to giving up your life to protect the gryphon and the curse. The question is whether you are willing to give up the boy's life as well?" Chase nodded to the gargoyles, one of which grabbed Sam from behind and pulled him into a tight, almost suffocating grip. The creature pressed a long, razor-sharp talon to Sam's throat. "I've wondered in these last several days how the child fit into the picture, and I'm beginning to realize that you, Knox, and Vantana don't have the foggiest idea either. So why don't I create a reason? Do what I ask, Guardian, or Sam London dies."

Sam struggled against the gargoyle's grip. The creature's talon bore into his skin, sending a stream of blood trickling down his neck. Tashi appeared utterly helpless. She looked at Dr. Knox, then at Sam, then back at Knox.

"Why do you insist on hurting this old man?" Tashi asked, trying to wrap her mind around the impossible situation. Chase shook his head, as if disappointed in her. He gestured for the gargoyle to continue. The creature readied its hand to slash.

"Wait!" Dr. Henry Knox cried.

Everyone froze.

"Then she must do as she is told," Chase insisted as he waved off the gargoyles.

Dr. Knox crawled to the side of the cage. He grabbed onto one of the iron bars and spoke to the Guardian. Sam strained to hear, but it was barely a whisper. Whatever Knox did say to Tashi appeared to have an enormous impact. Sam had never seen the stoic warrior look so dumbfounded. She appeared conflicted, then resigned. Tashi touched her shekchen to the stone stage, and Sam watched as electrical energy surged through the earth and crept up the side of the stage, darting across the stone floor until it converged on the shekchen and disappeared. Sam looked at Vantana, concerned.

"She's not going to—" Before Sam could finish his sentence, Tashi raised the shekchen, twirled it above her head, lowered it, and touched the tip to the doctor's frail hand. The entire surge of blue energy flowed through Knox's body. It jolted the old man, sending him convulsing across the cage.

"Nooooooo!" Sam screamed in horror.

Dr. Vantana struggled against his restraints, desperate to save his mentor and friend. Sam was again overcome with emotion. His eyes had not yet recovered from the cry he'd had earlier and promptly began shedding tears. He could see Dr. Henry Knox crumpled on the ground. His seemingly lifeless body lay still. Sparks of blue energy rippled through his skin. The entire audience was on the edge of their stone seats, leaning forward in wonder and curiosity. Chase was the only creature who appeared unfazed. He caught Sam's eye and winked. *Such evil arrogance,* Sam thought. Chase's eyes shifted back to the cage and Sam followed his gaze.

It was then that Sam London of Benicia, California, bore witness to the most startling sight anyone had ever seen. Though it was hard to believe anything could be more shocking than what he had already encountered these last several days, this moment put it all to shame.

Dr. Henry Knox began to change. The famed scientist's body twitched and shuddered, and then it grew. Slowly and steadily, Henry Knox expanded in size. His once-thin legs thickened and extended. His arms followed suit, lengthening and enlarging. His skin undulated before sprouting thick tan fur.

"What in the name of Sam Hill?" Vantana uttered in disbelief.

For a moment, Sam wondered if Dr. Knox was a tanuki. But that theory was quickly disproven when instead of fur on Knox's chest, feathers burst from his skin. Beautiful white feathers that encircled his head and covered his face . . . a face that was no longer human. Knox's nose shot forward, transforming into a majestic golden beak. Wings unfolded from Knox's sides, hitting the sides of the cage. His hands and feet morphed into paws with sharp, curved claws. There was no denying what Sam had just seen, nor could he ignore the unbelievable conclusion: Dr. Henry Knox wasn't just a friend of Phylassos. He *was* Phylassos.

Chapter 19
SAM'S GIFT

Tashi of Kustos stood on the amphitheater stage and peered down upon the frail human named Henry Knox. How could she strike this defenseless old man with a deadly weapon, as Chase had demanded? A shot from a shekchen would likely kill a human being. It would surely kill one in the doctor's weakened condition. Yet Sam's life was of paramount importance—this she had learned from her meeting with the gryphon during the Age of Mortality ritual. She could not let the boy die at the hands of the gargoyle. She had to act, but how?

The Guardian contemplated the alternatives. Her mind ticked quickly through a variety of ways she might extricate her human companions from this situation. She toyed with the idea of simply attacking and killing Chase before anyone could come to his defense. Perhaps with their leader dead, the crowd would acquiesce. Tashi worked out the scenario in her head. She would charge the shekchen and send a massive bolt of electricity into the cynocephali. As his minions prepared to retaliate, Tashi would leap forward, flipping in the air above Chase and touching down right behind him. At that precise moment, she would charge her weapon and strike the fatal blow. She was convinced this plan would work and was prepared to move forward with it when she heard Dr. Knox call out to her.

"Tashi?" he whispered. "Come closer." Tashi stepped toward the cage as Knox slowly pulled himself to meet her. He gazed up at the Guardian, locking eyes with her. "It is okay. I will be all right. Please . . . for Sam's sake, you must."

"But you will not survive," Tashi explained. "How can I choose one life over another? I can—" Tashi was poised to reveal her plan to the doctor when he said something totally unexpected.

"Do you not remember, Guardian?" Knox began. "I warned you such a day would come. A day that you would be forced to choose between my life and the boy's. That day is here, Tashi of Kustos. And you must choose Sam."

There was a twinkle in Knox's emerald-green eyes as he revealed this. Tashi's mouth dropped open as if in slow motion. She didn't surprise easily, but this was certainly worth her shock. The *gryphon* had warned her. He cautioned her that she would have to choose, but how would Dr. Henry Knox know of this? *Of course,* Tashi thought. The gryphon could change shape. After all, it was by changing his shape that he was able to trick Alexander the Great and curse humanity.

It was always right there in the story. . . . Alexander gave an old man a gift—an old man he believed to be his god but was actually Phylassos. It was at that moment that Phylassos took advantage of Alexander's folly. Namely, the often-forgotten magical rule that warns "Never give a gift to your enemy, for it can be used to gain power over you." The gryphon used his disguise to receive the gift and curse it.

Tashi knew the truth—a truth she should have realized years earlier. Henry Knox had visited the Guardians before. In fact, up until the day Dr. Vantana, Chriscanis, and Sam had entered the village, Henry Knox had been the only human visitor to Kustos. It made her wonder if any of her fellow Guardians knew Phylassos's secret. Yeshe must have known, she concluded, though he never let on.

The thought of Phylassos strolling about Kustos in human form this whole time was unnerving to the young warrior. She tried to recall any interactions she had with Dr. Knox that would have been disrespectful, given his true identity. This revelation continued to spur numerous questions. How long had Phylassos been in human form? Why had Dr. Knox disappeared? Why would Phylassos allow himself to be captured by Chase?

Those questions and the many others swirling in her head would have to wait for answers. Tashi had an order to obey. As a Guardian of the gryphon's claw, she could not refuse the gryphon's wishes, no matter the cost. Tashi had to strike Phylassos with her shekchen—the very weapon he had created for the Guardians to protect him and the curse. Although she knew it wouldn't kill the gryphon, she was unsure what sort of damage it might inflict.

When she touched the staff to his hand and sent the charge into his body, Tashi speculated on how the earth's energy might affect him. Energy from Gaia had a way of disrupting magic. She knew this from her studies. That was why it was such an effective weapon for the Guardians. Magical creatures, no matter how powerful, were not immune from Gaia's life force. As the charge pulsed through Knox's body and sent him crumpling to the ground, she wondered if the energy would interfere with his disguise and return him to his original form. Indeed it did . . . and in dramatic fashion. Tashi dropped the shekchen and kneeled in reverence.

Chase had discovered the gryphon's secret and sought to reveal his true form: to out Phylassos, once and for all. It would no doubt send the creatures in attendance into a frenzy. *What then?* Tashi thought. Would Chase destroy the claw? End the curse? Kill the gryphon? Whatever the cynocephalus's plan, Tashi was running out of options. She knew the Guardians would sense the danger but doubted they would reach her in time to help rescue Phylassos or maintain the curse. She did not enjoy this feeling of helplessness. It was the second time she had experienced it—the other was when she had briefly died after healing Sam. Tashi held tightly to the hope that there was a way out of this situation—and that it would come to her in time. The question was: would it come too late?

* * *

Upon the transformation of Dr. Henry Knox into the gryphon known as Phylassos, the gargoyle holding Sam released his grip. Apparently, it was just as stunned as Sam by the revelation that the world's foremost authority on mythical creatures was also a mythical creature himself. With the gargoyle's talon off his throat, Sam glanced over at Dr. Vantana to catch his reaction. The top ranger of the Department of Mythical Wildlife had been weakened by his time spent as Chase's prisoner, but at this moment he was totally alert and understandably taken aback.

"I had no idea, kid," he said, shaking his head in disbelief. "No idea."

"Behold!" Chase declared with a flourish of his hand. "The gryphon's trickery laid bare. The mighty Phylassos has been masquerading as a human. The so-called King of All Magical Creatures lowered himself to that pathetic form to appease the lesser beasts."

Phylassos roared and pushed against the iron bars, causing them to shimmer with a silver spark. Sam recognized that spark. It was the same phenomenon he had experienced on the dvergen subway ride to England. The subway car had passed through a silvery shimmer that caused it to speed up and ultimately led them to Smoo Cave in Durness, Scotland. It meant an enchantment was being used to keep the gryphon imprisoned.

"What are we going to do?" Sam asked with urgency. "We have to help him!"

"Frankly, I was counting on him to help us," Dr. Vantana

confessed. "We ain't exactly in the best of strategic positions at the moment."

"There must be something we can do."

"Well, I'd been holding out hope for the cavalry, but I reckon this entire place is hidden by an enchantment. Much like how they're keepin' Phylassos in that cage," Vantana explained. "The thing is . . . I can't imagine Chase is capable of such magic."

"Then who is?" Sam asked.

"Very few individuals," the doctor answered as he considered the possible suspects. "It doesn't matter now. Chase is the timber rattler that's starin' us in the face at present."

Tashi arrived back at their sides. She appeared distressed and displeased. The scowl on her face was the most pronounced Sam had ever seen it. But he wasn't about to forgive and forget what she had just done.

"How could you do that to him?" Sam asked angrily.

"Now, now," Vantana interjected. "Cut the girl some slack. She didn't exactly have a choice in the matter. It was your hide on the line, remember?"

"That is true," Tashi agreed. "But my actions were still unacceptable." Dr. Vantana shot her a confused look.

"You do realize I'm tryin' to defend ya," he said.

"That is entirely unnecessary," Tashi replied. "What is critical at this moment is helping determine how we can save you, Sam, and the gryphon."

"And you," Sam added.

"I am expendable. If it means you escape with my sacrifice, then so be it."

"Now, that is unacceptable," Dr. Vantana countered. "Any plan we've got has to include you getting out of here just as alive as us."

"That will depend. Please, tell me your proposals for escape," Tashi whispered. Sam and Vantana exchanged a glance, then turned back to Tashi with blank looks.

"I think I'm speaking for both of us when I say we're still working on it," Vantana admitted. The Guardian sighed.

Chase held the claw aloft, and Sam instantly turned his attention to the cynocephalus. What was this villainous creature going to do next? Sam wondered.

"How fitting that the root of the gryphon's injustice will now become the instrument of his destruction," Chase announced to the joyous crowd. "Shall we kill Phylassos with his gift to humanity? A gift that cursed us all to hide our true selves . . ."

Sam focused on one word Chase was repeating: "gift." He kept talking about Phylassos's "gift." Sam recalled that the claw was originally a gift from Alexander. He remembered Carl telling him, "Never give a gift to your enemy, for it can be used against you." Sam was considering those words when Dr. Vantana whispered to him.

"What we need is one of them big distractions, like we had in that yeti village," the doctor suggested. "If one of us could get up there and free Phylassos, even in his weakened state he'd be formidable and certainly cause a lot of panic among the attendees."

"I concur," Tashi added in a hushed tone. "But how? The cage is enchanted. Even if I could manage to retrieve my shekchen and disrupt the magic that keeps him imprisoned, he will need help, and we are unarmed. Against a horde of this size we would surely die."

"You got any extra shekchens or hologram devices hidden in that book bag, Sam?" Vantana inquired jokingly.

But Sam's attention was back on the gryphon. Phylassos stood up in his cage and locked eyes with Sam. It reminded him of the first time he'd seen the creature on that big rock in Death Valley.

"Sam? Are ya listening?" Vance asked.

Sam snapped out of his daze and looked at the doctor.

"My bag? No . . . ," Sam answered. "All I have is—" he stopped abruptly. A lightbulb switched on in the recesses of Sam's brain. And it was blindingly bright. "Wait," he said. "I think I have an idea." Vantana and Tashi looked at Sam as though they had already heard his idea and concluded it was terrible.

Back onstage, Chase was ranting about what he described as the "macabre manner" in which humans are able to see mythical creatures. "They steal our blood! They steal our magic! And the gryphon lets them. He encourages them!"

The crowd grew angrier. Sam tried focusing on relaying his plan to his friends, the noise nearly drowning him out.

"Tashi, when you healed me, you absorbed my injuries, right?" Sam asked, the gears in his head spinning.

Tashi nodded. "But I cannot absorb the gryphon's injuries or the doctor's. Not without the claw in our possession."

"I know that," Sam replied. "But what would happen if you did it to someone who was perfectly healthy?"

"I do not know," Tashi admitted, stumped by his question. "I would likely absorb their energy. It wouldn't make me stronger, if that's what you mean."

"That's not what I mean. Would it put someone to sleep?"

"It could," Tashi responded.

"Okay," Sam said, satisfied. "I want you to do it to me."

"Now, just hold on a moment," Vantana interjected. "Are you telling us you need a nap?"

"No. Well, not exactly," Sam replied. Tashi and Vantana eyed him skeptically. "I need to dream. Quick, Tashi. I don't have time to explain. You're just going to have to trust me." Tashi paused a moment and looked at the doctor, who shrugged. She reached out her hands and was about to touch Sam.

"Hang on," Sam said. He glanced back toward Phylassos, who was now being chided by a group of gargoyles while Chase watched in amusement. Sam shouted, "Just sleep, Phylassos. It won't hurt . . . and you might even dream."

"Interesting advice from the human child," Chase said. "Though I doubt the gryphon will be able to sleep through what he is about to endure."

Phylassos caught Sam's eye and Sam nodded to the gryphon. Almost imperceptibly, Phylassos nodded back. "Now, Tashi," Sam ordered. The Guardian quickly pressed her hands to Sam's chest. He smiled at her and then felt himself lose consciousness.

The instant Sam's eyes closed, he was transported to the place where it all began: Death Valley, California. This was where he and Phylassos had met, albeit briefly, in a dream, and then again in real life. Sam was thrilled—if his plan was going to work, finding himself in this dreamscape was the first critical step. His hand went to his shoulder to find the second critical step: his book bag. Sam launched into a full sprint. His target was the rocky hilltop where it all began. There was more riding on this meeting with the gryphon than he could have ever imagined. Time was of the essence. As he raced toward his destination, he hoped beyond all hope that Phylassos would be waiting for him. He wasn't sure if his plan would work, but it was their only chance.

Sam reached the bottom of the ridge and began his ascent. He had done this twice before and was prepared for every loose rock, each slippery surface. He finally got to the top and pulled himself over the edge. A plume of dust billowed up as he climbed to his feet. It swirled in the desert wind and then dissipated to reveal the gryphon perched on the summit, waiting for him.

"You made it," Phylassos said, a sense of relief in his weakened voice. "How did you know this would work?"

"I didn't. I hoped," Sam replied. "Are you okay?"

"I have been better," the gryphon answered. "My apologies for the surprise."

"Yeah. I didn't see that coming," Sam said. "I have a ton of questions, which I'll ask when we get out of here."

"You sound confident there will be a pleasant outcome to our predicament," the gryphon said. And then the creature suddenly lurched to his right side. "Hurry, Sam. I can't remain here long. If they pierce my heart with the claw, it will mean my demise."

"They really can kill you?" Sam asked, horrified by the notion. The gryphon nodded.

"I won't let that happen. I have an idea." Sam pulled off his book bag, unzipped it, and reached inside. A moment later he pulled out the package of NICE biscuits. There was only one left. Sam had been saving it for a special occasion.

"Your idea is cookies?" Phylassos remarked. "This is no time for jokes."

"This isn't a joke," Sam assured him. "I know they look like cookies and they taste as good as cookies, but in England they call them biscuits. It is the way they wound up in my possession that you will be most interested in." The gryphon narrowed his emerald eyes, intrigued. "They were given to me the morning after I met you," Sam revealed. "They were a gift from Chase."

Phylassos's eyes widened. "Did he say those words? Was it genuinely presented as a gift?"

Sam nodded. "He said, 'A gift for you, Sam London.' They're his favorite."

"Come closer," the gryphon requested. "Quickly." Sam stepped forward, the biscuit package in hand. When he reached Phylassos, he instantly noticed—

"You're bleeding," Sam said, eyeing a trickle of blood streaming down the gryphon's chest.

"They've pierced me. But not deep enough. You must listen closely." Sam nodded, ready for his orders.

*   *   *

When Sam awoke from his slumber, he found that much had changed since he closed his eyes. The roar of the crowd was now deafening—they had apparently been worked up into a frenzy. When he looked to where Vantana had been, he saw the doctor on the ground, unconscious. Tashi hovered above him, on her knees. She was also wounded. There was a deep gash on her shoulder that was bleeding steadily.

"You are awake," Tashi said quietly.

"What the heck happened?" Sam asked.

"They attacked the gryphon . . . and stabbed him," Tashi explained. Sam looked to Phylassos and found that he was fending off attackers and still bleeding from his chest wound. A mix of creatures stood goading him from outside the iron bars. Chase was now holding the claw; the gryphon's blood dripped off its tip. Sam spun back to Tashi.

"What did Dr. Vantana do?" Sam inquired.

"He could not sit idly by as they attacked. He lunged forward and attempted to protect Phylassos. So I knocked him unconscious."

"Wait. You did this?"

"He would have gotten himself killed," Tashi explained. "And we still had your plan to attempt."

"Okay," Sam replied, understanding. "Good call. What about your shoulder?"

"The gargoyle thought I deserved punishment for my action," Tashi said. "I am fine. What is needed of me?" she asked.

"If you had your shekchen, could it free the gryphon?"

"With enough charge, I believe so, yes."

"Great," Sam said. "Here goes nothing." Sam reached into his bag and retrieved the package of NICE biscuits. He held the last remaining biscuit in his hand and looked at Phylassos. Their eyes met.

Sam broke the cookie into three pieces and handed one to Tashi.

"What is this?" the Guardian asked, studying the treat.

"It's a cookie. A special cookie. You're going to eat it when I tell you. Wake him up," he said, gesturing to Dr. Vantana. "We're going to need his help." Tashi nudged the doctor, who slowly came to and focused on the Guardian.

"You hit me," Vantana said with groggy incredulity.

"It was for your own good," Tashi replied.

"It didn't *feel* good," the doctor replied, rubbing the back of his head. He noticed Sam. "Glad to see you're awake. Have a good rest?"

"I wasn't resting," Sam responded defensively.

"How's Phylassos?" Vantana asked, looking toward the iron cage.

"He cannot hold out much longer, I fear," Tashi said.

"He'll be fine. We're going to help him," Sam assured them. He handed Dr. Vantana the third piece of cookie. "Here."

"Now we're eating cookies?" Vantana asked as he took the piece. "Naps, baked goods . . . is this some kind of ridiculous picnic?" he added with irritation. "Dr. Knox—the gryphon—is dying."

"I know, but it's going to be okay," Sam said. "We need to eat our parts of the cookie at the same time." Tashi and Dr. Vantana followed Sam's lead and brought the cookies to their lips. Sam nodded to the two and they all popped the pieces into their mouths. They chewed and exchanged curious glances. One by one they swallowed.

A moment later, Vance was already impatient.

"Is the sugar rush going to save us?" he asked sarcastically.

"I do not feel any different, Sam," Tashi revealed, disappointed. Sam looked back at the gryphon, who was growing weaker by the second.

"It has to work," Sam said, almost to himself.

"What has to?" the doctor asked.

Suddenly, the gargoyle that was guarding them squawked that horrible squawk Sam had heard the day he left the hospital in Bakersfield. When Chase looked over, his canine face dropped like a hound dog's.

"Where are the prisoners?" the cynocephalus bellowed.

The gargoyle scrambled and the rest of the magical creatures in attendance began to stir. "Find them!" Chase commanded.

Sam's face burst into a giant toothy grin. He looked at Tashi and Dr. Vantana, who wore puzzled expressions.

"It worked!" Sam whispered. "We're invisible to magical creatures. The gryphon cursed the cookie, like he cursed the claw, but in reverse."

"You mean . . . they can't . . ." Dr. Vantana waved his hand in front of the face of the gargoyle guard, who was now busily scanning the area for a sign of them. The creature didn't react to the doctor's gesture.

"Well, I'll be," Vantana said softly in amazement.

"I don't know how long this will last, so we need to move quickly," Sam explained. "I'll grab the claw. Tashi, you free the gryphon. And Dr. Vantana, do you think you can find the entrance to this place?"

"Not sure I follow," the doctor replied.

"If there is some kind of enchantment keeping this area hidden, we may have some friends looking for us. . . ."

"And if I can find the hidden passage in, we might have help," Vantana completed Sam's thought. "Okay, then. Let's do this."

The trio split into different directions under the safety of invisibility. Dr. Vantana snaked his way through the crowd of bewildered creatures to the forested perimeter where Sam and Tashi had entered with Chase and the Beast of Gevaudan. Meanwhile, Tashi climbed onstage to retrieve her shekchen, which was still lying on the stone floor where she had dropped it. No one had dared pick it up, likely knowing that it would deliver quite a jolt. Sam approached Chase, who had grown steadily more paranoid in the last few moments. His eyes darted about nervously as he clutched the claw tightly in his hand like a security blanket.

"What are you up to, gryphon?" Chase asked Phylassos, eyeing him anxiously. Sam reached out for the claw but Chase's hand moved in the opposite direction. The cynocephalus walked to the cage, glaring at Dr. Knox. Phylassos met his gaze defiantly, which infuriated Chase even more. "Your tricks cannot save you . . . not anymore." Chase pulled back the claw, ready to strike with what would likely be the fatal blow.

"Tashi!" Sam cried out. She had already read the situation and let loose with a bolt from her shekchen. It hit Chase in the back and forced his body forward, slamming him into the iron bars. As soon as the effects of the charge subsided, Chase tumbled backward and released the claw. Sam ran and caught it in midair. Tashi then turned her weapon to the iron bars. She held the shekchen to the ground and pumped a continuous stream of energy into the cage. The stage was lit with blue light as it surged across the stone and into the weapon. Sparks sprayed the surrounding area as the bolt hit the iron bars, sending Chase's allies into a frenzy. Chase rose to his feet, now in a full panic.

"Stop her!" he ordered, pointing toward the blue energy. "Follow the blue light. Follow her shekchen!" The gargoyles and aswangs tried in vain to stop the Guardian as she poured Gaia's energy into the iron cage, but Tashi was simply much too quick for them. Sam watched as she leapt and tumbled and flipped, deftly avoiding her pursuers with superhuman agility. Even when the aswangs had surrounded her, Tashi was able to escape by quickly redirecting the shekchen charge in a circle around herself, hurtling the aswangs back several feet.

Although Tashi was able to elude capture, her ordeal made something suddenly clear: the magical creatures could see the shekchen. So even though Tashi was not visible, her weapon was. Sam came to a swift realization: the claw in his hands was also visible to the creatures. When he glanced upward, his fears were instantly confirmed. All the creatures, including Chase, were staring his way. The gryphon's claw must have appeared to be floating in midair.

"Based on the claw's height," Chase began with a knowing smirk, "Sam London, I presume?" Sam froze. "Clever boy," Chase continued. "But it is a little late for clever." Sam started to back away, toward the edge of the stage.

"Sam!" Tashi called out as she dodged a gargoyle. "Cover it up. . . . They won't see it." Sam quickly followed Tashi's suggestion. He cradled the claw in his arms, making sure to use his body to mask it. It must have worked, since Chase's expression turned angry and he was quickly scanning the stage and sniffing the air.

"I will find you, boy," Chase declared with a growing fury.

Sam slipped off the stage in an attempt to get some

distance from the cynocephalus. The creatures in attendance were clearly agitated by the sudden chaos that had erupted before their eyes. Sam had to simply stay out of the way and wait for Tashi to break through the gryphon's cage and free Phylassos while Dr. Vantana found the entrance and brought reinforcements. It seemed simple enough. The gryphon's cage was already glowing from the intense blue charge of Tashi's shekchen—it was just a matter of moments. But that was when things got complicated.

"Bête!" Chase called out. Sam had heard that word before . . . just hours earlier, when the cynocephalus had summoned his horrifying pet: the Beast of Gevaudan. The audience parted and the Beast began a slow, snarling approach. It was understandably unnerving; what made it even more so was how the beast was staring Sam's way, as if it could see him. But that was impossible! Surely the magic would render them invisible to all magical creatures. And then it dawned on Sam: the Beast was a hybrid creature. He hadn't considered that when concocting his plan with Phylassos. Chase had found a loophole; unfortunately, it was large and hairy with a scratch that was fatal.

"Tashi!" Sam bellowed, but the Guardian was in midleap.

"I am a little occupied at the moment," she replied, breathless.

"It appears you are not invisible to everyone," Chase snickered. The Beast was closing in fast. Sam tried the only move he had left: he ran.

Sam sprinted through the crowd, maneuvering around an

assortment of bizarre and terrifying creatures. But the Beast followed close behind. Once through the throng and out in the open, the Beast of Gevaudan lunged for him. Sam spun and lost his footing, along with the claw, which flew from his hand. The Beast leapt on Sam and reared back with its deadly sharp claws. He was done for.

Suddenly, the Beast was struck from the right side and thrown off Sam's body. Sam quickly got to his feet and found the creature wrestling with a figure. It was Vance Vantana! Sam panicked. The last time he had watched someone tangle with the Beast of Gevaudan, they'd wound up dead—or rather, absorbed by Gaia, as Tashi had explained. He had already lost Chriscanis to this nightmarish creature; he couldn't fathom losing Dr. Vantana as well. The two struggled mightily as Sam looked on in fear.

"Vance!" Sam yelled worriedly. "Don't let it scratch you!"

Then he heard a distinctly human groan, followed by a yelp from the Beast. The struggle abruptly ceased. Sam rushed over to find the Beast on top of Vantana. Both appeared unconscious. Sam wondered if the doctor had managed to kill the creature—but at what cost? Did he sacrifice himself in the process? When Sam saw the grass grow wet with blood, his heart sank. He could feel his entire body react to the thought of Vantana's death. It was like the world was spinning and he was losing his balance. He wanted to surrender to the sensation and collapse to the ground . . . and just give up. He shut his eyes, consumed by a feeling of total despair.

"Now, that is one big, mean ol' critter," Dr. Vance Vantana muttered under the weight of the Beast. Sam's eyes sprang open and his face erupted into the biggest smile he could ever remember smiling. "Reminds me of a mama grizzly I wrestled when I was ten. For fun, of course."

"Vance!" Sam said, overjoyed.

The doctor pushed the creature from his body and staggered to his feet.

"I found him guardin' the entrance," Vantana explained. "We took a tumble, and I managed to get a few good jabs in with my lucky knife, but the hairball refused to go down."

"Yeah," Sam replied. "It's 'cause he was half magical, I think."

"He almost had me until his master called him back."

"How did you—" Sam started to ask.

"With the only weapon that could do the job," Vantana said as he lifted up his hand to reveal the gryphon's claw. Its golden veneer was now stained with the Beast's blood.

Of course, Sam thought. The gryphon's magic was the only thing that could kill the Beast, but Phylassos's oath to protect magical creatures made this impossible.

"No!" Chase screamed when he saw his fallen pet. He turned back to the stage, enraged. "Kill the Guardian!" he ordered.

Sam could now see that the gargoyles and aswangs had managed to get ahold of Tashi. One had an arm, another a leg. Tashi struggled, still clutching her shekchen as they pulled and yanked on her limbs. Sam burst forward, charging toward the stage to help his friend.

"Sam!" Vantana called out in warning as he followed behind.

Sam jumped onstage and Tashi tossed the shekchen to him. "Once more!" she yelled. Sam caught the staff, touched it to the ground, and let another bolt of blue energy shoot from the shekchen into the gryphon's iron cage. In the process, Sam felt his body freeze up. It reminded him of the effects of the banshee cry, only ten times more painful. Fortunately, it was worth the pain. The electrical charge surged into the cage and triggered a massive explosion of light and sparks, which blanketed the stage in a gray, shimmering smoke. Sam was thrown back by the blast, his hair standing on end from the electrical current. Vantana caught him and held on as the two hunkered down and waited for the smoke to clear.

A second after, there was a rush of wind that blew Sam's and Vantana's hair back. It was followed by another, and then another, until there were steady and rhythmic gusts of air emanating from the now-dissipating cloud of smoke. The source of these gusts soon made its presence known in grand fashion. It rose above the cloud of smoke and emerged from the gray fog, quickly instilling terror in all who were gathered.

It was Phylassos! The gryphon was free from his prison and hovered above the stage; his mighty wings flapped as he released a deafening roar that ended in a birdlike screech. That was when the place erupted.

The magical creatures that sought the destruction of the curse and the gryphon himself had a sudden change of heart. With Phylassos free—and tremendously displeased—the crowd made a beeline for the exit. The melee following the gryphon's appearance sent the aswangs and gargoyles that were holding Tashi into a petrified stupor. It was enough to allow Tashi to break free and perform another of her perfect flying somersaults. She stuck the landing, coming down alongside Sam and Vantana.

"Well done, Sam," Tashi said. She fetched her shekchen and rejoined the two.

Phylassos swooped down and hung in the air a few feet above them. "I would request that the three of you cover your eyes," the gryphon instructed in a firm but friendly voice. Sam, Vance, and Tashi obliged. Sam wondered why the gryphon would ask that of them. Was it for their protection? What exactly was Phylassos going to do to these traitorous creatures? Sam covered his eyes with his hands, then opened them ever so slightly to catch a peek. He watched as Phylassos closed his eyes and the enchantment that was hiding the amphitheater sparkled and glowed a bright electric blue. The attendees of Chase's vengeance were now trapped inside.

"For those of you who wished to see the curse lifted and for those who wished to see harm come upon me," Phylassos bellowed, "I forgive you." At that, some of the creatures paused to look back at the gryphon. "But you will be punished for these crimes." This got the group panicked once again. As the creatures scrambled for safety, Sam noticed something, or rather, the lack of something. Both Chase and Capiz were missing. Did they escape before the gryphon could reverse the enchantment?

"Close those eyes for real now, Sam," Phylassos whispered. Sam turned a cherry shade of red and shut his eyes tightly. Yet even with his eyes closed, a blinding white light bled through Sam's eyelids. It was so bright he scrunched his face. When the light subsided, Phylassos spoke.

"It is safe now," the gryphon said in a solemn tone. "It has been done."

Sam opened his eyes, uncertain of what he would find, but awfully curious. The doctor and Tashi followed suit. The gryphon had landed and stood on the ground in front of the amphitheater stage. He appeared sad and still weak from the ordeal. Sam gazed back toward the amphitheater's stone seating area and beyond to find it was completely deserted. All the creatures gathered to watch the fall of Phylassos were gone. At first, Sam thought the blinding white light must have vaporized them, but then he looked more closely and noticed aspects of the landscape that had not been present just moments ago. Strange-shaped rocks, small grassy knolls, patches of overgrown weeds.

The gryphon had sent them all back to Gaia. Their punishment was to be reabsorbed by the earth itself.

"I'm sorry," Sam said to the gryphon, sensing the creature's sadness.

"Thank you, Sam," Phylassos replied. "Thank you for all you've done."

"I second that," Dr. Vantana added. "You saved our hides and protected the curse." Sam shrugged humbly. And then he remembered.

"Wait!" he exclaimed. "What about Chase and Miss Capiz? They disappeared before you sent those creatures back to Gaia."

The gryphon nodded. "Unfortunately, the aswang known to you as Miss Capiz eluded capture."

"And Chase?" Dr. Vantana asked. "I would have very much enjoyed settling that score with my bare hands."

"Ah, yes. Chase," the gryphon said. "He should be coming into view right about . . . now." Phylassos peered skyward. Sam, Vantana, and Tashi followed his gaze. A shadow passed across the sun and the distinct screech of the roc echoed through the valley. It was followed by a voice. . . .

"Help me!" the desperate voice cried out. It was Chase, and he was in the clutches of the roc as it soared across the valley and headed home.

"I thought it only fair," the gryphon explained. "After all, you did tease him with that yak in Tibet."

Chapter 20
CASE CLOSED

The cynocephalus known simply as Chase was not the criminal mastermind in the DMW case that came to be called the Guardians of the Gryphon's Claw. This seemingly contradictory point was stipulated by Dr. Vantana in the case notes and elucidated to the gryphon as the doctor stood in the creature's cave high above the Guardian village of Kustos.

Now alone with his mentor—recently revealed to be Phylassos as well—Dr. Vance Vantana divulged an interesting nugget of information he had kept secret since they had left Hérault. Once the enchantment broke over the area, the amphitheater was flooded by Guardians and several bigfoots sent by Carl. As they poured in, Vance noticed a curious figure standing atop a cliff, overlooking the valley. He could tell it was a woman. She had long black hair and a flowing black dress.

"Marzanna," Phylassos instantly concluded. She was the sorceress Vance and Sam had encountered in Cernunnos's lair. Vance nodded.

"I think the ol' dog was a pawn," he suggested. "Rotten to the core, but a pawn, nonetheless."

"We have had our share of run-ins with Cernunnos in the past, but this . . . this is something unique," the gryphon said.

"He's growin' more brazen," Vance asserted. "Our kidnapping was a bold move. If it hadn't been for Chriscanis . . ." Vance was suddenly reminded of the loss of his friend from the Agency for the Welfare of Mythical Beasts.

"I learned of his return to Gaia," Phylassos said. "He was a brave soul whose courage saved many lives."

"Including my own . . . and Sam's," Vance noted. Phylassos nodded.

"He's not dead, Vance," Phylassos reminded the doctor. "Not in your sense of the word."

"I know it, but . . ." Vance let his thoughts trail off. "So what do I call you? Henry? Doctor? Arrigo Busso?"

"I was first and will always be Phylassos," the gryphon replied. He stepped across the sea of golden treasure and eyed the gryphon's claw, which was back on its perch. "It is damaged, Vance," Phylassos revealed.

Vance approached to get a closer look. Sure enough, there was a crack in the gold-plated claw: a small but distinct zigzagging fracture about an inch in length.

"I reckon it must have gotten smacked around mighty

good," Vance said. "Question is, what does it mean, if anything?"

"Of that, I am uncertain. However, it is the talisman that retains the magic, that makes the curse possible," Phylassos noted.

"So damaging it might what? Compromise the magic?" Vance asked.

"That is one possibility," the gryphon answered. "But how it will manifest itself remains to be seen."

"Things aren't gonna be like before, are they, Doc?"

Phylassos shook his feathered head. "As you can probably surmise, I am quite old, Vance."

"Well, you look great," Dr. Vantana said with a smile. The gryphon smiled as well.

"It is time for me to retire my human identity for good," Phylassos explained. "I shall remain here, in my home, so I may preserve my strength and help when necessary." Vance's eyes met the gryphon's, the disappointment clear in his expression. "Apologies," Phylassos offered.

"None needed," Vance replied. "I understand, but you will be missed by everyone, especially me. I wouldn't be here if—" Vance was getting choked up, despite his valiant attempt to suppress his emotion. He was never a guy who was comfortable expressing his feelings and this conversation was making him all kinds of uncomfortable.

"I know," Phylassos replied. "This is not goodbye forever, just for a time. Of course, your new partner is much younger and much sprier than I ever was."

"New partner?" Vance asked with surprise.

Phylassos nodded. "I always knew that when it was time, someone would appear." Vance considered that a moment.

"You're talking about Sam. But he's just a kid."

"So were you at one time," the gryphon reminded him. "And there is more to Sam London than you know."

"But not more than you know?" Vance countered.

The gryphon smiled his great, kind smile. "There is a lot I know. Some of it need not be said. At least, not yet."

"Still keepin' secrets?" Vance chided him.

"Not keeping, Vance," Phylassos said. "Protecting."

Sam London had a multitude of questions for the gryphon. Questions about the dream that had started it all, about the sudden sight he developed, about the future—the queries went on and on. Sam met with Phylassos when they returned to Kustos and the gryphon thanked him for his efforts in exposing the conspiracy. Unfortunately, Phylassos had little to say regarding his sudden appearance in Sam's dream or the significance of Death Valley. He seemed as perplexed by these events as Sam.

"As I began my investigation into reports that the gryphon claw relics were disappearing from sites around the world, I asked the universe for assistance in determining the culprit," Phylassos explained. "The dreams with you started shortly thereafter."

"Where did you go after what happened at the gas

station?" Sam asked. "I saw you save Miss Hartwicke, but then—"

"Events took an unexpected turn in Death Valley, and with Miss Hartwicke's announcement on television, suddenly everyone knew the gryphon was back. That complicated matters. So I returned to human form and traveled to Kustos to meet with Yeshe, to let him know something was brewing. What, I could not say, exactly. On my way to the village I was apprehended by a group of yetis who were spying on the Guardians."

"Why did you stay in that prison?" Sam asked. "You're the gryphon!"

Phylassos smiled. "Revealing my secret would have hindered the search for those behind this rebellion. I thought it best if I allowed the conspirators to believe they had the upper hand. Perhaps they would reveal their identities and ultimate goal."

When Sam asked about suddenly receiving the sight during his altercation with the chupacabras, Phylassos theorized that the connection the two made via dream might have spurred some unintentional side effects. That left one remaining mystery Sam was anxious for the gryphon to clear up.

"I was bait, wasn't I?" Sam asked. "That's why you put the claw in my book bag."

"Yes and no," the gryphon confessed. "After the battle in the yeti village, I knew it was going to take something bold to expose the real force behind the conspiracy. I also knew the universe had brought us together for a reason."

"So you gave me the claw to see who would come for it," Sam confirmed.

Phylassos nodded. "My apologies for using you in this manner, but I believed it was the best way to draw whoever was after it into the open. Of course, it was not without its risks and clearly did not go as I'd hoped. I didn't realize the aswang was masquerading as your teacher, nor did I anticipate the ambush in the Philippines. Perhaps these are all clues that I'm losing my touch. A possibility that compels me to make a request of you, Sam."

"A request of me?" Sam inquired, surprised there was anything he could do for such a powerful being.

"As I've said, there is a reason you and I were brought together," the gryphon explained. "I believe part of that reason played out these last few days and culminated in your bravery and quick thinking in Hérault."

"What's the other part?" Sam asked.

"To join the DMW, become Dr. Vantana's protégé, as he was mine all those years ago."

Sam was overwhelmed by the idea. His inner voice immediately began throwing up obstacles. "But I have school . . . and my mom . . . and . . ."

"All things that can be worked out," Phylassos assured him.

"I would be honored," Sam said thoughtfully. This was an extraordinary moment in the life of Sam London. It was more than an honor; it was an affirmation that he had found his one thing. He was good at this. Not great, he cautioned himself, but good. He was certainly better at this than all the other things he had attempted over the years. And the best part was this counted; this made a difference. He was going to work alongside Dr. Vance Vantana . . . and he was going to have many adventures and meet fantastic creatures.

Yet in the shadow of this life-changing news, there was an unspoken sadness about a life cut short. Chriscanis was gone. Sam promised himself that he would never forget his friend. Their time together might have been brief, but they had shared a great deal about themselves. Sam would miss him. He hoped to meet Chriscanis's mother one day so he could tell her all about her courageous, selfless son.

After his meeting with Phylassos, Sam waited at the Guardian training ground for Vance. He watched as Tashi sparred with three of her fellow Guardians and easily bested them. It was only when the trio joined forces that they gained the upper hand on her, but even then she didn't go down without a heck of a fight.

"It's time to take you home," the doctor announced when he arrived. Sam grinned from ear to ear.

"That sounds great!" he replied. He was more than ready to return home, spend time with his mother, and eat her terrible food. "I just need to say goodbye to Tashi."

"That won't be necessary," Vantana informed him. "She'll be coming with us."

"Excuse me?" Sam said.

Tashi joined them, still out of breath from her training exercises.

"Dr. Vantana just told me you're coming with us to Benicia."

Tashi nodded.

"I was asked by Phylassos to remain close to you. For your protection."

"Are you going to live in the park again? Up in that tree?" Sam inquired, recalling Tashi's experience camped out in a city park the last time she'd traveled to his hometown.

"Nope," Dr. Vantana answered for her. "She's trading up. Miss Bastifal, your neighbor."

"The lady with all those cats?" Sam asked.

"She happens to be a child of Bastet," Vantana revealed. "She'll be taking Tashi in as a foreign exchange student."

"Student?" Sam said in surprise as he looked over to Tashi. She nodded her confirmation.

"Looks like you two are gonna be neighbors *and* classmates!" Vantana declared as he slapped both Tashi and Sam on their backs.

* * *

Sam London arrived in Benicia, California, later that night. Dr. Vantana dropped him and Tashi off outside Sam's home before returning to Redwood National Forest to brief Penelope on the events in Hérault. He assured Sam he would be back soon to check in. When the doctor drove away, Sam walked Tashi to her new home next door to his own. Sam's neighbor, Miss Bastifal, had always been known as the "crazy cat lady" around the neighborhood. She was unmarried, had a dozen or so cats, and was a professor at Stanford University. Little had Sam known, she was also a child of Bastet, a race of half-human, half-cat creatures descended from Egyptian royalty. When Miss Bastifal opened her front door, Sam finally saw his neighbor in her true form.

She was a cat version of a cynocephalus. She had a large feline head with piercing blue eyes, whiskers, and pointy ears. He'd always thought she spoke funny—slowly, with a tendency to draw out sentences toward the end. But hearing Miss Bastifal speak and seeing her true appearance provided a new understanding to this odd manner of speech.

"I always knew you were special, Sam London," Miss Bastifal whispered. "I always did."

"Thanks," a blushing Sam replied.

Miss Bastifal then turned to Tashi. "You must be the Guardian."

"Tashi of Kustos," Tashi announced with formality.

Miss Bastifal bowed slightly. "Welcome to my home. I shall do my best to accommodate you."

"I require very little in the way of accommodation," Tashi responded matter-of-factly. "A place to train and a place to sleep."

"What about a place to eat?" Sam asked.

"That would be fine as well."

"I think that can be arranged," Miss Bastifal said.

Tashi turned to Sam. "Good night, Sam London."

"Good night, Tashi. I guess I'll see you around." Tashi nodded and disappeared into Miss Bastifal's home.

Sam slipped back into his house with little fanfare. Nuks was ecstatic to see him and demanded details on all that had happened. Sam stayed up most of the night and obliged the tanuki. Afterward, Sam shifted the subject to how they were going to handle his mom. According to Nuks, when Ettie returned home the night of the aswang attack, Nuks had convinced her it was the dog that had caused the mess and he had the training school come and collect him. The question remained: How were they going to reintegrate Nuks back into the house in his natural form? How could they convince Ettie he was not going to rearrange the furniture again?

Before dropping him off, Sam and the doctor had discussed a means of communication that would help them avoid an explanation to Ettie. Dr. Vantana suggested telling Ettie he was a state psychologist charged with checking in on Sam following the incident in Death Valley. But Sam thought this was a terrible idea. He knew it would freak Ettie out and lead to more worry and questions. Sam told the doctor he would think about it and come up with a better solution. In practical terms, Sam and Vantana would communicate via Sam's new DMW badge. It had been designed as a two-way communication device that enabled rangers to contact each other when necessary. One would simply tap the badge and say the ranger's name, and it would alert that ranger, wherever he or she happened to be.

It wasn't long before Ettie learned Miss Bastifal was hosting a foreign exchange student. Once she did, she invited them over for tea and cookies and insisted Sam come down to meet their new neighbor. Sam found it particularly amusing that, after all they had been through, he had to pretend not to know Tashi. He could tell the Guardian found it equally entertaining.

Sam and Tashi exchanged knowing smirks while Ettie

asked questions like "So what's it like in Tibet?" and "Have you visited America before?" or said things like "You stick with Sam; he'll show you the ropes at school, and he can be quite chivalrous if any of those other boys give you trouble." Little did Ettie know, this quiet new girl next door could take down every boy at school, at the same time, with one hand tied behind her back.

The moment Sam found the most amusing was when his mother admonished him in front of the company for taking too many cookies.

"Sam, you've had too many cookies. They're not good for you, remember?"

"Where I come from, cookies have been known to save lives," Tashi said, sneaking a wink at Sam.

"Oh . . . is that right?" Ettie said with astonishment. "Those must be special cookies."

"Yes, I suppose they are," Tashi replied, while Sam tried his best not to burst out laughing. An awkward silence ensued. Uncomfortable, Ettie quickly filled it in.

"Why don't you go show Tashi your room?" she suggested.

Once the two were upstairs behind closed doors, Nuks emerged from his hiding place and leapt into Tashi's arms.

"Tashi!" the tanuki exclaimed.

"Hello, tanuki," she replied, petting him. "I mean, Nuks." Her use of his name made his day.

"Sam?" Nuks said. "Your badge has been beeping."

Sam grabbed the badge from beneath his pillow and tapped his finger on its shiny metal face.

"This is Sam London." He couldn't help feeling a little strange talking to a badge, but a few moments later the familiar voice of Dr. Vance Vantana was heard.

"Sam?" Vance said. "I was in the neighborhood. Have you come up with a cover story for Nuks yet?"

He hadn't, but as he looked at Nuks, the solution was suddenly clear.

"Yes. Yes, I think I have."

* * *

When Vance knocked on the front door an hour later, he was holding Nuks. The shape-shifting raccoon-dog had slipped out Sam's window and met up with the doctor around the corner. Sam raced down to answer the door. Ettie emerged from the kitchen a few seconds later to see who was visiting.

"Mom, this is Dr. Vantana. He's an animal trainer."

For a moment, Sam's usually effusive mother was silent. She eyed the doctor.

"Have we met before?" she asked.

"I . . . don't recall ever havin' met," Vantana replied haltingly. "But please forgive me if I don't remember."

"It's just . . . you look so familiar," Ettie said, sounding truly confounded. "Are you sure?" Sam wondered if Ettie recognized the doctor from the hospital in Bakersfield. He didn't think she had seen him, but he supposed she might have caught the smallest of glimpses. "I guess it doesn't matter. We're meeting now," his mom continued. "I'm Odette London, Sam's mother." She offered her hand. "Nice to meet you." Sam couldn't remember the last time his mother had used her whole name when introducing herself. It was always Ettie. Vance took her hand and gently shook it.

"Nice meeting you as well, Miss London. Pretty name, by the way. Reminds me of *Swan Lake*."

"A favorite of mine . . . and my parents, I guess." She smiled.

"Maybe you're right and we have met before. My memory isn't the best. I'm pretty sure I've forgotten what I was up to for whole years," Vantana added with a grin.

"I know what you mean," Ettie said. There was that silence again, and Vantana still had Ettie's hand. Sam decided it was up to him to interrupt the awkward moment.

"Nuks is all trained now."

Ettie pulled her hand back. "Trained?" she said with a healthy dose of skepticism.

"Yes, ma'am," Vantana responded. "My apologies for what happened earlier. We had some extra training sessions we were supposed to complete before releasing him from our care. But he's extremely well trained now."

"And what if he has a relapse?" Ettie asked. "Not that I'm agreeing to take him in again; I'm just curious."

"That's a legitimate concern, Miss London. But I'd be stopping by every now and again to check up on him."

"You would?" Ettie brightened at the mentioned of the check-ins.

"I would. I might even bring him in for some training updates," Vantana explained.

"How much?" Ettie inquired, her skepticism still firmly in place.

"Sorry?" said Vantana.

"How much will it cost us, if we keep him? Which I am not saying we are, but if we do, what will it cost for all this special training?"

"Oh . . . it'd be free," Vantana answered. "Nuks is a rescue dog, and, well . . . we just like to see our dogs taken in by a good family. We help to facilitate that as much as possible. Plus, he helps us train the other dogs in our care."

"Watch this, Mom!" Sam exclaimed. He then proceeded to deliver a series of basic commands to Nuks. He had him sit up, beg, roll over. Ettie was marginally impressed, so Sam decided to turn up the volume. "Go fetch the mail!" Sam ordered the raccoon-dog. Nuks hesitated, as if unsure. He glanced over at Vantana, who shrugged subtly. Nuks took off down the walkway.

"Sam . . . ," Ettie said, embarrassed by her son's request. But sure enough, Nuks scampered to the curb, leapt up to their mailbox, opened the flap with his mouth and leapt again to retrieve the mail. If that wasn't enough, he leapt a third time to close the mailbox flap before returning to the front door and placing the mail at Ettie's feet. She was too stunned to speak.

She finally managed to address Vantana. "You're an extraordinary trainer, Dr. Vantana," Ettie said.

"Well, thanks. We do our best."

"Please, can we take him back?" Sam begged.

"I suppose we can give him a second chance, but if—"

"It won't," Dr. Vantana assured her. "Thank you. If it's okay, I'd like to give Sam some instruction on how to communicate with Nuks, like the trainers do."

"Oh, sure," Ettie said. "It was nice . . . meeting you."

"My pleasure, Miss London."

"Odette."

"Odette," Vantana said with his most charming smile.

Ettie disappeared back into the house and Sam closed the door behind him.

"Clever idea," the doctor complimented him.

"Do you think she saw you at the hospital?" Sam asked.

"I don't know," the doctor answered, as if still trying to figure it out.

"Well, hello there!" a voice bellowed. They turned to find a man walking toward them from across the street. He spoke with a British accent and seemed oddly familiar.

"The name's Christopher Canis. Just moving into the neighborhood." He gestured to the moving truck parked on the other side of the street, a few houses down. Sam and Vantana exchanged the same dumbstruck expression. The new neighbor walked up and offered an outstretched hand. Vantana shook it tentatively.

"Nice to meet you. I'm Vance. This here is Sam."

Christopher offered his hand to Sam, who shook it. As he did, he immediately noticed a small white patch of skin on the man's arm. Sam couldn't take his eyes off it, even continuing to clutch the man's hand to get a better look.

"A family birthmark," the man explained. Sam nodded in

disbelief. "Do you attend Benicia Middle School?" he asked. Sam nodded again. "Well, then I will likely see you there. I'm the new teacher."

"New teacher?" Sam asked.

"Yes. I will be replacing Miss Capiz. She needed to move from the area. Something with her family, I believe."

"She was my teacher," Sam responded.

"I suppose that means now I'm your teacher," he said. "Fancy that! I've met my first student. And we're neighbors. I have lots of fun things planned for the class. Do you like field trips?" Sam managed another nod. "I love a good field trip." Sam had heard those words before. "I should probably return to the laborious task of unpacking. It was nice making your acquaintance, Sam, and . . ."

"Vance," the doctor reminded him.

"Right. Vance. Cheerio."

As Sam's familiar new neighbor headed back across the street, Sam spun to Vantana. "Was that . . . ," he began.

"Phylassos said the return to Gaia is different for all creatures," the doctor noted.

"His courage granted him his wish," Sam concluded. The doctor looked at Sam, uncertain of his meaning. "He always wanted to be human," Sam explained.

"I reckon he did," Vantana said. "Well, kid, it's been a hoot. You keep that badge close now, ya hear? I might be needing your help sooner than you think."

"I hope so," Sam replied.

Realizing this was goodbye for an undetermined amount

of time, Sam felt a surge of emotion and sprang forward to give Vance a great big hug. Of course, the height difference between the two made it more of a torso hug.

"Goodbye, Dr. Vantana."

With all they had been through, Sam was really going to miss the ranger. Vance was caught off guard and nearly fell over. He let out a surprised chuckle and gave Sam a hearty pat on the back.

"Take care, Sam."

They parted and with a wink and a smile, Sam's new mentor and friend was gone.

* * *

That night, as Sam lay in bed, he contemplated his extraordinary new life. There was now a girl living next door who was a fierce mythical warrior sworn to protect him at all costs. Sam's former schoolteacher turned out to be a monstrous creature from Filipino folklore who was replaced by a reincarnation of his late friend—a dog-man who had risked his life to save him. And if all that wasn't enough to keep Sam's head spinning, he was now a member of a secret government agency that protected creatures no one knew or would ever believe existed.

Dr. Vance Vantana would return soon to recruit Sam's help on a new case. It was on this investigation that Sam would happen upon shocking information about his family. Sam London thought the craziest revelations regarding the world around him had already been revealed. Little did he know, he was in for the biggest surprise of his young life.

EPILOGUE

It was late afternoon in Redwood National Forest when Ranger Penelope Naughton heard a robust knock on her cabin door. She answered it to find Carl, the bigfoot, standing before her. The orange glow of the setting sun radiated from behind the legendary creature, giving him an almost heavenly appearance.

"Hello, Penelope," Carl said.

Following the events at Hérault, Ranger Naughton finally learned the cause of her amnesia. Carl the bigfoot, who had long been aware of Dr. Knox's true identity, had been meeting with the doctor to discuss the threat to the claw and the doctor's secret plan to investigate. When a suspicious Penelope tracked Carl to a remote area of the park, she witnessed Knox's transformation into Phylassos and, in the ensuing shock, revealed her presence. Concerned this knowledge would put Penelope in danger or compromise the investigation into the gryphon's claw, Phylassos erased her memory. Carl avoided Penelope when she returned to the park because he feared that seeing him might prompt her to recall what she had seen and heard that day in the woods.

But all that was behind them now. Carl had come calling this day at Penelope's request. The reclusive bigfoot found a ranger who appeared both shocked and confused.

"You called?" Carl said.

Penelope nodded. "I did. It's about Sam London's DNA," she revealed, clearly unsettled. "I took a sample of his blood when he was here and, well, it's—"

"Magical in nature?" Carl suggested.

"Partially, yes," Penelope replied. "But it's the human part that's even more surprising. It's an exact match for—"

"Yes, I am aware," he interrupted, speaking in a loud whisper, as if the trees were eavesdropping.

"You are?"

"It's a complicated story, Penelope," Carl replied in a hushed tone. "One the gryphon has managed to keep secret. For the boy's protection as well as his parents'. If the Maiden Council found out, there would be a harsh punishment."

"But shouldn't Sam know his father?" Penelope asked.

Carl smiled warmly. "In a way, he already does."

* * *

Sam London will return in *The Selkie of San Francisco*.

GLOSSARY OF MYTHICAL CREATURES

Department of Mythical Wildlife

Memorandum

Date: ███████████

To: DMW Rangers & Administrative Personnel

From: Dr. Vance Vantana

Subject: Creatures linked to Case SL001

The following is a list of the mythical wildlife connected to Sam London's first case. At my request, the department's forensic arts division has provided illustrations for reference.

Aswang

Origin: Philippines

Known Abilities: Shape-shifting

Favorite Food: Human children

Comments: These things make vampires seem like sweet, cuddly puppies.

Banshee

Origin: Ireland

Known Abilities: Emitting paralyzing scream (also known as "keening")

Favorite Food: Tea with lemon and honey

Comments: Don't forget your banshee blockers!

Bigfoot

Origin: American Northwest

Known Abilities: Super strength, heightened senses

Favorite Food: S'mores

Comments: They will smell you coming a mile away.

Chupacabra

Origin: Central and South Americas, Puerto Rico

Known Abilities: Night vision, enhanced olfactory sense

Favorite Food: Blood (preferably human)

Comments: Worst. Breath. Ever.

Cynocephalus

Origin: Southern Asia

Known Abilities: Enhanced senses

Favorite Foods: Peanut butter, biscuits

Comments: The Chihuahua types are tough hombres.

Gargoyle (Gargouille)

Origin: France

Known Abilities: Flight, transmutation

Favorite Food: Rock lobster

Comments: Stone-hearted, literally and figuratively

Redcap

Origin: Scotland

Known Abilities: Unrelenting stamina

Favorite Food: Wayward travelers

Comments: Check your ego and call for backup. They cannot be outrun.

Tanuki

Origin: Japan

Known Abilities: Shape-shifting

Favorite Foods: Nuts and berries

Comments: Excessively affectionate, but loyal

Troll

Origin: Scandinavia

Known Abilities: Enhanced strength

Favorite Food: Whatever a friend is eating

Comments: Share a cookie with one and you'll have a friend for life.

Yeti (aka Abominable Snowman)

Origin: Himalayas

Known Abilities: Super strength, heightened senses

Favorite Food: Yak

Comments: Big and angry. That about sums them up.

Additional creatures (pending verification):

Barghests

Origin: Northern Engla—

—

—

—

TRANSMISSION INCOMPLETE.

DMW FILE CLASSIFICATION

DMW case files are presented in the following format: #XXXXX-XXX-XX.X. This ten- or eleven-digit code consists of both letters and numbers.

The initial series of letters and numbers represents the investigating ranger and the case number involving that ranger. These particular files are associated with Sam London (SL). As this is Sam London's first case, the files are designated as 001.

The second series of three numbers indicates the applicable DMW offense code. In this instance, offense code 180 is used. This code encompasses those crimes defined as sedition. In the department's use, sedition relates to any and all attempts to undermine or subvert Phylassos's Law.

The final number pertains to the section of the file for those files with multiple sections. Numbers that appear after the section and are separated by a period indicate subsections.

SUBJ: This is the subject or subjects of the section.

SOURCE: This notes the source or sources of the information included in a particular section. These sources are designated by an abbreviation. Below is a list of relevant abbreviations:

    SA: Special Advisor

    MC: Mythical Creature

    ODB: Operational Debriefing

    MR: Medical Records

    SR: Surveillance Records

    BG: Background Investigation

    WS: Witness Statement

    PR: Public Record

DATE: This is the date on which the incident or inquiry took place.

FORMS: In some instances, case files include forms used by DMW personnel to record information from witnesses or intelligence sources related to an investigation. For example, FD–11 is an Activity Report that draws on information procured from witnesses, informants, and surveillance to monitor important persons related to a case.

SPECIAL CLASSIFICATIONS: Files that are administrative in nature are given a classification code in the 400s. For example, classification 470 is reserved for personnel records. Specific file numbers of these records have been withheld due to privacy concerns.

PARKS TO VISIT

Death Valley National Park
California, Nevada
nps.gov/deva/index.htm

Great Smoky Mountains National Park
North Carolina, Tennessee
nps.gov/grsm/index.htm

Redwood National Park
California
nps.gov/redw/index.htm

Shasta–Trinity National Forest
California
www.fs.usda.gov/stnf/

Shey—Phoksundo National Park

Nepal

dnpwc.gov.np/protected_areas/details
/shey-phoksundonationalpark

Kuapnit Balinsasayao National Park

Philippines

abuyogleyte.gov.ph/about-abuyog/places-to-visit
/kuapnit-balinsasayao-national-park/

Support America's National Parks

National Park Foundation

Official Charity of America's National Parks

nationalparks.org

ACKNOWLEDGMENTS

I think of an acknowledgment as a metaphorical tip of the hat, but for the following folks I'd have to take the hat off and fill it with chocolates and flowers and eternal gratitude:

Dolores for making it possible.

Tiffany for making it heartfelt.

Valentina for making it worth it.

Lacy Lalene Lynch and Dabney Rice at Dupree/Miller & Associates for making it happen.

Random House and Delacorte Press for making it real.

Krista Vitola for making it (way) better.

Colleen Fellingham for making it betterer. (Stet!)

Sarah Hokanson, Kevin Keele, Julius Camenzind, and Chris McClary for making it beautiful.

Monkey Max for making it magical.

And all the family and friends who encouraged, supported, and humored my aspirations over the years, thank you for helping make a dream come true.

ABOUT THE AUTHOR

When he's not hammering out the next Sam London novel on his 1935 Royal Deluxe typewriter, Todd Calgi Gallicano is a ██████████████████████ Despite pressure from the media and the government, Todd remains tight-lipped when it comes to questions about the Department of Mythical Wildlife and his sources within the secret organization. He lives with his wife in ██████████████████ where he helps raise his daughter and tries to steer clear of gargoyles, chupacabras, and other nefarious creatures. Visit mythicalwildlife.com for more top-secret information.